Emly...
Stormy Crime ... ...e spent his ea... ...
travelling around Asia and pouring drinks in London f...
the likes of Sylvester Stallone and Princess Anne, before
joining the Curtis Brown literary agency and having his
first crime novel published aged twenty-five, his second
a year later, and then co-writing seven comedies with
Josie Lloyd, including the Number One *Sunday Times* best-
seller *Come Together*. He set up and launched the UK and
US paperback crime fiction imprint Exhibit A for Angry
Robot, and now lives in Brighton with Jo and their three
kids. You can find out more about him at emlynrees.com,
or follow him on Twitter @EmlynReesWriter.

Praise for *Hunted*

'*Hunted* gives new meaning to the phrase "fast-paced".
Filled with clever twists, stylishly written and populated
with characters who are as real as our friends and family
(and enemies!), this thriller moves at breakneck
pace from first page to last. Bravo!'
Jeffery Deaver

'Fast and furious from the very start,
Hunted is a shot of pure adrenalin.'
Sam Bourne

'*Hunted* reads like Simon Kernick and Jeff Abbott
have joined forces to write an action-packed,

WANTED

EMLYN REES

Constable & Robinson Ltd
55–56 Russell Square
London WC1B 4HP
www.constablerobinson.com

First published in the UK by C&R Crime,
an imprint of Constable & Robinson, 2014

A copy of the British Library Cataloguing in
Publication data is available from the British Library

ISBN 978-1-78033-035-8 (B-format paperback)
ISBN 978-1-47211-350-4 (A-format paperback)
ISBN 978-1-78033-554-4 (ebook)

1 3 5 7 9 10 8 6 4 2

Printed and bound in the UK

To my father, Richard,
for always being there as solid as a rock.

ACKNOWLEDGEMENTS

To my editor James Gurbutt, and Martin Palmer, and everyone at C&R for their monastic patience, and occasional 'prompts', over what was a glacially slow delivery. Thanks also to the very talented Hazel Orme and Clive Hebard for tightening the ride. And to Kev for general cleverness. And finally to Jo, Trees, Rox and Min for, well, you know, everything.

CHAPTER 1

CAUCASUS MOUNTAIN RANGE

Valentin Constanz Sabirzhan arrived exhausted at the edge of the snowbound forest and raised a gloved fist. The two masked men behind him stopped dead in their tracks.

Valentin coughed and spat. He didn't need to look down to know that there would be blood in his phlegm. He smoked too much. Cigars. Like some big-shot Moscow *Bratva* crime lord – that was what his wife always said, knowing how it riled him to be compared to such filth; she hoped the insult might shame him into quitting. Not that it would. He was too old to change his habits. Death could take him as he was. He would not live his last years in fear. All he hoped – all he'd ever hoped – was what every soldier hoped: that his end, when it came, would be fast.

He willed his heaving chest to be still and listened. He heard nothing. Not so much as a breath of wind stirred in the frosted branches above his shaven, hooded head. He remembered the roar of the helicopter that had dropped him and his unit in the forest clearing two kilometres away.

Standing there now, poised in the silence like an exhibit in a museum, it seemed impossible to Valentin that no one had heard them arrive. But the pilot, still waiting in the clearing, had been adamant that the snow and terrain had masked any sound.

Valentin's eyes glinted darkly as he stared into the valley. His expression hardened.

A bright crescent moon illuminated the village cradled below. It was a nothing place: fifty-nine properties, mainly residential, with a nursery school, a grocery, which also served as the village bar, a carpenter, a butcher, an animal feed shop, and a pharmacist beside the dairy and slaughterhouse, which employed nearly every able-bodied man and woman within a ten-kilometre bus ride.

The outline of a grey, gritted road snaked between the shabby buildings, leading to other similarly isolated towns and villages further up and down the treacherous mountain range. Valentin thanked the God he had never believed in that he had moved to the city long ago. He'd have drunk himself to death through boredom if his life had been confined to a shithole like this.

He checked his watch. It was an hour before sunrise. None of the buildings was lit. Even in a hard-working farming community like this, everyone was still asleep. The only sign that the village was inhabited was the blackness of its roofs, betraying the heating inside.

Valentin's leather boots creaked in the snow as he shifted his legs. Cramp cut deep into his muscles. As a young man, he'd been able to march in weather like this for days. But those times were long gone. He sucked cold, pine-rich air deep into his heaving lungs. His shoulders ached for the comfort of an armchair or a hot bath.

The sooner I'm back in Moscow, the better, he thought.

He pictured his wife, Anitchka, at home, beneath the thick blankets in the bed they'd been given thirty years before as a wedding gift from her parents. He imagined himself beside her as he drifted off to sleep, and remembered her as she'd been when they'd first met, when they'd danced and kissed and fucked and had fallen in love . . .

He raised his night-vision binoculars, magnifying the available ambient light by a factor of twenty thousand. The world switched from black-and-white to green-and-grey as he zoomed in on the buildings.

The village had been under geostationary satellite surveillance for the past six hours, ever since it had been decided to send Valentin and the retrieval unit here. Only as a precaution, Valentin reminded himself, in case someone had dared to steal the weapon that he and his comrades had hidden there.

Valentin's view of the village through the binoculars matched his memory of the last satellite photograph he'd studied in the helicopter. It looked the same, but he double-checked, rolling his thumb slowly across the binoculars' control wheel, booting up a Sentinel app, until the last photograph appeared now as a ghost image over the real-time view.

The smart binoculars compared the two images,

matching vehicle placements and searching for anomalies to confirm that nothing had arrived or moved during Valentin's twenty-minute march there.

Something had. A dairy lorry: the binoculars now highlighted its long articulated shape in pulsing red, revealing where it had been reversed into an alleyway between the square concrete block of the dairy and the end of the row of shops.

Valentin ignored the vehicle. According to his intel, it had been scheduled to arrive during the last quarter of an hour, as it did every morning, to siphon the milk from the dairy's holding tanks.

He switched the binoculars from night-vision to profile-guided infrared and scoured the valley again. But the only heat signatures he picked up other than chimneys were those of the dairy's generators and the lorry's still warm engine.

It seemed there was nothing to worry about. It looked as though he and his comrades had been mistaken: no one had come here to steal from them.

So where is the relief I should be feeling? Valentin wondered. Why instead had the queasy sense of apprehension that had dogged him all day spiked into a peak?

Lowering the binoculars, he turned to the two Arctic-camouflaged men lurking in the shadows behind him, Lyonya and Gregori. Both were recent graduates of the FSB Academy in Michurinsky Prospekt in Moscow, where Valentin presided, and where he'd recruited them into the clandestine organization on whose orders they had come here tonight.

Nothing about the village looks wrong, Valentin considered, but something about it feels wrong . . .

He decided to take no chances and ordered his two subordinates, with a swift series of hand gestures, to approach their target from the front, while he would circle around and approach from the rear.

He watched the younger men fading like ghosts into the tree line, envying them their athleticism and grace, then continued his descent alone, cursing his sciatica, which lanced through his right leg at each heavy step. Less than halfway down, he stumbled and slid, jarring his hip against a frozen tree stump.

I'm getting too old for this, he thought, wincing as he picked himself up and pressed on. But deep down he knew it wasn't only his age – he'd just turned fifty-eight – that was making this journey so hard.

No, what was slowing Valentin most of all now was fear. Fear of what it would mean if the weapon hidden in the village ever ended up in the wrong hands. Fear that someone might be on their way to steal it. Fear, not for himself, but for all those he might lose.

His wife, Anitchka.

His children, Stefan, Tamryn and Bepa.

His grandson, Mishe.

Everyone he loved.

CHAPTER 2

SCOTLAND

Paper, stone and scissors: God would not rest until they had choked, bludgeoned and torn Danny Shanklin apart.

God – for that was how powerful he believed he truly became at times like these – arranged the twenty newspapers in symmetrical rows across the heavy-duty plastic sheeting he'd nail-gunned to the kitchen floor.

Each front page from the last two days bore a different headline but the same face stared out from them all. It was the face of a cancer, one that had dared to gnaw into God's own flesh since he had spilled his own blood in the snow.

Every hour of every day that God had spent in the penitentiary, he had pictured this face before him. He had pictured it weeping with blood. He had come so close to killing Shanklin that he could still taste his blood.

One winter's night seven years ago, he'd followed Danny Shanklin and his family to their cabin in the Nevada woods. The next morning he'd watched as Shanklin had taken his nine-year-old daughter out hunting. By the time they had returned, he had been ready and waiting inside.

Paper ...

God remembered killing Shanklin's wife. He remembered pouring the tiny balls of scrunched-up newspaper into the rolled-up magazine he'd rammed down her throat. He remembered the noises she'd made as she'd jerked and spasmed and choked. He'd lost count of how many times he'd replayed these sounds in his memory, of how often they'd soothed him to sleep.

The memory of Danny Shanklin struggling to free himself from the chair he'd been strapped to ... *Ah, yes* ... God remembered the rage, the hatred, but, above all, the impotence in his eyes.

Stone ...

Shanklin's little boy had refused to play God's game. He'd been too stupefied with fear. He'd kept his tiny fists clenched like stones.

Scissors ...

He had shown the boy no mercy. If he would not play by the rules, then neither would God. He'd used shears. He'd watched Shanklin screaming as the child had twitched and bled out.

After that Shanklin had begged to be killed. But God had refused. Because God had known that Shanklin had hidden his daughter outside among the trees. And God had needed Shanklin to witness him killing her too, to witness him taking her and doing with her as he wished.

He'd needed Shanklin to see. Because it was only then,

when he saw the complete submission in Shanklin's eyes, that God himself could truly believe he was now all-powerful, and that the *BITCH GODDESS*, who had once ruled him, was now truly dead.

But Shanklin had tricked him. When God had gone out into the trees to find Shanklin's daughter and drag her kicking and screaming back in, Danny Shanklin had somehow got free.

God still remembered the snapping of that twig out there in the woods, like the fracturing of one of his own bones. He'd turned to see Shanklin – bloodied from where God had plunged the shears deep into his thigh – lurching towards him through the brambles, trailing his blood through the snow.

Like a demon, God had thought. As if Shanklin himself had been a creature resurrected, sent up by that *BITCH GODDESS* to—

God had raised his Browning pistol to kill Shanklin. But – impossibly – Shanklin had been quicker. His knife had lanced deep into God's shoulder. There, among those spiny winter branches, Shanklin had severed God's nerves, so that even now the fingers of his right hand were numb.

Too late – here, in this kitchen, in this house he had come to visit – God now saw his hand shaking and realized his shoulder was throbbing. And, too late, he felt *HOT RAW FEAR* ballooning like a black hole inside him. And the *SICKNESS* and *EMPTINESS*, the life he had once lived, were widening and stretching and opening up to swallow him.

Screaming, God screwed up his eyes. But even in the heart of his darkness he saw that she – the *BITCH GODDESS* – had already sensed his weakness and had come to claim him once more.

He felt himself falling and writhing, powerless before her. He begged her to stop but she showed him no mercy. He recoiled – so weak! – as her blackened, broken teeth began to grind and her mouth to snarl and roar of *PAPER* and *SCISSORS* and *STONE*.

'NNNNUUUUGH—'

Screeching, he prised open his eyes. Gasping for air, he saw light. He scrambled across the plastic sheeting, retching and reaching for the table, as though he were clawing his way up from a pit of wet clay.

He hauled himself upright. Snatching a fresh scalpel from his medical bag, he tore off his clothes. First he slit the shoulder scar Shanklin had given him. Then he sliced open the other scars – the older scars, the ones he'd been given by *HER* – the mesh of pulped flesh and white hieroglyphics engraved and battered into his ribcage, chest and what remained of his genitals.

He opened each wound, like an oyster, like an eye. He nicked with his scalpel again and again, and watched each cut weep red tears, until each scar filled, becoming a blur of red. Until a flare of hope – so strong! – leaped inside him that he might soon truly heal.

The *BITCH GODDESS*'s snarling faded. It became the whispering of dead leaves blown away by a breeze. And then – with such triumph, such joy! – he sensed her retreating into the darkness, dispersing, like blood drops in a stream, choke by choke, cut by cut, bruise by bruise.

Until she was gone.

Only now did he once more truly believe that she, the *BITCH GODDESS*, was dead and that he alone was all-powerful.

He remembered the others then, those he had come to claim, the family whose house this was. He turned to face them, tied to a row of chairs that he'd nail-gunned to the floor. A father and a mother. Three children. Five iron links he would soon prove to be water. He focused on the short, shallow gasps of their breath. A tingling in his groin. A tightening of skin, of pleasure *and* pain.

Each would give him what was his. Each would soon also believe.

CHAPTER 3

CAUCASUS MOUNTAIN RANGE

As the forest trees thinned at the edge of the village and Valentin moved stealthily through the shadows cast down by the tall trees and outcrops of rock, the crackle of mud and ice gave way to the reassuring crunch of grit and gravel beneath his boots.

Valentin released the safety catch of his AS Val and crouched. Two decades had passed since he and his closest friend, Nikolai Zykov, had illegally raided the top-secret Biopreparat repository. It had housed the hybrid smallpox formulations developed for the Soviet biological-warfare programme during the Cold War.

Correctly fearing the imminent collapse of the Soviet Union, and dreading the subsequent neutering of Russia's security and power, Valentin and his fellow loyalists had stolen those weapons with the intention of preserving them for the future exclusive use of the Russian state.

They'd got away with it too. None of them had ever been linked with the raid, or even questioned. The six separate smallpox variations they'd taken had never been found, or even publicly reported as missing. Each had been carefully hidden in remote places such as this village. Valentin had selected it and delivered the vial.

The smallpox formulations they'd taken had never been needed or used, either as weapons or bargaining chips, because Mother Russia had prevailed without them in carving out a powerful new place for herself in the post-*Perestroika* world. Mother Russia had prevailed without them in carving out a powerful new place for herself in the post- Perestroika world. She had gone from strength to strength, as witnessed by the recent triumph of both the Olympics and her rampant intervention in Ukraine.

Even so, they had decided to keep the six vials in reserve for the day when they might be needed. And while he had never forgotten their existence, each year he had thought of them less.

Until now. Because now Nikolai Zykov was dead.

The British Intelligence post-mortem file, of which Valentin had seen a stolen copy, claimed that Colonel Zykov had died of natural causes. A heart attack. Two days ago. In London's Ritz Hotel.

Valentin would have been more inclined to believe it of his hard-drinking old friend, if the world's outraged media hadn't claimed that Nikolai had suffered his fatal heart attack after first attempting to start a war.

The media claimed that Colonel Nikolai Zykov had assassinated a Georgian peace envoy, who'd been in London to protest to the United Nations Security Council about Russia's continued occupation of the disputed border territories of South Ossetia and Abkhazia.

Valentin believed that his friend had been set up. By whoever had been in that hotel room with him. By whoever had carried out the assassination. By whoever had wanted a Russian like Nikolai to be found dead and to take the blame for the massacre and the hit.

The world's media claimed that an American mercenary, named Danny Shanklin, had helped Nikolai. But Valentin had further intelligence, which suggested that Shanklin, too, had been framed.

Furthermore, not only was Nikolai dead, but so was his daughter. Katarina had been tortured and murdered by a psychopathic rapist in Moscow, only a few hours before her father had died.

It was this, above all else, that had brought Valentin to the village tonight. First, Katarina had been his goddaughter, and second, he didn't believe she'd been randomly killed by a rapist. He suspected that she'd been tortured in an attempt to get Nikolai to surrender the secret whereabouts of the six stolen smallpox vials.

Five had been successfully recovered during the last few hours by Valentin's comrades from other locations in Russia. The one in this village was the last.

Valentin hoped that Nikolai had done his duty and had taken the secret of the vials' locations with him to his grave, regardless of how his daughter had suffered. He hoped, too, that whoever had broken into Nikolai's office in the Russian Embassy on the night of the London massacre had left with nothing of use.

But he had come here to make sure.

A feathering of fresh snow was beginning to fall. Valentin moved wraithlike through the outskirts of the village, adrenalin overriding fatigue, powering him on through the shadows and past the small school, until he reached a tree-shaded playground at the rear of the shops.

No one must know he was there. As well-funded and influential as his clandestine, hardline organization was, he had no official business there. He needed to retrieve the vial, which did not officially exist, and fade back into the mountains.

Ahead he could see the silhouettes of the dairy and slaughterhouse rising up into the twinkling night sky. A dog howled in the distance. Closer, a diesel engine grumbled out a muffled, monotonous tune. *The dairy lorry*, Valentin supposed.

His face glistened with sweat as he wove between the swings and slides, momentarily picturing his grandson laughing last summer, as he'd stabbed his tiny finger towards a jet plane bisecting a clear blue Moscow sky.

Valentin slipped through the playground's gate and ghosted past the back yards of the shops, until he reached the last. The tump-tump of the diesel engine was louder now. He could even see the back of the lorry, red tail-lights glowing, a suction pipe running from its roof to the taps set into the dairy wall.

Valentin scoped the shadows with his rifle's night-sight. Nothing. He peered through a gap in the fence of the building he'd positioned himself behind. A thin line of yellow light beneath a ground-floor curtain indicated that someone inside was awake.

The pharmacist. Valentin's last contact with him had been less than twenty-five minutes ago, just before the helicopter had dusted down. By now he should have taken the vial from its refrigerated storage unit in the concealed safe room and readied it for transportation. In less than two minutes, Valentin hoped, Lyonya and Gregori would be in, out and gone.

'Report status, Alpha Two,' Valentin said softly.

'At rendezvous now.' Lyonya's voice came crackling back through his microbead earpiece. 'All quiet except one civilian in the cab of the lorry. Looks like he's pouring himself a coffee from a Thermos.'

The driver, Valentin thought. He'd be keeping himself warm while the truck's tank filled. Valentin hunkered down, peering again at the building, cursing the pain in his lower back and leg.

He checked the back door. No signs of forced entry. None of the windows had been tampered with. The only footprints were child-sized and iced over.

'Proceed to target,' Valentin said.

The snow was falling thicker now, spiralling dizzily to the ground. Valentin waited, eyes trained on the back of the building.

He pictured Lyonya and Gregori entering its front. There'd be no greeting, no words. The pharmacist would hand over what they'd come for. Then Lyonya and Gregori would leave.

But there . . . Valentin felt it again: the swelling of apprehension, the prickling sensation at the back of his neck. His sixth sense for danger. 'Look at you, twitching like a cat . . .' Wasn't that what Nikolai had always said to him in the old days whenever they'd gone into combat together?

A half-smile softened Valentin's face, as he remembered his old comrade. But then his smile died.

Had Nikolai betrayed the vials' locations before he'd died? Within minutes he would know.

He checked the luminous dials of his watch. Enough time had passed, surely, for Lyonya and Gregori to be reporting back.

'Status, Alpha Two,' Valentin said.

Nothing.

'Status,' he repeated.

Still no reply.

He felt a fresh surge of adrenalin, of nerves. But it might just be the weather, he reminded himself. Or the terrain. Either was more than capable of interfering with their comms . . .

He checked his Bluetooth microbead's placement, but it was fine. He peered up at the trees through the thickening snow. It was turning into a whiteout. Not even the satellite his comrades in Moscow had covertly accessed would be able to see him now.

Meaning that he was truly alone.

'Status,' he tried one final time, knowing that if there was no reply, he would have to go in.

A shadow moved across the slit of yellow light in the ground-floor window. Valentin waited for the curtain to be raised. For Lyonya or Gregori to look out. Nothing.

He had no choice. He slipped through the delivery gate and moved swiftly, silently, to the back door. He listened, hoping to recognize one of his men's voices. He heard nothing.

Crouching, poised, weapon at the ready, he reached up for the door handle and gently turned it. A click. It wasn't locked. Still no noise inside. No voices. His sixth sense was a siren wail inside his head.

He edged the door open, listening, perplexed, as the drumming of the diesel engine grew louder not softer, watching as a widening slice of the pharmacy's storeroom was revealed.

A second door was already open inside, leading out into the alleyway where the dairy lorry had been parked. He realized that what he had thought was a shadow on the floor was a growing pool of blood.

The red dot of a laser sight rose swiftly up his chest towards his head.

He had been right to be afraid. And his comrades had been right to send him here. Because whoever had set up Colonel Nikolai Zykov for that assassination in London had also succeeded in extracting the codes for the locations of the smallpox vials from him before he had died.

CHAPTER 4

SCOTLAND

Cleaning his wounds, God bandaged them tightly, careful not to step past the perimeter of the plastic sheeting, beyond which no one's – neither his own nor his victims' – blood must flow.

He sealed his bloodied clothing and the scalpel into a Ziplock bag, pulled on a new plastic jacket and surgical mask, then a fresh pair of gloves.

He set about tearing the photographs of Shanklin from each of the newspapers. He folded each image lengthways, then lengthways again, and ripped them into squares. He screwed each square into a tiny ball, then gathered them into the box he'd placed beside the rolled-up magazine, the surgical scissors and the jagged shard of rock.

No longer fearing the EMPTINESS . . . no longer fearing HER . . . he turned back to face the family . . . and stretched out his arms like the rays of the sun . . . and let them, his worshippers, behold their true God.

The TRUE GOD need fear no one. Not even the

BITCH GODDESS. Because the TRUE GOD cannot be defeated. The TRUE GOD will always prevail.

Even after Shanklin had attacked God with that knife in the woods, even when he'd tried to shoot God with God's own pistol, he had failed. Because God had been mightier. God had summoned a snowstorm, which had gathered around him like a cloak. Before Shanklin's disbelieving eyes, God had disappeared.

At the base of the mountain on which Shanklin's cabin had been built, God had found a place to hide. He'd crawled into an agricultural drainage tunnel and had daubed himself in black mud as the snow had continued to fall. He'd stayed there for two days until the police and their dogs had gone away.

It had been another two days after that when a security guard had tried to restrain God, after he'd caught him attempting to steal antibiotics from a doctor's surgery across the border in Canada. God had left the guard for dead. But the guard had not died, and a day later God had found himself pulled over in a stolen car by a highway patrol unit. The maimed guard had later identified God as the man who'd attacked him. CCTV footage from the surgery had confirmed that God had been there.

God had been found guilty of assault and attempted robbery. But he'd not been accused of any of the many other crimes he'd committed before that. The police and the lawyers had made no connection between him, paper, stone and scissors, or with the attack on Shanklin's family across the border.

Once more he had prevailed.

He'd been sent to prison for what he'd done to the guard. Each day he'd counted off the hours and had pictured Shanklin's face. And had pictured the guard's face. And had pictured Shanklin's daughter's face. Until the three had become one.

After his release six weeks ago his first task had been to track down the security guard. The man had moved jobs several times since, but that had not been enough to keep him from God. It was regrettable that the guard had lived alone, without any family. But God would still never forget the look on his face as he'd rattled his last shuddering breath.

Paper . . .

God had then dedicated himself to tracking down his cancer, so that he could at last cut it out at the root.

He'd made a study of Danny Shanklin. He'd learned that he was from a military family. His bastard of a father had been chief combatives instructor at the United States Military Academy. His half-English, half-Russian whore of a mother had lectured in Russian. Shanklin himself had gone to West Point. After graduating from NYC with a master's in modern languages, he'd then joined the US Army Rangers. The CIA had come next. Langley. Special Activities Division. Camp Perry. Special Operations Group.

Oh, yes, Shanklin had been reared in a nest of vipers indeed . . .

It was when Shanklin had been seconded to the FBI

that he'd first come to God's attention. He had attempted
to trap God. But he had failed. And it was then that God
had hunted him down and had followed him and his
family into the woods, where he had killed Shanklin's wife
and son.

During God's subsequent time in prison, he'd now
learned, Shanklin had stopped using his old bank accounts
and known addresses, and had liquidated his assets. He'd
set himself up instead with a complex web of financial
aliases, no doubt assuming that his whereabouts would be
untraceable.

But God had once worked for the American government, too, and still had many contacts there. So God had
soon discovered that, over the last few years while God
had been in prison, Shanklin had resurfaced. As a personal
security consultant here. A hostage negotiator there.
Always using a fake name. He'd made a business out of
helping people. He'd stopped them getting hurt.

But in all Shanklin's attempts to drop off the grid and
disappear from public view, he had made one terrible error.
Even though he'd moved her to England, he'd allowed his
daughter to keep her own name. Perhaps because – like the
FBI – he had come to believe that God, having vanished
for so many years, was dead. Or perhaps, through some
sentimental attachment to his dead wife and son, he had
tried to keep their family name alive.

Shanklin's daughter's first name was Alexandra. She
was now seventeen and in her final year at a boarding
school in London. According to her Facebook profile,

her nickname was Lexie and she had 117 friends. Her interests included sport, books and films, and she was in a relationship with a young man her own age, who liked football, rock music and skateboarding.

God had not wasted any time. He'd arranged false identification and had booked a flight to the UK so that he could snatch the girl. Snatch her and use her as bait. Bait to catch Shanklin. So that God could finish off what he had started in the woods.

But God had arrived at Heathrow Airport two days ago to be confronted by the spectre of Danny Shanklin's face staring out at him from every TV screen he saw.

God gazed down now at the newspaper headlines on the floor, which said that Shanklin and a Russian diplomat, Colonel Nikolai Zykov, had assassinated a United Nations envoy in London and had simultaneously massacred the civilians who had been walking past the Ritz Hotel at the time. Colonel Zykov had died of a heart attack in the hotel room shortly afterwards. Danny Shanklin had fled across London, the subject of what was now being described as 'the Biggest Manhunt in History'. He had somehow foiled half a million CCTV cameras, nine intelligence agencies, 33,000 cops – and escaped.

God did not care if Danny Shanklin had done what the newspapers said. God did not care why Danny Shanklin might have decided to kill all those people. Or whether he had even done it.

No, people killed and were killed every minute of every day, and God did not care about them.

What God cared about was that Danny Shanklin now had a price tag of ten million dollars on his head. And was at the top of every global security and intelligence agency's Most Wanted list. Which meant that Shanklin would once again be doing everything in his power to vanish from the face of the earth.

What God cared about most was that Shanklin had got to his daughter first and had taken her into hiding with him – and had thereby taken her from God.

Anger flowed red. It flowed like fire through God's veins. And, there, again, he felt her slithering up from the black – the *BITCH GODDESS* – probing, searching for weakness, trying to seep back into his mind through the gaps. But this time he blocked her. He turned to the family. He focused on them instead.

He focused on paper and stone and scissors . . .

He went for the older girl first and stretched out his clenched fist. She was in her late teens, around the same age as Danny Shanklin's daughter.

L

E

X

I

E

God's tongue flickered hungrily across his lips as he savoured each letter of Shanklin's daughter's name, like a fresh and wondrous taste in his mind.

CHAPTER 5

CAUCASUS MOUNTAIN RANGE

A sound like running water. Vibrations. A numbness like dental anaesthetic. A booming echo. A soft and sensual moan.

Am I dreaming? Valentin Sabirzhan strained to see through the blurred slits of his eyes. A shiny surface ballooned, then distorted and shrank in the weak light. What was it he could see? Some kind of wall? Whatever it was, it was curved. *Where am I?* A cave? No, the surface of the wall was too reflective. It's metal, he thought. And – *yes, right there* – he could see rivets running upwards in a line.

A gasp. Laughter. Another moan. Of what? Pain? Delight?

Valentin tried to move. Couldn't. His body wouldn't respond to the commands his brain was frantically sending out. Every part of him felt numb, cradled, and seemed to be tingling, as fuzzy and here-and-yet-not-here as his mind. *What's happened to me?* Panic ripped through him. *Have I broken my back? My neck?*

'See how he's trying to blink away the blood,' a woman's voice said in Russian.

Blood?

Another gasp. Of pain. Oh, yes, there was no mistaking it this time. More laughter followed. The sound was so near, yet Valentin knew it was not directed at him but at somebody else.

'Look . . . see how hard he is trying, even though his eyelids are no longer there . . .'

No longer there?

Fear. Valentin felt it then. This was no dream. No nightmare either. He would not wake from this. It was real.

He tried again to move. Desperately now. But it was like trying to will a body frozen in ice to move. Only this time – yes! – even though he couldn't move, he did at least feel something. A tightness at his wrists. In his knees and ankles too.

Not paralysed, then . . . I've been *tied*. My *wrists* have been bound to my ankles behind my back. *But how? By whom? And why?*

A blur of memories hurtled through his confused mind, like a section of film flicked to fast forward: icicles glinting in the branches of a tree; a snowbound village in a valley at night; and danger – yes, the sense of danger – was everywhere, all around.

He became aware of another sensation cutting through the numbness: a throbbing in his neck, as steady as a pulse, yet painful and localized and *wrong*. Heat was radiating outwards in waves from that point, as if he'd suffered a terrible burn. Or had been shot.

His whole body jolted. His stomach lurched. At first he thought someone had hit him, but then he realized he'd been shaken from below. Gravity, he felt that now too. He was curled up like a foetus on his side.

Another jolt. And that hissing sound he'd heard before, along with those vibrations – weren't they coming from beneath him as well?

A memory from fifty years ago solidified in the confused mists of his mind. He was racing on his bicycle down a steep road in the small town in which he'd been born. He was trying to catch up with his big brother, Yan, when his front wheel had hit a rut. And suddenly there he was: airborne, exhilarated, whooping with delight ...

A rut, a rut in the road – was that what had jolted him just now? Yes, I'm in some kind of a vehicle, he thought. I'm in some kind of ...

Truck.

The word hit him like a brick to the back of his head. He remembered everything then, as if he'd just turned on a burning white light in a previously pitch-black room. The journey from Moscow. The helicopter dusting down in the forest. Lyonya and Gregori. The pharmacy door. The spreading pool of blood. That red dot of a laser sight creeping up his chest.

That's it, Valentin thought – too late. That was what it was about the view of the village that had felt so terribly wrong.

After he'd switched his binoculars from night-vision to infrared, a heat signature had shown on the milk truck's tank as well as its cab. It had been warm when it should have been cold. Because – yes, he understood everything now – refrigerated milk wasn't being pumped into it: people had been concealed inside. Whoever it was who'd tied him up. That was how they'd got into the village without being observed by the satellite. And that was how they were fleeing it as well.

This miserable realization was followed by an even darker one. Valentin's old friend Nikolai Zykov had not managed to keep his secret. These people had found the vial.

A clanking of boots on metal. A shadow stretched out, enveloping him. Then pain. Ripping through his kidneys. Someone had kicked him and now they stamped hard on his back.

A roar exploded inside him. But only a guttural growl emerged. He felt himself choking. He tried to open his mouth. No good. He prised his front teeth apart with his tongue and probed between his lips. Stickiness. His mouth had been taped shut. He sucked sour air in through his nose. He felt his chest shudder and heave.

Again he heard the woman's voice, but it was closer now, right beside him: 'It looks as though Granddad's awake . . .'

Granddad? She meant him.

He fought to suck oxygen into his lungs. He waited for the next bolt of pain. Instead came more clanking.

More echoes. A torch beam flickered. He braced himself as her shadow fell across him again.

Instead a rush of ice-cold water smashed into his face. A boot pressed down hard on the side of his head. A terrible pressure that did not let up. Surely his cheekbone would crack.

The torch beam was thrust down towards him. He blinked too late. His vision blistered red. A man barked a single syllable. Someone – two people? – seized Valentin and jerked him upright. Silhouettes shifted left and right as the torch beam withdrew.

Whoever had hold of him twisted him round, forced him to his knees and gripped him by his elbows and throat. The ceiling . . . it was barely a foot above his head . . . He tried to struggle, but he couldn't move. Even at full strength, he doubted he would have been able to throw them off. Enfeebled as he was, he didn't stand a chance. He sagged, electing to conserve what little energy he had, his only idea being to advertise his weakness as best he could to make himself appear even less of a threat to them than he already was.

A tranquillizer. That explained the swelling in his neck and his inability to move. They must have shot him with a tranquillizer in the pharmacy. Anything else at that range and he'd have been dead.

What about Lyonya and Gregori?

Had they been tranquillized too? Hope leaped inside him. What if they – or the pharmacist – had escaped? They'd have alerted Valentin's comrades by now. Help might already be on the way. Even now this vehicle might be being tracked and his ordeal would soon be at an end. And then – then he'd get hold of these *sisterfuckers*, he'd get hold of them and—

The glare of the torch beam receded. Valentin opened his eyes, stared through the dancing blizzard of retinal flashes and saw his hopes crushed.

Lyonya and Gregori were framed in bright torch light, illuminated like exhibits in a museum for Valentin's benefit, trussed up on their sides and gagged, bound like him with their ankles and wrists tied behind their backs.

Both men had been badly beaten, Gregori the worst. Sickened, Valentin looked away from the younger man's bloodstained eyes, eyes that Gregori would never again be able to shut.

Valentin lurched forward. The road this truck was travelling along had just grown steep. The men holding him tightened their grip. The woman returned, hunkering down on her boots before him.

She was as pale and smooth-featured as if she'd been carved out of ice. Her fur-collared combat jacket was dusted with snow. A single short blonde lock of hair curled down across her brow from beneath her hood.

Without any warning she punched Valentin hard in the face. He absorbed the pain. He went with it as he had so many times before. He would not give her the pleasure of seeing him wince. Instead he glared back. She punched him again, harder than before. He still did not react.

She laughed. It was the same laugh he'd heard before, when she'd been mocking Gregori's inability to blink away the blood from his eyes. He'd make her pay for that. If he got the chance, he'd make her pay with her life.

No, he thought. Not if. *When* . . .

He knew he had to believe this or he might as well give up now.

The blonde woman leaned in as if to kiss him. She was beautiful. He could see that, in spite of the hatred he felt. She pressed her cold cheek to his, sniffing at him hungrily, like a dog would a bitch. And he could smell her too. He could smell her sweet perfume.

He shuddered as she trailed her lips lingeringly across his cheek. Something about the sensation horrified him. It was so clearly a promise that was about to be denied. His mouth felt as dry as autumn leaves.

When her lips reached his ear, she whispered, 'Your friend, Colonel Zykov, pissed himself like a child before he died.'

Then she bit him. Her teeth snapped deep into the cartilage of his ear. Until they met. Pain lanced his skull. He bellowed through the tape. He tried to break free, but he still could not move.

With her teeth still clamped together, the blonde woman jerked her head sideways, like a wolf ripping at the flesh of a lamb. She tore Valentin Sabirzhan's ear clean off.

White pain.

Red pain.

Pain that would not stop.

He gritted his teeth so hard together that he heard them beginning to crack.

Breathe! he ordered himself. Breathe through your nose or you'll choke!

The side of his head felt wrong, as if someone had punched a hole clean through it. Gobbets of hot blood trickled down his throat. He'd bitten through his own cheek and lips.

Breathe.

Breathe, dammit, breathe.

A mesh of torch beams flickered across his face, across his body. In a moment of clarity, he glimpsed the tattoo of the fist and the star on his right arm.

Remember who you are. *Spetsnaz*. Remember your strength.

His nostrils flared. His breath came in growls. The woman remained squatted in front of him, her head cocked to one side, watching him curiously, as if searching for understanding, as if trying to learn and comprehend what might be going through his mind. Her mouth looked like a gunshot entry wound. Blood drops patterned her jaw like holly berries.

My blood, Valentin realized. Not hers.

She spat hard at him. Something wet hit his cheek and momentarily stuck, before dropping to the floor. He didn't need to see it to know what it was.

Now her eyes were smiling. They were shimmering. No longer seeking to understand, already *knowing*, already satisfied. They were shining with something less like triumph and more like sex.

The first chance I get, I'll wipe that smile off your face *whoever the hell you are*, Valentin promised her, with his eyes.

And perhaps somehow she read his words. Because something in her expression altered. Her ecstatic mask cracked.

'When you die, old man,' she said, 'I will be the one who slits your throat.'

A click.

The red beam of a laser sight shot out from the pistol she was holding. It settled on his neck as she aimed.

The click of a trigger. Pain tore into his neck.

CHAPTER 6

RUSSIA

Darkness. Valentin tried to scream as he woke, but he could not.

Pain was spreading outwards from his head and enveloping his whole body now. He felt as if he were about to catch fire.

And if he felt this bad now – with whatever drug they'd given him still in his system – how much worse would he feel once it had worn off? Hopelessness gripped him. Was this it? Was this the place where he would die?

And *where* was he? He stretched out with all his senses. The air was cool. But he couldn't feel motion, not like in the back of that truck. Only stillness. And silence, silent like the grave. He could smell nothing. But he could hear breathing. Was it just him? Was someone else here?

Hello? Hello! Hello, is anyone there?

His words came out as a growl. He couldn't open his mouth. But the breathing – the other breathing – heightened. It became whimpers. It became gasps. And clinking. A *clinking* sound. It started up and did not stop.

I am not alone. I am not alone. But who? Who else is here?
Believe, he told himself. *Hope* . . .

A thunder of footsteps. A terrible creaking sound.
A burst of bright, flickering light. Valentin's eyes screwed
up involuntarily. He had to fight just to open them, to make
himself look. A terrible glare. Bare bulbs on the ceiling. An
open door. Dark shapes coming through it. Towards him.
One reached down and jerked him to his feet.

No.

The bitch.

She shoved him into the arms of someone else. They
gripped his neck from behind. As she moved aside, a
man took her place, stood before him and observed him.
Behind, a wall loomed into focus, damp brickwork, no
decoration. What was this? A cellar? Where had these
people brought him now?

The man watching Valentin was hooded, his face deep
in shadow. But as one of the bare bulbs above his head
flickered, pale yellow light flashed across his hooked nose
and gaunt features, making him look like a gargoyle, like
some devilish chimera, half remembered from a childhood
fairy tale, half hawk and half human.

'In case you were wondering,' the man said in Russian,
'we have already succeeded in securing the smallpox vial.'

His accent was Muscovite, educated, just like Valentin's.
Do I know you? Valentin searched his memory. *Have I*
worked with you? Are you military, just like me?

'The man you left there to protect it, the pharmacist,
he did his best to lie to us, but he was a family man and,

well . . .' the man sniffed dismissively as he waved his hand '. . . he simply was not up to the task.'

Valentin pictured the statistics, the ones about smallpox, the ones that had worried him each year more and more as he'd watched his own children grow up and have children of their own.

The effectiveness of the vials had increased exponentially over time because the otherwise globally eradicated small-pox virus was no longer vaccinated against. Conservative estimates, based on the recent computerized projections he had seen, suggested current national and international quarantine regulations and existing ring vaccination pro-grammes would fail to prevent a global pandemic, were the virus to be purposefully released and propagated. Many millions would die.

'I'm going to take the tape off your mouth now to enable us to talk,' the hawk-faced man said, 'but if you start shouting, I'll set her on you again. She will, of course, take your other ear. But, trust me, that is probably the least she will do.'

Valentin believed him. He felt himself nod. And there – right then, in his moment of spiritual resignation – a sudden hope surged through him. Because his head had moved, even if it had done so only fractionally. He'd moved it himself.

The hawk-faced man pulled back the hood of his jacket, revealing ice-blue eyes and a shock of white-blond hair, which dispelled Valentin's previous nightmare vision of some beast culled from a childhood story. This man's eyes shone with intelligence, with a kind of enlightenment, even. There was something about his bearing that was studiously refined.

Without warning, he tore the duct tape from Valentin's mouth and waited patiently as Valentin heaved air into his lungs.

'You,' Valentin said, ignoring the pain, his voice little more than a rasp, his tongue so swollen he could barely speak. 'You killed Nikolai . . .'

The man gazed evenly back. 'Zykov? Yes.'

'You set him up, so that it would look like Russia was behind the assassination of that envoy.'

'Quite so. Bravo.'

'And Shanklin?' Valentin said.

Danny Shanklin . . . Even now, even here, in so much agony, his training was kicking in, compelling him to gather whatever intelligence he could. In case he ever made it out alive. And Valentin had to know. Was his source right? Had Shanklin also been framed for the London massacre? Or had he been working with these monsters too?

'Shanklin should have been dead by now,' the hawk-faced man said.

Should have been . . . Valentin almost smiled. So this man who held him captive now *was* fallible, after all. Somehow Shanklin had disrupted his plan. Instead of lying there alongside Nikolai Zykov in a London morgue, set up and then disposed of like poor old Nikolai had been, Danny Shanklin had escaped.

'Why—' Valentin started to ask.

'Are we doing this?' The hawk-faced man's eyes showed only disdain. 'You are a man of so-called principle. You'd never understand.'

For profit, then, he guessed. For money. They're going to sell the smallpox to whoever will pay them the most.

Again he pictured his family. His heart grew cold as steel.

'As you've no doubt already guessed,' the man said, peering into Valentin's eyes, 'Zykov told us everything we needed to know about locating the smallpox vials. You will now aid us similarly, telling us exactly what intelligence you think you have on us, and how you are planning to hunt us down.'

Strength. Valentin felt it then. His right hand made a fist. He felt his calf muscles flexing too. The drug they'd used to incapacitate him was finally wearing off.

'Go fuck yourself, traitor,' he said – not only because he knew Lyonya and Gregori were listening but because he was certain that, once he gave these people the information they wanted, he'd be useless to them. He'd be dead.

'Traitor?' The man gazing into his eyes smiled thinly. 'To what? To Russia? Which Russia? Your Russia, old man? The one that no longer exists? Or today's Russia? The oligarchs' playground? What has *that* Russia ever done for me? Has it invited me onto a private yacht where prostitutes with legs longer than gazelles' suck my *hui* until I'm dry? Has it even bought me a ticket to see dumb shitting Chelsea play Manchester United in the cup? No, it has given me fucking nothing at all.'

The hawk-faced man gripped Valentin's jaw and twisted it sideways, examining his mouth in the same way he might do with a horse he was considering buying or having put down.

'But you know what?' he said, letting go. 'You look like a tough old bastard, eh? And time is short. So I'm thinking that perhaps we should leave you for now and we'll start with your colleagues instead.'

'They will tell you nothing either,' Valentin said. It was a warning, as much as a hope.

His interrogator ignored him. He slid a foot-long cylindrical metal contraption from inside his jacket. 'In the temporary absence of SP-17,' he said, 'I'm afraid we're going to have to resort to more primitive methods to get the information we desire. And, luckily, back there in that slaughterhouse, there was something just as good.'

Fresh adrenalin coursed through Valentin's veins, making them stand out on his neck like wires. SP-17 was a sodium pentothal-based truth serum, which had been developed especially for the Russian Foreign Intelligence Service, the SVR. To have had access to that before, these bastards must have had contacts within the SVR, or had even been Russian intelligence agents themselves.

And poor Nikolai, Valentin thought. The effect of SP-17 was irresistible. If these bastards had used it on him, no wonder he had talked.

The blonde woman moved close to the hawk-faced man, her body pressing up tight to his. He did not move away, Valentin saw. Meaning they were lovers, he assumed. Not only did they kill together, they fucked.

The hawk-faced man handed her the metal contraption, and as he did so, Valentin saw something pass between them, the same ecstasy he'd seen in her eyes before, that same frisson of desire.

'Do you know what this is?' she said, holding up the cylinder for Valentin's benefit.

He said nothing.

'A stun-gun,' she said. 'It fires a recoil-action stainless-steel bolt and is used to kill or knock cattle out cold, depending on what velocity it's set at, so that the beasts do not struggle or feel pain while they are being drained of their blood.' She slowly licked the contraption's metal tip, as if she were tasting ice cream. 'I'm guessing it'll make a big fucking mess of your friend.'

She moved out of sight.

The hawk-faced man's eyes stayed locked with Valentin's.

A whimper.

Valentin's eyes flicked right. Gregori and Lyonya. He saw them then. Both had been stripped naked and were manacled to a wall.

The *clinking* noise . . .

Both men were gagged, their heads lolling, their wrists and ankles bloodied where the metal manacles dug in. Their muscles were inflamed and black with bruises. How long must they have been struggling to break free? And how long had he been there too? How long had they kept him drugged? What were they going to do next?

A terrible thought occurred to him. The fact that they were no longer in the truck meant that these people had escaped from the village where they'd stolen the vial. Wherever they were now, it was possible that no one else knew they were there.

As the woman drew nearer, Gregori's body twisted hard against the wall, as if he were somehow attempting to force himself through. Fresh blood poured from his wrists and ankles.

Valentin saw a flash of white, as his red raw eyes rolled backwards in their unprotected sockets. The blonde woman was on top of him now. She pressed the barrel of the stun-gun to his head. A high-pitched whimper escaped Gregori's bound mouth. But instead of depressing the weapon's primitive firing mechanism, she turned back to Valentin.

'Don't worry, Granddad, we're not going to kill him just yet. We're just going to hurt him.' She smiled. 'A lot.'

Without warning, she rammed and twisted the stun-gun hard between Gregori's legs.

And fired.

A hiss of compressed air. A dull thud.

Gregori's face froze like a mask, then contorted in agony as he started to writhe.

Animal.

Valentin fought the urge to try to tear himself free from his bonds. Instead of being manacled, like the others, he was still hog-tied. If he tried to tear himself loose, he would fail, he knew. And in so doing he would give away his recovery.

Slowly, he commanded himself. Do not let these *sooki* see, but now slowly test what you can do. So he tried. And, yes, right there, he felt his wrists turning, twisting one against the other, probing at their bindings, trying to break free. Not long now, he told himself. A few more minutes and you'll be strong enough to fight.

As his wrists continued their hidden dance, his eyes searched desperately for some kind of a blade or sharp surface to speed matters along.

I will not quit. I will not surrender hope.

A shriek of duct tape.

A gargling of blood and air.

'Anything,' Gregori screamed. 'Anything. I will tell you anything you want to know.'

Before Valentin could stop himself, he reacted. He could not help himself. He twisted right round to face Gregori: if the younger man talked, they were all doomed. These people would butcher them like cattle. They'd have no reason to keep them alive.

'Shut up,' he shouted.

The blonde moved so fast, he hardly saw her coming. But then she was on him again. On top of him. She bared her teeth. She rammed the stun-gun into his squirming groin, and Valentin wished then that he was still gagged. If he had been gagged, then at least he would not scream.

But it was the girl who screamed first.

She was jerked backwards. But, even then, she refused to let go. Her nails clawed blood from his neck. The hawk-faced man gripped the scruff of her neck. Then he pressed a pistol to her head. Eventually she became still.

'Not yet,' he told her, soothingly now. 'I have a much better use for him first.'

Valentin's hope almost deserted him. The way the hawk-faced man had spoken . . . The look in his eyes . . . The way even the woman – this bitch – now looked sated by his words . . . He knew then that whatever the hawk-faced man was promising her, it was going to be so much worse than death.

CHAPTER 7

PRIPYAT, UKRAINE.

Hunting.

That was what this reminded Danny Shanklin of, the pounding of blood in his veins, the thickening of spit in his mouth. It had got him thinking back to when the Old Man used to take him hunting in the woods.

Danny had been a kid when his father had taught him how to kill, first with slings and bows, then with firearms. Many years later, after Danny's parents had passed away and he'd finally plucked up the courage to set about clearing out his childhood home, he'd found a faded Polaroid that the Old Man had kept tucked inside his Bible in his bedside drawer.

It had pictured Danny swamped in a camouflage jacket way too big for his skinny body, leaving him looking like a scarecrow, with his scruffy blond hair all messed up like straw, his knees and elbows sticking out. He'd been grinning, proudly holding up a dead wood pigeon. The bird had been shot clean through the head, mid-flight. An inch-perfect kill.

The Old Man had been a soldier, just as Danny would later become. Hunting had been in his blood and he'd wanted his boy raised the same. He'd taught him to trap and shoot small game, then skin, pluck and gut his kills for food. But the first time Danny had ever tracked, stalked and shot something as big as himself, it had been a deer.

Fleetingly, in his mind's eye, he now saw the young deer again. A stag, skin the colour of raw liver. It had been standing silhouetted against a blood-red sky, gnawing at lichen on the bark of a tree.

Danny hadn't waited for the Old Man's permission. He'd crouched and steadied himself. Then he'd done as he'd been taught. He'd locked his entire body as he'd aimed. He'd slowed his breathing and relaxed. As he'd squeezed the trigger, he'd exhaled, imagining the round he'd just fired first impacting and then snatching away its target's last breath.

Danny had been nine years old that morning. More than four decades had passed since then. Time enough for him to have married and had two kids of his own. And all the horrors that had happened since.

In spite of that, Danny still felt the same now as he had done on the morning he'd gone out after the deer. That same catch-breath of anticipation before the kill, that same deliberate unfurling of a bridge between life and death, and the same first step on it: he felt all that now and knew there could be no turning back.

And for that he was glad. Because, make no mistake,

the group he'd tracked here, the same terrorists who'd planned to torture and murder him and Lexie, he no longer thought of them as human. They were nothing but prey.

A voice like river grit being sifted through a coarse steel sieve cut clean through his thoughts.

'So are we going to do this shit, or what?' Spartak said.

All six foot seven of Spartak Sidarov was crouched low in the moonlight beside Danny in a thicket of brambles on the rusted railway track, about as subtle and as small as a tank.

Spartak's grizzled shovel of a face was pressed up to his ear so that he could make himself heard above the rain and the howling wind. So close that Danny could smell the stink of tobacco and salt liquorice on his breath.

Danny lowered the telescopic night-sight he'd been looking through. He gazed down at the Geiger counter strapped to his wrist. The digits were still spiking up into the red, meaning the radiation level remained dangerously high – even for the Zone.

The Zone of Alienation had been established in 1986, following the Chernobyl nuclear-reactor disaster. The entire population from the surrounding area had been evacuated at the time to protect them from the fallout, and most had never come back.

More than 600,000 recovery workers, known as liquidators, had been drafted in to work here between '86 and '92. Their job had been to hunt out the worst of the radioactivity and bury any materials particularly affected where they found them. Thousands of liquidators had died in these places, or had later become severely disabled as a result of the radiation poisoning they'd suffered.

The worst hot spots were still potentially lethal today. And the Geiger counter on Danny's wrist left no doubt in his mind that he and his team were crouched dead centre in the middle of one now: Pripyat, Ukraine. The faster they got this done and got the hell out, the better it would be for them all.

'Ready?' he said, turning to Spartak.

Spartak's crooked teeth glinted ghoulishly in the green neon glow of the GPS locator cupped in his enormous gloved hand. He pushed his tangled mop of thick black hair back from where it had been plastered across his wide brow by the rain.

'I was born shit fucking ready,' he said. 'Ready to rumble and ready to roll.'

Danny smiled wryly. Languages had always come easily to him, and he spoke a half-dozen fluently, including Spartak's native and learned tongues of Ukrainian and Russian. But the big guy preferred practising his English whenever Danny was around. He had ambitions to move to America one day, marry a Californian girl, with 'an ass as firm and as smooth as a peach', and go into politics the way Schwarzenegger had done.

Danny hadn't yet told him that the only real impediment Spartak needed to overcome for this plan to work was that he'd been raised on pirated American action flicks back in the eighties so he thought that cursing like an extra from *Full Metal Jacket* or *Hamburger Hill* was perfectly fine. He hadn't told him, not because he wanted his plan to fail but because he enjoyed hearing him talking that way.

Spartak turned to the two other men lying flat and silent in the dirt to his left. '*Rukhatysya*,' he told them, in Ukrainian, meaning, Time to fucking move and earn your supper.

Like Spartak, the two younger Ukrainians were ex-military turned mercenary. And, like Spartak, their loyalty in the recent political upheavals between Ukraine and Russia was to Russia, the motherland in whose army they had served, and where many of their extended family still lived. But while Spartak was there out of friendship and a shared history with Danny – each of them had saved the other's life – the others were there for cold cash.

They were dressed, like Spartak, from head to foot in black Gore-Tex assault gear and radioactivity vests. Both carried AK-9s, fitted with silencers. State-of-the-art retinal-targeting night-sight goggles glinted in the shadows of their hooded, visored caps, revealing patches of sallow, surprisingly boyish freckled cheeks and chins. Neither man spoke as they slithered up from the ground into a crouch.

'Meet Viktor and Vasyl, my cousins from my mother's side.' That was how Spartak had introduced the twins to Danny two days before, in the concrete cancer-riddled Ukrainian tower block where Danny had been hiding.

The names were so ridiculous that Danny knew they had to be bullshit. He guessed the family connection was more than likely the same. Neither of these youthful trained killers bore any familial resemblance to Spartak. For one thing, they were nearer Danny's height at around six foot. And for another, they were lithe, also like Danny, and built like middleweight boxers, not endowed, like Spartak, with all the suppleness and agility of a rhino.

But if Spartak vouched for them, that was good enough for Danny. The big guy had never let him down before. Which was why – along with the fact that he was Ukrainian and originally from around here – Danny had brought him to help with this take-down.

Danny had Spartak to thank for smuggling him across Europe as well. As the British police and intelligence agencies had continued to comb the UK for signs of his presence and monitor all points of exit, Spartak had kitted him out with a fresh Russian ID, an oxygen mask hooked up to a respirator, and a set of green hospital robes. He'd then stuck him on a gurney in the back of a private ambulance that had shipped him across the English Channel, then driven him through Europe.

The driver and attending medic had been introduced to Danny as 'a friend of a friend of a friend', and neither had asked him a single question the whole way there. 'They're used to moving things,' was all Spartak had said, when Danny had asked him who they were. *Things*: bodies, stolen art – he hadn't cared or probed any

further. He'd just been grateful at last to have the help
of a friend.

'*Now*,' Danny said, in Ukrainian, for the benefit of
the twins.

The four picked themselves up out of the dirt and rose
as one, then started running forward, fanning out across
the open ground.

CHAPTER 8

Gore-Tex scratched against thorns. Boots crunched on earth. Danny's weapon felt light, felt right in his hands. He ignored the fatigue in his limbs. He knew it was only temporary. Only a matter of seconds now before adrenalin kicked in.

Picking up speed, he snapped his night goggles down over his eyes. Autofocusing, retina-guided and smart-chipped, they fed off light thrown down by the moon and the stars. Danny's view of the world switched to green and grey, as though he were now under water, a ravenous pike lancing in search of fresh prey.

He upped his speed again as he zigzagged across the deserted shunting yard towards the abandoned town. His peripheral vision and feet were working in tandem, almost entirely independent of his conscious thoughts, instinctively navigating him through the minefield of potholes, rail ruts, torn-down fences and cracked concrete slabs that littered this forgotten, forsaken corner of the world.

As well as allowing him to see what was in front of him, his goggles were also automatically tracking the other members of his team, casting them as three separate green pulses, designated with a number from one to three, against a rolling green grid of pixellated terrain.

Ten years younger than himself and Spartak, the twins – numbered two and three – were moving fastest. He watched the spacing between them rapidly increase as they continued to deploy into the approach pattern he'd ordered.

He forced himself to move faster too, imagining Spartak attempting the same. 'This growing-old shit, this thought of having our asses kicked and beaten by motherfuckers younger than ourselves . . .' the big guy had once said '. . . a part of me hopes I get killed before that.'

Danny knew the feeling. Once this was over, he was finished. No more. Not for himself and not for anyone else, no matter how good the cause. He was done. He wanted to be a father again. To make up for all of the lost time when he'd not been there for Lexie. He didn't want to have to prove himself any more. He just wanted to be alive and allowed to grow old.

But first he had to finish *this* . . .

Reaching the crumbling concrete plinth of the decrepit station platform, Danny took the ten steps to its top in four swift strides. He ran on through the desolate, wind-whipped waiting room, with its mosaic of broken tiles, forgotten seats and smashed glass.

He'd been braced for the strangeness of the place, but

it still freaked him out. It was just so . . . *gone*. Nothing remained. Not even memories. No one had stayed behind. All gone. Everyone who'd ever lived there. Parents watching that their kids didn't stray too close to the tracks . . . Workers smoking cigarettes, waiting for the train to take them home . . . All their hopes and dreams, the everyday worries clamouring inside their heads. This wasn't even a ghost town. It was too dead now even for that.

Danny rushed on through the ticket office, past the creepers and curling timetables on its cracked, weather-beaten walls. Then on down into the car park at the front of the station. There, up ahead, was the old entrance to the town. His muscles were aching, screaming, but he could not afford to slow. Not out in the open. Seeing his own shadow running before him, he inwardly cursed the brightness of the moonlight. Danger pulsed through him. Adrenalin flowed. He wondered, *What if I've already been seen?* If he had, he'd know soon enough. Or, rather, he wouldn't. Because he'd be dead.

Using whatever cover he could – saplings, overturned bins and skeletal cars, each stripped down, twisted and cannibalized for parts by whichever crazed criminals and professional looters had been high, greedy or desperate enough to plunder a hot spot – he made it as far as the railway station gates.

He stopped there, breathless, and hunkered down low. He checked the open street beyond: more desolation and decay; a row of shops with cracked windows; a tree growing up tall through the busted windscreen of a rusted bus in the middle of the road.

But he saw no threats. No people. No life. Not even a stray dog or a rat. The only heat signature his goggles picked up now was of Spartak forty metres away.

The howling wind continued to blow. Ice-cold rain drilled down. Didn't matter how tight you wrapped yourself up against the elements, water always got in. The same cold water that could seep down granite crevices, expand and crack them apart, trickled down his neck now.

And while he wouldn't normally have given a damn, with his Geiger counter still high in the red, each fresh blast of wind and cold drop of rain came at him like a forceful tap on the shoulder, reminding him that he and the others were at risk of contamination too.

'*Tut*,' Danny said into his mike, meaning he was now in position.

'*Tut*,' the three others echoed. They were awaiting his orders.

The building Danny had travelled all this way for was now less than four hundred metres away. According to the basic commercial satellite images he'd studied, and the limited reliable map work available for the area, he'd concluded it was an abandoned telephone exchange, which had once been the town's main employer.

He and the others had been over their plan of attack a dozen times already. Attack? He hoped it came to that. There was still the grim possibility that the birds he'd come here to capture had already flown.

Of the unit of six mercenaries who'd assassinated the Georgian-sympathizing UN peace envoy in London ten days ago, there were now only three left alive: their leader, known only as Glinka, and on whom Danny had so far been able to turn up zero intelligence; his woman, a blonde, whose face he would never forget; and Adam Fitch, a.k.a. 'The Kid'.

Until ten days ago, Danny would have described the Kid as one of only three people left alive whom he'd have trusted with his life. Until the moment when the Kid had pulled a Glock 18 machine pistol on him and had told him that, unless he stole the secret locations of six smallpox vials from Colonel Nikolai Zykov's office in London's Russian Embassy, he would execute Danny and his daughter.

Danny had done what Glinka and the Kid had asked of him. But instead of being released, as he had been promised, he and his daughter had been handed over to three cold stone-eyed killers, whose job it had been to get rid of them in any way they saw fit.

Things hadn't worked out like that. The three men who'd been left to murder Danny and Lexie had ended up dead themselves.

Danny had made sure that the last of them to die, the torturer who'd planned to practise his despicable art on Danny and Lexie, had told him everything he knew during the final, prolonged and increasingly agonizing moments of his life.

He had confessed that certain elements of the Georgian

Secret Service had paid Glinka to assassinate the UN peace envoy and blame it on Colonel Zykov so that the UN would perceive this as an act of Russian aggression and would therefore once more demand the withdrawal of Russian troops from the former Georgian border territories of South Ossetia and Abkhazia.

The dying man had also told him that Glinka had set Danny up to take the blame for the London massacre and assassination so that he could publicly run him through the televised, police-choked streets of London, like a fox before a baying pack of hounds. Danny would gain international media attention and condemnation for the terrorist atrocity, and occupy the cops long enough for the real killers to get clean away.

The torturer had told him, too, about the smallpox. About how, after selecting Zykov to take the fall for the assassination – he was a high-standing member of the Russian Embassy staff in London – Glinka had recognized him as the same scarred soldier who'd raided the Biopreparat chemical-weapons facility at which Glinka had been stationed as a guard back in 1990.

Glinka knew Zykov had stolen the smallpox all those years ago and had decided that, as well as framing him for the assassination, he would take it for himself by torturing Zykov to discover the vials' current whereabouts.

The last thing the dying torturer had told Danny was what had brought him to this wasteland: the date and the GPS coordinates of where the torturer had intended to meet up with Glinka, the blonde and the Kid.

Namely here.

Tonight.

Bang centre in the deadliest part of the Zone.

CHAPTER 9

'Move, Two and Three,' Danny said in Ukrainian.

He pictured the twins – silent, lethal – moving like missiles towards their target.

He began counting down from thirty.

The plan was for the twins to close in on the abandoned telephone exchange from the north and the west. Danny and Spartak would move in from the east and the south. Danny wanted them to surround the building simultaneously, which meant the twins needed a small head start.

Tensing, ready to go, he again scoped the streets and buildings for signs of life. Still nothing moved. The one advantage to being in a hot spot like this: he didn't have to worry about the law. Even the MVS and the Ukrainian State Border Guard Service, whose job it was to police the Zone, kept away.

Because only a madman would set foot there voluntarily. Only a madman or someone out to catch one.

Rain beads zigzagged across Danny's goggles. Scoping

the street again, he noticed his hands were trembling for the first time since he'd said goodbye to Lexie three days ago. He'd finally got her somewhere he was still praying was safe.

Concentrate on here, on now, he ordered himself. Not on Lexie. Not on then. Concentrate on getting your team in and out alive. Concentrate on doing what you do best.

But he knew that this wasn't what he did best. What he did best was prepare and strategize, leaving nothing to chance. That was why he was good at his job: he never went into anything he didn't know his way back out of. The same as anyone else in his line of work. Anyone who wanted to stay alive.

But tonight he was barely prepared at all. Spartak had seen to their equipment and weapons, and Danny hardly knew the other half of his team. And only had the most basic intel on where they were heading. Not even a floor plan for the telephone exchange. No surveillance. No knowledge of what weaponry, or how many people – if any – might be waiting inside.

Which was maybe the real reason he was trembling now, he thought. His whole life he'd been one of the good guys, with the might of government and all its resources at his back. Now that safety net had been ripped away. For the first time, Danny Shanklin was operating on the wrong side of international law.

Ten, nine, eight . . .

Danny wanted this done with now. He could feel his energy levels dropping. Hardly surprising. He couldn't remember when he'd last had more than two hours' straight sleep. And Spartak, even though he'd never admit it, would by now be tiring too. They'd marched five and a half kilometres to get there tonight, having first penetrated the Zone's security perimeter on foot. They'd had no choice. If the people he'd come for really were there, they'd be on the lookout for approaching vehicles.

He forced himself to sharpen up and focus on what was to come.

He told himself that soon there would be blood.

Three, two . . .

The thirty seconds was up. And so was Danny. Mobile. Out through the gates, then heading right, sticking as close to the deserted buildings as he could. He sprinted up the street, counting off the alleyways either side, relieved to find their spacing matched the Soviet map of the area he'd memorized that morning.

'One – move in,' he radioed, unleashing Spartak too.

Danny switched left into the fifth alley. More of a side-street, he saw, as he raced on past a dozen arched wooden doorways set into a crumbling grey brick wall. A forgotten place. Gutters hanging at crazy angles. Blistered paintwork. A rusted tangle of bikes. Faded signs for cobblers, mechanics and furniture repairs.

At the end of the street, grim as a Gothic castle in a rainstorm, the two-storey utilitarian concrete block of the abandoned telephone exchange loomed into sight. In between lay what had once been a municipal car park, but which looked now like a junk yard full of abandoned cars.

Danny slunk into the shadows of a stack of warped pallets and peered through the dripping rotten slats. He scoped the exchange and the ivy-snaked buildings around it. Dark, empty windows stared blankly back.

He felt it then. In spite of his exhaustion. The same buzz of imminent action he had always felt at times like this, as if he'd been strangely transmogrified and was now a spider sensing a twitch at its web or a wolf picking up the scent of freshly spilled blood . . .

He moved swiftly to the edge of the car park, keeping low, edging along a row of corroded cars. Peering through the lashing rain as it rattled like hail across the car roofs, he scoped the surrounding buildings again. Moving forward, he felt the ground shifting beneath his feet, growing softer, turning from concrete into dirt and mud.

He slowed, no longer just worrying about threats from above and around but searching warily beneath him. As he kept edging forward, his eyes sifted through the green darkness for telltale signs of surveillance and IEDs: trip-wires, plastics and recently dug patches in the ground.

He hoped to hell he'd find none. Not because he couldn't circumnavigate them but because failing to have laid out perimeter defences would indicate that Glinka wasn't expecting unwanted visitors. Which would mean that, even if he'd guessed Danny and Lexie had escaped being executed in England, he didn't think Danny had the knowledge, means or determination to come hunting for him here.

'Always credit your enemy with greater intelligence

than yourself.' One of Danny's father's favourite sayings. One that would cost Glinka his liberty and even his life, if it turned out he'd ignored it now.

'*Tut*,' Danny hissed into his mike. He was now in position less than twenty metres from the exchange.

Then he froze.

Something wasn't right. Something in his field of vision. At first he couldn't see what it was. His goggles revealed no thermal traces, nothing living, as he slowly scoped the buildings and surrounding cars, hunting for glimmers of red.

Yet something had snagged his attention.

Just in time, he saw what it was. A sliver of vehicle ten metres to his right up ahead. Something about its shape was all wrong. He edged closer, widening the angle between himself and it as he did so. There, he saw confirmation of what his peripheral vision had flagged up.

The vehicle's black paintwork was rust-free and glinted slick as spilt oil in the moonlight. He recognized the model as well. A Honda SUV. A shape not even dreamed of when Chernobyl had gone up and the people who'd lived there had fled.

A click. A hum. Light blazed down.

CHAPTER 10

Danny shut his eyes just before his goggles massively magnified the intensity of the sodium searchlight on the Honda's roof. He crash-rolled left, between two hulks of cars, then flattened, tearing the goggles from his eyes, blinking in frustration as retinal flashes flickered over his vision.

The world swung back into focus as the first boot thumped down out of the Honda. The remote possibility that some civilian might be there on legitimate business vanished, as whoever it was took off right, racing away from the Honda towards the row of decrepit vehicles beyond.

He swung his AK-9 round and snapped off a shot. But his vision wasn't up to it. He missed.

The weapon's sound suppressor kept the noise down to a *phut*. The round, though, pinged off the hubcap of the van the Honda guy had just darted behind and echoed into the night.

He rolled left again, then spidered, crawled, crouched

and finally ran. He had to get away from the last position he'd been in. Flank the guy quick and he'd still be in with a chance.

He moved just in time. A drumming sound, louder, harder than the rain. A skittering of metal on metal. Rounds fired from another silenced weapon ripped into the car he had been hiding behind, sparking off its metal and thumping into the dirt all around it.

A high cyclic rate. An assault rifle, Danny guessed. If he'd stayed where he was, he would have been ripped in two.

He dropped low and rolled – once, twice – in rapid succession across the gap between the rows of cars. Thank God for the wind and the rain, and that whoever he was up against had a silencer fitted too. Whoever was inside that telephone exchange might not yet have realized what was going on.

But Danny knew that the Honda guy more than likely had comms: every passing second was a widening of their window of opportunity to call in and raise the alarm.

'Danny?'

He heard Spartak's voice in his earbead. The big guy must have heard him panting and known something was awry. He ignored him. Spartak was too far away to help him now.

Movement. Due south. Danny was staring through the slit beneath the corroded bottom of the car he was lying beside and the ground. Two cars further away, almost merging into blackness beside a flattened tyre, a new shape had just emerged into the grain of the driving rain.

This time his eyesight was clear. He scoped in until he could see the thin black line of the lace pulled tight to the eye of the boot.

'Sleep tight.' His lips framed the word silently as he squeezed the trigger.

The round fired from his AK-9 smashed through his target's ankle at such a velocity that it ripped his leg from under him and sent him crashing hard to the ground.

Danny waited. He watched. The man didn't move.

It was possible, he supposed, that the velocity and the round's impact alone had been enough to send his target into shock, or even kill him outright by inducing a heart attack. But while Danny wanted him alive to question, the risk of his victim being alive enough to send comms to anyone inside the exchange was just too big to take.

His target's body bucked twice in the mud as he loosed off two more rounds. One to the chest and one to the head.

'Danny?' Spartak's voice came again.

Still no movement from the fallen target.

'Hold your positions,' Danny whispered into his mike, in Ukrainian, eyes still locked on the stationary body. 'I've got one hostile down. I think he's alone.'

Silence, except for the drumming of the rain and the wail of the wind. Danny rolled right and came up slowly, snapping his goggles back up from where they'd been hanging by their strap around his neck. He wiped the mud from the lenses and checked the front of the exchange.

It was lifeless as the grave.

He nudged the body with the toe of his boot as he reached it, ready to shoot. He clocked the bloodied hole in the side of the Honda guy's hood and knelt. The dead man's finger was trapped in the trigger guard of his APS. Danny eased it free, inspecting the weapon.

The APS was old, but clean. A favoured weapon, then. This guy had been a pro and it might just as easily have been Danny lying face down in the mud.

He rolled the body over, his hands shaking now, as another burst of adrenalin rushed through him. Not from the kick of the kill, or from how close he'd come to winding up dead himself, but from who this dead man might be.

The body was too skinny for the Kid and too broad for the blonde. But how about Glinka? The exact right size for him, Danny reckoned. He peeled back the hood to reveal . . .

Someone else. A dark-skinned guy in his late thirties, whose face meant nothing to him.

Disappointment flooded him. But then came relief. Because the plain fact was that, no matter how much he might want Glinka dead, he still needed him alive to confess to what he'd done in London. To prove Danny's innocence of the crime.

He checked the dead guy's pockets for ID, his neck for military tags, but got nothing.

The Honda's door was still open when he reached it. No one else was inside. But he saw the dead guy's screw-up. His comms were lying on the dash beside the smouldering joint he'd been smoking when Danny's shape had first loomed in his vision from out of the dark.

There was nothing to identify the man either. The glove compartment and door pockets were empty. The same went for the boot.

Danny switched off the car's searchlight and took the keys. He ground the joint out in the mud. Then he radioed in the specs of the dead man's weapon and comms to the rest of his team.

'Status,' Danny said.

Spartak came back first: 'There's a fire exit half open on the south side. The windows above it are choked with vines. It looks as good a motherfucking way in as any other.'

The twins each reported they'd seen no one. Neither suggested a better way in.

'Converge on One,' Danny ordered.

He worked his way quickly back into the side-street and looped round to where Spartak lay in the rubble of a collapsed building. The twins were already there, in position ten yards either side.

Danny had a clear view of the exchange. Twelve blacked-out ground-floor windows, two hogged with ivy and vines. The promised ground-floor fire exit stood dead centre in between, its door hanging twisted off its frame.

'Anyone we knew?' Spartak asked, referring to the dead man Danny had left behind. No doubt he wanted to know if it had been Glinka or the blonde or the Kid.

'No.'

Danny slammed in a fresh magazine. He'd already told the others that once they were inside they were to try to avoid headshots and disable the targets instead. Again a command he wouldn't normally have given, because there were few things more dangerous than a wounded armed man. But again he had no choice.

He needed to take one of these bastards alive.

CHAPTER 11

A rumble of distant thunder barrelled across the swirling black sky, flicking a switch in Danny's mind and bringing a memory of tube waves rolling in and enveloping the bright white sands on the Caribbean island of St Croix where, for the last several years, he had made his home.

Warmth: a memory of it assailed him. Warmth, and the smell of the sun on his skin, the glint of his board, and the prickling of water droplets drying on his shoulder blades as he stretched his arms wide and dug his nails into the sand.

Rain pissing down washed the Caribbean vision away, making it fade and disperse, like squid ink in the sea. Danny grimaced, wiping the raindrops from his brow, determined. Once this was over, he'd take Lexie to St Croix. How could he not have done so before? He should have spent all the years that had slid by teaching his daughter to surf, fish and fly kites. How could he not have mended what had been broken between them? And how could she have grown up so fast?

In the final few seconds of waiting – slowing his breathing, readying himself for what would come next – he felt a burst of hatred for himself, for the selfishness of his grief. He'd wallowed in self-pity when he should have stood tall. For Lexie. No matter how ruined he'd felt inside, he should never have let her move to England to be with her grandmother. He should never have stepped back from being her father as he had.

Lightning split the sky. He raised his hand and jabbed three fingers forward twice. The twins moved in on his command, a pair of pincers closing in at either side of the fire exit. No wonder Spartak had vouched for them. Danny couldn't fault their work.

He moved in too, joining the twin on the left – Viktor, the over-display on Danny's night goggles told him. No eye contact passed between them. They were focused on what was ahead, on keeping themselves and each other alive. The only acknowledgement the twin made of his presence was to shuffle sideways, so that Danny could be nearest to the building's looming entrance.

Danny slid the goggles from his face so that they hung round his neck. He slipped a convex-lensed telescopic mirror from his sleeve and breathed on it, then wiped the condensation off the lens with the dry palm of his hand.

He edged the mirror forward inch by inch, using it to check through the gap left between the fire-exit door and the wall into which it had once been squarely set. Through a blur of reflected moonlight and raindrops, he saw that the space immediately on the other side of the door was empty. He stared into the darkness beyond, searching for signs of movement, but saw nothing.

He tilted the mirror down, eyes straining to filter useful information from the moonlight, looking for footprints in the first few feet of the damp corridor inside, and searching for signs of IEDs. Again, he got nothing. So far so good.

He could order the twins into the breach. He could let them take the risk. Maybe he should. That was how plenty of leaders he knew operated, considering themselves their most precious tactical asset and those beneath them in rank as expendable.

He knew neither twin would complain. He'd already wired money anonymously from one of his numbered Swiss accounts into one of theirs. They'd follow his orders. He owned them for as long as his money was good.

But a part of him wanted, *needed*, to be first in. Not only because he trusted his judgement and experience above theirs, but also because he wanted to be first to confront whatever might be waiting inside. He remembered the dead who had been littered across the London street as he'd looked down on them from that hotel balcony. The adults, yes, but mainly the children, thin-limbed and broken, as if frozen in a two-dimensional montage of impossible twists, turns and somersaults against the hard, cold concrete backdrop.

Danny thought of his own dead son too. His dead wife. In the cold vortex of the wind and the rain, he reached deep into his memory, and there he saw her as she'd once been, and remembered the slow, sensual curl of her smile as they'd walked through a park, her laughter as she'd played catch with the kids, or the sound of her yawning in the morning, as she rolled slowly onto her side to face him, in a tangle of crisp white sheets, her eyes opening, her hand reaching out to touch his, before pulling him into her soft, sweet embrace, as if he were falling through a perfect, never-ending summer sky.

It had been so long since he'd seen her and Jonathan alive. A thousand lifetimes was how it felt. They were gone. His brain told him so, but his heart, his soul, could not accept it.

Instead he dared hope. He dared pray. He dared to believe that if he died, they *would* be there. And all this might fade, like a dream, and he would find himself awakening once more in their arms.

A crackle from his radio. Danny slid the mirror shut and hooked it into his jacket. Snapping his night-vision goggles back on, he switched on his flashlight and gripped it on the barrel of his AK-9, then slithered flat on his belly through the gap between the door and the ground.

His mud-spattered clothing rustled on the concrete. He stared ahead, ready to fire, but no one leaped out of the shadows. The corridor terminated fifteen feet away and was clear. The stink of mildew clogged his nostrils. His skin burned with sweat.

He stilled himself and listened hard, wary that someone might even now be reaching for the handle of the door, wanting to maintain the element of surprise. He waited for it to creak, for a muffled voice to be raised. But then, hearing nothing but the whip of wind and the drumming of rain behind him, he moved in further, away from the entrance, deeper into the dark.

Halfway along the corridor, he trailed a gloved finger across the floor, leaving a clear line in the muck gathered there, which his goggles picked out just as surely as if it had been written in black pen. But that was the only mark there was. It seemed that no one had set foot there for years.

He studied the closed door at the end of the corridor. No light showed around its frame. Was it sealed? Or blocked off? Or even bricked up from the other side?

He crouched, then stood, weapon up, safety off. He moved quickly to the end of the corridor, again cursing the fact that he was operating outside the law. He was low on equipment. Had no fibre-optics or micro-drills to enable him to search for sounds of occupation in whatever room lay beyond this door. No way, even, of telling if the door was alarmed or wired to explode.

He examined it up-close. Its paint had long since peeled away. He pressed his hand against it. MDF, he guessed. Still dense and solid to the touch. Dust rimmed its dark frame, but there were no corresponding build-ups of dust on the floor directly below, which suggested that the door had not been recently opened. Might not have been opened for decades, he supposed.

He used a hand-held metal detector to scan the door frame, searching for signs of sensors. Then he pressed the small plastic amplifier, with which Spartak had provided each of them, against the door. Its needle barely moved above its tenth percentile. What fluctuations it did make, Danny attributed to the storm outside.

He squeezed himself tight to the wall and waved his hand across the door's dark keyhole. He did it again, half expecting a sudden gunshot to punch a zigzag of splinters into the corridor.

But no shot came. Danny pushed himself slowly off the wall and brought his head level with the keyhole. When he peered through, he saw only darkness. He stood upright and tried the handle. It didn't budge. Meaning the door was locked or corroded, most likely both.

He dug into his zipped jacket sleeve pocket. The one item of high spec equipment he'd brought with him from England was the lock-buster. A gift last year from an old Company friend who now consulted for a European security-accoutrements firm.

A shiver chased down his spine. The green world seen through his goggles had just darkened, the change of light implying nearby movement. Danny swivelled round, instinctively bringing up his AK-9 as he did so.

Then he lowered it. Spartak had either grown bored of waiting outside, or sick of the weather. His hulking silhouette ballooned as he continued to squeeze himself between the door and the wall, then moved along the corridor towards where Danny stood.

Danny twisted the lock-buster's nozzle into the keyhole and pressed himself tight to the wall. If someone was there and awake or waiting on the other side, then there was no way they wouldn't hear what was coming next, and chances were they'd react by pumping a few hundred rounds through that MDF into the corridor.

If someone was asleep, he might get lucky. Maybe they'd put down to the storm the noise he was about to make. Luckiest of all, no one would be there.

He glanced back over his shoulder, but Spartak didn't need any telling. He was already on the floor, his weapon trained on the door, doing a pretty good job for an elephant of making himself as small a target as possible by wedging himself against the wall.

Danny pulled the lock-buster's trigger, wincing as its gears whirred and ground. It took two seconds, but it felt like ten, before a single note of snapping metal rang out.

No shot came this time either. No splinters of wood or eruptions of shouting from the other side of the door. He used the handheld plastic amplifier again to check. Its needle remained low. The loudest thing he could hear was his own heartbeat thumping a whole lot faster than he'd have liked.

He turned to see Spartak grinning at him, now crouched, his weapon still trained on the door, ready, *wanting*, to move in.

Danny, too, felt the urge for it all to kick off. He pictured Glinka on the other side. Glinka and the Kid. *Please, God, let them be there.* The two of them drunk on whisky, their weapons out of reach, easy pickings. The scenario stretched out in his mind. He pictured them later, too, cuffed, trussed up in the back of a van, just as they'd trussed up Lexie. He pictured them being hauled out into the glare of a searchlight to the snarling of dogs and barked orders from whichever security service he chose to hand them over to, once they'd confessed to what they'd done.

Get a grip.

Who was he kidding? This would never be as easy as that. He needed to get real, bite back his desire for vengeance. The need for closure too. All that could come later. Vengeance for the dead civilians they'd left scattered across that London street and the grieving families. Closure because they'd murdered his friend, Alice De Luca, for trying to help Danny and his daughter escape.

For now he had to be a machine with a heart of stone. Like Spartak. Like the twins. Later, this could be personal. *Would* be personal. But not yet. This was nothing but work.

Danny used the amplifier again. Still nothing. He slowly turned the handle until it clicked, then began to force the door open, using his shoulder to pile on pressure, tension ratcheting inside him as the rusted hinges squeaked in protest, every bit as excruciating as the bark of the lock-buster's gears.

No gunfire. No voices. Was nobody home? He pushed the door another inch, then two more, raking the growing gap with his unblinking eyes for alarm wires. Five inches, ten . . . enough to peer through properly into the dark space looming beyond, his finger poised on the AK-9's trigger.

His goggles picked up nothing. No heat signatures. Danny kept on pushing until the gap was big enough for him to slip through. He glanced back at Spartak, who was already creeping up silently behind.

Dropping into a crouch, he edged through the gap, scoping the room once more, just to be sure. An administration centre, it looked like. A row of ten windows to his left. Thirty or more desks. Antique, pre-digital equipment. A thick layer of dust lay across the floor. No footprints. Two doors led off, one dead ahead, the other to the right.

Sheet lightning flashed outside, illuminating the opaque, grime-smeared windows. Details leaped out: telephones on desks, staplers, stacks of paperwork, left undone. Danny pictured a different time: he heard the sound of typing and people talking, smelt cheap coffee in the air.

But now there was nothing. This place was as derelict and rotten as the station waiting room he'd hurtled through earlier.

He signalled Spartak to go ahead.

'*Vvodty*,' he told the twins, ordering them to abandon their wait outside and enter the building.

Danny moved in on the door to his right, went through the process with the amplifier and turned to see Spartak doing the same at the other. A flicker of movement in his peripheral vision. The twins had now entered the room.

He tried the handle of the door he was at. It moved easily. Wasn't locked. He waved the nearest twin to him.

The younger man crouched, covering the door from an angle that would allow him to see into the room beyond as it came into view.

Danny flattened himself against the wall on the hinge side, stretched out his arm and began pushing the door open.

A long, drawn-out creak.

Then silence.

The watching twin edged forward, stopped and signalled that the next room was clear. Danny waved him through, then followed.

He found himself in what looked like an old delivery bay. But even as he was looking round, the twin's hand shot up in warning, and Danny dropped into a dead-still crouch. A shiver of electricity rippled across his shoulders as the twin pointed at the floor.

There were boot prints everywhere, fresh, like astronauts' prints on the moon. And not just one shape, grip and size. Several. And not just leading in one direction, but many.

Apart from the doorway through which Danny and the twin had just entered, the only way out appeared to be through a closed set of double wooden swing doors ahead. To Danny's left, there was a smoked, bevelled-glass window at waist height, against which the rain battered and raged.

His goggles picked out more signs of life and recent habitation. A row of cigarette butts stood on the windowsill, which was wet and slick with water – the window must have been recently opened. A plastic bottle of Coke stood on the floor, a couple of inches of black liquid still in it, with carbonated bubbles rising.

A rustling. Danny spun, pumped up, ready to fire. A black rat scuttled across the area. Its sharp eyes glared fearlessly at him, before it buried its snout in the remnants of some food inside a crumpled, discarded plastic package.

Another burst of adrenalin. Danny whipped round to face the double doors. There, at the limit of his hearing, a noise had just registered. A thudding. Muffled. Distant. More a feeling, in fact, than a sound. A vibration. Switching on and then off. Coming from somewhere deep below.

At first Danny thought it was some kind of machine. A flash memory hit him of the New York apartment he'd grown up in and how the clothes-dryer there had shaken and thumped so loudly in the last minute of its cycle that he'd always watched it, mesmerized, expecting it to tear itself free from its brackets and march across the floor.

But this sound was too irregular to be mechanical. Boots, he decided. That was what it sounded like. Boots on stairs. Someone was coming towards them.

Viktor could feel it too: he was staring at Danny in wolfish anticipation. Danny signalled him to hold his position and keep the double doors covered. Then he turned to see the other twin and Spartak emerging from the administration centre. He motioned them back through the doorway and signalled for them to shut the door behind them.

Wordlessly, Danny and Viktor, now alone in the delivery bay, positioned themselves either side of the swing doors. Through the thin gap between the frame and the door, Danny now detected the faint glow of artificial light filtering from somewhere deeper in the building.

The footsteps kept coming, closer and closer. One person, Danny decided, which gave him and the twin the advantage in numbers as well as surprise. The timbre of the noise changed now, the boots no longer thudding on stairs, but clacking towards them across wooden tiles.

Danny hooked his weapon over his shoulder and reached into his jacket pocket, as whoever was heading their way started whistling tunelessly. A sentry's whistle, a whistle of boredom. A whistle of someone inattentive who'd be easy to take out. Hardly the hallmark of Glinka, or even the Kid.

Nothing's ever easy, he heard an echo of the Old Man's voice say.

The light through the frame gap brightened. A flashlight beam? Then *whoosh*: the double door furthest away swung open, obscuring the twin behind it.

Whoever he was – he was six two, and big with it, about the same size as the Kid – he strode through the doorway and into the delivery bay.

Danny stepped in smartly behind him, ramming the Taser hard against the back of his neck. He pulled the trigger. A snap. A buzz. The man's body switched from being as rigid as a board to wilting, as if it had been filleted. Releasing the Taser's trigger, he caught the man as he fell, supporting him upright.

Viktor slipped round fast from behind the open door, which the downed man's body was preventing from swinging shut, and helped take his weight, even catching the flashlight as it slipped from his fingers, preventing it hitting the floor.

Danny unhooked his weapon from his shoulders and turned to look through the open doorway into the stairwell beyond. No one else there. The man had come alone.

They laid him on the floor. Danny checked his face. He had never seen him before.

As Danny rose, Viktor tied and gaffer-taped the man before the effect of the Taser wore off. Danny fetched Vasyl and Spartak, then stepped through into the stairwell, as the twins worked together to drag the already moaning and twitching captive into the administration centre and out of sight.

The wooden tiled floor of the stairwell was warped and buckled in places. But that was where the decrepitude ended. On the left – set into the external wall, Danny surmised, the one overlooking the car park – there was a modern steel blast door, with galvanized bars locked across. An RFID keypad winked red from its top right corner, showing it was locked.

No one would fit a door like that unless what was concealed inside the building was of extreme worth. But Danny took heart that no one had yet raised the alarm over the guard he had killed. That and the fact that the guy he had just Tasered hadn't exactly been on high alert. He thought that the door was working to his advantage: it made whoever was in here feel too safe.

Deciding which way to move next was easy. Even though this was the ground floor of a tall building, there was no up. At least, not where this stairwell was concerned. The way up was blocked, had caved in, and was nothing but a mass of impenetrable rubble and plaster.

But there was a way forward. Straight ahead there was another set of double doors. But they weren't wooden swing doors, like the ones Danny had just come through. They were state-of-the-art blast doors, like the one to his left. Also like that, they were controlled by an RFID keypad.

With no direct access to the locking mechanism, the lock-buster couldn't help. And while Spartak was carrying plastic explosives, enough possibly to take this door out, who knew how deep the facility went? Or how many people were inside? Or how well they might be able to react to a full-frontal assault?

Footsteps. Danny turned to see that Viktor had returned. 'I need the code for the door,' he said to him, in Ukrainian. 'Make him talk.'

CHAPTER 12

Alive.

Danny felt that way himself right enough. Alive and kicking. Buzzing with it. The proximity of death – the possibility that at any second his own life might end in a situation such as this – made him aware of each heartbeat, each breath, hearing, touching, seeing in a way he never did in his day-to-day existence.

That was why people like him, Spartak and the twins got addicted to this. To danger. To risk. Because beside this vibrancy, immediacy and sheer precariousness, the rest of their lives felt monochrome and slow.

Or that was what he used to think. Back when he was young, before he'd met Sally and had become a father to Lexie and Jonathan, and had been blown away by their births, the joy of their smiles and the light dancing in their eyes.

They'd changed everything, his family. It was them he'd started thinking of at times like this, no longer thrilling to the danger he was putting himself into, no longer being seduced by it, but dreading it, wanting it gone, wanting to be safe at home with them.

And that was where he wanted to be now. With Lexie. With the only family he had left.

'Four, nine, two, three,' Viktor's voice crackled in Danny's earpiece.

Footsteps. He turned to see the twins closing in on him and Spartak.

Turning his back on them, he punched the keys into the pad. The lock clicked. He hauled open the door and Spartak moved through.

'Clear,' the big man said.

Danny walked in behind him. Nothing to right or left. Just a staircase leading down.

The building they'd initially encountered might as well have been on another planet. Through this doorway they stepped out of the Cold War and into the twenty-first century. The whitewashed walls were spotless, with bright electric ceiling lights of a much more modern design than a building of this age could ever have been fitted with. Someone had spent a lot of money kitting the place out. And recently too. The dust-covered mausoleum of the upper floors was nothing but a memory now.

Moving aside, Danny slipped his goggles round his neck. He motioned the twins forward to take point. They moved swiftly and silently down the steep flight of stairs, around the first bend and out of sight.

Music. Somewhere below.

What the hell?

Spartak shrugged his huge shoulders and smiled thinly.

Danny counted to ten in his head, listening over the music for any sign that the twins had made contact or had been detected. He wanted to leave enough space between himself, Spartak and them to diminish any possibility of their entire party being wiped out by an IED. But impatience gnawed at him with each passing second because he no longer believed there would be any additional security between here and wherever the guard had come from. The man's relaxed attitude couldn't have spelled out more clearly that Danny's team was now well within the operation's security perimeter.

Ten . . .

Danny began his descent. The music got louder the further underground he went. Something classical, it sounded like. A swell of strings, no beat. It was so surreal that, under any other circumstances, like Spartak, he might have smiled. But it sent a shiver through him. It was too domestic, too *normal* a sound. It felt so out of place that he couldn't help wondering who the hell had switched it on.

At the bottom of the first flight of stairs he found the source of the sound: speakers and a laptop. The table on which they stood was flanked by the twins and was positioned in front of a row of flat-screen wall monitors, showing views of the building outside . . . including the car park.

How the hell could anyone who'd been sitting there

have missed Danny's firefight outside? Sure, the music would have muffled any noise and the storm might well have covered his team's insertion through the back of the building, but the muzzle flashes from his running battle with the guard he'd killed would have lit these screens like the Fourth of July.

Unless, of course, no one had been watching. Danny rounded the desk to see a sleeping-bag on the floor. The remains of a bottle of vodka, too. The guard he had Tasered upstairs should have raised the alarm, but he'd failed. He'd been too drunk, too lazy, and now he was paying the price.

Two corridors branched off, left and right. Midway between them, beside the surveillance desk, there was another blast door, this time with a small round observation window set into it.

As the twins and Spartak covered the two corridors and the way back upstairs, Danny edged towards the door, wary that someone might even now be approaching from the other side. But when he peered through the window, he saw nobody. Only another set of well-lit stairs leading further down into the bowels of the building.

The view was slightly distorted: whatever material the window was made of was inches thick, and he could see that there were two layers, with what he supposed might be a vacuum between.

He'd visited scientific and medical facilities with contamination barriers like this before. Methamphetamine and cocaine laboratories, too. Anywhere people wanted to be cut off from the civilian world outside.

But places like this cost money. He wondered who had originally equipped it and who controlled it now, if they were indeed the same people at all. Could be the Russian government or military, or a foreign government, investing in this as a rendition facility. Or even some criminal organization in need of a little privacy to do whatever they needed to do.

But *the smallpox*. That was Danny's first thought. Were these precautions because of that?

He set off along the corridor to the right, knowing that whatever was being protected here would, more than likely, be further below, but wanting this floor cleared and his route of withdrawal secured first.

Spartak followed, past the desk and the sleeping-bag. With the computer and its speakers behind them, a different noise began to assert itself. The thrum of an engine – a generator, it sounded like. And there, up ahead, was just that. Floor-to-ceiling and noisy as hell up close. The guard had tried to drown it with the music in an attempt to get some sleep.

Danny's first instinct was to switch the generator off. Do that, and it was possible he'd kill the power to the entire building, including the lights, giving him and his team with their night-vision goggles an instant and massive advantage. It might not even raise the alarm: whoever else was in the building might mistake it for an accident, rather than a deliberate act of sabotage.

Then he remembered the RFID-controlled doors leading down and up. Kill the power and he might inadvertently kill those too, trapping himself on this floor at the mercy of whoever was controlling the operation from the outside.

'Clear,' Spartak said, having finished checking the dark recesses behind the vast generator.

Danny set off back along the corridor, past the surveillance desk, and on down the corridor leading left.

Immediately, he slowed. This corridor wasn't featureless like the last. Instead it consisted of a row of what looked like cells. With modern wheel-locking mechanisms, fish-eye peepholes and feeding hatches set into each of the reinforced doors. He and Spartak checked them one by one. All eight were locked and empty.

But inside Danny, anger was rising, not just aimed at Glinka and the Kid, but exacerbated by the building itself. He didn't need to believe in ghosts to know that people had suffered here and died. He tried to ignore the sensation, as brittle as autumn leaves, shivering down the back of his neck. But he could not.

It wasn't fear. It was a memory. He'd been in a place like this before back when he'd still been on the Company's payroll. After one of his fellow operatives had been kidnapped from his home in the dead of night at the height of an African summer in 2004.

The girlfriend of the man who'd been taken had been left dismembered across the bedroom floor of her apartment as a warning that her boyfriend's abductors should not be pursued. But Danny had followed. He'd tracked his fellow operative to an out-of-town industrial facility just like this, with its own warren of subterranean and hidden rooms, locks on the outside of the doors. Rooms with drains on the inside just like here. Rooms that could easily be sluiced clean of blood.

He had finally found what was left of his friend behind one of those doors. Too late. What his captors had done hadn't been simply for information. The electrical burns and injection marks alone would have seen to that. No, the rest had been done out of some kind of sickness. Some kind of evil.

And that was what he couldn't get out of his mind now, as he returned to where the twins were stationed and the music was still playing. Evil resided here. And always had.

These passages ran too deep. They'd been part of the original design. He doubted any part of this building had ever served as a telephone exchange. More likely, it had always been a front for whatever had gone on underground. Before Chernobyl had gone up. Back in the Soviet days. And right through to today. For whoever was funding it now.

Danny punched the code into the next door leading down. Another soft buzz. Another click. The door's hydraulic hinges hissed as he pushed it open and headed down. He was leading from the front now. He needed to know what this facility was and who was controlling it. He needed to be the first to see.

Because whatever sickness was going on here, he was going to make damn well sure that he was the cure. *Evil?* Oh, yes, Danny Shanklin believed in the existence of evil all right. He'd seen for himself that there were no limits to the darkness of the human heart.

CHAPTER 13

As Danny moved slowly down the stairs, he felt the cool air straight away. The product of an industrial ventilation system running off the generator above. He heard more music too. No longer classical. Rock. His finger closed gently round the trigger of the AK-9: confrontation was near.

He checked the Geiger counter again as he stood at the top of the next flight of stairs. The reading, he saw, had dropped. An acceptable risk. Glinka and his friends had chosen this building well. A high count above ground, but safe below. Perfect for keeping other people away while you went about your work undisturbed.

He slowed. There, just above the rising sound of drumbeats and guitar, he could have sworn he'd just heard somebody laugh. And, yes, he could smell food now too. Paprika. Coffee. It smelt like a damn restaurant down there.

The music cut. A snatch of DJ chatter betrayed that a radio station was playing. So far underground, it had to be WiFi. More money spent here recently, then. But for *what*?

Another burst of laughter. Nearer this time. Was someone coming up? He couldn't be sure. He crouched, froze, perspiration trickling down his back. Aiming down, ready to fire, he visualized what would happen next. He imagined his target coming into view, whoever they might be. He readjusted his aim, so he could snap off a body shot that would hopefully leave any target disabled but alive.

But no shadows stretched out towards him to indicate that someone was on their way, no footfalls, nothing. As another song started playing, a grim smile crossed his face. He'd recognized the tune: Blink-182's 'American Idiot'. He hoped to hell he wasn't about to prove those lyrics right.

Reaching the next turn in the staircase, he slid the telescopic mirror from his jacket pocket and, inch by inch, extended it to its full length, until he could deploy it to look around the corner of the staircase and down.

He got a fish-eye view of what awaited him below. The staircase terminated in a vast room. Much bigger than anything he'd been expecting. Shiny walls. Bright lights. A clutter of workstations and scientific equipment. A laboratory of some sort.

Three people were sitting at a table, their shapes too distorted by the mirror for Danny to be able to tell their gender, let alone whether they were packing weapons or not.

Two looked as if they had blond hair. The same as Glinka and his woman. The third person's hair was dark. The same as the Kid's.

None was currently facing the stairs. One might turn before Danny was in a position to cover all three. And even though he would still probably get the drop on them, chances were it would spill into a firefight and fast.

Which might leave all three of them dead. Himself too.

Withdrawing the mirror, he signalled Spartak and the others to retreat back up the stairs, then followed. They grouped at the last of the vacuum doors they'd passed through and Danny slipped a stun grenade from his belt. He set and primed its digital fuse, then signalled to the twins to continue their retreat through the door, spiralling his finger in the air twice, telling them he wanted them on ground level, securing their exit and watching for anyone who might attempt to enter the building from the outside.

Spartak gripped his AK-9 with his ham-like fists and stood grim-faced to one side, as Danny flexed his arm back into a throwing position. For a fleeting second a memory struck him of teaching his son Jonathan how to pitch. Danny had been a baseball fan all his life. He'd always joked with Sally about how one day their boy might grow up to play for the Red Sox. But instead he'd been murdered by the Paper, Stone, Scissors Killer when he'd been just six years old.

Danny's eyes darkened as his memory of Jonathan's

smiling face faded, obliterated by what had happened to him. He pulled the pin and silently counted down.

Three ...

Two. ..

One ...

Then threw.

He stepped smartly back behind the wall next to Spartak, already hearing the echo of the grenade pinging off the bottom step of the staircase and skittering across the floor of the room below. Danny closed his eyes and covered his ears.

Just in time.

WHOOMPH.

A ground-shaking bang signalled the grenade detonating. The stun grenade, or flashbang, as it was more commonly known, produced 160 decibels of sound with a blinding mercury and magnesium flash equal to 300,000 candlepower. More than enough to disorient, induce severe dizziness and generally terrify ten shades of shit out of anyone unfortunate enough to be in close range.

WHOOMPH.

Just to be on the safe side, Danny had programmed it to go off twice. Because if any of those three people down there were real pros, then, like Danny and Spartak, they'd have been partially conditioned to the effects of flashbangs during training.

Twice, though, would give anyone a headache. Twice gave Danny edge.

Ceiling lights flickered above his head. One bulb

had burst, but the others powered right back up. No problem with the generator, then. The lights would still be functioning below.

Danny charged down the stairs. An acrid stink of magnesium. A pall of smoke. His goggles saw through it, picking out the thermal images of three bodies straight away. All were down, immobile. He closed in fast, weapon up, finger hooked round the trigger, ready – itching – to squeeze.

He could see two out of three of the faces of the fallen occupants of the room. Both were men. One early twenties and skinny, the other ten years older and fat as an ox. The skinny guy was out cold, must have cracked his head on something as he'd floundered in the wake of the detonation. The older man had his hands clamped to his ears, and was wheezing pneumatically through his mouth and flaring nostrils. His eyes were scrunched tight shut, as if he wanted nothing more than to make the world disappear.

He located the third person too, a little way apart from the others, his arms outstretched, so still he might have been frozen.

A blur of motion to the right: Spartak had entered the room. He crouched beside Danny, scanning for signs of life. Danny did likewise, but picked up no additional thermal images.

He swivelled, focusing on the man with the out-stretched arms. He was big, like the Kid. Dark-haired too. But the wrong kind of hair. Not dreadlocked like the Kid's. His was thin and greasy, trailing down his muscular neck.

The fat, hyperventilating guy started to puke, bringing up great gobbets of whatever he'd just consumed onto the pristine white material of what Danny now saw was a laboratory coat. This guy and the one lying beside him, he realized, were medics or scientists, unarmed by the look of it. Civilians. No weapons anywhere near them, or anywhere in evidence on the now overturned table they'd been sitting around. Playing cards littered the floor, alongside overturned metal food bowls and soft-drink bottles and cans. This looked more like a frat party than a war council.

The skinny scientist started coming round, with a moan. He coughed, choked and threw up too.

'Motherfucker,' Spartak said, as the guy sprayed spew all over his size-fourteen boot.

Danny shouldered his weapon and whipped out his Taser, leaning down to the muscular man, who was dressed like the sentry he had Tasered upstairs.

He still hadn't moved. He was dead, Danny realized, when he turned him over. He shone a pen torch full beam into his wide-open eyes. The retinas failed to dilate.

There were no entry wounds that Danny could detect: the shock had been too much for him, triggering heart failure or a cerebral haemorrhage. He had been a heavy smoker, Danny saw, glimpsing yellowed fingertips. Should have gone into another line of work.

Danny checked through his pockets. No ID. Nothing

but a disposable plastic lighter and a half-packet of cigarettes. He tossed both up to Spartak, who snatched them out of the air without a blink.

'Status, Two and Three,' Danny said, louder than he needed, in Ukrainian, watching the look that the two live captives exchanged as he did so. It told him not only that their hearing had come back but that they'd understood what he'd said.

'Clear,' the twins radioed back one by one, their voices faded, two floors of concrete all but wiping out the radio signal.

'One: hold your position. Two: get back down here,' Danny said, again in Ukrainian. 'We have captives here, secured for interrogation.'

The elder of the two civilians, the overweight guy with the asthmatic wheeze, wasn't slow to react. 'Please . . . I beg you . . .' he said. 'We had no choice.' Heavy tears ran down his face.

Footsteps.

Danny spun towards the sound, swinging his rifle smoothly into a firing position.

But it was Vasyl who emerged at the bottom of the steps. Danny looked back at the two men grovelling on the floor.

'Apart from you two and him,' Danny said, kicking the dead man, 'how many others are in the building or guarding it outside?'

'Two.'

No hesitation. And there was no way this man could

have known that he had already disabled the two guards he'd encountered. That suggested he was most likely telling the truth.

The elder man now clasped his shaking hands in the prayer position. 'They would have killed us if we hadn't done what they'd said,' he pleaded.

What? Danny was about to ask. What did they make you do?

The man's eyes gave him his answer, flicking towards the back of the room.

Spartak had witnessed the tell too. He and Danny turned their backs on the two civilians, leaving them to Vasyl, and stared through the thinning dust cloud. Spartak switched on the powerful beam of his flashlight.

The scientific and medical equipment Danny had glimpsed from the stairs now shifted into focus. It was the kind you found in field hospitals – and God knew Danny had been in enough of them over the years. Drips on feeders up against the wall. Needles. Plasma bags. A defibrillator station.

Three gurneys also. With restraint straps. The kind used in ambulances by paramedics to transport the critically ill. A retinal image of the corridor of cells on the floor above flashed through his mind. He remembered what kind of building this was, what went on here . . .

At the very back of the room he could see what looked at first like a smooth, polished dark wall. But then, as the smoke and dust continued to clear, he realized it was made of glass.

And then his heart leaped. Because that was when he saw it. A flash of movement. Like a fish glimpsed through the murky waters of a storm-tossed pond. Then violent red. A piece of meat. That was what it looked like. It was as if someone had just thrown a piece of bleeding, raw meat hard against the other side of that glass.

CHAPTER 14

Spartak fired first. Damn near got himself and Danny killed in the process too. The round ricocheted off the glass and embedded itself in the concrete wall just to the left of Danny's head.

It was lucky Spartak's weapon had been on semi not fully automatic. Because otherwise it would have already spat out enough lead to turn everyone in the room into sieves. But, as it was, Spartak had time to react to what was going on before his disbelieving eyes and not squeeze off another shot.

And what was going on was this: something human – humanoid – had emerged from the darkness on the other side of that glass. And not only was there now what looked like a piece of bleeding meat smudged up against the glass, but above it was an approximation of a human face too.

Approximation. That was the word that went through Danny's mind as he stared unblinkingly at the red raw eyes glaring out at him. Because what he was looking at could just as easily have been simian, some kind of an ape, or even something alien, something from a nightmare, something not really there or even possible at all.

He had seen plenty of burns in his career. From acid, fire and mustard gas. In Iraq and Afghanistan. In Africa and Bosnia. He'd seen what weaponry could do to human skin and hair. And what torturers were capable of.

But this was something else. Scales. It looked like some kind of reptilian scales. Not dry like a gecko's . . . this skin was wet, oozing, and looked as if it might shuck itself off entirely, leaving nothing but raw flesh and exposed bone.

As Danny forced himself to move forward, knowing he had to determine what kind of a threat he was up against now, he caught his own half-reflection in the glass, his night-vision goggles, hooded head and mud-smeared clothing. He saw he was still holding up his weapon, still aiming, still primed to fire.

He tried to lower his arms, but couldn't. Not because he wanted to attack: he knew now that this barrier was blast- and bulletproof, and would bounce back whatever he loosed at it. No, what kept his arms and weapon frozen in place was an irresistible, primitive urge to protect himself. He did it because he was afraid.

The man imprisoned behind the glass pulled back his bleeding fist and hit the glass wall again. But whatever noise he had been expecting was absent. Soundproof. As well as being blast- and bulletproof, that glass divide was soundproof too.

A hole – a *mouth* – opened in the centre of the face.

It stretched, weeping blood at its corners. Its teeth were barely discernible from the swollen mass of gums. The lips moved, dripping blood. The jaw clenched and unclenched.

'It's trying to tell us something,' Danny said.

It. He had meant to say 'he', because he had guessed that what he was looking at had once been recognizable as a man. A pitiable man. A prisoner. Someone who'd been experimented on. Someone – he knew it already – who'd been injected with the smallpox hybrid to see what it would do. But what he saw before him was so different from himself that a part of him was still refusing to accept it as of the same species.

Tears. Danny saw them then, as Spartak pressed his flashlight up against the glass and switched it on, illuminating the man's face and forcing him to squeeze his eyes shut against the glare. Tears. He watched them flowing down the face of the man on the other side of the divide.

Danny's horror left him because – right there, crying – the other man changed. He was no longer alien or bestial. All Danny could see was a person in terrible pain, who was crying out for help.

Clothes . . . He registered next that the filthy garments the man was wearing were military. Winter combat clothing. Stained, crumpled and bloodied.

The man's fist pulled back, then lurched forward again. This time the movement was weaker, and instead of the fist remaining bunched, it unfurled, its fingers pointing to Danny's right.

Danny's eyes tracked the movement. At the far edge of his side of the glass wall, he registered what appeared to be a doorway, a bulge in the glass, a chamber through which it might be possible to gain access to the space beyond.

Two long wooden desks formed an L in front of it. Some kind of control desk. Two lifeless plasma monitors fixed to the wall above stared blindly out across the room.

Danny crossed quickly to the control centre, passing other desks littered with cameras, notebooks and charts.

In the centre of the L-shaped desk, there was a row of monitors and keyboards. Judging from the scratches and smudges on them, they'd been there a couple of years at least. There was also a spanking-new state-of-the-art Mac. A ponytail of cables ran down from it into a series of hard drives, routers and junction boxes stacked in descending order of height on the floor.

His heart thudded. He couldn't be certain, but the last set-up he'd seen like this had been the Kid's, back in that old industrial redbrick in south London, which Glinka had used as his command centre on the day of the London attack and from which the Kid had orchestrated and tracked Danny's movements across London as they'd run him before the cops.

He also saw cigarette butts on the floor. Along with a crumpled packet of Marlboro Reds. The Kid's brand. And there, right next to it, as if any more confirmation had been required to prove that the Kid had been there, lay two crumpled, chocolate-stained doughnut boxes. The Kid's favourite.

Danny switched his attention back to the Mac. Its power light glowed in its casing like the pulse of some hibernating beast. But he wasn't tempted to open its lid and wake it. Not yet. Because if this really was the Kid's handiwork, he knew, too, that the Kid was no slouch at explosives. It was perfectly possible that he'd have wired this computer either to explode the second anyone touched it, or if a password was entered incorrectly or too slowly.

Six strides, and he hauled one of the two cowering men – the younger one, with better eyesight – to his feet. 'You fuck with me,' he told him, in Ukrainian, ramming the silencer of his weapon hard into the man's gut, causing him to double up in pain, 'and I will execute you. Understand?'

The man whimpered a single syllable that he took to mean yes.

'Who else was here with you?' Danny said, jerking him upright. 'Who imprisoned that man behind the glass?'

'I – I don't know their names.'

The older, heavier man, huddled like a terrified toddler on the floor, spoke next: 'Their programmer . . .' he was blinking frantically, as if he'd just been hauled from beneath a rock into the naked light of day '. . . they called him Glinka. They weren't meant to not in front of us, but I heard them . . . I heard them call him that name.'

Glinka. Danny felt darkness growing behind his eyes even at the sound of the name. A flurry of images from the day he'd been set up rushed through his mind. The TV footage of the hawk-faced man – Glinka – his face covered with a balaclava, out on the balcony at the front of the Ritz Hotel, firing into the crowd of panicked civilians, gunning them down as casually as if he'd been mowing a lawn. Then Danny pictured Lexie in the back of the Kid's van, blindfolded and tied. Glinka had personally held a gun to her head.

That was when he'd made this personal. Not just professional. Danny Shanklin now wanted his scalp.

CHAPTER 15

'Please,' begged the skinny man, 'we wanted no part of this. They said they would execute us. They kidnapped us from Kharkiv University. They took us in the middle of the night . . .'

Kharkiv. The name meant nothing to Danny. He glanced across at Spartak, who was still staring transfixed at the man imprisoned on the other side of the glass wall, still aiming at him, just as Danny had before him, as if he still didn't dare to leave himself open to what he could not yet comprehend.

'Kharkiv National Medical University,' said Vasyl. 'A science university.'

'Is that what you are?' Danny asked. 'A scientist?'

'A – a researcher, at the Institute of Clinical Genetics . . .'

'In what?'

'Contagious disease.'

'Like smallpox,' Danny said, not missing a beat.

And right there, along with the terror in the skinny

man's eyes, he saw something else, something even worse: shame.

Until he'd learned about the existence of the stolen smallpox, Danny had known little about the disease. Like the Black Death, he'd thought it had been consigned to history, eradicated in the last century, a conquered disease that was no longer a threat to anyone.

But since he'd discovered that he'd been used by Glinka and the Kid to steal the locations of six vials of weapons-grade hybrid smallpox developed by the former Soviet Union, he had dug up as much about the deadly disease as he could. A disease that was historically responsible for a third of all blindness, and the direct cause of 500 million deaths in the twentieth century alone. But a disease that had been eradicated in 1979. One from which we were now meant to be safe.

He had looked up symptoms too. Blindness. Lesions. Respiratory malfunction. And he'd found plenty of photographs online of smallpox victims from epidemics. And he knew now that the glass wall wasn't just there to imprison whoever was on the other side, it was there to quarantine them too, to keep what they had been infected with at bay and to allow them to be observed.

'The man on the other side of that glass. You infected him with the smallpox Glinka gave you, didn't you?' he said.

To test the hybrid Glinka had stolen, to find out if it retained its potency after all these years.

It was the only possible explanation for what had

occurred here. This building had probably been set up for exactly this kind of work back in the dying days of the Soviet Union, a place where human experimentation could be continued out of sight of any watchful, disapproving post-*Perestroika* eyes, separate from any official Biopreparat station.

And somehow Glinka and the Kid had learned of its continued existence and had come here to avail themselves of its facilities. Through military or criminal contacts, Danny supposed. More likely the latter. Because, in spite of the money that had been sunk into it since its likely initial abandonment after Chernobyl, the security would have been far higher, the staff levels too, if it had been a military installation.

Which left three questions. Which criminal organization was bankrolling the place? How did they know Glinka and the Kid? And what had they been promised in return for their help?

The last question was the first to which he could hazard an answer. A share of the profits. Because what had already been demonstrated here – one only had to look at the prisoner – was that the smallpox hybrid was still potent. In fact, not only did it still work, but its symptoms appeared to be even more horrific than anything the original disease had been capable of inducing.

This was a weapon that could bring not just one man but a nation of men and women to their knees. It could make whoever controlled it not only powerful, but rich beyond belief.

'Didn't you?' Danny said, gazing unforgivingly into the skinny man's eyes.

But he was now staring, transfixed, at Spartak, who seemed about to rip him limb from limb.

Danny stepped between them. The last thing he needed was Spartak cutting loose on these two before they'd told Danny everything they knew.

'They said they would kill our families, if we refused,' said the skinny man. More tears streamed down his face. 'They told us that if we did not work for them, they would—'

'Work,' Danny interrupted.

The researcher's face crumpled. He'd just realized his mistake.

'In other words, as well as getting kidnapped,' Danny said, 'you got paid.'

'Please,' begged the researcher, 'they said those men were criminals, the ones behind the glass. They said they were child murderers and rapists who—'

'*Men?*' Jesus Christ, was there more than one? He crossed quickly back to the glass wall. Pressing his face up against its chill surface, he peered deep into the gloom. And saw something. A body. Prone on what looked like a bed. Other beds too. Were more people trapped inside?

He shouldn't have moved from between Spartak and the researcher – a guttural, frenzied roar tore through the room behind him.

Turning, Danny saw Spartak crashing across the

room, smashing furniture aside. He seized the cowering researcher and dragged him to the wall, then hurled the man two-fisted across a paper-strewn desk, as if he were made of nothing more substantial than straw. The researcher landed in a twisted heap of limbs, and began desperately squirming away as Spartak thundered towards him.

'No!' Danny shouted.

But Spartak was beyond listening to orders now. He tore his goggles from his face and snatched up the screaming researcher. He locked his giant fist around the smaller man's beanpole of a neck, as papers fluttered around them to the floor.

'Look!' he roared in Ukrainian, slamming the man's head against the glass divide and pinning it there, so that the researcher now found himself eyeball to eyeball with the man he'd experimented on. 'Look at what you've done.'

The researcher was silent now, rigid with fear. His breath came in short, sharp gasps. His shoes weren't touching the ground. Urine flowed freely down his legs.

'You fucking scum,' Spartak spat. He shifted his grip to lift the man with both hands and dash his head against the wall of bulletproof glass.

But Danny threw himself between the researcher and the glass. Gripping the man's torn coat and shirt, he pushed back with all of his might.

Spartak's eyes were two black beads. Danny had seen him like that before – three years ago, when he had hired him to help retrieve a US senator's daughter from a South American kidnap gang. The drop-off and handover had been compromised by the local police. By the time Danny's team had reached the location where the girl had been held, she was dead. Dead and used.

'Don't,' he ordered Spartak now, remembering again what Spartak had done to that girl's kidnappers when they'd eventually tracked them down. 'Stop. We need him alive.'

Spartak spoke through gritted, gold-capped teeth. 'He's Spetsnaz.'

'What?' Danny stared at the guy shaking in their hands, at his baby-smooth white skin, his thin neck and wrists, and the fingers that looked about as strong as a spider's legs, as if they'd done nothing more strenuous than type.

'No,' Spartak growled, 'not him. *Him*.'

Danny twisted his head towards the glass wall, as he followed Spartak's furious stare. The bigger man was looking past him into the room on the other side of the glass.

And that was when he finally noticed what Spartak had already seen. There, directly behind Danny, stood the bleeding, infected prisoner. Even through the mess of his flaking, disintegrating skin the tattoo on his right forearm, which he'd pressed up against the glass, was visible. And unmistakable. It was of a fist and a star. And it was identical to the one Spartak had on his own arm, the tip of which was showing even now where his sleeve had been pulled upwards during his struggle with the researcher.

The tattoo was Spetsnaz.

Which meant the prisoner was Russian Special Forces.

CHAPTER 16

Spartak tightened his grip around the man's throat. The researcher's face darkened in a rush of blood. His eyeballs started to bulge.

'No,' Danny said.

Spartak's expression stayed hard as concrete. His neck tendons flexed.

'Let him go,' Danny ordered, trying to twist Spartak's hands away from around the terrified man's throat, ramming his face up towards Spartak's and staring into the bigger man's eyes. 'Let him fucking go. He might know how we can help them.'

Spartak's face grew so red it looked like it would burst. But then he blinked. His fist slackened. He lowered the choking researcher so that his feet were once more touching the ground. But he didn't let go of his throat. Flecks of spittle hung from the man's lips and his eyes streamed tears.

Danny glanced back through the smeared glass at the infected soldier. A sudden brightness had filled his eyes.

A keenness. He was staring at the tip of Spartak's tattoo, which was now plainly in sight: he knew Spartak was his brother-in-arms.

But something else was growing in the prisoner's eyes too. Hatred and hunger. A thirst for revenge, which made Danny glad the screen was there. And thankful it was soundproof. Because if the prisoner were to say what was clearly now on his mind, Spartak would obey him. He'd kill the scientist. He'd snap his neck on the spot.

Spetsnaz were every bit as lethal and elite as the British SAS or the US Navy Seals. And even though Spartak Sidarov had left their ranks more than ten years ago to become freelance, he'd still owe a debt of loyalty to the other man. In circumstances such as this, for him he'd willingly kill.

The researcher hung trembling off Spartak's out-stretched arm.

'Put him down,' Danny said.

Finally Spartak obeyed. He let the scientist go and stepped back.

The man slumped against the glass divide, massaging his throat and gasping for air.

'Listen to me,' Danny said, stepping towards him and pressing his AK-9 against his chest. 'My friend here wants you dead. And not only dead, he wants you screaming in pain as you die. Your only chance of getting out of this is to give me exactly what I want.'

'Anything.' The scientist sounded as if his windpipe had cracked.

'When did they leave? The others who were here?'
Danny said, gripping a handful of his hair and twisting it
so that it nearly ripped out. 'Answer me. Now.'

'Yesterday. Yesterday afternoon.'

Danny gritted his teeth, furious to have missed them
by so little. In England, had the dying torturer lied to
him about when he could meet up with Glinka? Had he
snatched the last laugh by sending Danny here just too late?

'How many others were there?' he said. 'Not including
the two men upstairs.'

'Six.'

'Any women?'

'One.'

'What colour was her hair?'

The man looked confused, as if the question might be
a trick.

'You heard.'

'Blonde.'

'Her name?'

'I don't know.' The man's face tensed. Clearly he was
sensing that this failure might lead Danny to let Spartak
off his leash.

Danny pictured the blonde as he'd last seen her, walking
with Glinka to that Cessna light aircraft, leaving Danny
in the English farmhouse with those men whose job it
had been to torture him and his daughter to death.

'What about the hacker?' he said, his dark eyes angling
towards the L-shaped desk. 'The Englishman. The one
who set up that computer.'

The researcher seemed shocked that he knew such details at all. 'I did not know he was English. He spoke . . . many languages . . .'

Many? Could they be talking about the same person? If it were true, then it confirmed just how deep the Kid's act had gone. It also begged the question, what other secret skills did he possess? And how might he now deploy them to prevent Danny hunting him down?

'His name in English,' the scientist was saying, 'I think it was . . .'

Two words followed, in mangled English, but clear enough for Danny to translate, and to confirm his suspicions one hundred per cent.

The Kid.

He still didn't know why the Kid had betrayed him to Glinka. For money? For power? Or because he'd had no choice? Had Glinka been blackmailing him in some way?

He no longer cared. He just wanted to get his hands on the Kid. He wanted to make him confess to everything he'd done. To force him to tell the authorities the truth and, that way, to give Danny and his daughter back their lives.

Danny shoved the researcher hard into Spartak, who snatched him up in his arms. 'Bring him,' he ordered, crossing to the L-shaped desk.

Spartak obeyed, visibly shaking, a volcano about to erupt.

'Sit him down,' Danny said.

Spartak rammed the researcher into the seat, as if he wanted to push him right through it. He kept him gripped by the back of his neck.

'Is the computer rigged?' Danny said. 'Is it alarmed or wired in any way?'

'No.' The researcher frantically shook his head. 'We use it continually for our – for our work.'

Work. That word again. The neutral catch-all that could somehow excuse all *this*.

Danny watched for 'tells', for any sign he might be lying.

'I swear it,' the man said, starting to weep again. 'We use it to control their environment – the lighting, the heating, their water supply . . .'

Their. Danny felt a shiver run down his spine, as he peered through the glass, past the infected soldier, who was still hovering, like a distorted reflection in a tarnished mirror, into the gloom beyond.

'And each subject – each patient,' the researcher hurriedly corrected himself, 'this computer is monitoring them also.'

Patient. Spartak's fist had clenched so tight at the word that the veins on the backs of his hand had stood out as taut as iron wires and the researcher's air supply had once more been cut off.

Danny glared at Spartak, a warning not to hurt the researcher any more. His hand slowly relaxed, releasing another series of gasps as the man gulped more air into his lungs.

'Each of them also,' the researcher said, in a hurry now to please Danny, 'has been fitted with a diagnostic collar to relay physiological changes – their temperature, heart rate, their sickness . . . the extent of the disease . . .'

A collar, like a chimp in a vivisection lab.

A movement to the left. Vasyl, Danny saw, was talking into his radio. And moving. Fast. He'd dragged the other researcher to his feet, and was now marching him forward to the glass barrier, the barrel of his weapon rammed into his back. The young mercenary had pulled his goggles off his face. His expression was as dark as Spartak's. It was the face of someone who wanted blood.

Of course, Danny thought. The twins were more than likely ex-Spetsnaz too. That was probably how Spartak had recruited them. Through an ex-special forces network. They, too, would regard the infected soldier as one of their own.

Vasyl slammed the second researcher up against the glass just as Spartak had done with the first. He held him there, forcing him to behold what he had done.

'Log in,' Danny told the researcher at the desk.

'But—'

'What?'

A bead of sweat ran down the skinny man's brow. 'It will activate the cameras,' he croaked, as the pressure of Spartak's grip bore down.

'What cameras?'

'The ones that he . . . set up to transmit the images . . .'

'Images of what?'

'Of them.' The man's eyes were flickering, terrified, towards the glass wall and back. The soldier had moved across. He was now right in front of them, and staring. 'To demonstrate the effects of the virus,' the researcher gabbled, his voice fluctuating with fear, 'to enable the people – the buyers – to observe for themselves the effects. That is why they have kept us here – to keep transmitting these images, along with the data reflecting the changing condition of the patients, onto a private access website every hour so that the buyers might continue to see how truly effective this hybrid continues to be . . .'

Buyers.

Danny could hardly believe what he was hearing. Glinka and the Kid had been advertising their work, had been demonstrating the virus's effects on human test subjects over the net. His eyes were already scanning the walls. It didn't take him long to spot the cameras. Two of them, one bolted to each wall at either end of this side of the glass divide. High up. Close to the glass.

Spartak took two steps sideways and twirled his rifle, like a majorette's baton, smashing the nearest camera clean off its pivot with a single blow.

Vasyl was moving swiftly too. Forcing the older researcher to his knees, he cracked him hard across the back of the head with the barrel of his weapon. A warning that nearly knocked the man out. Grabbing a chair, he stood on it and battered the second wall camera to pieces with the butt of the Glock pistol he'd been wearing across his chest.

Glass rained down on the man, who curled up into a foetal position with his face to the wall, as blood trickled down his neck.

Danny focused back on the skinny researcher and the laptop at his side, hearing it chime its welcome. Start-up software booted up, splitting the screen into five windows. Two of them he didn't understand. Computer code, it looked like. The Kid's first language, not his. The other three windows showed medical graphs. Vital signs. Each had a different name at the top.

The heart rates of the first two graphs had already flat-lined. Meaning probably that two of the so-called patients were already deceased.

The only patient left alive, the man staring out through the glass at them now, was ...

'Commandant Valentin Constanz Sabirzhan,' Danny read.

CHAPTER 17

Beside him he heard Spartak's breath catch.

'What?' Danny said. 'You know him?'

'No, but . . .'

Danny saw the colour had drained from his old friend's face.

'But I do know of him,' Spartak said.

Spartak stared into the infected man's eyes with increasing outrage as he told Danny who he was. A hero. The commandant of the FSB Academy. A personal adviser to the Russian prime minister no less.

'Then what the hell is he doing here?' Danny said.

And why was he dressed for combat? As if he'd come here looking for a fight. Did it mean Sabirzhan had somehow known that Glinka had gone hunting for the smallpox? And he'd tried to prevent him getting it? Or, after he'd got it, he'd attempted to take it back? Perhaps not even here at all? Somewhere else. Somewhere cold and remote. Somewhere Arctic clothing such as he was wearing would be required.

Hope flared momentarily bright inside Danny. Because if someone else – someone as influential as Commandant Sabirzhan – had worked out what Glinka was up to, they might also have worked out, or at least might have come to suspect, that Danny was innocent of the London attack.

'I need to know how he ended up here, who he's working for,' he said.

'First we get him out.'

Spartak was already at the bubble doorway set into the glass wall. It consisted of three separate chambers, one on this side of the glass, one on the other, clearly locked from the inside with the third between them. It had a vacuum funnel running upwards from its roof and jets studding its walls, with pipes leading down. A decontamination chamber. A safeguard to allow someone wearing protective clothing and breathing apparatus to pass safely into and out of the partitioned room beyond.

'No,' Danny warned, as Spartak grabbed the door's round steel wheel-handle with both hands.

The skinny researcher had leaped to his feet. 'You can't. If you breach that door, we'll all be killed.'

'The hybrid,' Danny snapped, rounding on the smaller man. 'How is it transmitted?'

Just how contagious is it?

'It is airborne,' the researcher said. 'Even standing in the same room as a carrier, even breathing their air . . . That is how it was transmitted between the three patients. We only injected the first.' The researcher stared desperately up at Danny. 'Please,' he begged, 'I swear it. Not only will we die but so will everyone we come into contact with. All of them will sicken and then . . .'

The statistics flashed through Danny's mind of what a smallpox pandemic might do. Of how many might die. He saw Lexie with the infected soldier's face.

Spartak screamed at the researcher: 'Where are the fucking suits? Where is the clothing I can put on to allow me to pass through to the other side?'

'It won't do you any good,' the man pleaded, cowering now in a ball on the floor. 'He is dying.'

Danny stepped quickly between them. 'There must be something we can give that man – something we can inject him with,' he said.

The researcher wrung his hands.

'A cure. A fucking antidote for you to give him.'

'No, there is nothing. Not here. Other scientists, that was their work, but they are not here now, and I do not even know if they were successful in their goal. You cannot help him. There is nothing any of us can do.'

Us. Danny had nothing in common with that man.

Spartak's shadow engulfed the researcher. 'In which case, there is no longer any reason to keep you alive.'

But Danny had already drawn his Taser. Part of him wanted to let Spartak do as he wished. God knew these men deserved it. He remembered them playing cards. He remembered their laughter. But another part of him needed them. Their existence might not prove his innocence but it was a start. And who knew what other evidence of Glinka and the Kid's involvement he might uncover from further interrogation? Who knew what they might have forgotten or have chosen to keep secret? He might yet gather enough evidence from them and the guard upstairs to convince the authorities he'd been set up.

He steadied himself to fire. He'd need to take Spartak in the neck at least, he knew. Even then, though, he was far from convinced that the Taser would be enough to take him down and keep him there.

And then there was Vasyl. Danny could sense him moving in his peripheral vision even now. With whom did his loyalty truly rest? To himself, the man who was paying them? Or to Spartak, to the man he trusted more, the man who'd brought them in, who might even be family as he'd claimed?

Before he could find out, Spartak's shoulders slumped.

But it wasn't because he'd noticed Danny standing there with the Taser. It wasn't because his temper had cooled. It was because he'd heard something. A tapping sound.

And turning now, with Spartak, to look at the glass, Danny saw that it was Commandant Valentin Constanz Sabirzhan who had stopped him. He was knocking on the glass, each time spotting it with blood from his raw knuckles. And now that he had their attention, he began repeatedly pointing at the wound of his mouth. And then at his ear, which Danny saw had been torn clean off. Then, with a sudden glimmer of determination in his eyes, he looked across at the laptop.

Commandant Valentin Constanz Sabirzhan was

telling them something. And as he pointed once more at his mouth, then at his ear, Danny kicked himself.

Commandant Valentin Constanz Sabirzhan wanted to talk.

Danny wheeled on the researcher. 'Is there an intercom?' he snapped.

The researcher nodded rapidly.

'Where?'

'The computer. The laptop. The machinery down here was crackling so the hacker – the Kid – he routed it through that . . .'

'Then switch it on,' Danny said, slipping the Taser back into its holster. 'Now, before my friend here makes you wish you'd never been born.'

CHAPTER 18

The first thing Danny registered, as the neon strip lights flickered into ghoulish life on the far side of the glass, were the bodies of not just one but two other prisoners. They'd been laid out prostrate on two of six cast-iron beds chained to the walls.

He could not see their faces. They'd been covered by bloodstained sheets. Out of respect, it looked like. By their comrade Valentin Constanz Sabirzhan, Danny supposed.

According to the graphs on the computer, their names were Lyonya and Gregori. One had died yesterday morning, the other the night before.

Danny's disgust only increased as he looked further round the space they'd died in. Rotting food. A leaking chemical toilet. Blood and excrement and God only knew what else across the white-tiled floor.

He sensed Spartak's growing fury. And Vasyl now had the barrel of his weapon pressed up to the back of the fat researcher's neck. He kept glancing across at Spartak, as if awaiting an order to fire.

Danny was tempted to give it. To unleash his team on the two researchers who'd helped commit this atrocity. Because, no matter what they said, no matter how much they pleaded that they'd been forced into it, he would never forget that they'd both accepted payment for it.

He lowered his hood so that Sabirzhan could see his face. He picked up the desk mike, switched it on and spoke.

'Commandant Sabirzhan,' he said in Russian. 'We are not here to hurt you. We are here to help.'

In reply, the desk speaker crackled. At first Danny thought it was static he was hearing. Then he realized it was the commandant's laboured breathing.

Sabirzhan said nothing. He turned from Danny to the tip of the star of the Spetsnaz tattoo still visible on Spartak's arm.

Danny passed Spartak the mike. 'It's you he wants to talk to, not me.'

Spartak raised it to his lips. 'Tell me what I must do to help,' he said.

The commandant pointed to himself and slowly drew his finger across his throat.

'There must be some way . . .'

Sabirzhan shook his head. With his swollen fingers and thumb, he mimed putting a pistol to his head and pulling the trigger. He stared into Spartak's granite-black eyes. And again Danny saw that hunger. Only this time it was his own death he was begging them for.

Spartak nodded grimly. 'I understand,' he said.

He clicked off the mike. The anger, Danny saw, had gone from Spartak's face. In its place was resignation. The certain knowledge that he could not save or even help the man.

'We must allow him to do this,' he said. 'We must spare him more suffering and give him his dignity. He is Spetsnaz.' Spartak said the word softly, with deep gravitas, as another man might the name of his god in prayer. 'I must see to it myself that he is given what he needs. You understand?'

As Sabirzhan's eyes closed heavily, what looked like a tear rolled down the swollen side of his face. But it was blood.

Spartak was still waiting for Danny's response. *Not* for his permission. Danny knew that. He would defy Danny if he had to. He did not want to, but he would.

'First we find out who brought him here,' Danny said. 'Who did this to him. Why.'

Spartak turned back to face his dying comrade. 'The people who did this,' he said into the mike, 'I vow to you now: I will hunt them down and they will die in extreme pain. But first we need your help.'

Sabirzhan opened the bloody maw of his mouth and once more came that rattling of his lungs. Danny thought of his son, of the Paper, Stone, Scissors Killer and that cabin in the woods. He thought of his failure too, of how he'd struggled to free himself from the chair to which he'd been strapped but had looked away rather than watch his son die, and how, in that one act of personal cowardice, he'd condemned Jonathan to die alone . . .

Danny forced away the hacking sound of the PSS Killer wielding the shears.

Then Sabirzhan responded. Not something that could be mistaken for a buzz of static this time. Something stronger, enraged. A single word. A war cry. Then another.

London?

England?

He stared into the weeping eyes of the commandant, as he clutched at his throat. But no more words came. What had he meant? That he recognized Danny from the television reports, now that Danny had revealed his face? Or was he saying that he knew of the Kid and Glinka's connection to the assassination?

Danny's heartbeat stuttered as he stared at the shadow of a man behind the glass. *Talk*, he willed him. *Tell me. Every fact you know. Give them to me as you would bullets to a gun.*

But the effort of talking was too much. Valentin Sabirzhan could not stop shuddering and wheezing. Flecks of blood flew from his nostrils and lips, spraying against the glass.

'He cannot,' Spartak said. 'The sickness has destroyed his ability . . . It is rotting him inside as well as out—'

'Wait,' Danny interrupted. 'Look . . .'

Sabirzhan was coughing, clutching at his chest, but he was now slowly moving too, pointing past the contamination doorway to a waist-high series of interlocking reinforced glass drawers, each with ventilators running upwards into the ceiling.

'You,' Danny snapped at the researcher. 'What is that?'

'A sterilization chamber,' the researcher answered. 'To allow us to pass objects through.'

'And it's safe?'

'Yes – at least, it is meant to be,' the researcher stuttered. 'Infected air is evacuated before and after the drawer is opened from either side and irradiated and incinerated in an electric furnace above.'

Danny watched Spartak staring up into the funnel that led into the ceiling. He didn't need to see his expression to know what he was thinking. The pistol. He'd pass it to Sabirzhan through the contamination drawer, to allow the commandant to blow off his head.

Locking eyes with Spartak now, clearly sensing the approach of this opportunity to end his misery, Sabirzhan began miming writing. A thumb pressed to two swollen fingers moving back and forth against a flattened, oozing palm.

'Pen and paper,' Danny barked at the researcher. 'Get them to him now. And clean food and water – and this . . .' He tore a primed morphine syringe from the medikit in his thigh pocket and thrust it into the younger researcher's shaking, outstretched hand.

He saw Spartak taking his pistol out of its holster. 'No,' he mouthed at him. 'Not yet . . .'

Vasyl kicked the other researcher into action and harried both civilians, threatening them with death, until they'd gathered up what Danny had told them and had inserted the items into the first of the sterilization chamber's compartments.

The drawer's mechanisms ran smoothly, silently, operated not by the Mac, but by a series of power switches set into the nearby concrete wall.

Spartak and Vasyl stared with fixed hatred at the researchers, as the ventilators hummed into life and the interlocking drawers of the mechanism began to open and close in a series of automated movements and the supplies were slowly shuttled across by the mechanism's rolling floor.

A gobbet of blood stretched like drool from Sabirzhan's blistered lower lip as he opened the drawer on his side. No wonder he wanted to die, Danny thought. He was falling apart in front of them.

And yet, in spite of his suffering, Sabirzhan ignored the water, the morphine and the food. He went straight for the pad and pen.

He dropped to his knees. Pressing the pad on the floor, he tried to write. But his fingers were too weak, too swollen. He resorted to gripping the pen pitifully in his fist instead.

He wrote slowly, painfully. Then he pushed the pad up

against the glass divide, smearing the fine mist of blood he'd coughed onto it before.

Spartak read his words out loud: 'The same people who set you up, they captured me and did this to me also.' Spartak glanced back at Danny. 'He must mean you. He knows who you are . . .'

Which also meant, Danny calculated, that Sabirzhan had been captured some time after his own face had been broadcast across the planet's media. And that the virus had done this to him in that time.

So much for his attempts to disguise himself over the last few weeks – the beard and dyed hair. Even with his failing eyesight, Sabirzhan hadn't been fooled.

Kneeling down, Sabirzhan scrawled on the pad again. Then pressed another page against the glass with the bleeding, peeling palm of his hand.

'He overheard them talking,' Spartak read, 'soon after he was captured . . . They thought the tranquillizer they'd used on him had not worn off.'

'What?' Danny said. 'What did he hear?'

Sabirzhan started writing again, weaker this time, using the pen now as if he were scratching with a rock on a wall. When he had finally finished, Spartak once more read his words aloud.

'"The buyer for the smallpox",' Spartak read, '"is a terrorist organization that has every intention of using it. We have to stop the exchange taking place."'

'What exchange? You mean he knows where the sale's going down?'

This time Spartak didn't need to use the mike. The commandant was already scribbling, his limbs moving awkwardly now as he grew more exhausted. Lurching forward, he pressed a third piece of paper silently against the glass divide.

Danny stepped in smartly beside Spartak, not wanting Vasyl to be able to read the new note. Even though the man had given him no reason to distrust him and even though he'd made obvious his disgust at what had happened here, the fewer people who knew where Danny might be heading next, the better. The fact remained that this bioweapon and the whereabouts of those who controlled it were worth more than enough money to turn anyone's head.

'A date and an address,' Spartak said.

Danny stood beside him and translated the address for himself. It was a warehouse on a wharf in the Port of London.

'It's where Glinka's heading next,' Spartak said.

'And soon,' Danny said.

Sabirzhan lurched back towards the contamination drawer on his side of the sterilization chamber. He fumbled with the syringe, gripping his neck, searching for the right place to inject, before plunging the needle in.

Danny watched the agony subside from his face as the morphine did its work. He knew the feeling – of surrender, of bliss, of forgetting – from the three times when he'd treated himself or had been treated

by others, once in a hospital for at least two weeks. He
hoped it would be strong enough to relieve the man of
his pain.

A crash. A burst of footsteps. A shout.

CHAPTER 19

Danny turned to see the older researcher stumbling for the stairs. He wasn't the only one. His younger colleague, clearly terrified too, had also seized the moment when Danny and his team had been staring transfixed at the commandant as his last chance to escape.

Vasyl had reacted quickest, had already wheeled round, and was racing after them.

'Don't shoot,' Danny shouted, seeing Vasyl already lining up the younger of the two men.

Too late. He had already fired.

But – thank God, Danny thought – he'd missed. Against the odds, the two researchers had made it as far as the stairs and were now scrambling up them out of sight.

Slowing, Vasyl glanced back, his eyes burning. But he'd heard Danny now, and stepped aside to let him race past.

Danny wove through the furniture and hit the stairs at a full sprint. He reached the first doorway at the top, just as it was swinging shut. He burst through onto the next

floor and on up the next flight of stairs. Then an alarm bell
rang inside his head. Not because he was worried about
catching the two men – they were unfit and unprepared
and panicking. No, what he'd just realized to his horror
was—

'Don't!' he yelled into his mike.

But even as the word left his mouth, it was drowned in
a savage clatter of gunfire from above.

Then all he could hear was the sound of his own
footsteps echoing off the walls and the thumping of his
heart.

His spirits sank as he reached the ground floor and
the wooden swing doors came into view. It wasn't that he
thought the researcher downstairs had lied when he'd said
there were no more of Glinka's people left in or around
the building. It was because he already knew what he'd see
waiting for him in the next room.

Viktor. He'd ordered him to guard the way in and out
of the building. And he already knew that Viktor had just
opened fire.

'Stand down,' he warned in Ukrainian, slowing to a
stop as he reached the doors. Edging them open with one
hand, the first thing Danny saw was the slick of blood
spreading across the floor. Then he saw shoes, twisted legs,
a thin white-coated torso, torn and bloodied from where
the rounds from Viktor's magazine had ripped into it. The
thin researcher would have been dead before he had even
hit the floor.

The fat man's bloodied body came into view next as

Danny pushed the door wider. In spite of his weight, it seemed he'd made it to the ground floor ahead of his scrawny colleague. And his prize for coming first? To take the full brunt of Viktor's fire.

'Hold your fire,' Danny ordered.

A barked affirmative crackled in his ear, as he stepped into the doorway to see Viktor kneeling against the wall to one side of the bevelled delivery-bay window.

Far from having stood down, Viktor was staring along his weapon sight, his forefinger hovering on the trigger, covering both the window and the doorway that led to the abandoned administration centre, ready to shoot whatever other strangers might rush him next.

Danny knelt beside the two researchers and checked their pulses. Nothing. Both men were dead. The first shot clean through the head, the second twice through the chest. 'I told you that once we were inside you were to try to disable people – that we needed them alive,' he said, but even as he did so, he knew it was pointless. It was already too late.

It's my fault, he thought. How was Viktor to know what was coming at him through those doors? If anyone was to blame, it was himself. He should have seen the risk sooner. He already knew from Spartak exactly how well the twins were trained and how lethal they were. The instant the researchers had bolted, he should have radioed Viktor and told him that the two men coming his way were unarmed.

Danny stared hard at the floor, at the slick of bright

red blood he was kneeling in. Footsteps. A warning. Vasyl appeared through the doorway. Then Spartak.

'Go check the prisoner upstairs,' Danny ordered both twins.

'And be quick about it,' Spartak added. 'Dead?' he asked, looking down at the two corpses, as the twins hurried away.

Danny nodded.

'No matter. All is not lost. Thanks to Sabirzhan, we know where Glinka and the others are going next.'

'If it's the truth,' Danny said.

'You think Sabirzhan is lying to us?' Spartak's face darkened.

'No, but that doesn't mean he wasn't lied to,' Danny pointed out. 'Sabirzhan may be right. Maybe he did get lucky and overhear their plans. But, equally, he may be wrong. They could have tricked him into thinking he knows what they're planning next.'

The big man stared at him pensively. 'But why?'

'Just in case.'

'In case what? They have him in a cage and he is dying.'

'In case someone like us turned up here looking for them and found him still alive. Then he could pass on any disinformation he'd been tricked into believing.'

'And send us on a . . .' Spartak's eyes narrowed '. . . *wild goose chase*, yes? That is how you say it?'

'Yes. Or into some kind of a trap.'

Because that was possible too. Glinka and the Kid might have believed that someone would track them soon enough, and if that person was Danny, they might also have seen this as a chance to trick him once more and lure him to London to be either captured or killed.

'Or Sabirzhan really *is* telling the truth,' Spartak said.

Yes, and Danny hoped more than anything that he was. But he had no way of knowing. All he did know was that Glinka was no fool. In fact, the way Danny saw it, the only mistake his adversary had made so far was in not killing him when he'd had the chance.

'So what now?' Spartak said.

Darkness fell like a veil across Danny's eyes. 'I find out what that guy upstairs knows,' he said, already rising.

Spartak nodded grimly. 'And the commandant?' he said. 'Sabirzhan?'

'Go back and find out what else he needs.'

Spartak inhaled deeply, as he steeled himself to walk back into that subterranean slice of hell. 'And then?' he asked.

'Then I'll make a decision,' Danny said. About what is best for him, he thought. And what is best for us.

Spartak turned away and pushed back through the double doors. Danny picked up his weapon and walked quickly through to the administration centre where their prisoner was being held.

As he approached the room he'd last seen the prisoner taken into, he heard urgent whispers. On edge, he switched off his flashlight and pushed the safety off his AK-9.

The door to the administration centre was ajar. As he neared it, he saw Viktor and Vasyl crouched on the floor at either side of the prisoner. Vasyl held a flashlight in one hand, illuminating them as though the three were huddled out of doors beside a campfire. It showed deep slashes sliced across their now dead prisoner's face.

It showed the blood too, dripping from the serrated combat knife gripped in Viktor's hand.

CHAPTER 20

'What the hell happened here?' Danny said.

The two mercenaries fell silent. Neither would meet Danny's eye. He'd not lowered his weapon, even though there was no one else in the room. Instead he kept it trained on the two frozen members of his team.

In addition to the gleaming knife, Viktor had his rifle across his lap as he crouched, his left hand on it. Vasyl's AK-9 was on the floor by his side. But still in easy reach. And Danny had already seen for himself how fast the twins could move.

'Spartak,' he said, toggling his mike. 'Get up here.'

No answer.

'Spartak,' he tried again.

No reply.

'Shine that light across his face,' he told Viktor, unwilling to risk moving his hands from his weapon to put his night-vision goggles on. 'Do it now.'

Viktor obeyed. The torch beam traversed slowly across

the prone guard's face, picking out the blood spattered there and his dark dead eyes.

The signs of torture, which Danny had first glimpsed as he'd come through the doorway, were now unmistakable. The man's smile was slick and obscenely wide, where the knife's blade had clearly been pressed hard into it, slitting his cheeks.

'Now the body,' he said.

Another slow traverse, even slower than before. It did not reveal fear or shame, but something more like satisfaction . . . pride.

The man's hands were not tied, as Danny would have expected. His left wrist had been slit. The worst of the blood, pints of it, had clearly flowed from it. He looked like a suicide, but that was clearly impossible.

Danny had seen enough to know that the twins could no longer be trusted.

'Both of you,' he said, 'put down your weapons and push them out of reach.'

He didn't need to warn them to do it slowly. They knew the drill and, fast as they both might be, they knew how ruthlessly Danny had dealt with the guard in the car park outside.

'Now roll him over,' Danny said.

Because even though a lot of blood had pooled around the dead guard's wrists, there wasn't enough for him to have died from simply bleeding out.

A soft groan – air being expelled from the dead man's lungs as the twins pushed him onto his front.

'Shine the flashlight,' Danny said.

An exit wound, glistening scarlet and white with blood and bone, was clearly visible in the pale glow of torchlight at the base of the prisoner's skull.

'He tried to run,' Vasyl said.

'It's true,' said Viktor. 'Look there. He had a blade on him – he cut himself free and must have cut his wrists in the process.'

A stiletto blade lay beside the dead man's open fist.

'We got back here just in time,' Vasyl said, nodding to where the rifle was propped against the wall.

Viktor: 'He was running for it.'

Vasyl: 'That was when I fired.'

You're lying, thought Danny. Both of you. And not just because the exit wound in the dead prisoner's skull meant he'd been shot close up through his mouth, which could not have happened if he'd been running away.

But also because of the amount of blood. Pints of it. Meaning his heart had kept on pumping for quite some time after his mouth and wrist had been slit. Whoever had done it had wanted him to think about it. They'd wanted him to know that he was dying. They'd wanted him to feel his life force draining away.

Revenge for his part in what had happened to Commandant Sabirzhan downstairs. That was Danny's first thought – that Vasyl, having witnessed downstairs what had happened, had marched up here and summarily tortured and executed the prisoner for his part in it.

But for there to have been this much blood? It didn't

make sense. Vasyl had had just a couple of minutes' head start on Danny. There hadn't been enough time.

Meaning that the wrist and mouth wounds must have been inflicted on the guard while he, Spartak *and* Vasyl had been downstairs. So it must have been Viktor who'd set about torturing the prisoner.

But why?

What did Viktor know that Danny did not?

Footsteps behind him. Danny moved sideways in an arc, keeping the twins covered. Spartak entered the room and stared down at the twins beside the corpse.

'What's going on?'

'They say he cut himself loose,' Danny said, 'then ran for his rifle. But he's been tortured. Vasyl would not have had time. Viktor is responsible.'

Spartak didn't question his analysis.

'Why?' he asked the twins.

A shared look between them. A mutual nod of acquiescence.

'I told him to,' Vasyl said.

'What?' Spartak asked.

'When?' Danny said.

'The moment I found out who was down there, I radioed him . . .'

Danny remembered how Vasyl had been talking into his radio.

'The commandant,' continued the twin. 'We met him once when we were students at the FSB Academy. We both shook his hand.'

'This man deserved to die,' Viktor said. 'For what he'd done.'

'I needed him,' Danny snapped, his professionalism leaving him now, the weapon trembling in his hand as anger pumped through his veins. 'I needed to know what he knew.'

'And that is why I tortured him before I cut him loose,' said Viktor. 'He knew nothing. Not even the names of the people he worked for. He was locally hired. Nothing but a gangster.'

'And so you executed him,' Danny said.

'I put him down,' the twin answered, 'like the animal he was.'

There was no apology in the younger man's voice. In neither twin's expression did Danny see regret. Only pride.

He thought fast. What had happened here – the torture, the execution – was wrong. But the man was dead. There was no way of bringing him back. And even though the twins had lied to him once about what had happened, he did not believe they were lying to him now. Not in front of Spartak. He did not believe they would dare.

'Idiots,' Spartak said. 'I should shoot you both now.'

But in the way he'd said it, Danny heard something else: an undertone of respect. Yes, Spartak was angry with them for what they had done, but he understood – sympathized – with why they had done it.

He turned to Danny. 'What do you want to do?' he said.

Danny knew Spartak would back any decision he made. But at the same time, he knew there was no point in attempting to discipline the twins for what they had done. Spartak would do that in his own time and way. Maybe they'd still get fully paid for what they had come here to do, or maybe not. Maybe they would never work for Spartak or any of his associates or contacts again.

'We move out,' Danny said. 'As soon as we're clear, you call in whoever you think might be able to help the commandant. Do it anonymously. Tell them where he is and what has happened to him.'

'I don't understand,' Spartak said. 'The researchers said there's no cure.'

'But what if they're wrong? The Soviet government made that virus. There may still be someone in the Russian government today who knows a way to cure it too.'

Spartak said nothing. A look of incomprehension, then surprise spread across his face.

'It's all right, I know what you're thinking,' Danny said. 'That whoever you tell will come here and talk to the commandant and, of course, you're right. If they do reach him before he dies, he'll probably tell them exactly what he told us about where the people who did this to him are going next.'

Both twins were now staring at Danny, wide-eyed with surprise. They, too, knew that by calling in the Russian authorities to help the commandant, Danny was burning his only lead.

'The other choice we have,' Danny said, 'is to give the commandant what he wants, a weapon to kill himself.' But choosing not to help . . . That would make me no better than Glinka, he thought. No better than the others who'd helped him murder the people in London.

Spartak opened his mouth to speak, but the conversation was over. Danny had made his decision. He would not trade the commandant's life for his own freedom. He'd find another way to track Glinka down. Yes, it would be harder, but he still believed he might be able to find a way to get to him through the Kid. And in the meantime, he would pray. He'd pray that any agents sent by the Russian authorities to London after Glinka and the smallpox would simultaneously uncover the truth of Danny's involvement in the affair.

But as Danny turned to go, he heard Spartak clear his throat.

'You're wrong,' the giant Ukrainian said.

The certainty in his voice made him stop and turn. 'About what?' he said.

'You think that because you've chosen to help the commandant, you will now no longer be able to go to England to try and capture Glinka yourself.'

'Yes,' Danny said.

'No. Because no one is coming to help the commandant. Because I will not be calling anyone. Because the commandant is already dead.'

Spartak lowered his eyes. And only then did Danny see it: there at his waist: an empty holster where his pistol should have been.

'It was what I promised him,' Spartak said, 'and what he begged for. I looked into his eyes. He was dying. Trust me, even if I had managed to contact someone who could have helped, they could never have got here in time . . . Only I could help him . . .'

Danny remembered then the gesture, the way Sabirzhan had mimed a gun with his fingers and had then pressed it to the side of his head. 'You passed your pistol through the contamination drawer,' he said.

'It's what he wanted. It's what I would have wanted him to do for me.'

The twins were both staring at Spartak, not shocked, Danny thought, just accepting. It was a look he'd witnessed a thousand times in the eyes of men at war. Death was death. Once it had happened, there was no use in discussing it. It was already done.

'And so you see,' Spartak said, 'now we can go to find out if the information he gave us is true or not. And then if you capture Glinka, at least the commandant's death will not have been in vain.'

The huge man forced a smile when he said this. But behind it Danny saw deep regret, even horror, at what he had just been forced to do. And a thirst for something else. Revenge. 'So you think I should do it?' he said.

Spartak nodded. 'We go where he told us. And we hope we really do find Glinka, that fat fucking pig the Kid, and whatever motherfucking terrorist cell they are planning on dealing with there.'

'To England, then,' Danny said.

But even as he spoke, the words sounded remote. And not just because of the distance between here and there, but because London was just about his last lead and not one he trusted.

Crane. The word leaped into the forefront of his mind, as it had done on so many occasions in the last few days. Crane was Danny's agent, his handler, the person who'd always found him work. Crane had resources and plenty, was quasi-governmental. But could Crane be trusted to help Danny once Danny's own leads ran dry? And would Crane even want to help, or believe that Danny was innocent of the crimes he'd been accused of? Crane had always been able to help find people. Perhaps he could help Danny find Glinka and the Kid. Perhaps contacting Crane was a chance he would soon have no other choice but to take.

'To England.' Spartak agreed. 'Land of warm beer, fog and fish and chips.'

'Not you,' Danny said.

Spartak's wide brow creased into a frown. His dark eyes glowed like coals.

'I'm sorry,' Danny said, 'but I can't risk us both. Not on what might be a trap.'

'But I like risk.' Spartak smiled.

'I know, but there's something else I need you to do.'

CHAPTER 21

SCOTLAND

Ray Kincade gazed out of the hire-car window into the night, inhaling appreciatively on cigarette nineteen of pack five of the ten soft packs of Lucky Strikes he'd brought with him from the States two days ago.

Thirty years of experience in the game had taught him that there were plenty of downsides to stake-outs, but getting to smoke as many cigarettes as he wanted without getting nagged by his wife, Suzie, sure as hell wasn't one of them.

Ray was parked on a deserted farm track in a patch of Scottish woodland. He'd been there two hours already and pretty much nothing had moved, other than leaves shifting in the breeze, and dark clouds slowly scudding across the waning moon.

He wriggled his toes in his stiff new hiking boots, glad of the thermal socks he'd picked up that afternoon in the nearest town's outdoor-activity store. It was summer in the UK, but no one seemed to have told the Scottish Highlands that. He wished to heck he'd picked up more than just one Thermos flask. Another shot of hot sugary black coffee would have warmed him and given him just the jolt he needed, but he was out.

He adjusted the upturned collar of his jacket tighter round his neck, wanting to shut the car window but knowing he couldn't. It wasn't the smoke that bothered him – hell, the more the merrier, was the way he saw that, kind of like the good old days when you could still get your nicotine fix in a bar without even needing to light your own cigarette. No, the windows were open to stop the windscreen steaming up so that Ray could see out.

He'd been staring at the view for so long now that it had become almost like a screensaver, and every few minutes he'd taken to pinching himself hard on the back of the hand – a childhood habit he'd picked up in church as a kid – just to keep himself from falling asleep.

The stone farmhouse stood half a mile away on the brow of a forlorn hill against a star-studded sky. It still had just the one light on in an upstairs window, with its curtain not properly closed.

The binoculars Ray had purchased at the store could hardly be described as professional quality, and they'd proved practically no use after dark. Even so, he was ninety-nine per cent certain that the farmhouse was empty and that the light had been left on for show.

He peered down at his lap, pushing his grey fringe back from his brow. He'd got his iPad's backlight turned down low so as not to signal his whereabouts to anyone who might be passing, or watching the farmhouse, like him, or even waiting patiently inside it looking out. He surfed the news again. Plenty of headlines about Danny Shanklin, but no real updates to speak of, no one yet trumpeting that they'd finally caught him or run him to ground.

Ray checked his email, hitting the 'fetch mail' icon even though he knew full well that this was something the device did automatically. Nothing new there either. Nothing to prove that Danny Shanklin had got the email Ray had sent him four days ago.

None of which surprised him one bit. Because, even though he was now six years retired, he was still ex-FBI, and would always think FBI. He'd once hunted fugitives like Danny Shanklin for a living and knew exactly what Danny would be currently up against in terms of hostile government resources.

All of which meant that Ray fully expected Danny to have been either captured or killed.

He hoped he was wrong on both scores. He didn't believe what the news media said about Danny being a terrorist and a murderer. He'd known him too long. Danny wasn't the type, was how Ray saw it. In fact, if anything, he was the exact opposite to the way he'd been portrayed in the press.

Ray considered Danny a family man at heart. A protector of those weaker than himself. In his professional opinion, the only time a personality type like Danny Shanklin would attack a complete stranger was in defence of someone weaker than himself. And he would never shoot an unarmed civilian. That would go against everything he believed.

Which was why Ray had ended up in this ass-freezing, wind-whipped, remote Scottish village tonight. He'd refused to believe that Danny Shanklin had had anything to do with the recent London assassination and massacre. He'd sided with Danny and had therefore felt no conflict whatsoever in coming here to continue the work that Danny had first tasked him with such a long time ago.

In fact, even if any of Ray's well-placed sources were now to inform him that Danny Shanklin had already been neutralized by one of the several intelligence agencies currently attempting to nail him, Ray would still see the assignment through.

In part, he'd do this because he liked Danny but also because he felt he owed him: Danny had paid him a generous annual retainer these past five years to pursue the case. But mainly he would do it out of plain old curiosity because, like every good investigator he'd ever known, Ray Kincade had a pathological inability to let a good lead slide.

The first article about the recent multiple Scottish murder, already dubbed the 'Clan Killings' by the sensationalist UK press, had found Ray, rather than the other way round. He wasn't as hot on computers as he'd once been, but luckily his kid, Sam, who worked for the military, was.

Five years ago, when he had first begun working for Danny, Sam had fixed him up with a web filter, which would continually and automatically trawl through the world's media sites in search of articles within which certain key words had been grouped.

Key words such as:

Paper . . .

Asphyxiation . . .

Stone . . .

Bludgeoning . . .

Scissors . . .

Throat cuts . . .

Ray had worked on the original Paper, Stone, Scissors killings in the US, back when the serial killer had still been known in the American press as the 'Director', and had become the FBI Elite Serial Crime Unit's top priority.

The Director had murdered eleven families in six different states in a North American killing spree that had lasted sixteen months before Danny Shanklin had been seconded from the CIA to the FBI to help hunt him down.

The way things had turned out, though, it had been the Director who'd got hold of Danny and his family first.

Danny's wife and six-year-old son had been the last murders chalked up to the Director in the US. And it was only thanks to Danny and his daughter's survival that the Director's signature – forcing families to act as an audience, while each member was choked, stabbed and bludgeoned to death – had been finally explained.

It was a game. The killer had been making his

victims play Paper, Stone, Scissors for their lives, as he'd watched and played God, deciding when and how they'd die.

But before he'd had a chance to finish off Danny Shanklin, Danny had freed himself. It had already been too late for his wife and son, but at least he'd saved his daughter, and badly wounded as he'd been, out in those frozen woods, he'd not only knifed the killer in the shoulder, he'd also got a shot off at him as he'd fled.

No one knew if Danny had hit his target. The Director had faded like a ghost into the snowstorm that had been raging around the log cabin where Danny and his family had been holidaying. He'd vanished off the face of the earth. There'd been no more Paper, Stone and Scissors. No more tortured mothers and children. No executed fathers, who'd first been made to watch.

Two years after Danny's wife and son had been murdered, the FBI had begun to theorize that the 'PSS Killer' – as the press had now taken to calling him – was dead.

Only Danny had refused to believe this. Instead he'd hired Ray Kincade, who'd just retired from his position as an FBI investigative profiler. He'd asked him to keep hunting. To keep trying to fit the pieces together. To cross-reference any and all convictions that might tally with the PSS Killer. In case the only reason the killer was no longer attacking was because he was already doing time. And Danny had also asked Ray to keep searching for similar assaults or homicides, in the US and abroad, to see if the PSS Killer was still active. He'd told Ray he didn't care how much money it cost. All he'd asked was that Ray never stop looking.

And Ray never had.

The perennial grim joke between Ray and his son during the last five years had been whether the media filter Sam had designed was truly effective. Because the fact was that during the entire time it had been up and running, in spite of all its clever algorithms, it hadn't flagged up a single result.

Until now.

Two days ago, as Ray had stood at the bottom of his front yard, dragging deep on another of those Lucky Strikes he'd sworn blind to his wife he'd already quit, his iPad had pinged him a new mail, an automated one from Sam's filter program.

A match.

The key words and phrases flagged up had included: 'murder'; 'family'; 'bludgeoned'; 'throat'; 'missing body parts' and on – right the way up to a total of sixteen.

Of course, the way the victims' bodies had been found – stripped naked, outside, with petrol poured over them and burned – in no way looked like the work of the PSS Killer. And the British cops, so far as the copy of the confidential reports a contact of Ray's had snagged him suggested, hadn't yet made any connection between the murders and the PSS Killer.

But the key words Sam's filter had flagged up had been too much to ignore. They'd suggested only one thing to

Ray: that the PSS Killer might be back. Which was why he'd come here: to see if he was right.

He continued to gaze out into the night at the stone farmhouse with the solitary light burning at the upstairs window, where the Scottish family had been murdered. It sure as hell looked like no one was home. But he'd give it another hour, just to be sure.

And then he'd break in.

CHAPTER 22

WALES

The lorry's diesel engine idled as it pulled up at the edge of the small Pembrokeshire village. Danny Shanklin thanked its driver and got out.

It was a warm, starry night and he stretched, exhausted after the long journey, as he watched the lorry accelerate away, its red tail-lights fading into the dark. Further back in the village they'd just driven through, he had caught snatches of laughter and conversation from people heading home after an evening in the pub.

He hoisted his backpack onto his shoulders and set off in the opposite direction, following the same silent, unlit road the lorry had disappeared down.

He scratched irritably at his face. He hadn't shaved since he'd been forced to go on the run in London. His beard was unkempt and stiff with dried sweat. His dyed hair was tangled and matted – he looked like he'd spent the last few weeks sitting on a beach somewhere smoking grass, rather than running for his life and tracking a pack of psychopaths across Europe.

He'd rounded off his current look with cheap, generic service-station shades, scruffy jeans, scuffed Dr Marten's boots, a shapeless waterproof jacket and a faded Ramones T-shirt. Hardly his usual taste in clothes or music, it had to be said. He was more a surf shorts, flip-flops, Hank Williams and Van Zandt kind of a guy. But this was all he'd been able to find in the second-hand Rosslare store he'd switched clothes in yesterday.

No matter. His get-up made him look exactly how he wanted to be perceived: forgettable. On the ferry that had brought him over from Ireland to west Wales earlier that evening, there'd been plenty of other foot passengers just like him, migrating to the UK for the summer music-festivals, most of them with backpacks and rolled-up tent mats just like his. No one had given him a second glance.

It had been the same at Customs. A cursory exercise, less thorough than anything you'd find at an airport. They'd scanned and then leafed through his seemingly above-board British biometric passport. Danny had looked both the Customs official and the camera staring over his shoulder dead in the eye, relying on his changed hair and beard, and the fissured contact lenses with which Spartak had supplied him to trick any biometric and retinal databases his image might be fed into, assuming the cameras were indeed linked to a wider system, which was by no means necessarily the case.

The passport was in the name of Mark Rawlings, a nobody, an invention. It was one of several flawless fakes Danny possessed and trusted to withstand any

level of scrutiny. Spartak had fetched it for him before
their trip to Ukraine. He'd picked it up from where it
had remained secured for the past twelve months in a
left-luggage locker in London's St Pancras station, along
with a functioning set of credit cards, linked to cash-rich
ghost accounts, and a valid driving licence. It had needed
some Photoshop work to match it to Danny's current
appearance, which Spartak had arranged through his
own London contacts.

Danny's other counterfeit IDs were currently out of
reach. One was stashed in a steel box buried in the garden
of his main home on the United States Virgin Island of
St Croix, a second in a locker at JFK airport, New York,
while the last was in Switzerland, in a safe-deposit box
near the apartment he kept there.

His passport in St Croix, he suspected, had already
been compromised. He'd heard, in horror and revulsion,
on the news that the FBI had raided his home there on
the old tobacco plantation out at Grassy Point, which
he'd been renovating and clearing these last several years.
Maybe their dogs had sniffed out his hidden IDs and his
stashes of weaponry. No doubt the property would be
under surveillance now too.

On top of all the other grief that Danny was being forced
to deal with, he hated that his privacy had been wrecked.
His London houseboat and his Caribbean home had been
registered in his own name. Once the Kid had leaked that
to the press, God only knew what Sunshine Day, Danny's
elderly, kind and caring St Croix housekeeper would have

thought after everything she'd must have read. The same went for his St Croix neighbours and the flotsam and jetsam of surfers and travellers he hung out with during his down time at the beach.

Danny had never given any of them so much as an inkling of the fact that he'd once been CIA and now worked private sector as a gun for good people to hire. Instead he'd always told them he was a yacht broker with offices in Miami and St Tropez. Anything for a quiet life. Anything to stop people prying and thereby keep his home life partitioned from the otherwise sometimes dirty and difficult work he did.

But Glinka and the Kid had now stolen that sanctuary too. They'd detonated Danny's safe haven sky high.

Danny shook them from his mind. He didn't want to think about them now. Didn't want to think about his own frustration either. The last thing he wanted where he was going was anger etched all over his face.

He picked up his pace and marched faster down the road. He could now smell the sea. He could sense it too, over to the west, a roiling black mass. He turned left off the main road onto a dark muddy track that headed towards the sea. The further along it he walked, the safer he felt. No engines, no footsteps, no signs that anyone had tailed him from the port.

He should have felt a corresponding sense of relaxation, he knew. But instead he felt increasingly wired and apprehensive and – even though every muscle in his body was aching for sleep – he knew he could not stand down until he'd reached his destination and had determined it had not been compromised.

The track steepened. The air became heavy with the scent of heather. The land round here was too inhospitable for houses, but he still found himself thinking back to the people he'd overheard in the village. He imagined them safe now inside their homes, doing all the things that normal people took for granted: watching TV, fixing snacks, going to bed. And suddenly it swept over him: a craving for that normality, so powerful that it hurt. Right now it felt like the most unattainable thing in the world.

A campsite sign jutted out into the lane ahead, ghoulishly reflecting the moonlight, like a disembodied arm. Danny turned into the gateway just beyond. The shapes of ten dilapidated static caravans stood as silent as sleeping cows in rows, one above the other, on a sloping hill facing the sea.

He walked past the cracked concrete shower block and mud-spattered washing-up area, and headed for the furthest caravan, the one up in the top left-hand corner of the small field. A couple of the others were occupied and, as he passed by, he saw TVs flickering behind their closed curtains.

But any sense of exclusion he might have felt was now instantly wiped away. Because there she was: Lexie, his seventeen-year-old daughter. And right now, she was the closest thing to home he had left.

CHAPTER 23

Danny had been carrying a picture of his daughter in his head ever since he'd said goodbye to her when he'd headed for Pripyat. She was the point of all this. Her, and the freedom he wanted to give her back.

She flinched, noticing his approach, and stood – looking suddenly older than the schoolgirl she still was – wrapping her arms protectively around herself. She didn't smile. It was his fault she was there. He'd had to hide her from the government agencies who'd come looking for her. They'd have used her to get to him. They'd have hurt her. And she knew it. But she still blamed him. It was his work that had led to the PSS Killer murdering her mother and brother. And his work that had led to her then living apart from him, with her grandmother, in London. And now his work had destroyed the new life she'd built for herself in the UK.

I love you, he wanted to tell her. But he knew the words would only make her angrier. Instead he hugged her as he reached her, but she pushed him away.

'I thought you were dead,' she said. 'I thought you weren't coming back.'

'It took longer than I thought.'

'Did you find them?'

Them. The people who'd set him up, the same people who'd tried to kill her.

'Did you?'

Did you kill them? her eyes said. Because – oh, yes – she'd seen what he was capable of. She now knew her father could do that.

He said, 'No.'

'So it's not over, is it?' she said, her eyes full of scorn.

'No.'

'You didn't find any of them, did you?'

She knew that was why he'd gone away with Spartak, but she'd had no idea where. He'd told her that by the time he returned he hoped to have captured the people who'd set him up. He wasn't going to tell her about the horrors he'd encountered in the Zone, but he would not lie to her about the outcome. And the outcome was this: he had failed.

'No.'

'Then we're fucked.'

'No, we're not. I'm not going to give up.'

'Just don't, OK? Just fucking save it.'

For a second, she looked as if she was about to cry. Instead, she lit a cigarette. He hated to watch her do it, just like he hated to hear her swear. But what right did he have to play the guiding father when all he had brought her was grief? He stared at the tiny freckles on her cheeks, the ones that never left her, even in the coldest and darkest of winters, the ones that had patterned her little brother's skin too.

'I'm sorry,' he said.

'I'd hoped . . .' But whatever she'd been about to say dwindled away. She blew out a long, miserable breath. Then looked around her. At the weather-beaten caravan, the ripped camping chair and the near-dead fire. Her meaning was obvious: *What now?*

'I did everything I could,' he said. 'For now . . .'

But she was already one step ahead of him. 'We're going to have to move again, aren't we?'

'Yes.'

'When?'

'Tonight.'

They'd taken every precaution they could since they'd fled together. The chances of anyone tracking them down were pretty much zero, but Danny also knew that the longer you stayed anywhere, the more likely it was that someone was going to start asking what you were doing there and why.

Or to put it another way: *A moving target's much harder to hit.* That was how Danny's Old Man would have put it.

'Where?' she said.

He wished he could tell her somewhere beautiful, somewhere there were people they could trust, somewhere she could tell people her real name and they'd know what she was going through. But no such place existed.

'I don't know yet. Somewhere else like here.'

'And what about you? Are you going away again?'

He thought back to the lead he'd got from Commandant Sabirzhan.

'Yes,' he said. Then, seeing her face, he realized how keen he'd sounded and how wrong that must have seemed. He added, 'I don't mean that I want to. I don't. Leaving you at all, especially on your own, is the last thing I want to do in the world.'

She stared into his eyes, but he saw no love there. Only resignation.

'The fire's nearly dead,' she said, gazing past Danny now as she'd used to when he'd visited her at her school, as if he wasn't really there.

Turning her back on him, she picked up a pan of water that was sitting in the dirt by the barbecue and tipped it over the coals, leaving them hissing and spitting, sending clouds of steam into the cold night air. 'I'll go and pack,' she said.

'Good,' he said. 'I'm putting my gear in the car now. I'll put yours in too.'

'How long until we have to leave?'

'An hour. Maybe two.'

'Then I'll sleep in the car,' she said.

He marvelled at her toughness, this toughness she'd had to develop so fast to survive. It was all his fault.

He followed her into the worn-out half-wreck of a vehicle. The supplies he'd bought before he'd left her – clothing, packets, tins and bottles – remained methodically laid out and stacked just as he'd left them. Hardly touched. The same went for the selection of second-hand paperbacks he'd bought and lined up on the caravan's crooked shelf. None had been moved.

He didn't know what he'd been expecting. Maybe Coke cans and crisp packets strewn all over the place. Or some other sign that a normal teenage kid had been living there. But not this. It didn't look like she'd really been living at all. Just waiting for him to return. Waiting for the rest of her life – her real life, the one without him – to continue.

They packed in silence, leaving nothing personal behind. He boiled a kettle and made them tea.

As she squeezed herself behind the small table in the dining area, the blanket she'd had round her slipped and he saw she was clutching a mobile phone, one of the cheap ones he'd left with her that wasn't capable of accessing the internet.

Since he'd been gone with Spartak, he'd messaged her each day on one of ten such basic disposable phones he'd left her with to let her know he was safe. And each day he'd instructed her to remove the battery and SIM card from whichever phone he'd contacted her on and destroy it.

He wondered now if she'd called anyone else – her friends. But he couldn't ask: she'd interpret it as him saying she couldn't be trusted.

'You look terrible,' she said.

'I'm guessing I don't smell too good either,' he said. 'I should grab a shower.'

'There won't be any hot water,' she said. 'The old guy who runs the field only switches it on for an hour at six in the morning and the same at night.'

Danny remembered him – he had to have been around eighty, with thick glasses and a shock of nicotine-stained white hair. The evening they'd got there, Danny had watched, from behind the tinted windows of the busted-up old car he'd bought for cash and had switched the plates on, as Lexie had paid him a month's rent up front for the caravan.

He went into the short corridor that led to the two bed-rooms. He glanced in at Lexie's room as he passed. A sleeping-bag and pillow. He felt another shiver of worry. What had she been doing since he'd gone to Pripyat? Just staring at the wall? Again, he found himself gazing at her phone.

He took a brand-new towel off the shelf in in the next room, where his own brand-new sleeping-bag lay on the bare mattress, not yet unfurled. Back in the kitchen, he took a block of soap from the sink, flinching at the sound of Lexie popping a can of Dr Pepper.

'You got a better phone?' she said. 'One I can go online with?'

'What for?'

Her face flushed with anger. His fault. Wrong tone.

'Just to see what's happening.'

'Where?'

'Out there. Outside that damned field.'

Say no and he'd make matters intolerable between

them. Just trust her, he told himself. Trust her and she
won't let you down.

He put the iPhone Spartak had secured for him on the
table. She stared.

'Just news sites, OK?'

She didn't answer, but he didn't ask again. She already
knew the score. Social networks. Facebook, Twitter, Bebo,
Instagram and whatever the hell else was fashionable
with kids her age right now: all of them were forbidden.
Because that was all it would take: her popping up on
one of those sites for a chat with her buddies. Anyone
looking for Danny and her – cops, journalists, government
agencies, maybe even the Kid and Glinka – would already
have infiltrated those sites, and would have laid down
spyware to hunt for either of them surfacing so they could
trace them to whatever location she'd accessed the sites
from.

'And don't spill any of that drink on it either, OK?' he
said. 'There's something important I need to do on it when
I get back.'

Important. Damn right, he thought. He was going to
pack up their stuff and get ready to go. And then he was
going to contact Crane. And try to work out if he could
still trust him, then see if Crane would be willing to help.

CHAPTER 24

SCOTLAND

Ray Kincade checked his watch: time, he decided, to make his move.

He reached across the passenger seat into the footwell for the climber's ice pick he'd bought. A ridiculous weapon, he was aware, but there hadn't been a great deal of choice.

And, what with airport security being as tight as it was now on both sides of the Atlantic, it had been out of the question to bring along anything more powerful, like his usual weapon, an ACP single-action pistol, or a short-barrelled pump-action shotgun, which he'd have preferred to be packing tonight.

He got out of the car, quietly closing the door behind him, knowing from his own upbringing in rural Kentucky just how far sound could travel in the country at night. He walked halfway along the crunching, caked mud track towards the road, then set off into the woods, warily, without using his flashlight, choosing instead to use the light of the moon.

He worked his way slowly east, keeping parallel to the
road until it turned into a dogleg bend, where he crossed
out of sight of the house, then followed a thick, curving
hedgerow to the right, until it brought him to a five-bar
gate guarding a paddock at the back of the farm.

He could make out the shapes of what looked like oil
drums and poles; a horse jump. He remembered from one
of the articles he'd read that the older girl who'd died here
had hoped to ride in the Olympics one day. Ray had a
daughter of his own. Away at college now in New York.
She was his life.

He stayed there in the shadows for five minutes, not
moving, barely breathing, cold fingers of breeze stroking
the back of his neck. His eyes kept scanning the farm
buildings and the back of the house. Partly because he
wanted to make sure that the locals, who were sure to be
jumpy, and might even be keeping some kind of sporadic
watch on the property themselves, weren't anywhere near.
But also because he was aware of the propensity of serial
killers to return to their crime scenes in order to relive and
even re-enact what they'd done. Some were drawn there
by narcissism, trying to understand their own actions more
deeply, others simply because of the feeling of power such
places held for them.

Ray heard nothing but the scratching of some tiny
creature in the hedgerow and the far-off cry of a night
bird.

Ready to move, he gripped the ice pick that little bit
tighter and checked the hunting knife already hooked

into his belt, reassured by its weight, and picturing its wicked sharp edge.

The FBI's policy on guns was that you didn't pull them to threaten, you pulled them to kill. Ray believed the same went for blades. And the devil he was here to hunt would never come quietly. If their paths ever did cross, any chance Ray got to kill him, he'd have to snatch it with both hands. Or he'd wind up dead himself.

Not that he thought it would come to that tonight. And not that he'd want it to. Not without back-up.

The latch on the field gate was open – a sign in itself on any working farm like this that something had gone badly wrong. Ray slipped silently through and on past the jumps to another hedgerow and gate, then into the farmyard beyond, with its empty cowsheds and silent, dark machinery.

There was plenty of cow crap on the ground, he saw, but not an animal in sight. He guessed one of the neighbouring farmers must have taken the herd. Hadn't been able to face milking them here. Not after what had happened.

Murders didn't usually occur in backwaters such as this, he supposed. They were more likely confined to Edinburgh and Glasgow – urban rat runs full of drugs and thugs and killings – according to the well-thumbed crime novel he'd found and wryly leafed through in his hotel room.

But in the case of the PSS Killer, the remoteness of this place fitted. He got off on the sound of his victims' screams. He liked to take his time.

Ray edged past the farm buildings, sticking like glue to

the shadows wherever possible, wishing for cloud cover, shrinking from the pools of bright moonlight emblazoned on the ground. A horrible self-awareness was creeping over him, making him feel somehow absurd, like an actor in an escape movie, darting between searchlights, pretending his life depended on it, when it fact it was all just make-believe.

Because this could just be make-believe, he thought. Because no one might be watching at all.

But then he froze.

He'd felt something, a shift in texture, beneath the soles of his boots. He'd smelt something too. Burned ground. Ash. Looking down, he saw he was standing at the centre of a wide patch of charred earth.

The bodies of the family who'd lived here, Ray had read in his pilfered report, had been discovered in the main yard at the back of the house, twisted and blackened and burned, having previously been soaked in some kind of accelerant — most likely turpentine, the forensic investigator had said — then lit.

The UK police had found no evidence to suggest that the victims had been killed anywhere but right here where Ray was standing. The inside of the main house and the surrounding farm buildings had betrayed no signs of struggle or other forensic indicators that the murders had taken place there. Similarly, the surrounding gardens and countryside had been scoured, but nothing had been discovered to suggest that anything untoward had occurred there either.

He raised his eyes from the ground and stared up at the dark house. In spite of the complete lack of forensic evidence to suggest otherwise, he did not believe the victims had died out here.

The pathologist's report, a copy of which he had also read, had stated that the husband and wife's skulls had been smashed prior to death.

Stone.

The daughter's actual cause of death had yet to be determined. Her body had been severely mutilated. She'd been cut from neck to waist, and her throat and lungs were missing.

Paper.

While the son had been decapitated and his skull left between his legs.

Scissors.

Several other body parts had been missing: fingers, a tongue, a heart. The pathologist had no way of telling if they had been eaten by wild animals either before or following the burning of the bodies, but some of the missing body parts appeared to have been chewed off. With one exception. The mother's ear had been severed with the same blade, the pathologist had concluded, that had been used to decapitate the boy.

Parts of each of the PSS Killer's American victims – all of whose case histories Ray knew so intimately that he might as well have been staring at them right now – had been missing. Danny Shanklin's wife's ear had been severed and never recovered.

That the murderer of this family had taken the throat and lungs of the daughter convinced Ray that this was the PSS Killer's work. Because that removed any possibility of forensic investigators realizing that she would have been killed in the same way as many of the PSS Killer's other victims: by having a magazine inserted in her throat, then hundreds of pieces of screwed-up paper forced down it until she'd choked.

Ray gazed up at the house. Every single one of the PSS Killer's known victims had been murdered inside their own homes. Which was why Ray needed to get in there. He knew that, if this had been the PSS Killer's doing, it was inside, not outside, he might find proof.

He backed into the nearest outbuilding, a chicken shed, as quiet and empty as all the other outbuildings he'd passed.

He took out his phone. You never could be too cautious, was the way he saw it. He scrolled down his contact list to an email address he'd not used since he'd first been given it, one he was only meant to use if he discovered firm evidence concerning the PSS Killer's whereabouts.

The account belonged to Danny Shanklin. Ray started punching a message with his thumb. Just in case, he told himself. Just so someone at least knows that you're here.

CHAPTER 25

WALES

Still shivering after the freezing shower, Danny pulled on a jumper, sat down at the caravan kitchen table and took a slug of steaming tea.

Lexie was already in the car, wrapped in a sleeping-bag, with the light out, either asleep or feigning it. She was probably as keen to get away from here as he was.

He'd already checked her room, but she'd left it spotless. Nothing there that could help anyone trace them.

As well as his own belongings, he'd packed enough food and drink into the car to get them to where they were going next: a remote seaside town he'd picked out, in the opposite direction from the ferry ports and airports that anyone who tracked them here might imagine he'd go.

His phone was on the kitchen table where he'd left it, as though Lexie might not even have picked it up. As he cradled it now, he tried to resist the urge to check his web browser's history to see whether she'd obeyed him or not, but failed.

He still remembered the brief encounter he'd had with her boyfriend the day he'd collected her from her school just before M15 had got there to snatch her. He remembered how Lexie had looked into the kid's eyes and couldn't help linking the yearning he'd witnessed then to the expression she'd been wearing when Danny had got here tonight.

But as his eyes scanned down the list of the URLs the phone had recently been used to visit, he saw she'd kept clear of social networks, sticking to news media sites, along with YouTube.

On Google, she'd typed in his name and hers, searches that would have resulted in next to nothing a few weeks ago, but which now led to entries that scrolled down seemingly indefinitely. Danny checked the first few pages, but there was nothing he hadn't seen already. The only news was old news: the whole goddamn world still wanted his head.

He felt a pang of guilt because, on the surface, it didn't look like Lexie had been trying to contact her boyfriend or any of her other friends. But he knew she was smart. So, just to be sure, he visited each URL she had and scanned any comment boxes beneath the articles she'd been reading, and even the tunes she'd been listening to on YouTube, just in case any were forums where she and her friends regularly hung out online.

He read the most recent comments on each, ignoring the quirky pseudonyms under which most people posted. He looked for recent dialogues between site visitors, searching for any sign that they might be coded messages from Lexie, revealing how, or even where, she was.

He found nothing. But instead of feeling relief, all he truly felt was an ache of disappointment. He should have trusted her. She'd done nothing wrong. He hated having become someone who snooped on his own child.

Only one thing left to do when you're forced into a corner: fight back.

Danny had been seven years old the first time the chief combatives instructor of the United States Military Academy, a.k.a. his Old Man, had first stuck him in the ring to spar. As he'd goaded Danny on, he'd blocked his wild punches to begin with, hadn't hit him back. But he'd cornered him against the ropes all the same.

Danny typed 'InWorld™' into the Google search box, as more than three hundred thousand other players would have done today. Normally, when Danny visited the online gaming site, he logged in as 'F8', the same avatar he'd been using until now. And normally when he visited InWorld™, it was to meet Crane.

But Danny's F8 avatar was useless now. Prior to the assassination in London, the Kid had hacked Danny's InWorld™ account to gain access to his contacts, then hijacked Crane's avatar and used it to relay false instructions to Danny to manipulate him and eventually frame him for the terrorist attack in London. Pretending to be Crane, he'd tricked Danny into going to the meeting at the Ritz Hotel and had continued to run him, like a puppet, for the rest of that day. Danny couldn't trust Crane's old avatar any more than his own.

He set about creating a new avatar for himself. He decked it out in the free clothing made available to new players: grey shorts and a white T-shirt, non-logo sneakers and a non-affiliated baseball cap. He named it Jackal, after the Jack Russell dog his mother had bought him for his fifth birthday, an animal that had been more stubborn and determined than a mule. Then he pulled up the InWorld™ map and scanned it to choose a location to teleport into.

The InWorld™ playing area consisted of four virtual continents and twenty-eight diverse virtual cities. Each city contained many thousands of virtual streets and buildings for players to explore. In the guise of F8, Danny normally chose to visit the city of Noirlight, which was where Crane's preferred hang-out, Harry's Bar, was located. But Harry's Bar had also been hacked by the Kid and was a no-go area now.

He zoomed in on the city of Steem on the onscreen map and homed in further on its most central point. He tapped the teleport icon and watched as the map faded to be replaced by a swirling digital vortex, which solidified into an image of Jackal in the middle of a computerized portrayal of a Victorian railway terminus.

Passengers in top hats, derbies and suits, bonnets and wide dresses bustled up and down the main concourse. Hansom cabs rolled by on the roads servicing the station. Danny popped his earphones into the iPhone's socket and turned up the volume. A rich and diverse soundscape synched with the action on the screen. Street traders hustled and hawked their wares. All around he heard the clank and whirr of cogs and clockwork, hissing steam, occasional gunshots, screams and the clip-clop of hoofs.

He used Jackal to explore the area, gliding across the concourse and outwards. To the north, a leaded stained-glass roof stretched into the distance. Several trains stood at platforms, as passengers embarked and disembarked, and luggage was loaded and taken off. To the south, the terminus opened out onto the Victorian brickwork of Steem city.

Ignoring the attempts of other newbie avatars to engage him in conversation and ask for directions, Danny moved his thumb across the iPhone's screen, scanning the nearby businesses. Settling on a café called Rest Cure, he used a gesture to zoom in on its sign and double-tapped. Rest Cure's InWorld™ location coordinates popped up on his phone and, with another swift gesture, he copied them.

He then dragged Jackal through the crowd to the right of the ticket office, to a Public Contact Board. This was a feature common to all InWorld™'s central locations, enabling any game player to post a message where others could access it from any other part of the virtual world. There were thousands of messages, which you could sort by category. It was a useful way to find other players with similar interests to your own. And it was a perfect way to establish covert contact with someone too.

Danny typed: *LOST HOOK SEEKS FISHERMAN.*
LOST HOOK'S NAME IS JACKAL. He attached the
Rest Cure's game location, so that anybody reading
the message, or monitoring the contact boards for its
appearance, would know where they needed to go to
continue the conversation.

That done, he disengaged from the Public Contact
Board and dragged Jackal over to the Rest Cure's doorway,
where he double-tapped his screen to gain access to the
establishment. The smoked-glass door swung open and
Danny moved Jackal inside. It was busy, with plenty
of other players' avatars sitting at wooden tables with a
variety of healthy drinks before them – anti-viral software
for which they'd have paid to protect their avatars' in-game
integrity, or potions to endow the avatars consuming them
with abilities such as strength and temporary invisibility,
anything that might progress them in the wider quests
available in the game.

Some of the avatars' conversations were visible to the
public, floating in tiny speech bubbles above their heads,
which you could click on to enlarge. Others sat in seeming
silence, but were more than likely communicating privately
using global Instant Messaging, which was hidden from
view and protected from electronic eavesdropping by
standard InWorld™ text encryption software.

Danny had never actually met Crane in the flesh. Didn't
even know his real name or if he was in reality a she. He
had always only communicated with him online here in
InWorld™. But since his and Crane's old avatars had been

hacked by the Kid, there was no way Danny could just meet up with him here as he'd used to.

Which was why he'd needed to come up with another way to contact him. And what he'd done was this: before his trip to Pripyat with Spartak, Danny had used a fresh dummy email account to email Brian Nowak, an old CIA buddy who'd introduced him to Crane. Danny had told Brian he'd been set up. He'd also asked him to forward the message 'LOST HOOK SEEKS FISHERMAN' to the real-life Crane, and tell him to monitor the InWorld™ Public Contact Board system, where Danny would post a message once he was ready to communicate.

It was a sound enough plan, he knew, but it was still a risk. For one thing, Brian Nowak might have chosen not to accept Danny's protestations of innocence. Instead he might have gone to the CIA with Danny's email, which meant it would be the CIA, not Crane, who'd be monitoring InWorld™ and waiting for him to appear.

Similarly, even if Brian Nowak had believed him and had passed on the email to the real Crane in good faith, the real Crane might have decided independently that Danny was guilty as hell and contacted the CIA himself.

Danny's only hope was that Crane had believed his message and had kept it to himself. And had since been willing to help him in any way he could. In which case, any second now, the real Crane, as some new avatar, might walk through the virtual café door on Danny's screen and make contact.

Danny glanced at the dark window of the closed

caravan door. If he had been betrayed by either Nowak or Crane, someone might already be coming for him in the real world. Because the second he'd surfaced on InWorld™ and posted his message, any government agency that had been tipped off would have set about tracing the location of the phone he'd sent that message from. And the second they found it, they'd trigger the nearest hunter-killer team to close in on it.

If that was the case, he did not have long. It would take a team on standby no more than an hour to be here from London. Less if they'd been assembled at an airbase closer by.

Danny checked his watch. In fifteen minutes, whether he'd heard from Crane or not, he'd need to destroy his phone and leave with Lexie. And his last chance to contact Crane would have been well and truly blown.

CHAPTER 26

SCOTLAND

Ray had circled the house, pausing and watching every couple of yards, checking in each ground-floor window he passed that didn't have its curtains drawn. Having seen no movement either inside or outside, he knew he should feel confident that no one was there. But still a warning chimed in his head. *Confident? Hah. Sure. Just try convincing your thumping heart and sweating skin of that.*

He was now at the wooden back door, his ear close to its chipped paint, listening, slowing his breath. Hearing nothing untoward, he crouched and slid a lock pick into the keyhole, then twisted, turned and twisted again. There was a click as it gave. He pushed aside the strip of 'POLICE DO NOT CROSS' tape, wincing at its sudden rustle as it fluttered to the ground. Then, slowly, he turned the handle and stepped inside.

A ticking sound. Ray moved slowly: he needed to rely on his night vision, at least until he'd satisfied himself that there really was no one else in the house or watching him from outside.

He kept his back to the door, as he closed it behind him. He peered into the gloom. He was in the kitchen, an L-shaped room. Shafts of moonlight shone down through a row of skylights set at a forty-five-degree angle to the house. Six matching windows below, each with their blinds drawn tight shut, would look out over the back of the property. A cooker and cupboards occupied an alcove to the left of the door through which he had just entered. Then there was the main part of the room, with an open doorway at its far end, blackness beyond.

Other objects slowly swam into focus. An American-style fridge with moonlight shimmering on its stainless-steel casing. A grandfather clock on the wall: the source of the ticking. And in the centre of the room: a dining table, with six chairs – the first things Ray would examine as soon as he got the chance.

But before that he gave himself time to listen. He stilled his body. It was cold as hell in here, colder than the night outside. He could feel it lancing his bones. He started to shiver, then couldn't stop.

He listened to the tick of the clock. He counted to one eighty. And only then did he feel his grip on the ice pick relax. Three minutes he'd been standing there and, apart from the clock, he'd not heard a damn thing.

Even though his eyes had already grown accustomed enough to the dark to be able to discern the various pieces of furniture, he needed to be able to examine this place in greater detail than that.

He switched on a pen torch, not powerful enough to

give off so much light that it might be picked up from outside via the skylight, or the open door that led into the rest of the house.

He surveyed the kitchen in more detail. In spite of the forensics report saying they'd found no evidence to suggest the family had been killed inside, a part of Ray had still expected to be confronted by a grim montage of blood-spray patterns, as had been left behind at Danny Shanklin's cabin and in every other North American home that the PSS Killer had defiled.

Or, more specifically, every North American *kitchen*. Because that was why he'd been so keen to come here: it had always been in the kitchen – in the beating heart of family life – that the PSS Killer had done what he had to the people he'd killed.

But there was no blood here and no sign there'd been any. No scrubbed stains or patches on the walls. Nothing immediately visible on the floorboards.

Ray probed the extremities of the room with his torch beam, still half expecting to see blood there also, suddenly screaming out at him, dripping in gobbets from the wooden ceiling beams and the white plastic chandelier.

But there was nothing to indicate that anything violent had ever occurred. Everything looked perfect. Like a show home. Like no one had ever lived there, let alone died.

He scanned the work surfaces next. They were pristine white and clear of crockery. The same went for the table. The whole place was spotless.

In part, he knew, this would be down to Forensics.

They'd have dusted everything down, bagged, tagged and shipped out whatever they thought might shed light on what had happened to the family outside.

But he had worked enough crime scenes to know that this didn't *feel* right. Everything, right down to the cookery books on the shelf by the sink, was *too* perfectly aligned. It looked tidied. It looked *cleaned*.

He checked the dark doorway at the back of the kitchen, leading with the torch beam, his grip on the ice pick tightening again. *What if someone's through there? What if they're waiting and watching and readying themselves to—*

It led into a short, spotless tiled hallway with a closed front door at the end, and stairs leading up into more darkness. Another open doorway to the right. A living room.

Stepping inside, Ray scoured it with the pen-torch beam. All too perfect again. Another pristine, show-home room, with two sofas, two armchairs and two occasional tables arranged in a perfect semicircle in front of a gaping black granite hearth.

Even the newspaper beside the wicker basket full of logs had been neatly folded and set at a right angle to the whitewashed wall.

Paper . . .

His breath shortened as he stepped into the room and slowly made his way across to the hearth. Kneeling, he examined the paper up close with the pen torch. The sports page was face up, an article about a tennis championship from a week ago.

He slowly turned the paper over and – there – the second he saw its front page, he knew. He *knew* it, dammit. He'd been right to come here. He'd been right.

Because the PSS Killer *had* been here.

Because the front page of this newspaper had the headline 'HUNT FOR DANNY SHANKLIN CONTINUES' emblazoned across its top. But below it, where the remainder of the article should have been, the paper had been torn in a neat horizontal line, leaving nothing at all . . .

Someone had deliberately taken the remains of that article . . . And the photo of Danny Shanklin that should have been there could have been screwed up and forced down the poor girl's throat . . .

Ray stood, hearing the creak of cartilage in his knees, and feeling the ache there too. As he turned back to face the doorway leading to the hallway and the kitchen, his heart was pounding, his mouth dry as dirt.

He walked slowly and silently back through the kitchen, a primal part of him noting a shift in the atmosphere, a sense of sudden pressure bearing down, as though he were under water or wading through oil. But he refused to let it undermine or paralyse him. He recognized it for what it was. It was knowledge. It was fear. With an effort, he forced it from his mind.

He warily crisscrossed the torch beam over the room. Then he got down on all fours and turned it on the wooden floor. He began crabbing slowly across the room, checking each bare board as he went, part dreading, part *knowing* what he would find.

He got nothing on the first few, but then he saw it. Yet more confirmation that he'd been right to follow his gut instinct and come all this way.

Tiny vampire tooth-marks in the floorboards. There, in the board near the centre of the room. In four groups of four, where four chairs with duct tape strapped to their legs could have been nail-gunned to the floor.

A square of tooth-marks, where the father would have been positioned to face his family. And three squares in a row opposite, where his wife, son and daughter would have been placed to face him.

So that, as in the homes of all the other victims Ray had visited, the father would have had no choice but to *watch*.

The marks were small enough not to catch the attention of Forensics, particularly when they didn't think a crime had been committed in here.

But why was there no blood? If the PSS Killer had restrained, tortured and killed them right here, there would have been so much that these boards would have had to soak it up; they would have been stained.

Yet they were pristine.

Ray swept the torch beam round. He left the pattern he recognized. He searched for something new. And didn't have long to wait. Because – by the wall – he saw additional tiny tooth-marks: running in a straight line along the floorboards, up against the wall, spaced evenly, six inches apart: the kind of marks that might have meant a carpet had once been nail-gunned there . . . or that instead confirmed to Ray that the freak he was hunting had called.

He noticed something else and shuffled quickly across to get a better look. A glint like glass. Snagged right there on a tiny shard of wood in one of the vampire tooth-marks.

He knelt down closer. It was plastic. A tiny rip of plastic. Holding the pen torch in his teeth, he laid the ice pick on the floor, then removed an evidence bag and tweezers from his jacket pocket. He unhooked the plastic and studied it up close. Heavy-duty industrial polythene. He bagged it up.

A tapping sound.

His heart skipped a beat, as he glanced to the row of windows by the back door.

But then the pattering got a little louder. It was rain. Fat drops splashed onto the skylights and spread.

Edging forwards now, he followed the straight line of nail holes. He found another rip of plastic in one. Then another. He bagged them. The line of nails ran round the perimeter of the room. And the table – he saw underneath it where the floorboards' varnish had recently been scuffed.

Ray felt a stir of further conviction deep inside him. Because he'd worked out what this new pattern – this unexpected variation in the PSS Killer's signature – was.

The rips and the nails. The only explanation for their presence – and for there being no blood – was that the PSS Killer had laid down plastic sheets before he'd begun his sick game.

But why? Why had he wanted to keep the place clean?

In each and every one of his North American attacks, he'd always left the blood, and so much of it, there for all who came after to see. He'd revelled in so doing and not only that. It was Ray's firm belief that having other people witness what he'd done was part of his motivation, his *need*.

Just as Danny Shanklin, the only man to have survived such an attack, had told the FBI: the PSS Killer needed others to *see* what he was capable of. Which also explained why, each time he'd killed, he'd left the families he'd butchered arranged in the same way: mutilated and blood-drenched in their chairs, so that those who came after would know that he had done it.

Why keep this crime scene clean? Why dispose of the plastic sheeting, which had nowhere been mentioned in the cops' reports? Why go to so much trouble to deceive the police about where the family had died? What, carry – for if they'd been dragged, the police would surely have noticed the marks – the bodies outside and burn them? And why deliberately disguise how the girl had died? Why rip out her throat and lungs?

The answer to all these questions dropped into Ray's mind like a pebble into a well, sending ripples through everything he'd been certain of before.

The PSS Killer had done all this because, far from wanting police attention, he'd wanted them not to realize he'd come back.

But what could possibly be so important to him that everything about *who he was* had suddenly realigned?

Ray used the tweezers to grip another piece of torn plastic and held it up before the flashlight beam. And, as it glinted in the light, another question entered his mind. If the PSS Killer had indeed changed his method to disguise the fact that he'd become active again, why had he left behind this evidence of it?

Because of all the serial killers Ray had ever hunted, the PSS Killer had always been the most precise. In fact, until he'd run into Danny Shanklin, and Danny and his daughter had survived, he'd not left the FBI a single lead, forensic or otherwise.

Bagging the plastic and continuing to edge sideways as he scanned the floor, he cast his mind back through the police report and newspaper articles he'd read, racking his brains, not for the gory facts of the 'Clan Killings', but the incidental details that had surrounded them.

The night of the murders, a neighbour had called round and rung on the door, but had not received an answer.

Which meant any killer inside the house might have been disturbed. And might have panicked. And might not have given himself sufficient time to clear up as thoroughly as he otherwise would have done.

In other words, Ray concluded, perhaps the PSS Killer *hadn't* overlooked or forgotten these tiny rips of plastic.

And if he hadn't forgotten, he might have also realized that they remained loose ends, capable of giving away that he was killing again.

And if he had realized that, then a killer as precise and

as thorough as he was would have no choice but to return and remove every trace.

Tap.

Ray's heartbeat spiked.

More rain?

He looked up at the skylights, but the raindrops had stopped.

He switched off his pen torch. He froze.

Scuff. Scuff.

Not inside. No. But near, dammit. Just outside the back door.

What was it? A footfall? Or nothing? Just some creature? The flap of a wing against a wall? Some kind of a rodent? A rat?

His eyes turned slowly to the door. It still looked shut. But was it? Had he locked it behind him? Had he? Had he even shut it? Shit, he couldn't even remember that.

Another *scuff*.

His heart thudded hard. No doubt about it: someone – *something* – was there.

Ray slowly edged backwards, first one foot, then the other, telling himself to keep calm, concentrating desperately on mapping the room in his head, forcing himself to think back and remember its contours. There was nothing behind him, right? Right? Not for at least another three feet? And then there should be that door leading through to the hallway and living room? Right, goddamn it? *Right?*

Slowly he rose into a crouch. He took two more steps

back. Then half a pace more, all the while staring fixedly towards the kitchen door he'd come in through.

Scuff. Scuff.

Right there – magnified to a monstrous size by the light of the moon – stamped black as a gateway to hell against the pale, drawn kitchen blind, he saw the unmistakable silhouette of a human torso, and a head.

CHAPTER 27

WALES

Danny Shanklin was still gazing at his iPhone screen, where his InWorld™ avatar, Jackal, remained idling at a table in the Rest Cure café in the city of Steem.

None of the nearby players had yet approached him. Neither had Danny been sent any direct messages from other off-screen players who might be on their way to meet him.

Jackal was being ignored by the players in the immediate vicinity but that came as no surprise. The more time players spent in InWorld™, the richer they became, at least in terms of Inwad™, the virtual currency they accrued either by working for richer players who owned cafés like this, or by questing for plunder across the game's four virtual continents and twenty-eight virtual cities.

The wealthier players were, the more they tended to advertise it by splashing out on customizing and accessorizing their avatars. Which was why even the waiters and waitresses here were ignoring Jackal, on account of the generic way in which he was attired: they had rightly guessed he didn't have enough money to buy himself a virtual coffee, let alone leave a tip.

Fact was, Danny wouldn't normally have given a damn that no one wanted to talk to him, but the exhaustion he'd felt earlier as he'd walked to the camp site from the edge of the village was now threatening to suck him into sleep.

And that was something he couldn't risk. Not only might it cost him his one chance of hooking up with Crane, but possibly his liberty and life too, if he'd already been betrayed.

Just damn well stay awake . . .

He gouged at his eyes with his knuckles and took another swig of Coke. But even that wasn't touching his exhaustion.

A shot of bourbon would do the trick, he thought. A little something to sharpen you up . . . A smoke, too . . . A Marlboro Red, your old poison of choice. Or even one of Lexie's . . . Hey, maybe she's left them lying around.

But even as his eyes set about raking the kitchen surfaces, he shook his head and turned away. Jesus, he had to be bordering on delirium to be thinking about going back on the drink and the smokes.

He knew where this kind of thinking led. Smokes and drink. Smokes and pills. Drink and pills and smokes. Every time Danny had fallen off the wagon, he'd ended up back where he didn't want to be. And every time he'd thought he wouldn't. He'd thought it would be temporary. And he'd been wrong.

Biting the inside of his cheek, he tasted blood. It was an old trick he'd learned way back to stop himself dozing off. A nasty little habit, he knew, but one that sometimes helped.

He gazed into the tiring glare of the iPhone at the virtual café's door and the system status grid at the bottom of the screen, where any incoming DMs would arrive, and where any of his other email accounts could be accessed if he so desired.

He thought back to the many other times he'd come to InWorld™ to meet up with Crane. Whenever Danny had been left waiting, he'd used to toggle between his various email accounts – business and personal – ticking off bits of admin that needed doing as he went along, checking in with people he knew.

But since this whole shit grenade had blown up, with him at its epicentre, he'd resisted checking his email. Not because he'd been worried that his accounts might have been hacked by journalists or government agencies because that was almost impossible: anything reaching his master email address, from which he could access all the others, would already have been automatically filtered through a number of unhackable torrent sites, which would have deconstructed, then reconstituted, all mail sent to him.

No, the reason Danny had steered clear was because he'd dreaded what he'd find: emails from just about everyone he'd ever known, via the various email addresses he'd given them for whatever identities they might have known him as or worked with him under – bombarding him with questions, wanting to know what the hell was going on.

Anna-Maria: when he'd left her on the morning he'd been set up in London, he'd hoped to meet her for dinner later that night.

Frank De Luca: when Danny had left Lexie with Frank's wife, Alice, later that afternoon, he'd done so because he'd thought the pair would be safe; an error that had cost Alice her life.

And the Kid – would the Kid have been in touch? To taunt? To see if Danny would respond? To see if he could bait him into giving away his whereabouts?

And maybe it was tiredness, or frustration. Or perhaps it was simpler than that. Perhaps it was just plain old curiosity, or a need to get away from himself, to reach out into a wider world where normal people still lived.

But whatever it was, something made him do it. Something made him tap the icon at the bottom of the screen to trigger the phone's search app. Something made him shuffle this new window across his screen so he could still monitor what was going on in InWorld™. And something made him log into a previously set-up email account – he'd delete it as soon as he'd checked what had come in – and trigger it to feed off his master email account.

He took a deep breath, regretting his impetuosity: hundreds, maybe even thousands, of emails, which had accumulated in his master account since the worldwide manhunt for him had begun, waterfalled down the mail window.

Changing his mind, unable to summon the energy necessary even to begin processing this amount of information, Danny moved his thumb towards the corner of the window to close it down.

But his thumb froze and his heart juddered. It wasn't any of the people he'd been wondering about whose name appeared at the top of the list of emails. The last email had been sent to him from a contact he'd almost given up hope of ever hearing fresh news from, news of a kind he dreaded and yearned for in equal measure.

The name was Ray Kincade.

And the email had been sent only minutes ago.

CHAPTER 28

SCOTLAND

Sweet Jesus, you've got no gun . . .

That's what a voice inside Ray's head was screaming repeatedly at him, like an alarm, as he stayed in the farmhouse kitchen, locked in a half-crouch – *For how long now? A whole minute? Maybe more?* – his calf muscles practically shrieking from the pressure, feeling as if, at any second, he might overbalance and fall with a thud onto the bare wooden floor.

But he couldn't move. He *mustn't* move. Not with that hulking silhouette of a man continuing to stand outside the farmhouse back door. Move and the man might hear him and know that he was there.

At least now he had the hope that his presence had not yet been detected. Because whoever was out there, they couldn't see in, *right?* The blinds were drawn. There was no way they could know that he was there unless . . . Oh, shit, Ray thought. What if whoever this was *had* been watching him outside, as he'd cased the joint and broken in?

Ray still had the ice pick in his hand. He gripped it

tighter – so tight that his tendons felt like they were going to snap.

Still the figure didn't move. Sweat blistered across his brow. His mobile phone was right in his inside coat pocket. But who the hell was he going to call? He didn't even have a number for the local cops. In any case, they were probably miles away. Plus, how the hell could he call them when he was breaking the law? When whoever was out there might just be a civilian? Or even a cop on the snoop?

The silhouette still hadn't moved.

Yeah, Ray told himself. Maybe that's it. Could be it's just some farmer, some goddamn nosy neighbour. But then why aren't they moving? Why are they just standing there? Why would they be doing that unless they were listening as well? And what the hell would they be doing here at this time of night in the rain?

Ray couldn't handle the pain in his calves any longer. He'd cramp up, he just knew it. Instead he decided to risk another half-step back.

Concentrating again on remembering the room's layout, desperately trying not to make a sound, he made his move. And – *there!* – he felt it, the back kitchen wall right where he'd guessed.

Which meant there should be that doorway leading to the rest of the house, just behind him, to his left. He could move through it into the dark embrace of the hallway, where he could crouch in the darkness, watch, and make his next play – whether to stay put or perhaps sneak out through the front door. It would buy him some breathing space. It would mean that, even if whoever it was decided to enter the property via the back door, they'd still not see him right away.

Not that they'd yet given any indication that they were planning on coming in. Not that they'd even moved.

A drumming sound. The rain was back, falling harder than before. And yet the man – oh, yes, Ray was convinced it was a *he*, all right – at the window still failed to move. Who wouldn't take shelter?

Only someone who already had good reason to stay. But why weren't they coming in? Because they'd already called for back-up? It was a possibility Ray couldn't ignore. He needed to get out of there. And quick.

But even as he continued edging back towards the hallway, even as he felt a stirring in the stillness around him, a minuscule change in air pressure that sent a sudden shiver chasing down his spine, Ray thought of another reason why the man outside might not be coming in. Because he didn't need to.

Because somebody else was already there.

He looked back just in time to see another silhouette. This one was moving. Fast. Coming at him. A blur in the darkness of the hallway, rushing at him, growing huge.

He twisted round and stood as fast as he could, a blot of adrenalin rushing through him, as he swung the ice pick back to strike. But his heavy new hiking boots made his feet move slowly. He got himself tangled in the doorway. In an agony of panic, he stumbled sideways and fell.

Which more than likely saved his life.

The intruder hurtled past, tripping over Ray, hitting him so hard with his knee that he actually heard his own rib crack.

Whoever had rushed him sprawled headlong into the kitchen, tumbling across the floor into the table, so terrifyingly fast that it felt to Ray as if the very air had just been vacuumed out from around him, leaving him gasping for breath.

Now that the dam of silence that had previously reigned over the house had burst, a torrent of noise filled the room. A clattering of furniture, as the intruder rose, hurling a chair aside as though it were made of balsa. A scream of fury. A guttural growl that chilled Ray's blood.

He already knew it: this was no cop or neighbour. There was only one person this could be.

Fear gaping inside him, Ray watched as the other man rose, scrabbling up from the floor, gathering himself once more to attack.

And also there – even as Ray struggled to get to his feet – he caught a glimpse of the silhouette of the man outside the back window, which, impossibly, it seemed, still hadn't moved . . .

Ray snatched up the ice pick with his right hand, while the grasping fingers of his left fumbled with the pen torch. He nearly dropped it but, *thank God*, didn't. *Use it to blind the fucker, whoever it is*, his racing mind screamed. And then: click. The beam shot out like a fist into the dark.

Ray caught only a glimpse of the man's face, but it was enough for him to know for certain who this was.

The man crouched in the beam of Ray's torch, even now rocking back on the heels of his mud-spattered running shoes, flexing his legs and readying himself to spring, had a blue-paper gauze surgical mask covering his nose, mouth and his jaw. But other than that he matched the description Danny Shanklin had given. Right down to the same shaved head and eyebrows – proof, Danny had claimed at the time, that whoever this psychopath was, he knew all about the dangers of DNA and forensics.

But it was the eyes, which matched Danny's description of the man, that really took Ray Kincade's breath away. They were more reptile than human. They contained no mercy, no empathy. They spoke of nothing but feeding on death.

Only then did Ray catch sight of the weapon – the *two* weapons – gripped in the PSS Killer's neoprene-gloved fists: a cosh in his right and a pistol, fitted with a sound suppressor, in the left.

So why hasn't he already shot me? And why isn't he firing at me now, when again he so easily could? Because – Ray straight away answered his own question – *he wants to use the cosh on you instead . . . He wants to subdue you with that so then he can find out who you are and what you know . . .*

The PSS Killer did raise the pistol then, almost as if reading Ray's mind, as if sensing his growing understanding and trying to smash it down.

But it was too late. Because now, instead of doing what

the killer might have expected, instead of surrendering or trying to escape, Ray chose to gamble with his life that his instinct was right – that the PSS Killer had no intention of shooting him at all.

Ray didn't surrender.

Ray didn't turn and flee.

He did the one thing the killer wouldn't be expecting. He threw himself upright and ran at him.

Ray's adversary might be twenty years younger than him, stronger than him and faster too, but none of that would count for shit the second the ice pick was embedded in his head.

CHAPTER 29

SCOTLAND

The second Ray was moving, his torch beam was off the killer. But, damn it, Ray still had locked in his mind the exact spot he needed to strike.

Two paces into the kitchen and he brought the ice pick swinging round fast in an arc, aiming on driving it down as hard as he could into the other man's face or neck.

He hit neither.

He hit nothing at all.

Instead the pick, rather than slamming into flesh and bone, just kept accelerating, bringing Ray's torso pivoting round with it.

Then – *crack*.

Ray lurched sideways. From what? A punch? A cosh? It felt more like a sledgehammer thundering into the side of his skull.

He reeled. His legs gave way beneath him as if he'd just stepped into a hole. He hit the floor face down, and heard the ice pick skittering across the wooden boards, before he even realized it had slipped out of his grip.

But somehow he'd kept hold of the pen torch. Its beam lurched maddeningly across the furniture, walls and cciling, as he floundered and tried to right himself. But his balance was off. He couldn't even tell which way was up.

You're screwed, he thought. *You're dead.*

A sudden weight pressed down on him, driving the air clean out of his lungs. He struggled and managed to twist onto his back, lashing out with his arms and legs. But the killer was on top of him now and pinned Ray's flailing right arm to the floor.

For a split second, the beam of the torch – still gripped in Ray's left hand – illuminated the PSS Killer sitting astride him. He braced himself as the killer's arm came swinging round.

Crack . . . Another blow from the cosh, onto Ray's left arm this time, a wave of agony shooting through his body, and sending the pen torch tumbling across the floor.

The killer's arm whipped back to strike again. But this time Ray managed to move. Only a fraction, but enough. The blow would have knocked him clean out if it had connected with his head, as the killer had intended, but instead it struck his shoulder.

And the killer had made another mistake. In failing to restrain Ray's left hand, he'd enabled him to get a hold on the grip of the knife he had tucked into his belt, using the PSS Killer's motion to disguise his own.

Ray knew he wouldn't get another chance. Mess this up and he'd wind up tortured to death.

He sucked air into his lungs and used every last ounce of his strength to twist his body right, and buck the killer off balance just enough to give himself the room to thrust the knife up as hard as he could into his attacker's chest.

He didn't miss.

A gasp of pain, loud enough to make Ray think he'd rammed the blade in hard enough to rip right through the killer's jacket and plunge into his flesh. Ray twisted the knife as fast as he could anticlockwise, picturing the wicked curve of its embedded barbed hook, using all his might to try to drive it in deeper.

He was rewarded with another – deeper – gasp of pain. Even better, the next blow he'd been expecting from the cosh never came. Instead, he felt the killer's weight lifting, first off his right arm, where the killer's knee had previously pinned it, and then off his chest, where the killer had been squatting astride him.

Enough, Ray suddenly realized, for him to throw himself forward and upwards, as if he wanted to launch himself right off the floor, as if he wanted to fly.

The hard thick slab of Ray's brow smashed full force into the PSS Killer's face. And elicited not just a gasp this time, but a scream. And then another. And not just from the impact of the head butt, but from the knife, which Ray was still twisting hard into the killer's side.

He registered a swift, dark blur of movement immediately above him. The cosh, he guessed, again twisting hard to his side, using the force of the movement to drive the knife in harder too.

The cosh missed Ray entirely and, this time, it was the killer's turn to be swept sideways by the momentum of his own swing.

He toppled clean off Ray and hit the floor with a clatter, and in the same movement Ray's knife was shucked free from his side.

The two men scrabbled to their feet, less than six feet apart. Ray almost fell straight back down, still struggling with his balance, feeling the floor beneath him shudder and shift. Lurching to his left, he reached out desperately to steady himself against the dark edge of the table. He held the knife up before him like a shield. By God, he managed that, all right. He held it in the shaft of moonlight, as the rain poured down outside. He made certain the PSS Killer could see.

Ray had expected the PSS Killer to rush him again. But instead he was standing unsteadily, too, breathing heavily, with one hand pressed tight to his side. To staunch the blood? How far in had the blade gone? What damage had it done?

Not enough, Ray saw. Because the killer took a step sideways then. Not a stumble. A much more controlled movement.

Ray tensed himself for the next attack. He'd already planned his move. A half-step back as soon as the killer moved forward. But that would be a feint. Ray would then lunge. One stride forward and strike. He'd meet him halfway and stab once more for the torso.

But instead of attacking, the killer's head tilted, as he looked down at the floor.

The pistol, Ray realized. Where the fuck was it? Was that what he'd heard clattering off into the dark? He glanced down too, hunting for a glint of cold metal, because whoever got that pistol first . . .

That was when the idea hit him, an idea he knew straight away might just save his life.

He took a step back. Then another. Out of the moonlight, which was fading now as the storm grew. Into deeper shadow. He didn't try to hide the movement. He did it for show. And then, once he was sure he had the killer's full attention, he dropped swiftly into a crouch – fighting and praying not to lose his balance – and made as if to grab something from behind the table leg.

Then, just as quickly, before the killer had a chance to move, or even work out what was happening, Ray got back up, using the speed of the movement to switch the knife from his right hand to his left, and turn it around.

'Put your fucking hands up,' he said, aiming the knife hilt forward into the gloom, as he would a pistol barrel.

The hissing of the killer's laboured breathing slowed, then stopped.

Ray couldn't see his face. He couldn't even guess what he was thinking. Had he bought it?

A flash of movement.

Something big, something solid, hurtled through the air towards Ray. He lurched sideways in the nick of time, as whatever it was lanced past his head, missing by mere millimetres.

A crash. A splintering sound. As Ray steadied himself

and looked back towards where the killer had been, he saw that he had gone.

A blast of cold air. Twisting to his left, Ray saw the kitchen door – half smashed off its hinges – was wide open.

His legs gave way, dragging the rest of him down with them.

'Get up,' he told himself. 'Get up, goddammit. Move.'

CHAPTER 30

WALES

Danny Shanklin must have read Ray Kincade's email twenty times. But in spite of its brevity and the fact that it was written in plain English, his brain was still having trouble processing it and taking the information it contained on board.

Ray had emailed to say he was in the UK, about to break into an isolated farm in a remote part of Scotland where a multiple homicide had taken place. Even though the Scottish cops had made no connection between these murders and the PSS Killer, Ray was convinced they were indeed his work.

He had written:

> I do not believe you are guilty of the crimes the papers say. Nor do I believe the PSS Killer is dead. Or in prison. I believe he is near here. In short, I believe the PSS Killer is back.

Everything that had happened to Danny since he'd

been forced on the run . . . This last sentence had blown it all away, taking priority in his mind.

All he could now see, as he stared into his iPhone's screen, was the disbelief in Jonathan's eyes before he'd been killed. All he could hear was Sally's choking.

It was as though the intervening years had not happened and he was now back there, tied to that chair with that madman making him watch, while Lexie hid outside in the snowbound woods and listened to her family's screams.

But as well as taking him back in time, the email, it seemed, had the power to take him forwards, to a future he had dreamed of and yearned for in the days, months and years after his wife and son had been killed. He couldn't count the ways he had imagined of bringing the PSS Killer's life to an end. Bludgeoning him, strangling him, decapitating him, stabbing him, shooting him, drowning him, torturing him – doing to him everything he'd done to others, making him pay, beg, scream and die.

But as the years had passed, these crazy, self-destructive fantasies that *would not bring Sally and Jonathan back* had dwindled, loosening their grip, until he'd seen them for what they were – not a way forward, but a way to prevent him moving on.

But he couldn't kid himself either. Even though he had made a semblance of a life for himself since, he'd not quenched the thirst for revenge.

Even though a part of him had always hoped that one day the PSS Killer would be brought to account for what he had done, and even though he'd still craved to be the one who made it happen, another part of him – a better part, he'd come to believe – had been grateful that the PSS Killer had failed to surface. Because his not being there had meant that other families had not had to suffer as Danny's had.

As much, then, as he had wanted to kill the PSS Killer, he'd come to hope that the PSS Killer was already dead.

But not any more. That hope had just been extinguished. And, in its place, his desire for revenge burned.

Believe: that was the word Ray had used. Not *know*. Just *believe*. And with anyone other than Ray, Danny would have taken that belief with a pinch of salt. But not Ray. He had chosen Ray to continue the hunt for the PSS Killer after the FBI Elite Serial Crime Unit had gone cold on it. And he'd chosen him because he was the best, and certainly not likely to ring a false alarm. As witnessed by his silence concerning any leads until now.

But in spite of Danny's burgeoning *hunger* that a day of reckoning might finally be at hand, his heart was pounding, not because of what Ray might find, but because of what Danny might lose.

He was worried sick about Lexie. What would it do to her to know that the PSS Killer was alive? And not just alive, but doing to others as he'd done to her brother and mother. And not just anywhere, but here in the country where Lexie had made her fresh start.

And his fears didn't stop there. Because if the PSS Killer was alive and at large, then he, too, would have seen what Danny had been accused of. He would have seen that Danny had been forced to snatch his own daughter and go on the run. He would have seen the photos of Lexie, of the beautiful young woman she'd become. And – this thought made Danny's fist close so tight around his iPhone that its frame creaked – he might decide he could finish what he'd started, that she might once again be his.

He thought of Lexie's school, its address compromised. He thought of her friends, several of whom had already been interviewed by the press. All of them were now compromised too. He thought of his homes in London and the Caribbean, their locations publicized across the world. Danny had known these people and places were off limits for as long as he was a wanted man, but he'd hoped that his life – and, more importantly, Lexie's – might return to normality at some point.

But now he saw this could not be. The PSS Killer would be able to find him and Lexie whenever he wanted. Far from the two of them happily surfacing in the event that Danny cleared his name, they'd now have to stay in hiding. At least until the PSS Killer was stopped. At least until he was dead.

But it wasn't only Lexie Danny was fearful for. It was Ray. How old was he now? Sixty? At least. He was tracking the PSS Killer without back-up – and there wasn't a damn thing Danny could do to help, even though he was in the same goddamn country.

No. That wasn't true. There *was* something Danny could do. Not to help capture the PSS Killer but to protect Ray from further danger. And to preserve whatever leads he'd discovered.

Danny could call him off. He could tell him to hold back and wait. Wait until he had cleared his name so that he could join him. Or, if not that, at least wait until Danny had been able to arrange back-up for him.

He began to type:

Do nothing. Await further instructions. Do not do this alone.

CHAPTER 31

SCOTLAND

Ray's head was throbbing. His vision was blurred and it was all he could do not to throw up. He staggered sideways, grabbing at the wall for support. But there, in front of him, he saw the gun. Right there, framed in a flicker of lightning coming through the open back door.

He grabbed it and lurched towards the door, wondering how badly the lunatic was injured. He'd moved fast enough just then, all right. But the knife Ray still had in his hand was slick with blood.

The blood, he thought. It was all the proof he'd need that the PSS Killer was back. He could match it to the sample taken from the snow outside the cabin where Danny Shanklin's family had been attacked.

But a body would be even better. You can do this, he told himself, taking the final stride to the open door. You can take the motherfucker down. You can bring him in dead or alive.

He froze in his tracks, as a deafening roar of sheet lightning crashed outside in the gathering storm, revealing that the silhouette at the window was still there. Ray raised his pistol to fire, then saw how he'd been tricked.

A scarecrow. The killer must have taken it from an outbuilding or nearby field. He must have seen Ray breaking in and used it to fool him, so he could sneak up on him from behind.

Ray heard him then, the crashing of metal. The killer must have run into something nearby, at the front of the house. He set off after him, but he was still reeling from where he'd been hit and was now feeling nauseous too. He was moving so slowly he might as well have been wading through water. He could feel every one of his sixty years.

But he would not quit.

Through a crosswind of rain, and a strobe of lightning, he glimpsed the killer on the driveway ahead moving even slower than he was, dammit, at a crazy angle, one arm clamped to his side, to staunch his wound.

Ray watched him stumble and fall. He's yours, he thought. You can still end this now. You can take this mother down.

But then – while Ray was still twenty yards away – the killer got up and set off again. Ray lifted the pistol and tried to aim, but his arm wouldn't keep still. Too weak. He needed to get closer if he was going to stand a chance in hell of hitting him.

Ray staggered after him, but with every step he felt his strength fading. He reached the spot where the killer had fallen and saw it was a deep pothole, half full of water. Something was floating on it – a piece of white paper.

He sank to his knees and picked it up. A fresh flicker of lightning illuminated it. A parking ticket, it looked like. He stuffed it into his pocket.

He puked then. A gutful. His skull felt all wrong, his hearing too. He was more than likely concussed.

Ahead, he saw the PSS Killer stumble again. Ray forced himself to his feet and lurched after him. Maybe he's dying, he thought. Maybe even right now he's breathing his last breath . . .

He pressed on, cursing as the killer reached a screen of trees near the end of the driveway. Got to get to him, he thought. Got to get to him fast. Got to stop him before he reaches whatever vehicle he came here in.

He put his hand into his pocket. His phone wasn't there. Must have lost it in the struggle.

He heard a car start up. He heard its engine rev and its tyres shriek, as it raced down the road, away from the village, further east.

Ray was panting. He felt disoriented. He sank to his knees and then rolled onto his side. He tried to sit, couldn't. He rolled sideways instead. Not just because he thought he was about to throw up again, but because he couldn't help himself. Something wasn't working. Some connection between his brain and his body had snapped.

Just for a second he was back on a camping trip as a little kid with his father. He'd crawled out of their tent in the middle of the night for a pee and, on the other side of their burned-down fire, he had stared into the coal black eyes of a bear. And Ray had frozen. Whatever impulse had normally fired his muscles into life had switched off. He'd frozen and the pee had run down his leg. The bear had watched him for a minute or more, before slowly turning and trudging away.

That was what he remembered now as he lay on his side, staring up at the flashing, booming sky. He remembered powerlessness. He remembered not knowing whether he would live or die.

CHAPTER 32

WALES

Even though Danny Shanklin hadn't asked Ray to reply, he couldn't stop himself toggling back to the email window on his iPhone screen over and over to see if he had.

But as the seconds trickled by, he heard nothing. Did it mean Ray had received his instruction to back off? Or had it reached him too late?

Tink.

He jolted in his seat. He looked first to the caravan window, thinking someone was there.

Tink-tink.

Then he stared at his iPhone, shut down his mail app and logged out.

The Rest Cure café filled his screen. Jackal had not moved from the table he'd been at before. But he was no longer alone. Another avatar, dressed in newbie clothing also, only distinguishable from Jackal by his blond hair, was sitting opposite him at the small corner table.

Tink-tink-tink.

The sound was the noise of someone attempting to

speak to Danny's new avatar, Jackal. He read the message scrolling across the dialogue at the bottom of the screen: *IF YOU STILL WANT TO TALK ABOUT FISHING, THEN FRIEND ME AND SWITCH TO DM.*

The avatar who'd sent it was named Melville. In spite of Danny's exhaustion, a smile crept across his face. Herman Melville, the author of *Moby Dick*. Some might say the greatest fisherman of all time, who'd sought the greatest prey.

The Crane Danny had dealt with over the years at InWorld™ had always displayed a wry enough sense of humour, which gave him hope. But so had the Kid. The Kid had always liked riddles and had known how to make Danny laugh. So this could just as easily be him.

Danny tapped Melville's avatar, bringing up the raft of basic details publicly accessible for any InWorld™ avatar. Melville had been created less than five minutes ago. Almost certainly as a reaction, then, to the message he had posted on the Public Contact Board.

He checked his watch. Minutes. That was all the time he had to establish whether this was Crane or not, and if so, whether to trust him and the integrity of this form of communication to request the help he so desperately needed. Bare minutes. Then he and Lexie had to be gone from here, with this phone destroyed, if they were to be sure of escaping any attempt to ensnare them that this online contact might already have instigated.

Pulse rising, he accepted the friend request from Melville, then hit the DM option. The Rest Cure café receded into the background, while the images of Jackal and Melville's avatar faces ballooned to the fore, until it was just the two of them filling the screen.

A cartoon bubble emerged from Melville's mouth, growing to accommodate the words that scrolled across it like tickertape.

Melville: 'Fate comes in many guises.'

Another pun, with whoever was acknowledging that Danny had got rid of his old avatar F8 and turned into someone new.

Melville: 'And shows itself in unexpected places.'

Whoever this was might mean that they were used to meeting Danny in Harry's Bar at Noirlight. But, again, this could as easily be the Kid as Crane.

Danny thumbed in a reply and watched as it scrolled across the speech bubble emerging from Jackal's mouth.

Jackal: 'Your old house is no longer safe.'

Melville: 'I know.'

If this was the Kid Danny was talking to, he'd know because he'd hacked Crane's virtual safe-house himself. If Melville was really Crane, he'd know because he'd have been locked out.

Time was ticking . . .

Jackal: 'What's the name of the first client I worked for you?'

A pause. One second, two . . . He watched the old speech bubble fade out next to Melville's head. The Kid had not been involved in the close protection of a Hollywood actress who'd been receiving death threats, which had been Danny's first assignment for Crane. But the real Crane would remember. He'd been meticulous with information from the start. Three seconds, four . . . His eyes flicked to the tiny log-out icon at the top of the screen, suddenly fearing this wasn't Crane he was talking to, after all. But then a fresh speech bubble appeared and letters began to scroll.

🖝Melville: 'Janey Stempleton.'

Danny breathed out. It was the right answer. He should have felt relief, but a renewal of tension tingled through him. Because this answer was not in itself proof enough that this was Crane. Danny racked his brain. *Had* he ever told the Kid about the Stempleton assignment? He thought not, but could he bet his life on it? No. He might have made some flip comment. Or there might even be some record of it out there. Close protection was as competitive as any other industry. And with a client that famous, somewhere, somehow, his name and the actress's might have been linked.

🖝Jackal: 'What date?'

He waited for a reply, but no speech bubble appeared to indicate that the real person behind the avatar was typing. Five seconds, six . . . He looked again to the door. As well as packing the car, he'd already memorized the route he'd take from here. Other than stopping to change the vehicle's plates en route, in case anyone here had made a note of the current ones, he was confident he'd be able to get far enough away quickly enough to slip through any net that might be closing in.

A bubble formed, then came words:

➡Melville: '16 March.'

Danny's mind raced. Could anyone other than the real Crane know that? Again, there was a remote possibility, but—

He watched more words scroll across Melville's speech bubble, and with each new phrase, any doubts he had were finally erased.

➡Melville: 'Fee: $60,000. Account fee paid into: CH9300762011623852957.'

Danny sincerely doubted anyone but Crane would have access to that information. And he remembered the fee because it had been his first as a freelancer. The account number was correct as well, the same account he'd always filtered his money from Crane through.

➡Jackal: 'I'm innocent.'

➡Melville: 'I believe you.'

➡Jackal: 'The Kid was working with the mercenary group who did this. They in turn were working for the Georgian Secret Service. They framed the Russian Colonel Zykov as well as me for the assassination of the Georgian peace envoy, who'd been in London to protest to the United Nations Security Council about Russia's continued occupation of the disputed border territories of South Ossetia and Abkhazia. They wanted Russia to get the public blame to renew pressure on them to return buffer.'

➡Melville: 'Why did they frame you?'

➡Jackal: 'Because they wanted to maximize publicity,

international outrage and condemnation for what they'd done. They deliberately kept me just ahead of the police in London so that the whole world would watch the chase.'

Now was the time for Danny to tell Crane about what they'd made him do next: steal the locations for the smallpox vials from Colonel Zykov's office in the Russian Embassy. But he said nothing.

Melville: 'How is Lexie?'

Jackal: 'Alive.'

Melville: 'Where is she?'

Jackal: 'Somewhere safe.'

Melville: 'I can talk to people. We can attempt to explain to them what really happened. We can bring you in.'

Jackal: 'No.'

Because, yes, it was possible that certain elements in the US and even the UK government might be willing to believe Danny, but there were others whose driving motivation would be to hang the London massacre on someone fast: all the hard evidence pointed at him, so why would they look anywhere else?

Melville: 'I'm here to help in any way I can.'

The offer, Danny knew, was huge. Not only in terms of how it compromised Crane, making him an accessory, but also in terms of scope. Crane's network of contacts and intelligence resources was unrivalled in Danny's experience.

But he had to be careful. Even though he was now satisfied that this truly was Crane, the possibility remained that Crane had already told the authorities about this contact and that the entire conversation was being monitored. He needed to find a way to get Crane to mine him the information he needed, without Crane or anyone else listening in and being able to work out from that information where he was heading or where he'd surface next. He needed to give Crane a jigsaw to work from, but with enough pieces missing so that he'd never see the full picture.

➡Jackal: 'OK, here's what I want you to do.'

Danny took a folded piece of paper from his pocket and started to thumb the carefully constructed sentences written there into his phone.

CHAPTER 33

PORT OF LONDON

Even being this close to London, where his pixellated face had been glaring out from every phone screen and TV shop window since the hunt for him had begun, was bringing Danny Shanklin out in cold sweats.

And seeing London laid out before him like this from a distance, as a vast concrete labyrinth, more than fifteen miles wide, reminded him of how trapped he'd been – and how lucky to escape.

Much of the city remained sunk in shadow, but already the first rays of sunlight were flaring across the towering tops of the Centre Point building and the recently completed Shard.

Danny craved some of that heat right now, as he had throughout the long night he'd been positioned there, lying flat on his stomach beside a humming industrial extractor fan on top of a tall refrigerated storage facility on Pier Twelve at the docks.

Still fearing that the lead he'd been given by Commandant Sabirzhan might be a set-up, and knowing that if it was the whole area would be under surveillance prior to any attempted sting, he had arrived early.

Nearly twenty-four hours ago, to be precise. A decent enough safety measure, of course, but the downside was that the adrenalin that had fuelled his breaking into the docks compound and preparing his exit strategy had long since faded, leaving him at first lethargic and now in a trance-like state.

In the old days, in the field with the CIA, he'd used amphetamines to keep himself alert, but since he'd sworn off all that, he had only the same taurine- and caffeine-rich drinks that helped clubbers stay up dancing all night. And the big problem with these, Danny had discovered, was that, on top of making his breath stink, they perpetually made him want to piss.

He thought of his phone in his pocket. How many times a minute had he been doing that? It was like an addiction. No, not *like*. The desire to call Lexie *was* an addiction. Was she OK? Dammit, this was what his whole life now boiled down to. He knew nothing about what he cared for most.

At least he'd heard back from Ray. Danny had contacted him again and this time Kincade had messaged him to say he was suspending any further investigation into the whereabouts of the PSS Killer until Danny gave him the go-ahead. *With me at your side*, he promised himself. *To make sure no one makes the same mistake I did the last time. To put that fucker in the ground for good.*

He readjusted the flattened cardboard box and tangle

of plastic sheeting that covered him, slipped the last
piece of his energy bar into his mouth and chewed it as
he rolled sideways, crouched close to the extractor fan
block and urinated into the gutter there. He was badly
dehydrated, he saw. Which meant he'd be slow to react, if
anyone did show.

Just keep alert. Concentrate.

Only forty minutes remained until the meet between
Glinka's people and the terrorist cell was supposed to take
place. Just forty minutes until he'd find out whether this
was a set-up designed to eliminate himself, a chance for
him finally to nail Glinka and the others or just another
dead end.

He felt his eyelids beginning to droop.

CHAPTER 34

Footsteps.

Danny woke, sweating. He blinked in the sunlight. Jesus, what time is it? Panic raced through him. He twisted his wrist to check his watch. How the hell could he have fallen asleep?

Six fifty-two. He nearly spewed with relief. Eight minutes remained until the meeting was meant to happen.

He wriggled forwards to the edge of the roof. Stretched out before him, this part of the port was a ghost town of warehouses, container stacks, storage facilities and transportation depots, fronted by a mile-long quayside, where stationary crawler cranes stood sentry, like giant herons, against the blushing London skyline and the dark, fast-flowing waters of the Thames.

He edged forward and peered over the building's guttering at the security foot patrol passing below. A man and a woman. Both had radios clipped to their utility belts, but there were no signs that they were anything other than the rent-a-cops their uniforms declared them to be – no telltale bulges of concealed weapons.

They weren't conducting counter-surveillance either. They didn't inspect the doorways they were passing, much less look up. Which again implied that they were genuine Docklands Authority employees and nothing more sinister.

Getting into the docks at night had been easy. This was no military base. The security outfit running the place was there to fulfil the freight companies' insurance requirements and check transportation dockets. They certainly weren't looking for lone intruders like him.

There'd been plenty of CCTV at ground level, though, but if anyone was searching for him now, using its hard-drive records, they'd have a problem tracing him to this roof: the first thing he'd done on entering the compound had been to disable the cameras along the route he'd taken, before doubling back and climbing up here.

He'd watched the cameras being repaired yesterday by electricians. He'd even listened to them bitching below. 'Some stupid kid,' was what they'd reckoned. With the CCTV restored, Danny would be filmed, of course, the moment he set foot back down there. But he'd made sure to take precautions already to deal with that eventuality.

Even better, shortly after he'd scaled the Docklands Authority's security fence and had entered the compound, he'd got lucky. A laundry van with its rear doors open had been idling outside one of the administration buildings. As its two complaining drivers had lugged the heavy fresh-uniform bags inside, it had been a simple enough task for Danny to take what he'd needed, before fading back into the dark.

He was now wearing the same blue rent-a-cop uniform as the foot patrol below. Not that it would help him explain what he was doing up there if anyone spotted him now, of course. But on the ground? Well, it might make all the difference between him being hauled up and detained, or being ignored and allowed to go on his way.

A waterproof pen and pad hung from a lanyard around his neck. The pad was littered with markings: timings, tithe marks and more esoteric symbols. It was a record of each and every movement he'd witnessed in the network of alleyways below over the twenty-four hours he'd been hidden there.

It confirmed that the two-person patrol passing now was the same half-hourly patrol that had been running like clockwork all night. Nothing out of the ordinary, then. Still nothing to indicate that any other pros, like himself, were staking out the area.

Turning his attention to the maze of alleyways and buildings to the west of his position, Danny zoomed in on Building 17. Two hundred yards away, it was there that the rendezvous between Glinka and the terrorist cell was due to take place. The double gantry doors remained shut. Nothing moved. There wasn't so much as a wharf rat in sight.

Glancing down, he saw the patrol rounding the building and disappearing from sight. A riverboat klaxon sounded mournfully across the Thames. Guided by two London Port Authority tugs, a container ship was moving steadily upriver towards the quayside.

His nerves hit a peak, screeching discordantly through his sleep-shattered mind. How long before that ship was due to dock? How long before the day shift of dockworkers was swarming across the quayside to prepare for the great ship's arrival, and the dull diesel grumble of the cranes started up?

There'd be too much interference then – vehicles and people moving – for Danny to be able to film any meeting that might take place from this distance. And too many potential witnesses if Glinka showed, a drop-off took place and Danny got there in time to disrupt it.

He searched the rooftops of the surrounding buildings. They remained free of surveillance. He checked his watch again.

Only two minutes remained.

For the hundredth time, Danny felt for the reassuring shapes of the Glock 30 pistol and the Taser in the dual holster strapped across his chest. The pistol, of course, was useless from here. But not if he closed in on that building in time.

If anyone showed . . .

He zoomed in on Building 17 again and wished also that he was staring instead through a rifle scope – then dismissed the fantasy of killing Glinka with a shot to the back of the head.

Instead he reminded himself that the reason he'd come was to capture video footage of the meeting and thereby establish a link between Glinka and whatever terrorist cell he'd meet, then send it to Crane to show his people, as further evidence to corroborate Danny's story about how Glinka and the Kid had set him up.

Or, even better, to film the Kid alongside Glinka, then either follow them to where they were going next or somehow take one of them captive.

And make him talk.

CHAPTER 35

Only one minute left now until the meeting was due to take place.

Activating the 'Record' function on the control pad of the same smart binoculars with which Spartak had furnished him in Pripyat, Danny once more swept the nearby alleys below, praying for a car, truck or unscheduled foot patrol to appear. His hopes were fading. Nothing moved, apart from the steadily approaching container ship and the promise of failure it bore.

The minute ran out.

An ache of desperation filled him. The doors remained closed. There was no meeting. And Danny knew Glinka: everything he did was on time; if he wasn't there now, he wasn't coming.

Maybe this was just a dead end. Perhaps Commandant Sabirzhan – Danny remembered his eyes, their fury and pain – had misheard the details of the rendezvous, or had got the time or even the place hopelessly muddled in his sickening mind.

Or – Danny's desperation peaked once more into fear – maybe it wasn't a dead end or a meeting. Maybe it was what he'd suspected from the start: a trap. Whereby Glinka had fed Sabirzhan that information, in case Danny had been ruthless and smart enough to track them to Chernobyl.

A beep.

Danny's heartbeat accelerated as he checked his phone: a new text message, from the package-delivery firm DHL. Danny scrolled across the screen, hit open and smiled.

He waited until, a few minutes later, the high pitched growl of a motorbike engine confirmed this.

Threading his arms into the straps of his rucksack, Danny watched the bike cruise past the end of the building he was stationed on and followed its progress along the quayside until it pulled up in front of Building 17.

Rolling his thumb across his phone screen again, he selected the icon of an app you couldn't buy in any store. Spartak had got hold of it for him and its instructions were in Russian.

Activating it, he watched a grid of squares balloon across the screen. Inside each square was a GPS location, each one corresponding to a position within a few hundred yards of where he was concealed. As his thumb tapped each of the squares, their colours switched from green to yellow.

He trained his binoculars on the bike and its rider and pressed record again. He'd called DHL and had them collect a brown-paper package from outside an office block on the other side of London. He had instructed them to deliver it here to Building 17, at exactly five past seven and not a minute before. He now watched the courier removing the same brown-paper parcel from his pannier.

You wanna know what's inside something? Give it a damn good poke.

Danny remembered the Old Man telling him that. They'd been on spring-break vacation in the woods. A hornets' nest had been hanging from the log cabin's guttering. He and his father had been watching what appeared to be three or four hornets sporadically arriving and vanishing into the nest, then re-emerging a few seconds later, each one as big as ten-year-old Danny's thumb.

The Old Man had told him that, come night, they'd need to bung the entrance of the nest with an industrial filler spray. The ones inside would suffocate, he said, while those outside would die of cold. There were too many of the insects already and they would become increasingly territorial, until it would be impossible for Danny and his father to approach the cabin at all.

Danny had objected, saying there didn't seem to be enough of them to do anyone any harm. After all, he'd reasoned, they'd only seen three or four. His father had walked back and thrown a stone at the nest with a precision Danny still marvelled at.

There'd been a *tock*-ing sound, as the Old Man had drawn Danny back into the safety of some bushes and a slow second's silence. Then a swarm had emerged from the nest. Maybe as many as fifty, a number Danny had thought it impossible such an outwardly small nest could contain.

The nest had been deceptive. There'd been a cavity in the wall inside which the hornets had built, they'd learned later. Where at first there'd appeared to be little to worry about, in fact there'd been great strength.

And now, as the courier removed his helmet and hung it over his bike's handlebars, Danny felt the same sense of anticipation as he had after the Old Man had unleashed the stone and Danny's keen young eyes had followed its perfect arc through the air.

Was this a hornets' nest too? Was there more here than met even a trained eye like his? He was about to find out.

The courier swigged from a water bottle, took a mobile phone from his pocket and made a call.

Danny thought of Spartak Sidarov, how he'd love right now to have him at his side or, even better, stationed nearby in a position from which he'd be able to run interference and misdirect anyone who might come Danny's way.

But Danny hadn't let Spartak come.

He'd asked Spartak instead to find out what he could about Glinka, based on the little information they had. The torturer Danny had interrogated at the farmhouse he'd been taken to on the day of the London massacre had told him that Glinka had known about the stolen smallpox because he'd been at the Soviet Biopreparet in 1990. Spartak was now using his contacts to trawl through the records of all the soldiers who'd been stationed there that year and would filter those results by age. Spartak had never seen Glinka, but so long as he obtained a shortlist of photo IDs, Danny was certain he'd be able to pick out the man.

And then? Once they knew who Glinka was, they could set about finding out who his current contacts were and whether he was still operating under his own name. Partnered with the Kid as he was, he was more than likely already a ghost, entirely wiped from the web. But he could have family, old friends, some emotional attachment that might lead Danny to him.

Danny readjusted the cardboard and other detritus he was using for camouflage. He flexed his legs, arched his back and slowly rotated his neck. Realigning his tired, cramped muscles, he thanked God as he felt a fresh burst of adrenalin.

He trained the binoculars on the courier again, then zoomed in on Building 17. In the middle of its huge double steel doors there was a smaller access door with a glass viewing panel at its centre.

The courier approached this now, and Danny watched as he pressed the door buzzer beside it.

Then all hell broke loose.

CHAPTER 36

The chugging of mechanized rotors. Birds tore into the sky. Danny watched an unmarked black Dauphin helicopter rapidly rise over the buildings at the far end of the docks and tilt its nose, then rush towards him.

He fought the dread that swelled inside him – that screamed at him to run. Moving as little as possible, desperate now not to knock the trash covering him or in any other way reveal his presence, he lowered his binoculars, fearful of sunlight bouncing off their lenses and giving him away.

The chopper raced directly at him, as though hauled on an invisible rope, but then, without warning, it slid to a halt mid-air and hovered directly above where the hapless courier was still standing.

Danny's worst fears had been confirmed: this *was* a trap. Glinka wasn't there. The meeting between him and a terrorist cell had been fiction, nothing but bait, a ruse designed to lure Danny there and take him down.

None of which explained who the hell was up in

that chopper now, of course. But Danny could hazard a guess. Had their situations been reversed and Danny had wanted someone captured, why risk doing it yourself?

Glinka had instead simply tipped off intelligence – either UK or US – to let them know that Danny might be there and at what time.

A wail of distortion and feedback. Inside the chopper, a loudhailer barked orders. Danny could make out two silhouettes positioned in its open doors – snipers, both holding rifles.

The courier was looking desperately around him, one arm flailing, the other clutching the parcel for dear life. For a terrible moment, Danny feared that the clearly terrified civilian would do something foolish, such as try to run. If he did, he would die.

Whoever the guys hovering above him were, their assumption would be that the courier was a pro, the same as themselves, and if he did run, it wouldn't be through panic, but through intent, because he was planning on either evading or in some way fighting back. Any sign of resistance to their will, and they'd use lethal force. That blood would be on Danny, too, for having brought the courier into this arena to begin with.

He willed the man to stay the hell where he was.

And the courier did. He controlled his panic. Instead he did what he was being ordered to do. He put the parcel on the ground, stepped away from it and lay face down, spread-eagled.

Danny didn't move. Not only might whoever was in that chopper see him if he did, but he could now safely assume that the whole area would be under geostationary satellite surveillance. Any organization that commanded sufficient tactical resources to scramble a Dauphin helicopter into view would manage that too, no sweat. Danny just prayed that the tangle of garbage camouflaging him would be enough, and thanked God he was far enough away from the rotors for it not to be blown clean away.

But the trap had not yet been fully sprung. Several sleek black Mercs emerged from other buildings, rushing in, blocking off the roads and alleyways to the north and south.

Their doors swung open, disgorging into the alleyways a number of men and women wearing civilian clothing – T-shirts, jeans, shades and caps. Weapons already drawn, they moved swiftly into a containment pattern, closing in on and then around the hapless courier, like a net, until he was completely surrounded, by men either crouching or standing, legs planted firmly apart, all adopting a firing stance, each ready to shoot.

The courier clasped his head with both hands. The operatives around him divided into two smaller groups, one tightening the circle they formed around him, like a noose round a condemned man's neck, the others turning their attention to the parcel he had put on the ground.

Something struck Danny hard then about one of the

men now pressing a gun to the back of the courier's head. There was something familiar about his gait as he'd moved, something about his current stance . . .

He didn't need his binoculars to know that he'd met the bastard.

His mind lurched back to his daughter's school. After he'd been set up for the massacre in London and publicly identified, he'd known that British intelligence would go after Lexie to use her against him. But as he'd fled with her through her school grounds in an attempt to outrun the intelligence agents who'd been in pursuit, two had caught up with them. Danny had taken one down easily, but the other had fought. He and Lexie had been lucky to escape with their lives.

And, staring down at the heavily muscled, black-haired agent now straddling the courier and pressing a pistol to the back of his head, Danny didn't need to see his eyes to know with absolute certainty that this was the same man.

He was dead certain of something else too. Mixed with the blood lust in the agent's eyes, there would now be a vicious, overwhelming thirst for revenge. The second he turned the prostrate courier's head around to face him, and saw that he was not Danny Shanklin, he would rip the place apart.

He'd have the whole docks searched inch by inch, until it was Danny whose skull that pistol barrel was jammed against.

'Well, screw you,' Danny said, switching one of the

squares on his phone's display screen from yellow to red.

The first of the bombs he'd set when he'd first brokem into the docks exploded with a deafening roar that drowned even the noise of the chopper and the screaming agents below.

CHAPTER 37

The two groups of agents on the ground broke apart, some remaining close to the courier and the parcel, others turning away, fanning out, covering the approaches, trying to work out where the new threat had come from, and whether it was just the beginning of a wider attack that would now close in and centre on them.

The chopper had reacted too, rising rapidly, attempting to gain a wider perspective from which it could assess what was happening. It turned now to face the direction the explosion had come from – a hundred metres east – where a thin plume of white smoke was now rising into the sky.

Impressive, Danny thought. The agents on the ground held their positions. None was panicking. But, then again, why should they? He could pretty much guess what was going through their minds. If the chopper was holding its current fixed position – as it was – and not engaging, or indeed beating a rapid retreat, the chances were they had nothing to worry about either, right?

Wrong. He pressed the second and third yellow squares on his screen simultaneously.

Two more explosions blasted out. Neither sounded harmless, but both were, as the first bomb had been. Home-made incendiaries designed to do nothing more than belch white smoke into the sky.

His thumb punched two more squares on-screen. No noises came this time. Instead black smoke billowed upwards from the two incendiaries he had detonated, which had both been concealed inside waterproof packages rammed with dry bedding and strips of black tyre.

Another of the Old Man's aphorisms echoed through Danny's mind: *The best way to panic an enemy is to make them believe they're surrounded, outnumbered – or, preferably, both.*

He allowed himself a grim smile now, as he watched those words take their grip on the reality below. It would be the black smoke, of course. Most of the agents would have been in combat at some point in their lives. The smoke, and the stink now hitting them too, meant that whatever those explosions were, they sure as hell weren't cars backfiring, ship flares being sent up or any other such innocuous shit.

Panic, absent before, now began to spread. And not just on the ground. The chopper rose higher, rotating first this way, then that, focusing on one column of black smoke, then another, torn between which threat to concentrate on first.

Both of its side doors were open now, with snipers

facing out either side, their rifles covering the multiple threats they'd now been presented with, swinging from one smoke stack to another, no longer looking nearly so confident or in control – no longer certain which their primary target was.

But Danny knew even more confusion was needed to allow him to escape. More incendiaries – a precaution he'd planned with Spartak, suspecting that this might be a trap.

Tap-tap.

He thumbed two more of the grid squares on his phone from yellow to red. Another two explosions rang out, further east – away from the direction in which he was planning to exit – each much more audible now that the chopper was so high.

The layout of the docks was playing into his hands now. The labyrinth of alleys and buildings made it practically impossible for the agents on the ground to work out from which direction the explosions were coming. Their only real guide was the chopper above them, but that was now switching focus even faster than before, giving no useful indication of where the main threat was based.

As a result, the agents' previously tight formations were continuing to break apart. Some were taking cover, bodies hugged tight against walls, or wedged into locked doorways, while others were frantically screaming at them, attempting to force them back into position.

Tap.

Bang went the 'Big Boy', as Danny had christened it. It had ten times the power of anything that had come before. He'd rigged it even further to the east. More black smoke filled the sky and he could smell the stench of burning rubber now. To anyone but himself, it looked as if several buildings across the compound were on fire, though none actually was.

Meaning it was time to get the heck out of Dodge . . .

As the first of the smoke reached his building, Danny began to edge away, watching the chopper to check it wasn't yet looking towards him. And just in case its pilot was thinking of turning.

Tap.

Another incendiary: this one launching a high-street rocket, which Danny had rigged inside a drainpipe. It streaked vertically into the sky. Fifty yards from the chopper, but close enough maybe to convince the pilot that he was now under ground-to-air strike.

The chopper lurched sideways in an emergency evasion manoeuvre.

Then it shuttled forward.

Before, finally, it raced away.

The knock-on effect on the agents was immediate. Any attempt to restore their previous pattern was abandoned. Maybe because of something the helicopter pilot had radioed down. Or because he had bolted – perhaps that had driven home the message that their assumed dominance had been stripped away.

Danny peered down over the edge of the roof a final time to see that the courier had now been pulled to his feet and was being dragged towards the wall of

Building 17. With the helicopter gone, he could hear shouts rising up. He could even pick out the accents. English.

Again his eyes narrowed on the dark-haired MI5 agent he'd fought off at Lexie's school. And for the first time since he'd triggered the first of his incendiaries, he felt a dart of panic.

Because the dark-haired agent wasn't running or seeking cover. While his colleagues raced this way and that, he was looking at the rooftops. And then he did what Danny had dreaded. Through the gathering smoke, Danny saw him stare directly at him, then point.

CHAPTER 38

Danny punched yet another square on his grid. A thud. The parcel, right there beside the agent, erupted into flames. Black smoke danced into the air. The dark-haired agent ran for the building.

Danny didn't wait to see what happened next. He slithered across the roof, heart stuttering with adrenalin, towards its back edge.

He'd never considered waiting it out there anyway. As soon as it had been confirmed that the courier was innocent and had been nothing but a dupe, the whole area would be cordoned off, and the rooftops – the vantage points – would be the first places to be searched.

Danny fought the urge to shake off the garbage that covered him, stand up and run, reminding himself that the area would still be under satellite surveillance, and while the smoke now billowing above him would at least partially obscure his movements, he still needed to do everything in his power to blend in.

To which end he punched the last three grid squares on

his phone, two of them detonating incendiaries further to the east, away from the direction Danny was planning to go, and one detonating outside Building 17.

Danny kept moving. Come on, he told himself, shuffling back now as fast as he could, reaching out with his feet, feeling for the end of the building, which he knew could only be a short distance away.

He couldn't stop picturing the dark-haired agent and his team rushing towards him, closing in on the building he was on, surrounding it and waiting for him to descend. *Could he really have seen me from that far away?* Had he really made eye contact, or was that just Danny's paranoia? Had he really been pointing at him or somewhere else?

He reached the roof's edge. Only then did he break cover, slithering out from under the rubbish that had been covering him and over the side onto the drainpipe that ran down the two-metre gap between the building he was on and the next. He slid down, moving so fast he was half falling, using the pipe almost like a zip wire, grunting in pain as he tore his right hand on a bracket.

He crashed to the ground, jarring his ankle, He got up, dusted down his uniform, took the peaked cap from his bag and pulled it on.

A flash of movement. There, at the end of the alley he was now standing in. Someone – one of the agents – had rushed by. Were they the first in pursuit or the last? Were the others already rounding the building to cut him off? How much longer did he have?

Stumbling to the east end of the alley, he peered into the wider service street beyond. Empty. He looked up into the sky. Plenty of black smoke billowing around. Even better, it was starting to rain.

He trotted, didn't run – like a man who was unnerved by the explosions going on around him, not like one who was desperate to escape – knowing if he was spotted now by any of the agents on the ground, or any eyes in the sky, his uniform alone might allow him to escape.

On the opposite side of the service road, which he was now halfway across, were another two high-sided corrugated-iron storage facilities and in between them another alley, like the one he had just emerged from, leading further east.

Five yards to go. Danny counted them down, ears straining, eyes flicking left and right, praying he'd make it into the dark mouth of the next alley before any agents arrived.

Four . . .

Three . . .

Two . . .

One.

The second Danny entered the next alleyway, he broke into a sprint. No shouts behind him. No footsteps. No shots.

But he knew he wasn't safe yet. There was still the danger of an agent having seen him but not wanting to alert him to the fact. They might be running parallel with him even now, either side of the two buildings he was sprinting between. Meaning they'd emerge into the next service street at the same time as he did. And if they wanted to, they'd gun him down.

The fact was, they might also be behind as well. He didn't give himself time to turn. What was the point? If they were that close, he was already as good as captured or dead.

As he sprinted, he stared fixedly along the alley, as if it were the barrel of a gun, imagining himself absurdly as a bullet, as something deadly that could not be stopped.

He made it to the end. Breathless, weakening from lack of sleep and proper food, he lurched out into the road beyond without stopping, and looked first right, then left to the end of the buildings he'd just run between, and saw—

Nothing. The street was empty. Both ways. Relief burst inside him, but was then snatched away.

Three men ran into the road from a doorway in the warehouse twenty yards to Danny's right. He slowed – at a loss. What the hell was he going to do now? They were running at him fast.

Even as he reached for his pistol, he knew he wouldn't shoot them. They were government agents, not terrorists, not crooks. No matter how much they might be his enemies today, on any other he'd be on their side. They were just people like him, doing what they thought needed to be done to make things right and keep the world safe. For Danny to open fire . . . well, that would make him one of the bad guys too.

But surrender? Not yet, not until he had no choice. His training kicked in. Even as they kept running, none of them had even aimed his weapon. Leaving Danny with a chance. He speeded up. He'd give everything he had. Every last atom of energy.

Even as he turned, though, an alarm was shrieking in his head. Something about those men giving chase, something that didn't make sense . . . He turned back for a second look.

And only then did he realize what had been staring him right in the eyes all along. They weren't wearing jeans or T-shirts, or even goddamn suits. The reason? They weren't agents. They were rent-a-cops. They were dressed in black Docklands Authority uniforms – just the same as him.

They must have heard the explosions. They were frightened. They were racing towards him – seemingly one of their own – to find out what he knew and work out what the hell was going on.

They were still ten yards from him and only twenty yards back from the corner of the building, where the agents chasing him, led by the dark-haired MI5 spook, would appear at any second.

Take control.

That was what the Old Man would have told him, dammit.

Danny did. 'It's a robbery,' he shouted, his accent English. 'Back there.' Louder this time, the sound of the chopper's rotors was rising. It was coming back. 'They've broken into Building Seventeen. They saw me trying to radio it in. They're coming this way. Quick! We've got to go.'

The rent-a-cops slowed, some confused, others scared. The taller of the three, a blond guy, his brow creasing now, was staring Danny dead in the eyes. Was he maybe realizing he'd never seen him before? Or thinking his uniform was two sizes too big?

Danny didn't give him any more time to think. In fact, he didn't have any more time to think because, at that moment, two agents appeared at the end of the building fifty yards to his right, just as he'd predicted they would.

Danny's blood ran cold. The guy in the lead was unmistakably the MI5 agent from Lexie's school. He'd rounded the corner, like a sprinter entering the home straight on a track. Danny didn't need to be a psychic to guess what was going on in his mind. He'd let Danny get away before. Just from the set of his jaw, Danny could see he wasn't planning on letting that happen again.

'There,' Danny barked. 'Behind you.'

The blond rent-a-cop, the tallest of the three, turned fastest. The rest of his crew followed. The guy on his left, short but wide as a barn door and looking like he'd been breastfed on steroids, flexed himself even wider as the dark-haired agent ran at him, screaming at him to get out of the way.

Only he didn't.

Danny's uniform, or the lack of any uniform being worn by the agents, had been enough to convince the three rent-a-cops whose side they were on.

From scrutinizing him, they'd switched to forming a human barrier between him and the agents, which the agents were going to have to circumvent or break clean through if they were going to stand a chance of taking him down.

As the dark-haired agent tried sidestepping the supersized blond rent-a-cop, in an attempt to cut off Danny, who was already turning to break west towards the next alley, the rent-a-cop showed a remarkable turn of speed.

He launched himself hard at the agent, ploughing into him and tackling him around the ankles, sweeping the man's legs from beneath him and bringing him crashing to the ground.

The last thing Danny saw was the look of pure disbelief on the agent's face. He didn't wait to see what happened next. He sprinted into the alley and only looked back when he reached its end.

It was clear. Which was more than could be said for the sky. The incendiaries were still pumping black smoke all around. But not only that. Heavier clouds had gathered. More rain.

He kept running. Further west. Across another road. Into another alley. Another glance back: still no sign of pursuit. What the hell had happened to that agent? The tackle must have been even more powerful than it had looked. Enough to have laid him out flat. It had been no martial-arts move either, he reflected, which was perhaps why it had taken the agent so much by surprise. It had been a rugby tackle, pure and simple, a sport Danny had never played but that would have a place in his heart from now on.

He ran on. The next road was clear too. Only this time, instead of running straight, he turned south, powering up to the next intersection between the towering storage facilities. You can do it, he told himself. He'd memorized this route. Just run. Don't quit.

His lungs were burning, his muscles tightening, seizing up from lactic acid. He knew he couldn't keep it up much longer, but he also knew he didn't need to. That knowledge was enough to give him hope and the renewed burst of energy that came with it.

The same went for the sky, which was growing darker. Not just smoke and clouds but a gathering storm. The rain was falling harder.

Keep on movin', don't stop, no . . .

His shoes pounded the tarmac like a bass drum. God bless the crappy British weather, he thought, as thunder boomed, lightning cracked the sky and rain sluiced across his face.

Turning left at the end of the alley, he followed the curve of a train track round to the right, into a warren of container stacks. This route had been his 'in' to the docks compound. It would be his 'out' too. Making sure his face was covered as he passed the CCTV stacks he'd circumnavigated on his way in, but had no time to avoid now, he slowed, his energy resources finally depleting as he reached the security fence.

Panting, he squeezed behind a pile of pallets and found the gap he'd entered in through. Crouching, he took his phone out once more and punched the last of the two yellow squares into red.

The rain was falling so hard now that he hardly heard the explosions. But the agents and rent-a-cops, who'd either still be fighting or would now all be searching for him, would hear them well enough, all right.

Well enough to slow them. Well enough to confuse them. Well enough to allow Danny to do what he did now, which was slip through the fence and limp into the drainage ditch beyond, then fade into the rain and out of sight.

CHAPTER 39

WALES

Danny had reached the small seaside resort on the west coast of Wales at gone three the night before in a car he'd rented using false ID before switching its plates for some others he'd stolen.

He'd let himself into the holiday apartment he'd left Lexie in three days before, accommodation he'd rented under a different false ID and had paid for up front with cash. He'd found his daughter asleep on the sofa in the living room with the remains of a pizza and an empty beer bottle on the glass table in front of her. The blinds had been drawn.

Beer. . . Jesus Christ, he'd thought. When the hell did she start drinking?

He'd not woken her. He'd quietly put down the bags he'd brought in from the car, except the one laden with weaponry, which he'd taken to his bedroom and stashed beneath the bed.

He'd woken from the blackest of sleeps this morning, just after nine. When he'd gone through to the living room, Lexie had disappeared. He'd checked the kitchen and bathroom, but she'd not been there either. Guessing she must have gone to the shops for milk or bread, he'd taken a bath, lying there for God only knew how long, letting the warm water work its magic on his tired muscles, trying his damnedest to think about nothing, and in particular what he was going to do next, a prospect that had been driving him out of his mind since he'd discovered that his last and best lead had been a trap.

Still, at least there was Crane, he supposed. Or Melville, as he was now known. It was possible he might still conjure up the information that Danny had tasked him to secure. Or maybe Spartak had found out something about Glinka or the rest of his crew. Maybe someone else had made a breakthrough where Danny had failed.

When he came out of the bathroom, wrapped in a towel, the first thing he saw was that the curtains leading out onto the balcony had been drawn back. The second was that his tech kit bag was open, his iPad lying face up on the table next to the empty pizza box.

He snatched up the iPad and swiped its opening bar to one side, then stopped. Lexie couldn't have accessed it, *could* she? Because she didn't know the password . . . Only, oh, shit, she did. Because the password he'd used on this machine, which Spartak had given him, was Lexie's name and date of birth combined. But would she have worked that out? He typed it in now, then went straight to the history section.

'Piece of goddamned shit,' he said, staring disbelievingly at the scroll of sites that had been visited since he'd been in the bathroom.

Tossing the iPad onto the sofa, only just resisting a sudden desire to snap it in half, Danny marched out onto the balcony into blazing sunlight.

The apartment was six floors up and overlooked the bay. White horses chased across the wide blue sea. Lexie was rapidly rising from the wicker chair she'd been sitting in. She looked up at him guiltily. He glanced down and saw she'd just stubbed out a cigarette.

'What the hell do you think you're doing?' he said.

'What?'

'Don't play innocent with me.'

'Oh, come on. You already know I smoke.'

Knew didn't mean he *liked* it, dammit.

'Not that,' he snapped. 'Or the fact you've been drinking . . .'

'Drinking? At my age?' Her lip curled into a nasty sneer that only fired up his fury afresh.

'I mean my damn iPad.'

'I don't know what you're talking about,' she said. But it was obvious that she did. Her cheeks were flushing. Quickly, she tried pushing past him, desperate now to get back inside.

He grabbed her wrist.

She tried shaking him off. 'Let me go.'

'Not until you tell me who you talked to.'

'No one.'

She tried again to break free, then stopped. 'I didn't speak to anyone,' she said. 'I didn't. I swear. It's fucking true.'

Danny winced at her language but there was no time to remonstrate now. If she *had* contacted someone, if she'd surfaced anywhere on the net, the iPad could be tracked, which meant this place was no longer safe and they'd have to run.

'You went on Facebook,' he said.

'So now you're spying on me as well?'

'As well as what?'

'As well as screwing up our fucking life.'

She spat each word. Danny almost physically reeled from the force.

'I was looking up something else.'

A lie. 'It was right there,' he said. 'In the history.'

'That's the same as spying,' she snarled. She was angry with him, but with herself too, for forgetting to wipe the history clean.

'Well?' he said.

'I just looked, that's all. Nothing else.'

'Looked at what?'

'Just stuff,' she said, avoiding his eyes.

'*Who?*' he demanded.

Because he'd already guessed. The boy she'd been with at school when Danny had taken her away. The curly-haired kid who'd fronted up to him and told him to leave Lexie alone. 'He's no one,' she'd told Danny later, when he'd asked. But she'd blushed as she'd said it and that had said more clearly than any words ever could that his daughter was in love.

'Just friends,' she said.

'What else have you done? Have you called anyone? Have you spoken to anyone at all?'

'No.' Adamant. Eye contact.

Was she really telling the truth?

I just wanted to see,' she said.

'See what?'

She didn't respond. Her eyes had turned glassy. She stared right through him, didn't blink.

'See what?' he demanded, shaking her now.

'My friends – everyone. I just wanted to see if they remembered ...' The fight left her. Her shoulders slumped.

'Remembered *what*?'

'It's my birthday.'

Danny stared. He didn't know what to say.

'I'm eighteen,' she said. 'You know?'

She looked up at him and, right there, she saw that he didn't. He'd not had a clue. 'Just like in your password,' she said. 'And that's why I wanted to see them. I wanted to see if anyone out there still even fucking cared ...'

She pushed past him. He didn't try to stop her. Eighteen? Sweet Jesus, Lexie had turned eighteen today and he hadn't even known. Anger at himself, at his own stupidity and selfishness, swelled inside him. And he pictured his wife, Sally. He saw her, suddenly, so clearly all those years ago in hospital, gripping his arm, her nails digging into his wrist, during the final push that had brought his beautiful baby daughter, kicking and screaming, into the world.

And as he watched Lexie vanish into the flat, he thought again of the boy he'd taken her from, the boy she so clearly loved. Because she was right. This wouldn't have affected only her, it would have affected everyone she knew. And he *had* screwed up her life.

'I'm sorry,' he said, following her. 'I should have remembered.'

She was standing with her back to him in the middle of the living room.

'Please,' he said, stepping close behind her, reaching out to touch her.

But she flinched.

His hand pulled back. He realized he was crying. Tears were streaming down his face. He wiped them, not wanting her to see. He went through to his bedroom and sank onto the bed.

Pull yourself together, he told himself. You can't do this. You can't crack up.

But everything in him was telling him it was over, that he'd failed.

He heard footsteps and forced himself to stand. He walked to the window and wiped his eyes with clenched fists. He heard the door creak behind him. Lexie was already in the room.

And he knew he had to tell her. Even now, when she was sadder than he'd ever seen her, he had to make her sadder still.

'Everything I've done,' he said, 'everything I've got wrong . . . I'm sorry, Lexie, I'm sorry for it all . . .'

'It doesn't matter. I know you've tried your best.' Her voice was placatory. She sounded beaten and tired.

Just do it, Danny told himself. He'd put it off long enough already. Too long. He should have told her before he'd gone to London. He'd put her life at risk because he'd been too afraid of how she might react. Do it *now*. Because he had to. Even though no father should ever have to do what he must now. He had to tell his daughter that her worst nightmare might be about to come true.

'No,' he said, 'you don't understand.'

He couldn't bring himself to face her. His voice caught in his throat, like gravel. His tears, he noticed, had dried. As he turned to face her, coldness filled him and turned his heart to stone.

'There's something else,' he said. 'Something I haven't told you. There's something you need to know.'

'What?' The reconciliation was gone from her voice. In its place was fear. She must have read something in his eyes.

He swallowed and tried to answer. He failed.

'What? What is it?' she said, her voice rising.

'He's back . . .' His words came out as a whisper.

'Who?' she said.

'Him.' Danny couldn't name him. He couldn't do *that*.

'Wh—' She stopped. She *knew*. Her eyes raked his. And she *saw*.

He reached out to her, but she held up her arms to block

him. She turned as if to march through the open bedroom door, only to stop in her tracks and wrap her arms around herself. She spun to face him, tears running down her face, her whole body shaking. 'How can this be happening?' she screamed. 'How can this be happening *again*?'

But Danny had no explanation. He stared mutely at her.

'He's dead!' she screamed. 'He's meant to be dead! You told me he'd not killed anyone. Not for years. You told me he was never coming back!'

Hoped. That's what he had *hoped.* But, yes, Lexie was right: that was what he'd told her.

She slapped him as hard as she could across the face.

He didn't follow her as she walked out. Two seconds later, the apartment's front door slammed so hard he felt it.

He was still standing in exactly the same position when she came back ten minutes later. It was only when she walked in and he saw the clock on the wall above her that he saw how much time had passed. He didn't know what he'd been thinking. It was as though he'd been standing there in pitch darkness, even though the room was golden with light.

'I'm hungry,' she said.

He nodded. The movement felt painful, as if he'd somehow seized up.

She said, 'I'm going to fix myself something to eat.'

He followed her to the kitchen in silence. She took

a jar of peanut butter from the shelf. He picked up the loaf of bread from the sideboard and put it on the kitchen counter. He took a wooden chopping board and laid two pieces of bread on it. She took a knife from the drawer and unscrewed the lid of the peanut butter. She spread first one slice, then the other. They each picked one up and turned their backs to the counter, leaning against it as they ate.

Just like we did when she was a kid, Danny remembered. Just like I did with her and her mum and Jonathan, when we were still a family, when we still lived in a world full of love.

'So what are we going to do?' Lexie said. Her voice was quiet but not weak. Not frightened any more. There was grit in her words. And she was asking him a question. She thought he could help. Or he had to believe she did. And he had to believe he could.

'We're going to adapt to make sure we survive,' he said.

'Meaning what?' Lexie said.

'You know how I told you before that if anything happened to me you were to contact Spartak?'

'You mean if they catch you or . . .' She didn't finish her sentence; didn't need to.

He nodded.

'You told me I wasn't to go to the authorities,' she said, paraphrasing the words he'd spoken to her before he'd set off for Chernobyl, 'because any reports of your death in the papers might have been planted there to lure me out.'

'That's right. Well, now if anyone contacts you, I want you to call Spartak and arrange to meet him.'

He went to one of the bags he'd left at the apartment before he'd gone to London, and took out the same disposable phone, the corresponding SIM card and battery, to which he'd given Spartak the number. He placed the phone in her hand and closed her fingers around it.

'You'll need these too.' He took her other hand and put the SIM card and battery in that. 'Don't put these in unless you know I'm not coming back.'

She nodded. She understood. 'And after I've used it, I should destroy it, right?' she said. The same as she'd done with the other disposable phones he'd given her.

'That's right. But with this one it's even more important, because there's a possibility that people might know the number is one I'm planning on using. Meaning the second you do use it, this phone will be easy to trace for anyone looking for its number going live. Anyone looking for *you*.'

Something in her broke. Tears flooded her eyes. She threw her arms around him and hugged him tight, as if she wanted never to let him go. She pressed her face into his shoulder. He hated himself for having reduced her to this, for fear now being a part of their love.

He rested his chin on the top of her head, closed his eyes and breathed in, cherishing not just this moment but a thousand others, remembering his little girl right back to the day she'd been born.

He'd loved her then with every atom of his being and

nothing had changed. He would protect her. He would give her back her life.

Even if it cost him his own.

CHAPTER 40

LONDON

Danny Shanklin was wearing a baseball cap pulled down low across his brow, and old-school wide-lensed Aviator shades, covering as much of his face as he could without drawing attention to himself. Along with his beard, he hoped this would be enough to prevent him getting ID'd by any of the couple of hundred thousand CCTV cameras incorporated into New Scotland Yard's facial-recognition surveillance system.

This was the first time Danny had been back in central London since the entire city had shuddered into gridlock on his account and its thirty-three thousand cops had focused on snatching him out of the panic-stricken crowds.

It couldn't have been be more different now. It was a warm, balmy evening and London was no longer a city in shock, terrified that a series of Mumbai-style attacks was about to happen. The commuters had gone back to commuting. Even some of the tourists had returned.

In fact, as Danny turned the corner into the quiet

suburban street he'd come to visit, for a fleeting moment, he almost felt normal being there.

How easy would it be to hail a cab and ask it to take him to see Anna-Maria? And how tempting. He thought back to the last night he'd spent with her on his houseboat, just hours before he'd walked into the trap that had been set for him at the Ritz. As he passed the bloom of a magnolia tree, he remembered her perfume and the feel of her smooth, hot skin against his.

How easy . . . but how impossible too. Danny's converted coal barge in north London's Little Venice, his home-from-home in the UK, where he and Anna-Maria had slept together the night before the attack at the Ritz, had already been picked apart.

He had seen it on the news. Even though the vessel was registered to a Swiss holding company, one of the neighbouring boat owners must have recognized his face from the TV mugshots and called in the cops.

Danny had watched the news footage over and over online, showing a steady stream of forensics officers confiscating boxes of his belongings and packing them into vans for further examination. It was a joke, of course. There wasn't a single item in there to incriminate him. The most suspicious thing on that boat was the previous owner's taste in flock wallpaper.

Not that the cops were interested in Danny's innocence. They just wanted proof of his guilt. The same went for the press. Rather than getting colder, the story had grown hotter with time. And in the absence of any sightings of

Danny, they'd spun his life into an inversion of the truth. Instead of painting his career in a positive way, they'd homed in on the negatives. On his alcoholism following his wife and son's death. On his turning his back on the intelligence community, which had trained him. They'd used words like 'recovering addict', 'rogue' and 'loose cannon' to describe him. They'd raked back through his entire past and he'd bet they were still out there, digging for more dirt.

Which was why he couldn't see Anna-Maria. Because she was probably being watched as well. No matter how careful they'd been over the years to keep their occasional meetings from her husband, it was more than likely that someone some time had noticed them together, and that they, too, would have gone to the police.

Cut it out, Danny told himself angrily. There was no point in dwelling on what a screw-up this all was. He needed to focus on making it right. He counted the numbers of the red-brick terraced houses he passed. There were odd numbers on this side of the street, evens on the other, meaning he was now only four doors away.

He took the stack of leaflets from his pocket. Menus from a Chinese takeaway he'd gone into ten minutes ago. He'd snagged twenty from the pile on the counter and now started delivering them, one through each letterbox of the houses on this side of the street.

He slowed as he approached number thirty-nine. The building was much like the rest, but with a fresh paint job

on its wooden bay window frames and door. A recycling box
piled high with empty bottles, mostly vodka and white wine.
The curtains weren't drawn. The living room was empty, its
lights out. Danny spotted a big flat-screen TV and what
looked like the spiked leaves of a marijuana plant on the
kitchen sideboard. He made a show of tying his shoelace on
the doorstep and listened, but no one was home.

The lock wouldn't be a problem. But he didn't want to
frighten the woman he'd come to see. He tugged a glove
onto his right hand, took a fingertip-sized mike from his
bag and pressed its adhesive back against the brickwork
behind the drainpipe.

Removing his glove, he slipped an audio bead into his
ear and continued his delivery run of menus down the
street.

A block away there was a small park. Danny sat
on a bench and unfolded a newspaper. To a casual
observer, he was reading, but in fact he was locked in
deep thought.

Considering that he'd once trusted the Kid with his
life, he sure as hell didn't know much about him. Like
a lot of ex-government intelligence operatives, both he
and the Kid had kept their private lives to themselves.
Danny's knowledge of the Kid's work history prior to
his meeting him was sketchy too. The first job they'd
teamed up on had been five years ago in Basra, where
Danny had been training executive protection units in
fieldwork, while the Kid had been honing their counter-
surveillance protocols. A mutual friend, now dead, had

introduced them. But that point of contact was all it had taken for Danny to start trusting the Kid too.

He'd seen what the Kid had been capable of: running the best surveillance and counter-surveillance ops Danny had witnessed outside his time with the CIA. The two of them had partnered on at least ten protection jobs and hostage retrievals since. Along with Spartak Sidarov, the Kid had become Danny's first port of call for back-up.

Before Danny had contacted Crane from the caravan to ask for his help, he'd made a list of everything he knew about the Kid that might help Crane track him down. It hadn't been long. He'd mailed it to Crane's new avatar, Melville:

First name: Adam

Surname: Fitch

Age: 35–40

Employment: British Army and GCHQ-trained cryptologist and coder; four years with the European Network and Information Security Agency; then private sector, working with me and God only knows who else.

Other than the Kid's age, which Danny had estimated, he no longer knew what, if any, of the other information was true. If the Kid had been prepared to kill him and his daughter, then Danny was guessing he wouldn't have much of a moral objection to lying through his teeth about the rest of his life.

Crane had got back to Danny yesterday, the portal of contact once more being a message posted on the InWorld™ Public Contact Board, which he had been regularly checking in on. The message he'd found there, tagged for the attention of Danny's new avatar Jackal, was: *FISHERMAN SEEKS LOST HOOK.*

The subsequent conversation Danny had had in the Rest Cure café in the city of Steem with Crane's new avatar, Melville, had gone like this:

➡**Melville:** 'The records of the EPU company you and the Kid worked for in Basra were compromised by a hostile virus less than a month ago. Whatever photos of the Kid were filed there, along with any links to other organizations he'd worked at previously or after, have now been wiped.'

Meaning the Kid had already set about removing all traces of himself from the net, and any obvious means by which Danny might trace him, long before he'd helped set Danny up at the Ritz.

But Danny had refused to be discouraged by this. Rather, he'd expected it and had instead comforted himself with the thought that, while the Kid hacking a private security company's files might have been within his capabilities, it would have been a hell of a lot tougher for him to tamper with any other records on him held by British Military Intelligence, GCHQ and ENISA – or any of the other organizations the Kid had claimed he'd worked for.

●Jackal: 'What did your UK and European government contacts dig up?'

●Melville: 'No employee named Fitch was on the payrolls of the British military, GCHQ or ENISA during the time the Kid was likely to have been there.'

Which meant that the surname Danny had always known the Kid by was a fake. Because if the Kid really had worked for these organizations, he'd have had to use his real name to pass their rigid security protocols.

●Melville: 'However . . . six employees named Adam of a similar age to the Kid *were* employed by British Military Intelligence. And of these Adams, only one of them, Adam Gilloway, went on to work for both GCHQ and ENISA.'

Danny's heart had begun racing right then, because this had meant that maybe the Kid had told him his real first name.

●Melville: 'My contacts sent me the photos of all three of the separate employee files held by these organizations for Adam Gilloway.'

●Jackal: 'Patch them through.'

Three jpeg icons had popped up on Danny's screen. Swallowing hard, he'd opened them one by one, each time feeling a surge of triumph rushing through his veins. Because, even though the photos been taken over a period of several years, they'd undoubtedly been of the same man.

A man Danny knew.

Adam Gilloway.

A.k.a. the Kid.

Jackal: 'That's him.'

Melville: 'I took the liberty of having a Company contact run the photos through the main European and North American law-enforcement databases, including Interpol and the DVLA. We also checked all the major social networks. But we got no matches for any of these photos either for Adam Gilloway or any other alias he might have used. So far we've uncovered no other online photographic matches of him at all.'

In other words, the Kid had pulled off the electronic equivalent of a Houdini disappearing act. He'd vanished into thin air.

Melville: 'Of course, we could try tracking him down through his name alone. But I've got to tell you, there's a whole bunch of people called Adam Gilloway living in the UK, and a whole bunch more in the States. To check them all would take a lot of manpower and a lot of time.'

Jackal: 'Neither of which we have. Plus, I doubt there's a chance in hell that he'd have registered a property, phone, vehicle or anything else we could trace him via in his real name . . .'

Melville: 'If we had a better idea of where he lives, then at least we could narrow our search and check out the Adam Gilloways living in that area.'

Jackal: 'But we don't.'

Melville: 'Right, so all I can offer is to keep trawling the net for image matches of him.'

Jackal: 'What about border crossings?'

➤**Melville:** 'There's no way my contacts could sanction that. Not without knowing who we're tracking and why.'

And that was the real trouble. On paper, the Kid had done nothing wrong. No one was looking for him or would waste resources on doing so. They were all too busy looking for Danny.

Danny had signed off.

It should have been a dead end.

But it wasn't. Because what Danny hadn't told Crane was that he'd made another list, detailing some other information he thought he knew about the Kid. And he'd not shared the second list with his handler. Why? Because even though he now believed he was in contact with the real Crane, there was still the possibility that the real Crane was being eavesdropped on by the US government, either knowingly so or not. And while Danny had needed Crane to help him discover the Kid's real name, he didn't need to risk sharing with Crane what he was planning to do with the information. Because if Crane had been compromised, that would only lead to Danny's capture.

His other list had been even shorter than the first. It had read:

Relatives:
a younger sister, who still lives in Hackney, a single
mother with a young daughter called Beyoncé.

One of the great advantages of no longer drinking was that Danny remembered conversations other people forgot. The Kid had been drunk when he'd mentioned his niece's name. He and Danny had been in a bar in Copenhagen, celebrating the successful conclusion of a job. Danny even remembered the Kid's smashed rendition of Beyoncé's 'Crazy In Love' making him laugh, when he'd let slip to Danny that his sister had just given birth to a little girl.

All of which had brought Danny Shanklin to this quiet park in Hackney, east London. Adam Gilloway might have disappeared into the ether, but Beyoncé Gilloway had been easier to find. In fact, the UK births database had listed only three in the whole of London, and he'd already visited the other two.

Of course, the Kid might have been lying about his niece's name. But Danny doubted it. It wasn't as if it had been part of a wider cover story the Kid had been feeding him. In fact, it was the only personal detail Danny remembered him ever having revealed about his background.

In other words, maybe this was what he had been praying for: a mistake.

Turning the page of his newspaper, he saw 'DANNY SHANKLIN SIGHTED IN VIENNA'. Below was a blurred photo of a man who looked nothing like him, as well as an interview with an Austrian woman who claimed to have recognized him coming out of a cinema.

Good news for me, he thought, allowing himself a

half-smile. The more people who thought he was there, the safer he was here.

A crackling sound in his ear. A jangling of keys. The turning of a key in a lock.

He folded his newspaper and dropped it into a bin as he marched towards the park gate.

It was time to pay Beyoncé Gilloway's mother a visit.

CHAPTER 41

The Kid's sister – if this was indeed her – was tall and lithe, Danny saw, as she answered the door. She must have been around thirty, with spiked, dyed hair, as red as her wrinkled, bloodshot eyes.

'Yeah, what?' she said, keeping the door half closed, as she looked him warily up and down.

He didn't take his shades off, or his cap, for fear of her recognizing him from the news, although she clearly wasn't the kind of person who would make a big point of keeping up with current affairs.

A gold stud glinted dead centre of her chapped upper lip. Pronounced muscles showed where her baggy white T-shirt had been cut off at the shoulders and where her denim miniskirt had ridden high up her thighs. This wasn't the kind of physique that came from hours spent in some uptown gym, though, Danny reckoned. More a symptom of dependency. Maybe just nicotine and alcohol. But probably something worse.

The nostrils confirmed it. Inflamed and red. Coke or

amphetamines. A dotting of scars on the inside of her right arm. Old track marks. Maybe so old she was now off whatever she'd been injecting, or maybe she'd just taken to injecting herself somewhere less noticeable now that she had a child and, maybe, social services people to deal with.

It would be easiest, of course, for Danny to terrify the information out of her. And he'd have been lying if he'd claimed the thought hadn't already crossed his mind. It would be fastest, too, to extract what he needed if he seized her by the throat and forced her back into her hallway, where none of her neighbours could hear her scream.

A patter of footsteps on tiles. A little girl appeared in the doorway, curling round the Kid's sister's legs like a cat, peering curiously up at him through beautiful big brown eyes.

Danny had read covert operational memos, detailing how young children could be used to coerce adults, and how the resistance of even the most militant extremists could be pushed to a point of collapse in the face of a threat to their offspring's life.

'Achilles Heels' – that was how one of Danny's former Company colleagues had referred to children. A man who'd had no children of his own, he'd perceived them as nothing more than 'flesh and blood crowbars, a God-given gift for prising open locked secrets from their murderous, wayward folks'.

Based on the accompanying case studies this man had not only cited, but had claimed to have been personally involved in, Danny had judged him as scum, with lower moral standards than a snake. And the fact remained that, no matter how badly Danny had ever needed information, he'd never stooped to such methods, and knew he never would.

'Hey, sweetie,' he said now, keeping his accent good and English, kneeling down so that his face was level with the little girl's. 'And you must be Beyoncé, right?' He tousled her hair. 'That's such a pretty name.'

The little girl's face lit up. 'Everyone calls me Bay,' she said.

'That's even prettier.'

Another bright, gap-toothed smile.

As he straightened, he saw the child's mother clearly wouldn't be so easily won over. She crossed her arms, still not opening the door. Those wary wrinkles around her eyes had tightened into outright suspicion. 'How d'you know my little girl's name?' she said.

Her accent was a match for the Kid's. Harsh and abrasive, it contained the same urban London grit that the Kid's always had, which no amount of money or working abroad had ever smoothed away.

'My name's John,' Danny said, using one of his old schoolteachers' names, 'John Morden. I'm a friend of Adam's,' he said, 'your brother – the Kid.'

'Yeah, I know what he's called,' she said, confirming everything Danny had hoped she would. 'But I don't know what he's doing giving you my address. Because he ain't here, if that's what you think.'

There'd been no stumbling in her speech, but too much

movement. A flick of her eyes to the left. A tightening of her forearms and the tendons in her throat. He would have put money on it that she was lying.

'In fact, I haven't seen or heard from him in nearly a year. He ain't even called.'

And now too much talking. Another sign of nerves. She'd seen the Kid all right. Or had had contact. This expensive address. The fresh paintwork. Somebody was paying for it and, from her bloodshot eyes and empty bottle collection, Danny guessed it sure as hell wasn't her.

'Where did you say you knew him from?'

'He's an ex-colleague.'

'Army?'

Danny said nothing, wondering what else she might give away.

'GCHQ?' she asked.

Again he didn't answer, smiling at little Bay instead, wondering if her mother might mention some other part of the Kid's subsequent career history he knew nothing about. But this time, she kept quiet.

'Something like that,' he said, with an apologetic smile.

The answer seemed to satisfy her. She nodded, sniffed, and seemed to reappraise him. 'Yeah,' she said, some of the harshness dropped from her voice. 'Well, he never much talks about his work either.'

Talks. Present tense. Not *talked*. Not the past. Meaning they weren't estranged. They were still in regular contact.

'I've got something for him,' Danny said.

'What?'

'Money,' he lied, choosing the one thing he thought would interest her most. And, right away, he got his reward: in his peripheral vision, he noticed her fingers tightening once more around her arm – a grasping motion. 'A lot of money. Cash. And something else.'

'What?'

'Something private. Something I've got to give to him in person.'

Again he saw that tightening of her fingers. Maybe all this – the new paintwork and bike – was just for his niece and the Kid's generosity didn't extend to funding his sister's lifestyle, too.

'So why don't you just call him?' she said.

'Because all the numbers I've got for him are dead. All I've got is this address.'

'He gave you *my* address?' She sounded surprised.

'He said he was thinking of moving, but that you were more settled.' A hint of flattery in his voice. She lapped it up. She smiled.

'Yeah, well, you know him. Always up to something. Never could sit still.'

What Danny needed – what he now *craved*, so much he had to resist just shouting it out – was a live number for the Kid. Dial that through to Spartak and his contacts could set about attempting to trace the Kid's location via his phone.

'I haven't got a working number for him either any more,' she said.

The disappointment must have shown on Danny's face.

'Last time we spoke,' she said, 'he told me he had to go away on business. And said he wouldn't be able to surface for a while.'

He ignored the contradiction, that she'd said before that she'd not heard from him in more than a year. Did this mean she was lying about not having a phone number for him as well? There was no way to tell. And no way of putting any additional pressure on her, not with her little girl there.

He thought of the bug in his bag. He needed to get inside and out of her sight line long enough to tap her phone, then wait for her to call her brother and get the Kid's number that way instead. *If* she had his number, that was, and *if* she decided to give him a call.

Only then she came up with something much better. 'I have got an address for him, though,' she said.

'Yeah?' He couldn't believe his luck.

'Yeah.'

'Well, that's great,' he said. 'So that thing I need to get to him, I can just could take it round there and deliver it.'

'Right.'

'Or I could even just post it,' Danny said.

'Sure.'

'So what's the add—'

'But the cash,' she interrupted.

Of course, he thought. Nothing in this world was for free.

'The cash?' he asked.

'You wouldn't want to risk putting that through the

letter box.' She was trying to play it cool. But that hand was grasping her arm again. 'You know, just in case he's got someone else staying there – or a cleaner goes in.'

'Oh, right, yeah, that's true,' Danny said, as if this had only just occurred to him. He frowned, as if confused as to what to do next, making sure also to pat his bag, so that she knew he really did have the cash on him right now. 'That would be a risk.'

'A big risk,' she agreed, unable to stop herself glancing at his bag.

'Hey,' he said, as if an idea had just dawned.

'What?'

'Maybe I could . . .'

'Yeah?' she prompted, smiling now.

'. . . just leave the cash here with you.'

'Exactly.' The corner of her mouth tightened, as she struggled against the desire to come right out with it and grin.

'Well, OK,' he said, looking as pleased and relieved as he could. 'I'll do that and then you can . . .' he unhooked his bag from his shoulder and began to unzip it '. . . give me that address, right?'

'Right. Of course.'

He reached past the Glock 30 pistol and took one of the ten sealed envelopes from his bag. Inside was five thousand pounds. He handed it over to her and watched the same hand that had been digging into her arm only moments before now close around it like a vice.

She weighed the envelope in her hand and smiled, all

traces of her former hostility gone. Then she looked him over, her eyes lingering a little this time, as they took in his waist and chest. 'You want to come in?' she then said. 'I was just about to fix myself a drink.'

A little way back in the hallway, the little girl, Bay, started to sing. Danny recognized the tune and the words. An old Burl Ives number: 'Ugly Bug Ball'. A half-smile crossed his face. He remembered Lexie singing it as a kid. Jonathan too.

'Thanks,' he said, 'but no. I'd better get going. Places to go, people to see.'

CHAPTER 42

The address was a west London red-brick mansion block, built in 1892, as the plaque on the wall next to its entrance proudly proclaimed. Judging by the row of delis, restaurants and boutiques opposite, as well as the Porsches, Aston Martins and Mercs parked in the residents' bays outside, this was something of a yuppie haven. Meaning there'd be plenty of alarms inside.

Danny set up camp in a small but busy café opposite and sipped his way through three espressos over the next hour, watching various smartly attired men and women step out through the building's entrance, and either get into waiting cabs or head west towards the nearest tube. It was getting dark and he swapped his Aviators for thick-rimmed glasses, to make himself even less noticeable.

The seat he had chosen was next to the window. No one could look over his shoulder, leaving him with ample opportunity to use his phone to zoom in on the mansion block's doorway each time it opened.

He saw the entrance lobby inside was too small for

there to be a doorman, which meant he'd only need to worry about other residents questioning his purpose in being there once he was inside.

It looked like there was some kind of party going on upstairs on the second floor. A guy and a girl were leaning out of the open window there, sharing what looked like a joint and swigging from bottles of beer. He could see other people moving back and forth behind.

Situations like that. Social gatherings. Even cafés like this, with people his own age sipping coffee and talking about their relationships, the movies they'd seen and the holidays they were planning, left Danny feeling more and more an outsider. And not just because of what had happened to him here in London, but because of who he was now, compared with the happily married man he'd once been. He had grown into the habit over the years of watching people as he would do a film in a language he did not understand. He felt as if he were on the other side of a screen that he could never break through.

He zoomed in on the panel of doorbells at the entrance to the mansion block, memorizing the names. There were twenty, giving him a one-in-twenty chance of getting busted for lying by one of the residents if he used the ruse he was planning, namely doorstepping the place and trying to slip in by telling someone coming out that he was going in to visit a friend.

But then the odds swung in his favour. A red-haired guy, late twenties, exited the mansion block and crossed straight into the café.

'Hello, Matt,' the friendly Polish girl behind the counter said.

As she fixed Matt a coffee, Danny wandered up to the counter to pay.

'Matt Jones, right?' he said, turning to face him, acting like he'd only just noticed him there.

'Er, no,' said the ginger-haired guy, looking confused. 'Matt Banks, actually.'

'Oh, right.' Danny kept his accent flat and English. 'Only I heard the young lady here say your name and I had a meeting with a Matt Jones. Meant to be here half an hour ago. Only he never showed . . .'

The ginger guy shrugged apologetically. 'Wrong Matt,' he said.

'Sorry to have bothered you.' Danny put a twenty-pound note on the counter and told the girl, 'Keep the change.'

He turned to go, and walked right into a tall woman with short dark hair coming in through the door.

'Sorry,' they said at the same time.

Annoyed, she brushed past him, adjusting her shades.

Still haven't lost the magic touch then, he thought wryly, as he headed out into the warm evening, glad to escape the Muzak and sickly sweet aroma of cinnamon and hot milk. He walked twenty yards along the pavement, then stationed himself on the next street corner. Leaning against the wall, he opened his newspaper and checked over its top to make sure he had a good view of both the mansion block and the café, then waited.

Matt Banks emerged five minutes later and turned left, away from the mansion block. Danny moved in towards its entrance. There were way too many people for him to risk using the lock-buster. Plus a CCTV camera was pointing straight at him from across the street. Instead, he positioned himself two yards from the block's front door and pretended to make a phone call, even though he'd dialled no one, making sure he kept his back to the camera the whole time.

Five minutes passed – long enough for him to be sick of talking to someone on the phone who wasn't there, and to be considering some other ruse to justify his lurking around – but then he saw the front door to the mansion block opening. He moved in quickly, almost walking slap-bang into the pretty young woman who was stepping out.

'Yeah, I'm here right now,' he said into his phone, plenty loud enough for her to hear, slipping her a friendly smile as he did. 'No, no need, Matt. One of your neighbours is just coming out. I'll see you in two secs.' He switched off his phone and stepped aside, holding the door open for the woman. 'Hi, I'm a friend of Matt's,' he said. 'Matt Banks, your neighbour.'

'Oh, yeah, right.'

She headed off into the night without a backwards glance. Danny moved inside. The door shut behind him and clicked as its lock sank home. Pulling on his gloves, he hurried up the stairs.

Flat four, he quickly discovered, was on the second floor. There was a dull throb of bass coming from the doorway to flat three on the opposite side of the landing. That would be the street-side window where he had seen the couple smoking.

He slipped off his glasses and tucked them inside his bag. He checked a third doorway at the end of the corridor, next to more stairs leading up. He ran a palm-sized metal detector round its door frame, checking for sensors, but it wasn't alarmed. He pushed the door's bar open to check it wasn't locked and stepped outside. Outside was a fire exit, a zigzag of metal steps leading up and down. At the back of the building there was a communal bin area, and a high wooden fence with a small door set into it. Beyond was an alleyway, an easy exit.

He shut the door and hurried to flat four. Again, he scanned for sensors, and again nothing showed, which surprised him. If there wasn't an alarm on, did that mean someone was in?

He pressed the same small plastic amplifier he'd used in Pripyat against the door. Its needle picked up nothing, not so much as the squeak of a mouse. Which indicated that the flat was empty, but in no way proved it.

It was possible, of course, that his metal detector had missed any alarm sensors on the other side of the door because they'd been positioned too far back or fixed on the other side of the thick walls.

If it turned out the place was alarmed, then he'd need to act fast. Good news on the bass-heavy party next door, then. It might buy him a little extra time to shut the alarm off if it had a siren. It might be wired direct to the cops too, but somehow he doubted it. The last thing the Kid would want was law-enforcement turning up here and snooping around, if the alarm was triggered accidentally.

Danny took out his lock-buster, waited for a fresh tune to start up in the apartment next door, then made his move. A twist. Then another. A familiar kick, bark and whirr.

He was in.

CHAPTER 43

Inside it was twilight, the kind of twilight that exists in every home in every city, where the light pollution of your fellow citizens and the sense of being a tiny part of something far greater is never far away. Danny eased the door shut behind him.

He was in a small, tiled entrance hall. Straight ahead an open doorway led to a kitchen. The pale orange light of a streetlamp outside glowed through the plain white curtains there, while in the hallway, two other open doorways led off to the left and the right.

Danny took out a long-handled South African police flashlight that doubled in terms of weight and size as a cosh. He turned and checked the front door behind him and the surrounding area for alarms.

And found one on the wall to the left of the front door. Its illuminated indicator buttons clearly showed that it had not been triggered or even set. Which meant *what*? Had the Kid forgotten to set it? Or just left in a rush?

The stink in the kitchen, as Danny crossed the hallway

and entered, indicated the latter. He swept his flashlight beam round the room. An open cardboard pizza box stood on the sideboard, a half-eaten pizza inside, looking like a mouldy jigsaw. There was a half-empty bottle of chocolate milk too. And, of course, a doughnut box. Empty. The whole flat smelt of cigarettes. Marlboros. The Kid's.

OK, let's get on with it.

He searched all the normal places first – the writing desk in the living room, the bedside drawers: places where normal people left important stuff. But there was nothing in any of them except dust. No big surprise there. The Kid wasn't exactly normal. So he tried the obvious places – obvious, that was, in terms of places someone with training like the Kid might choose to conceal items he did not want to be found.

First the kitchen. A refrigerator hummed. He checked the freezer compartment, slashing through the frozen vegetable packets he found there and upending them into the sink. There was a big chest freezer too, up against the wall by the long dining-room table. Danny peered inside, but it was empty, apart from a couple of frozen ready meals. Trust the Kid to have two freezers, he thought. Food, even more than money and women, had always been his obsession.

He checked under the sink, in the overflow, then searched in and beneath every drawer. Down on his knees, he crabbed across the wooden floor, expertly feeling for loose boards. He checked the tops of the units next, then behind, beneath and inside the appliances.

Nothing.

Half the problem, of course, was that he didn't know precisely what he was looking for – just something, *anything*, that might help him hunt the Kid down. It might be paperwork connecting the Kid to an alias he might now be operating under, or bills for a property he owned abroad. Or a mobile-phone bill, or a USB, or anything else that might contain data Danny could get one of Spartak's contacts to unravel.

He moved to the bathroom next. It was all but bare. He checked inside the cistern, but got nothing. He tried the back of the boiler too, but pulled up zip.

Next was the living room. A lamp had been left on in there. He switched it off, wary of shadows being thrown up against the curtains, betraying his presence to anyone who might be observing from outside on the street.

The room was carpeted so he set about working its borders first, seeing if any of the carpet was loose or not tacked down properly, where it might have been prised open to conceal documents.

As he knelt there with his back to the doorway, methodically working, he didn't see or hear his attacker. He *felt* them. A tiny shift in the air pressure to his right. Enough to alert him that he was no longer alone.

Enough to make him react.

CHAPTER 44

Someone tried to grab Danny, but he moved too fast. A knife blade slashed past, glinting in the twilight, barely inches from his face.

He crash-rolled left, glimpsing a blackened figure. Whoever had tried to slit his throat had clearly planned on grabbing him and keeping hold of him too, maybe breaking his neck or, at the very least, throttling him as he weakened and bled out.

Danny was already rising, turning, flexing, loading muscle tension into his legs. No time for defence. No time to pull out his Glock 30 either. This man wanted him dead. He had to neutralize him.

He struck out hard. A left hammer-fist. A body blow. Enough to drive the attacker back and maybe, he hoped, even smash the air clean out of his lungs.

Only Danny didn't just drive him back, he knocked him clean over. Whoever he was, he was lighter than Danny had expected for an opponent of such height.

It threw his whole attack sequence out of whack. He'd

stepped forward, expecting his attacker to be upright and within easy reach. He'd brought his heavy torch arcing round like a bull whip, intending to crack the other's skull. His arm tore instead through the empty space left by his fallen opponent. His momentum dragged his whole body pivoting round, throwing him temporarily off-balance and tossing a lifeline to the assailant.

Danny felt his legs swept from beneath him. The flashlight slipped from his grip and thudded onto the floor. As he fell, an elbow smashed hard and fast into his face. A flash of red pain. A cracking sound. His nose?

Blood cascaded into Danny's mouth, as he twisted out from beneath his attacker's outstretched leg, desperate to avoid getting trapped in a foot or body lock.

He searched frantically through the gloom. Did the guy still have the knife? Or had he dropped it?

Movement in his peripheral vision. Enough for him to locate the man: back and to his right. Face down, he pressed his palms flat against the floor, his whole body flexing as he kicked out. He got lucky. His right heel slammed full force into his opponent, throwing the other backwards with a cry of pain.

Stumbling. A gasp. A retching sound. Had Danny's foot somehow hit the solar plexus, the target his fist had earlier failed to find? It sure as hell sounded that way.

Danny grimaced, rising, wheeling round, left arm up to parry a second thrust from the knife.

There, in the twilight, he saw his opponent, already half

upright, but unsteady, not poised. And with nothing in his hands. No knife. Danny stepped in, intent on grappling the man, or throwing him hard to the floor. But instead of them closing, as Danny had expected, the other lurched sideways, deliberately throwing himself to the floor, stretching out an arm as he did so.

Danny saw why. The knife was illuminated in the shaft of white light stamped across the carpet by Danny's flashlight. But his attacker's reach came up short by nearly two feet. Wheezing, the man rolled left then right once more on his back, to gather momentum, and stretched out in a desperate attempt to snatch up the blade.

The delay was all Danny had needed. He stepped back, planted his feet apart in a shooting stance, slipped his Glock 30 from its holster and brought it round in a double-fisted grip.

Click.

Just as his attacker's fingers brushed against the glinting blade, Danny flicked the safety off his pistol and locked his aim. A single tap of the trigger. That was all it would take. A head shot. A double tap. He would not miss. But the click of the safety had been warning enough. His attacker had frozen.

A pro, then.

'Move your hand back. Do it slowly,' Danny said. His voice sounded all wrong, not just because he was panting but because of the blood still pouring from his nose into his mouth.

A moment's hesitation from the other. A wheeze of pain

and frustration. Then his attacker obeyed, withdrawing his hand from the blade and slowly turning his balaclava-covered face towards Danny, his entire body quivering now. From adrenalin? Fear? With resignation? Probably all three.

Danny sucked air into his lungs, swallowing blood. 'Roll slowly onto your front. Hands behind your back,' he said, stepping away, his flashlight beam illuminating his attacker.

Black jeans. A tight black leather jacket. Black running shoes. Whoever this was, they clearly weren't working for Benetton.

Whoever this was also knew the drill. As he turned face down onto the floor, he clasped his leather-gloved hands behind his neck.

'Are you wired?' Danny said.

'No.' The word came out as a rasp.

'If I find out you're lying, I'm going to shoot you in the back of the head.' He had the Taser holstered across his chest, but elected not to use it. He needed the man alert, not groggy, so that he could question him fast. Keeping his pistol trained, he took an industrial cord-tie from his jacket pocket and dropped it on the carpet two feet in front of his captive's head.

'Slowly bring your hands forward. Locate the cord-tie on the floor. Put your hands through it. Then use your teeth to pull it tight.'

He did as he was told, his breathing finally slowing. Maybe because he'd realized that what had seemed impossible only seconds before was now about to happen: Danny might not be about to execute him. *Not yet.*

Making sure to keep out of reach of those legs, and knowing it was just as easy to strangle someone with your hands tied together as it was with a rope, Danny edged carefully around his fallen attacker's body. He took another cord-tie from his pocket, knelt and noosed the ankles together.

Pressing the pistol to the back of the man's head, he quickly frisked him for weapons, comms and ID, paranoia making him picture scores of intelligence agents surrounding the building, and even now creeping stealthily up the stairs.

He found nothing. Nothing that indicated the guy was working as part of a team. Nothing that told him who he was or why he was there. His body shape, though . . . that came as a shock. Sleek, lithe and curved. Not what Danny had expected at all.

Rising, he circled round in to the man's head, again keeping well out of reach, and picked up the flashlight. Bright blue eyes shone back at him from the balaclava's eye holes. A curl of long eyelashes showed at a blink.

The truth hit Danny, like a brick to the back of the skull: the person who'd come here to kill him was a woman.

He thought of *her* straight away: the *blonde*. Glinka's woman. He remembered the first time he'd met her, when she'd searched him for hidden comms before the meeting at the Ritz Hotel.

She was late twenties with short blonde hair, tall and

athletic-looking. And pretty. In spite of the loathing he felt for her now, he remembered that. He recalled other details too. That she'd had a tiny green rose tattooed on her wrist. That she'd worn no make-up, and that her skin had been as pale as a corpse's.

The blue eyes Danny was staring at now had no make-up around them. This woman's height and build looked perfect too. Was it Glinka's woman? *Had* the Kid's sister tipped him off about his visit? Had the Kid then chosen the blonde as the instrument of Danny's doom?

She cried out and grimaced in pain as, without warning, he stepped on her tied hands and trod down as hard as he could.

Crouching, keeping his weight pressed on her, his skin prickled electrically with the buzz of adrenalin, as he watched her squirm. Leaning in, he tore the balaclava from her head, and jammed the pistol's sound suppressor directly into her right eye socket.

She bucked in shock, then grew still, as he kept his weight bearing down on her hands and the sound suppressor lodged against her eye. He shone the flashlight into her face and stared. And this time it was his turn to be shocked. Because it wasn't Glinka's woman.

This woman's complexion was much darker, Mediterranean. Her hair was raven black. The only facial similarity, in fact, with Glinka's woman was that she had cheekbones so sharp they looked like they could cut through coal.

'Who are you?' he said.

She blinked blindly in the blaze of the flashlight's beam and heaved air into her lungs. The fear in the bright blue eyes darkened into loathing, as she spat into Danny's face. 'Go to hell, you fucking murderer,' she said.

CHAPTER 45

Danny didn't know if it was a reaction to the fact that she'd just spat at him or to what she'd said. But something inside him snapped. Looking at her then felt like looking into the eyes of every TV journalist, government official and cop who'd maligned and slandered him since he'd been blamed for the London hit.

'Tell me who you're working for. Now,' he barked, seizing her by the jacket collar and twisting, so he cut off her air supply.

He let her choke for a second, two seconds, three – then released her.

'No one,' she gasped.

No one? What did she take him for? A moron? He tightened his grip and twisted again.

'Muuughthuugh,' she managed, through gritted teeth.

The garbled word slowly unravelled itself in Danny's mind. *Murderer.* The woman was choking, her face contorted in pain, yet still her hatred blazed. And there was something else. Something about her face seemed familiar. Danny sieved his memory. Had he seen her somewhere before?

'Last chance,' he said, flecks of blood from his mouth freckling her face. 'Who. Are. You. Working. For?'

Once more, he slackened his grip. Her head lolled forward and thudded against the carpet.

'You. Murdered. Her,' she croaked.

Her?

Who?

What the hell was she talking about?

He tightened his grip on the Glock 30's butt, making sure she felt the movement too, and would assume that he was about to pull the trigger.

'My mother . . .' A cobweb of saliva stretched from her lips to the floor, her face a mask of pure loathing. 'You murdered her. You shot her outside the hotel . . . You shot her in the back,' she spat, 'like the fucking coward you are.'

Danny could hardly believe what he was hearing. Or seeing. Tears welled in the woman's eyes. Danny's thoughts raced. He pictured the bodies on the street outside the Ritz. Her mother?

'Name,' Danny said, again tightening his grip on the gun.

'Ruth. My name's Ruth Silver.'

'Not yours. Hers.'

'Anya Silver.'

Danny knew them all, the dead whom Glinka, the Kid and his team had massacred. He had looked them

up since, every one of those who'd died or been hit. He'd
followed the links. He'd skimmed across their lives, like
an insect across a series of ponds. He seen – he'd *felt* –
what had been lost, yet he'd been powerless to change a
thing.

A thumbnail image of Anya Silver swelled inside his
mind. Dark hair, like this woman's. A dark complexion
too. A retired Israeli doctor on vacation in London, she'd
been on her way to meet her daughter for lunch when
Glinka and his accomplice had stepped out onto that
balcony and strafed the street below.

Danny slumped back on his haunches, stunned, finally
releasing the pressure on her hands. The Glock suddenly
felt so loose in his grip that he couldn't have fired it even
if he'd wanted to. Which he no longer did.

The flashlight slipped from his grip and rolled across
the floor, its beam pointing away from them, leaving them
in shadow. He listened to his attacker's breathing. Anya
Silver's daughter?

'Just fucking shoot me,' Ruth said, flexing her fingers
now, curling them. 'Get it over with. Do it now.'

'I didn't do it,' Danny said. 'I didn't kill her.'

'*Liar. . .*'

Her voice was as dry and dead as autumn leaves, as
though she were speaking for those from the grave.

She twisted then, her silhouette like that of a beast
determined to break free.

He moved back from her. He couldn't shoot her but he
couldn't afford to let her get too close. He didn't want to

hurt her again if he could avoid it. Not if she was innocent, as he now believed she might be.

In a desperate effort, she managed to raise her head off the floor enough to try spitting at him again. But she was too weak, too much in shock. She sank back down in a shuddering coughing fit.

'It's true,' he said. 'I didn't kill any of them.'

'You're Shanklin,' she growled, from the darkness. 'I watched you on TV. I saw everything you did. The whole world watched. The whole world saw.'

'What you saw was me running,' he said. 'After I'd been set up to take the blame.'

No words, just the sound of her breathing. No acknowledgement that she'd even heard him, let alone believed he might be telling the truth.

He picked up the flashlight then. He shone it obliquely across her face, trying not to blind her this time . . . and there he saw it: a seed of doubt, of confusion, in her eyes.

He said nothing. He walked back to the window, parted the curtains and checked the street outside. Everything looked normal. He looked back at the woman. What the hell was he meant to do now?

'I'm going to cut you free,' he said.

Silence. Even in the gloom, he could picture the expression of disbelief on her face.

But what other choice did he have? It was already clear that she'd tell him nothing, unless he beat it out of her, and he was no longer in a position to do that. But he still needed to get her to talk. He had to find out why she was there in case he could use the information to track the Kid down, or in case she'd found a way of tracking him herself, which others might now use as well.

He needed to win her trust, persuade her to talk and get her on side.

'But do anything stupid,' he warned, 'and you're going to end up back like this or worse. And if I have to shoot you, I will.'

Keeping the pistol trained on her, and making sure to keep himself at arm's length from her, he gripped the flashlight and her knife in one hand and cut through the cord-tie binding her ankles.

He walked round, making sure Ruth got a good look at the Glock, then sliced the cord-tie holding her wrists, and stepped smartly back.

As he'd expected, she rolled, rising in one fluid movement into a defensive stance, confirming once more that, even if she was there for reasons of personal revenge, she was a pro.

He kept his beam on her body so as not to blind her. He could still make out her features in the weak light filtering through from the kitchen. She looked from him to the door.

'Don't,' Danny said. Any attempt at fight or flight, and he'd have no choice other than to subdue her. 'I don't want to have to hurt you again.'

'Prove it,' she said, not missing a beat.

'Fine.' Slowly he slipped the pistol back into his holster.

Another gesture of good will. Another reason for her to trust him and talk.

The seed of doubt he'd seen in her eyes was flowering now into full-blown confusion.

'If you didn't kill my mother, then who did?' she said.

'How about first you answer me something?'

A hesitation. *Could she trust him?* He could almost see the question written on her face. Why would he have cut her free, unless he was telling the truth?

'How did you find me?' he said.

She nodded.

'I didn't,' she said. 'I found *him*.'

'Who?'

'The man who lives here.'

'The Kid?'

She stared at him blankly.

'Adam Gilloway?' he tried. 'Adam Fitch?'

'I only ever knew him as Martlett,' she said.

The name meant nothing to Danny.

'I employed him for a job three years ago.'

'*You* employed him?'

'The organization I work for.'

An agency then, Danny deduced. But which one? From her accent, he knew she wasn't British or American, although he reckoned she'd definitely spent time in both. She wasn't Eastern European either. He was familiar with enough Slavic languages to have picked that up right away.

'Mossad,' he said.

He made it sound like a statement, even though it was a guess. But it paid off. She didn't deny he was right. And something else, now he thought about it, made him feel he'd hit the mark. Her moves when they'd fought: a couple had felt familiar – Krav Maga, the martial-arts hybrid favoured by the Israeli Defence Forces.

And she'd said *work*, not *worked*. Meaning she was still employed by them. But could Mossad really have sanctioned her coming here? To assassinate someone without back-up on foreign soil? Danny doubted it. This was too personal. There was no way on this earth any operations commander would have let her off her leash for this.

'The man I knew as Martlett recommended your services,' she said. 'That's how I knew the two of you sometimes worked together. But the job we'd employed him for, we already had another enforcer lined up, so I never contacted you.'

'So after I got the blame for what happened in London, you decided that the best way to find me was to find him first?'

'Yes – in case he'd been working with you on it too.'

'So you tried to contact him,' he guessed.

'Yes, but all the contact numbers I have for him are now dead.' Her voice was still hoarse, but slowly softening with each word. 'We still had this address, though.'

'He'd given you this as a contact point?' Danny failed to keep the disbelief from his voice.

'I wouldn't exactly say *gave* . . .'

There, in the twilight, did he detect the trace of a smile?

'. . . it's more like we *took*,' she said.

Ruth stared at him in silence, her eyes fixed on the pistol in his holster and her knife in his hand, no doubt weighing up once again the fact that he hadn't killed her when he could have done, and wondering why he'd have cut her free if he really was the guilty man she'd supposed him to be.

'A woman,' she said. 'One of our agents. After we first hired Martlett – the man you call "the Kid" – in London, we had her follow him and pick him up in a bar so that we could find out where he lived.'

A honey trap. A common practice. Particularly with Mossad. And one that had targeted the Kid's predilections for drink and loose women.

Danny guessed the rest: 'So, after the London attack, you staked this place out?' he said. 'In case one of us turned up.'

'I didn't want to risk coming in here in case it was alarmed and I ended up tipping Martlett off that I was on to him. So I staked it out front and back instead,' she said. 'CCTV in a blacked-out car at the back, me parked in another car across the street . . . with a few spells inside that café you walked into earlier as well.'

Jesus . . . So that was why her face had looked familiar. Because he *had* seen her before.

'And that was why you followed me in here. Because when you saw me there, you recognized me.'

'That's right. So now why don't you answer me this?'

she said. 'If you're so goddamn innocent, what the fuck are you doing searching the home of your friend?'

'Because he's not my friend,' Danny snapped. 'He's the bastard who betrayed me. He helped kill your mother and all those other poor people. He's the one who set me up.'

CHAPTER 46

The moment Danny had said it, he wished he hadn't. It was information Ruth didn't need to know. He stared at her, confused. Why had he told her? Because of her mother? Or did he just want one stranger in the world to believe he could never be capable of something like that?

Enough. He levelled his pistol at her. He watched her tense, perhaps thinking about running, but deciding to stay where she was. *Better*, he thought. *Retake control.* He tossed another pair of cord-ties onto the floor at her feet. 'Put them on,' he said.

'*What?*'

'You heard.' She'd told him everything she knew. He'd earned her trust and used it. Leaving her free was too much of a risk. What if she changed her mind about him – went to the cops? 'I'll cut you free once I've finished searching this place,' he said. After I've Tasered you first, he thought. Leaving you here nice and groggy to stop you doing anything dumb like trying to follow me.

'But—'

'But *what?*'

'But I can still help you find him,' she said.

'No.'

'I found you, didn't I? I found out where the Kid lived?'

'Yeah, you did good. Congratulations. Now put the fucking cord-ties on.'

'But we're both after the same thing.'

He glared at her. 'No. I want justice. You're looking for revenge.'

'You think there's a difference?'

He opened his mouth to rebuke her again, but no words came.

'You trusted me enough to set me free,' she said.

'Only so you'd trust me enough to talk.'

And he was regretting it already. Discovering how she'd tracked down this address hadn't brought him any nearer to finding the Kid. This was the only lead she'd had and, unless he found another here, it would have proved a dead end.

'This is the last time I'm asking,' he said, flicking the Glock's safety off with another *click* just to encourage her along.

'OK, but there's just one problem with that plan.' She didn't move.

'What?'

'If you're really not the cold-blooded killer the press say you are, then you're not going to shoot me, are you?' She left a beat for this to sink in. 'And if you're not prepared to kill me,' she said, 'you might as well let me work with you because, I promise you, the last thing you want is the alternative.'

Danny didn't like the way this was sounding. 'Which is?'

'I go to the authorities here in London. I tell them you're here. And you end up getting hunted right across London all over again.'

Even in the semi-darkness, he could have sworn then that he saw another trace of a smile play across her lips.

'Plus,' she said, 'I also tell them your theory about our friend who owns this place being involved in the assassination so that they can go looking for him too. And guess what, Danny?' she said. 'With their resources, I'm betting they'll find him first. And maybe kill him and whoever he's with, wrecking any chance you have of getting them to spill and put on record that you weren't involved with them.'

Danny . . . She'd used his name in a way so over-familiar that it had made his skin crawl. But she was right, wasn't she? Because she did know him – well enough to be confident he wouldn't harm her, and well enough to have guessed, rightly, that what he feared most was someone else, someone better resourced, going after the Kid and Glinka.

Why? For the reason she'd just said: because they might kill them before Danny could get them to confess. But also because they might not find them, just scare them into vanishing even deeper underground, so that they'd never resurface. And then, of course, there was the other main reason that Danny hadn't tipped off the intelligence agencies about the Kid's involvement: because he knew any agency that got to Glinka and the Kid first would also find out about the smallpox. And once they did, their only priority would be to secure it for themselves. They certainly wouldn't give a damn about using it to prove Danny's innocence. In fact, he doubted they'd want any witnesses to its theft at all.

But even if this woman knew nothing about that, she still knew one thing: that she had Danny Shanklin by the balls.

Which meant that, like it or not, he needed to keep her on side. He watched now as she rubbed her neck where he had throttled her.

'So, have we got a deal?' she said.

He didn't answer. He didn't have to: she already knew she'd won.

'Start through there in the bedroom,' he said. 'I'll carry on checking in here.'

Just take back control, he told himself. Remember why you're here. He'd deal with this later. With *her*. A flash image of one of Spartak's twins watching over her filled his mind. Somewhere nice and remote. Yeah, he'd have her contained, all right, until this was over.

'Here.' He took a pen torch from his pocket and gave it to her. Their fingers brushed, and he felt a jolt somewhere deep in the pit of his stomach. Nerves. He felt like a car with a puncture, a computer with a fractured screen, a machine no longer working at its fullest capacity.

He watched her leave the living room and walk round to the left, towards the bedroom. He moved to the far side of the room, still watching the doorway, a part of him expecting her to reappear and come at him hard again. Every ounce of his experience told him not to trust her, yet a part of him did. A part of him made him turn eventually from the doorway and continue searching the room.

Nothing in the vases on the mantelpiece or taped up inside the chimney. He swept the flashlight beam across the walls. Nothing expensive. Posters not prints, none framed. Pink Floyd, Nirvana and, of course, the Kid's favourite, Aphex Twin.

Then – *BAM* – a wall of sound made him step back as if he'd just been punched.

Then came light. Bright white light. A massive rectangle of it. Right there in the corner of the room.

CHAPTER 47

Then came laughter, as the Kid's face appeared on the screen. He was sixteen stone and thirty-five years old, but baby-faced, practically wrinkle- and stubble-free, which was how he'd got his nickname. He was sitting on a swivel chair, lighting a smoke. He scratched at the part of his belly that was showing between his stained grey T-shirt and jeans, every inch the fat cat who'd just guzzled all the cream.

'Damn, Danny, it's good to see you,' he said, smoke cascading from his mouth, but not nearly enough to hide the grin on his face.

Movement to Danny's right. He swung round, expecting an attack, but all his flashlight beam picked out was Ruth in the doorway, rushing back into the room. Only it wasn't Danny she was coming for, he saw right away. It was the sound that had brought her. The thunder of bass.

'And all kudos to you, mate,' the Kid continued, his south London accent as pronounced as ever. 'Because I've got to say, you've got more lives than a cat. I mean, just look at you, still at large. Shit, you're good. You even escaped the welcoming committee we set up for you at the docks. And after all the effort we put into convincing MI5 to turn up and shoot you dead. That's right. It was us who arranged for all those agents and that chopper to be waiting for you. You didn't give us much choice after we found out you'd been to visit the good Commandant Sabirzhan on his deathbed. Just as well we'd left a false trail for you then, though, wasn't it? A shame it didn't finish you off.

'The thing I don't get is how you found our cosy little Cold War facility near Chernobyl at all, you sly old dog. I'm guessing you must have heard it from one of those fine people I left at that farmhouse to kill you and your daughter. Is that what happened? Did you beat it out of them, Danny? Did you make one of them cough up all that intel in blood?'

Danny said nothing. He was trying to work out if the video feed was some kind of recording that the Kid had previously set up, which had now been triggered by their presence. But in which case, how come the events it referred to were so recent? And how come it was addressed to him in person?

Unless . . . unless it was being transmitted *live* and—

'Get back!' he shouted to Ruth.

Too late, she was already by his side. Just as his worst fears were confirmed. And he'd got his proof that the Kid was watching them too.

'And – ooh,' he said, making a show of peering closer

into the screen, 'what's this, Danny? I see you've got
yourself a little lady in tow.'

If Ruth heard him, she gave no indication. Instead she
marched right up to the TV, got down on all fours and
used her pen torch to examine the nest of wires and metal
boxes beneath.

But Danny knew it was pointless: even if they did cut
off whatever cameras the Kid was filming them through,
it was already too late.

These images of him and this address would already
have been sent to the cops, MI5 and whoever the hell
else the Kid had felt like tipping off concerning Danny's
presence.

He turned back to the screen. The Kid was grinning.
His big fat face was almost split in two.

'That's right, Danny. I'm watching you watching me
watching you. And I know what you're thinking,' he said.
'How long have I known you were in my apartment? Am
I right?'

Danny didn't answer. Didn't need to. The Kid was right.
He knew Danny too damn well.

'And the answer is . . . *ta-dah* . . .' the Kid threw up
his hands like a magician '. . . I've been watching ever
since you fucking walked in. The motion sensors in the
hallway rumbled you the second you stepped through that
doorway. And, yes, I've been recording you ever since.'

Danny should have known better. The Kid had left the
lamp on in the living room to allow him to observe. Of
course he hadn't forgotten to set his alarm. He'd not set it

on purpose. He'd wanted Danny to come in here. Because this was a trap.

Danny started to turn. He had to get out. The fire escape. That was his best bet. If the Kid had already passed on his whereabouts to the authorities, they'd already be on their way *en masse*. Jesus, was this what all his efforts had come to? Was he now right back where he started? Trapped inside a building in central London with the police and intelligence forces closing in?

'*But*,' the Kid shouted, 'before you go running, I should tell you that I've *not* tipped anyone off about where you are.'

Not?

Danny broke his stride and turned back towards the screen.

'I mean, why would I?' said the Kid. 'Why would I trust the British law-enforcement authorities again when they made such a spectacular mess of failing to kill you last time? Why would I bother, when I can do that myself?'

A number superimposed itself over the Kid's face.

It was a ten. It turned into a nine.

'Run,' Ruth shouted. 'It must be a bomb.'

She'd already seen the numbers and was pushing him back, turning him round and driving him ahead of her.

'Seven.'

Danny could hear the Kid laughing.

'Six.'

Ruth reached the front door at the same time as Danny.

'Five.'

'Open it,' she screamed.

He tore the door open. She pushed him through.

'Two.'

It was the last thing he heard.

There was only darkness after that.

CHAPTER 48

LONDON

Danny woke to the sound of what he first thought was waves breaking on the shore. He'd been dreaming of water too, of being on holiday in Florida and teaching Jonathan how to swim. Sally had been standing in the shallows less than a metre from him.

Jonathan's swimming goggles had glinted in the sun as she'd launched him towards Danny. The little boy had ploughed through the water, carried by his momentum, not really swimming at all, but as he'd surfaced, spluttering, into Danny's arms, from the gasp and squeal of triumph you'd have thought he'd just front-crawled solo across the Atlantic.

Now, as Danny opened his eyes, he saw there was no blue sky above him. Jonathan and Sally were gone. His arms held nothing but the gaping hole of their absence.

His head and neck ached as he turned it to look round the room he found himself in. Perfunctory furniture. A full-length wall mirror. A trouser press. Drawn beige venetian blinds. A towel covered with blood.

He sat bolt upright, immediately regretting it. He saw the balaclava on the floor, with the black trousers and boots. The Kid's flat. The woman who'd tried to kill him. The Kid . . . He remembered the Kid laughing. Had the Kid really been there too? Shit. A bomb. Was that why he couldn't remember anything?

A wave of nausea washed over him. Retching, Danny leaned over the bedside and saw a bin had already been placed there. Tissues. More blood. A stick. No, he saw, not just a stick. A painkiller. A Fentanyl 'lollipop'. An opiate given to combatants who fell in the field.

Danny pictured the woman again. *Ruth*. Had she given him the Fentanyl? Had they both somehow made it out of there alive? She'd been behind him, hadn't she? As they'd tried to get out of the Kid's apartment . . .

He retched again, but nothing came up. The nausea passed. He laid his head back on the pillow. He saw he'd been dribbling. His spit was flecked with blood.

He rolled onto his back and stared up at the ceiling. A fan slowly turned. He let its breeze lull him, cooling his sweating brow. *How long have I been here?*

And where *was* here? A hospital? He needed to check, but he felt too sick to move. Instead he slumped back.

A moment of panic. Had the police captured him? Or, worse, MI5 or even Mossad? Was he about to find himself in the back of some blacked-out truck or soundproof crate on the way to who the hell knew where? Or had that already happened? Was this a cell? Was his run finally at an end?

No, he told himself. *No. If that was the case, you'd still be drugged or trussed up.* Someone had brought him here. It had to have been Ruth, hadn't it? She had to be here somewhere, didn't she?

He closed his eyes, his nausea steadily morphing into a splitting headache. More pain as well. In his shoulder. That's right. He'd been wounded there. There and his head. His *face*. He shut his eyes tight, part of him wishing he'd never woken up.

A click. Footsteps padding across carpet. A rustling sound. He turned as she was unwinding the clean towel from round her. Funny, but it was this he stared at almost as much as her smooth naked breasts and limbs. More so, probably, embarrassed at the prospect of being caught awake. He tried turning back before she saw him staring. But he was too late. The movement caught her eye and for a fleet second their gaze met. Eyes shut again, he faced the wall.

'You're back in the land of the living, then?'

'Urgh.'

He'd meant to say, *Yeah*, but his jaw was too swollen and his tongue too dry for him to form the word properly. Even with his eyes closed, he could clearly picture her combed-back hair, glistening after the shower she'd just taken.

'I hope you've got good dental insurance.'

He could no longer hear the static slide and rustle of her getting dressed, which he took as an invitation to turn back and talk. She was dressed, he saw. Or half dressed anyway. She had a crisp, box-fresh white shirt on and blue jeans, no belt, with the buttons not yet done up.

She took a compact mirror from her bag and handed it to him. He held it to his face and grimaced, bringing on a fresh bout of pain. He looked as if he'd been through ten rounds with a heavyweight pro. Yellow bruises. Black bruises. So many he lost count. He pulled his blood-black lower lip down, wincing at the touch. His nose was freshly broken too. He remembered he had the girl to thank for that.

'Ug,' he said, meaning *fuck*.

She passed him a glass of water.

'Drink. Gently,' she warned, watching him impassively as he winced.

He didn't listen. He drained the glass.

'Another,' he said, quickly adding, 'Please.'

She shook her head. He opened his mouth to protest, but then turned quickly from her to the bin as the water he'd just drunk rushed back up and out of him in a jet.

She passed him a tissue to wipe his mouth.

'Jesus wept.' He groaned loudly. 'Just give me a gun and let me shoot myself in the head.'

'No permanent damage to your vocal cords, then,' she commented. 'I guess I'll soon find out if that's a good thing or not.'

A joke. At least, he hoped so.

'You saved my life?' he said.

'Yes. Maybe cost you it too, though. Should have

checked sooner to see if his apartment was rigged. Once you told me he was part of what happened, that he was a terrorist, it should have been the first thing I did.'

Part of the group that had killed her mother, she meant. Anya Silver.

He propped himself up on his elbows, touched the back of his head and winced. He felt something shift as he applied more pressure and realized that whatever wound was there had been dressed.

'Don't worry,' she told him. 'It's clean. The explosion in the flat threw us both clean across the hallway outside. I got lucky, I guess, didn't even get a scratch, but you got smacked right into a wall . . .'

He gave another exploratory prod with his forefinger. A low red pain exploded across his entire back. Some kind of nerve damage. It hurt like hell.

'It could have been worse,' she said. 'Those British Victorians, they did things properly. It was only thanks to the thickness of the walls in that building that we weren't shredded on the spot.'

She was right, of course. They were both lucky to be alive.

'Pills on the bedside table,' she told him, buttoning up her jeans and crouching down to pull on a pair of brown leather sandals.

'Where am I?'

'My hotel room.'

'But how—'

The room lurched sideways. His skull felt as if someone

had tried to cleave it in two with an axe. A wave of nausea washed through him. He retched, but this time nothing came up.

'Well, that's a relief, at least,' she said. 'There's nothing left inside you.'

She swam into focus again. The beautiful woman who'd tried to cut his throat. She looked younger here in the warmly lit room. Early thirties? Her face was bruised, he saw that too. Her lower lip was cut. From the explosion? Or his own work? The former, he hoped.

'Ruth,' he said. 'Your mother . . .' he said. 'I read about her after the massacre . . . I read about them all . . . all of the civilians killed . . .'

'Why?'

'Why *what*?'

'Why read about them?'

To give me strength, he wanted to say. To remind me that this wasn't just about myself. To make sure I'd never give up.

'How did I get here?' he said. 'How the hell did we get out of that apartment block?'

'The bomb – a gas leak, the news is saying – blew the front room and the kitchen clean out.'

Danny felt his chest tightening. 'What else?' he said.

'What else *what*?'

'What else did the news say? About us? About me? About the footage of us that the Kid took?'

'Nothing.'

'Nothing?' He screwed up his face. It made no sense.

'But he must have leaked it. And if he had, every cop in London would be searching for us right now.'

'Well, they're not.'

'So what's your take on it?' He pinched his brow. He still felt groggy. He needed to wake up, to think smart.

'The way I see it is that, one, he doesn't want any spooks nosing round his flat having connected it to you. Maybe because he's worried they might link him to the attack.'

Which made sense, he agreed. 'And two?'

'Two: he might think he's already got us, that we're already dead,' Ruth said. 'Even if no fatalities have been reported from that apartment-block explosion, he might think that they recovered and ID'd our bodies, but just haven't gone public with that information yet while they're trying to figure this whole mess out.'

The Kid was certainly arrogant enough to think we couldn't have got away, Danny thought. 'And how *did* you get us out of there before the authorities closed in after the explosion?' he asked, his memory still hazy as hell.

'Speed,' she said. 'And smoke. And, trust me, there was a hell of a lot of that. I carried you out through the smoke.'

Carried him? He took in the tone of her muscles again.

'And on down the fire escape leading out to the back,' she continued.

So she'd spotted it too.

'That was where I'd parked my car,' she added.

'Who saw us?'

'No one.'

'You're sure?'

'As sure as anyone can be who had a bell the size of Big Ben ringing inside their head.'

Anger ripped through him. 'You stupid motherfucker.'

She blinked, surprised. 'And there was me expecting a thank-you.'

'Not you,' Danny said. 'Me. I can't believe I was so stupid. I can't believe that son-of-a-bitch nearly killed us both.'

He pushed himself up onto his elbow, swung his legs round and sat up. As the sheet slipped from him, he saw he was naked. He dragged it back up across his lap.

'Where the hell are my clothes?' he said.

'Gone,' she told him. 'After we got back here, I ditched them. They were pretty much dead from all the smoke and I couldn't risk taking them to a dry cleaner.'

Again he reached up and tentatively touched the back of his neck. He winced. 'You dressed it?' he asked.

'Yes.'

'How bad is it?'

'You'll live.'

'Without seeing a doctor?'

'You already have.'

He looked up at her, confused, then startled. This just got better and better, he thought, shaking his head carefully in response to the look of cool amusement on her face.

'Well, a fourth-year medical student anyway,' she said. 'I never did take those final exams.' She handed him another glass of water. And two pills.

'What are these for?' he said.

'To help you sleep. And when you wake, we'll talk about where we need to go next.'

'*We?*'

'Yes,' she said. 'Or didn't I make that clear? I got you out of there. You owe me now. And, the second you're fully *compos mentis*, you're going to start to pay me back. You and me, we're partners now.'

CHAPTER 49

Danny didn't know how long he slept, but when he woke, he was still in the same room, the only difference being that the bin had been emptied and the sheets changed, somehow without Ruth having disturbed him.

He saw she'd left new clothes for him on a chair by the bed, still in the shop's carrier-bag – jeans, a jacket, underwear, a couple of shirts. He got up, showered, careful to keep his dressing dry, then cleaned his teeth with the new brush he found on the basin. When he looked in the mirror, he didn't feel half as bad as the last time he'd seen his reflection.

He found Ruth sitting in a high-backed wooden chair in front of an oval glass table in the small sitting room of her hotel suite. She was staring into the screen of a brand-new iMac. USB wires trailed off it, linking it to various pieces of computer hardware that Danny didn't recognize.

She didn't see him at first, as he stood there watching her work. Damn, she really is beautiful, he thought, at the same time feeling a momentary pang of guilt, wishing he could at least get word to Anna-Maria that he was OK.

Ruth didn't take her eyes from the screen. Several different windows were open on it, he saw, as he joined her at the table. Numbers scrolled down the one she was looking at. The one beside it showed a map of the world.

'The thing with your erstwhile friend the Kid maybe thinking we're dead,' she said, 'gives us the edge, in that he's not going to be worrying about us coming after him now.'

'I guess. Or it would if we had any means to do that, if we had any leads.'

'Maybe we do.' Keeping her eyes glued to the screen, Ruth took her hand off the mouse and tapped a black metal box on her right.

'What's that?' Danny said.

'His router.'

'Whose? You mean ...'

'Yep, the Kid.'

He had a flash memory then of her holding something just like this as he'd spun her away from the nest of wires beneath the Kid's TV in his apartment, just before the grenade had gone off.

'And that video of him,' he said. 'It came through this?'

'Precisely.'

'Meaning he'd dialled through to us live right then?'

'Correct.'

'And routers keep records of what's come through them?'

'Not normally,' Ruth said.

'No? Then what use is . . .'

She faced him – and smiled. 'Someone needs to tell them to do that.'

'Someone?'

'Yes, Danny. Someone like me who knows what they're doing. Someone who's capable of thinking very fast and clearly under pressure. Someone like me, with only a pen torch for guidance, while a psychopath makes a speech about how clever he is and openly refers to me as a "little lady", before attempting to blow me to Kingdom Come.'

Danny leaned on the desk. He could feel his hands trembling. But this had nothing to do with the physical beating he'd taken. It was pure adrenalin. 'Are you telling me we can trace his call? We can find out where it came from?'

'Normally, no. That would be impossible.'

He had already learned that *normal* didn't appear to apply to this woman. 'And *ab*normally?' he asked.

She rewarded his attempt at humour with another polite smile. 'Abnormally,' she said, 'it's possible to do precisely that, but only if you possess some very expensive equipment. Of a type not available to the public. In fact, of a type available to very few governments' agencies.'

'Just tell me what it is,' Danny said. 'I still have contracts. I still have people who can get me things I need.' He was thinking of Spartak, of course. And, dammit, he needed to call him too. In case his own enquiries into Glinka and his team had come to fruition.'

'Unnecessary,' said Ruth, reaching forward and tapping another of the pieces of hardware plugged into the iMac's screen, 'because the kind of equipment needed for this is exactly the kind of tracking equipment Mossad agents based in the United Kingdom are issued with as part of their standard ops kit.'

Danny's eyes locked back on the iMac screen, specifically on the window showing the world map. A white line, he saw, was slowly scrolling down it. When it got to the bottom, it vanished, only to appear at the top of the window and commence the scan again, like a comb moving through hair.

'In other words,' Danny said, 'you're going to be able to show me where the Kid was when he made that call to us and where he might be right now?'

Ruth twisted round in her seat to face him. 'No,' she said.

'No?'

The spark of amusement that had been in her eyes just a moment ago had gone. A toughness, like tungsten, had taken its place. 'Not unless you tell me everything,' she said. 'Everything that happened to you the day my mother died. And everything you've discovered since.'

Danny's brow crumpled. Where to begin? With what the torturer had told him? About the smallpox? About what had happened in Pripyat? About the scientists he and Spartak had discovered there? About what they'd said of how Glinka and the others were planning to sell the hybrid to the highest bidders? About what they'd done to

Commandant Sabirzhan and his two colleagues? About what Spartak had been forced to do too?

He couldn't tell her any of that. Information was power. It was the only advantage he had. But there were other things he could tell her, information that would give her no advantage over him in finding the Kid or Glinka if her own methods floundered – in which case Danny would ditch her and move on alone.

He could tell her the truth about how he'd been set up. Nothing about the smallpox. Just about how Glinka and the others had killed the UN peace envoy, then massacred the civilians who'd happened to be there because they'd been paid by the Georgian Secret Service so that the Russians would get the blame.

He could tell her the truth right up to the point at which the mercenaries who'd carried out the massacre had gone on to uncover the existence of a lethal Cold War hybrid smallpox, which they'd made their own.

'OK,' Danny said.

He turned away to go and get dressed.

But Ruth hadn't finished. She placed a restraining hand on his wrist. 'One other thing,' she said. 'In case you're thinking of leaving out the bit about the smallpox hybrid, *don't*.'

Danny swallowed.

What? But how?

'I don't know what you're—'

Her grip tightened. 'I said *don't*,' she warned. 'Because most of that you've already told me.' Her eyes narrowed, their blue irises now as sharp as blades of steel. 'You see, that's the funny thing about Fentanyl,' she said, staring at him unblinkingly. 'As with most other opiates, even when people think they're fast asleep and dreaming, in reality they're just delirious and keen as hell to shoot off their mouth to anyone who might be there.'

CHAPTER 50

SCOTLAND

The seaside town Ray Kincade found himself in was around fifteen miles from the farmhouse where the young Scottish family had been murdered.

He was in his hire car, following the signs for the beach. The vehicle was a deliberately different colour and model from the one the PSS Killer might have seen parked near the farmhouse. It was raining and the streets were all but empty. A knot of school kids huddled round a shared cigarette or joint in a bus stop. A woman pushed a pram determinedly into the howling wind outside a tourist café.

The beach itself was deserted. Waves roiled along its wide eyelid of sand. The masts of fishing boats swung like metronomes in the small harbour to the east. The sky was an unrelenting swirl of grey clouds. The forecast said it would stay that way all week.

Ray counted eight cars and two vans in the car park he turned into at the edge of the town. As he cruised slowly up and down the rows, checking the makes and models of the vehicles, he remembered his first couple of years as an SFPD rookie, way back before he'd joined the CIA.

He smiled grimly to himself. The uniform and patrol car had been his be-all-and-end-all back then. Who'd have thought that same career path would bring him so many years later to Scotland, looking for the perpetrator of the worst string of unsolved murders in American history?

He didn't just suspect that the man who'd attacked him in the farmhouse was the notorious Paper, Stone, Scissors Killer, he *knew*. Not having the forensics contacts here to prove it empirically beyond any reasonable doubt, he'd carefully removed the bloodstained handle of the knife with which he'd stabbed his assailant and air-couriered it inside an evidence bag to an old colleague of his at Quantico.

He would have called in the Scottish cops when he'd been at the farmhouse. That had, in fact, been his initial plan once he'd become convinced that the PSS Killer had been there. Only then, in the struggle, he'd lost his phone. And by the time he'd got back to the farmhouse to recover it, he'd changed his mind. Because that torn newspaper and those nail-gun marks on the floor had proved to Ray that the PSS Killer had been there. As, of course, did the fact that the man who'd attacked him bore an almost total resemblance to the artist's impression of the PSS Killer furnished by Danny Shanklin. But none of that amounted to a compelling enough case to present to the Scottish police to convince them of what they were dealing with.

Ray had concluded that reporting straight into the

Scottish cops might have ended up getting him into
the papers, thereby tipping off the PSS Killer that his
involvement was suspected, giving him time and opportunity to disappear back underground.

No. Ray had decided back near the farmhouse, as he'd
sat in his car tending his bruised shoulder, cracked rib and
bleeding head, that when he involved the Scottish police,
he had to have incontrovertible proof. Which meant the
blood. The FBI already had a sample of the PSS Killer's
blood, taken from the snow outside the cabin where
Danny Shanklin's wife and son had been murdered. All
Ray needed now was a match.

The FBI DNA profiler to whom he had sent the sample,
simultaneously requesting he keep whatever he discovered
to himself for now, had come back yesterday with email
confirmation that it was indeed a match to that taken
from the PSS Killer's last known attack. His ex-colleague
had also come back with a question: *Where the fuck did
you get this?* Because for the FBI, of course, proof that the
PSS Killer was not only alive but active again opened up
a whole can of trouble for their Elite Serial Killer team:
they'd stopped actively hunting the PSS Killer several
years ago, having mistakenly put down his disappearance
and lack of new offences to the fact that he was dead.

Ray's ex-colleague had further written:

> And where the hell are you? You need to get back to
> me, Ray. I'm not going to be able to keep this under
> wraps for long. And you know better than anyone,

Ray: you don't want to go hunting this guy on your
own . . .

Ray hadn't answered the email. Not yet. For one thing,
he didn't work for the FBI any more. He worked for
Danny Shanklin. And, for another, he knew how the FBI
would react to the discovery that they'd made a mistake.
Not by trying to cover it up: too much time had passed
for that – the honcho at the Elite Serial Killer team who'd
called off the hunt had retired last year. The case would be
reopened by his successor. And with the chance of closing
a case file as notorious as this one, he had no doubt that
they'd throw everything they'd got into it. They'd descend
on that farmhouse like locusts on a fresh crop.

Which, again, Ray worried, would scare the PSS Killer
off.

The PSS Killer had avoided capture for so long because
he was smart. More than that, Ray reckoned, he was
professional. The way he'd fought Ray – even the way
he'd been dressed to avoid contaminating the crime scene
with his DNA – had all tied in with Danny Shanklin's
theory that the killer had been, perhaps still was, either
intelligence or police.

The PSS Killer knew how cops and feds thought. And
if a bunch of them turned up here and started snooping,
Ray had no doubt that he'd vanish just as surely as he
had done into that snowstorm outside Danny Shanklin's
cabin.

Ray wasn't keen on having the FBI snooping round

anywhere near himself either. They'd want to know why he was trying to track the PSS Killer. Out of purely professional interest? A sense of duty? Or a desire to lay the past to rest?

Even though all three of these motives were true, Ray knew there was no goddamn way the feds would stop there. They'd wonder who he was working for. And they'd look. And if they looked hard enough, they'd soon find his link to Danny Shanklin.

And no matter how appealing a catch the PSS Killer might be, the truth was that the US authorities were more interested right now in finding Danny. With the CIA, and God only knew how many other official and covert government organizations, they'd get stuck right into interrogating Ray and ripping his communications history apart to get a sniff of where Danny might be.

But even though Ray hadn't yet given away his location, he knew he was living on borrowed time. His ex-colleague, as he'd stated, would be able to keep quiet only for so long or he'd risk a severe disciplinary.

Were the FBI then to launch an intelligence investigation into Ray, they'd soon track his flight here and subsequent movements. They'd also more than likely do as he had – namely, cross-reference recent crimes against the PSS Killer's MO. They'd soon put two and two together and find the farmhouse. And it wouldn't take them much longer to find Ray.

None of which bothered him one jot, he thought, as he parked his hire car next to the ticket machine. Because the plain fact was he didn't need a lot of time. Just enough to follow this last lead. To find out where the PSS Killer was staying. And then he'd call the feds, the cops, and the entire goddamn British Army if he could. He'd do whatever it took to make sure the motherfucker did not escape justice again.

As he zipped up his jacket and stepped out into the gale, Ray pictured the photos in his study back home, the ones he'd copied before retiring, of the men, women and kids the PSS Killer had butchered. He saw the kids' names and the names of the schools they'd gone to, the lives they'd never had.

Do nothing. Await further instructions. Do not do this alone.

Danny Shanklin couldn't have made his orders any clearer. But aside from the fact that Danny had enough problems of his own and wouldn't be available any time soon, if, indeed, ever, to help with this, Ray had never been a do-nothing kind of a guy. He'd messaged Danny back to let him know that he'd hold fire. But even as he'd done it, he'd known he wouldn't. The PSS Killer was at large. He couldn't ignore that. He had to press on and do what he could to find him. Then he'd let Danny know, before he attempted to confront the lunatic.

He had to lean his whole body at a forty-five-degree angle to make any progress towards the ticket machine. He fed coins into the slot and took the ticket it spat out.

This was the third car park he'd visited in the last twenty minutes. As well as having the name of the town printed on it just like the other two tickets he had already bought, this one had a serial code that matched the parking ticket the PSS Killer had dropped as he'd fled from the farm.

That was proof of nothing in itself, Ray acknowledged. The PSS Killer could have stopped here for a rest, or a smoke, or to walk his goddamn dog down there on the beach.

But – he turned back towards the town, studying the holiday cottages and bed-and-breakfasts hugging the craggy hillside, with no vehicular access from the main road – it could mean the opposite.

It could mean the PSS Killer had been staying near here – *and still was.*

Ray fought his way back to the car and wrestled to keep its door open, stuck the ticket he'd just bought on the dash, then locked it and set off towards the holiday rental store and post office on the main road.

He'd start there. An old cop with old methods. He'd start by telling whoever worked there that he was looking for a friend, a fellow American tourist, whom he'd arranged to meet locally but whose mobile-phone number he'd lost. He'd tell them what his friend looked like: white, bald, powerfully built, over six feet tall, with slate grey eyes.

Oh, yes, if the PSS Killer was still here, Ray would find him, keep him under observation and call in the authorities. He'd watch the motherfucker being taken down. He'd watch and savour every second of that.

And Scotland Yard, the FBI, the CIA, MI5, and whoever the fuck else came for him, they could ask him whatever they wanted. By then, he'd have destroyed and ditched the laptop and phone he'd used to communicate with Danny Shanklin.

They could do their worst and it would make no difference. They'd have no way to get to Danny through him.

And Ray would face them, knowing he'd finally done what Danny had hired him to do. He'd have laid his own ghosts and Danny Shanklin's to rest.

CHAPTER 51

GERMANY

A hundred miles east of Berlin, Ruth parked the four-by-four Merc at such an angle that its German number plate couldn't be seen from the farmhouse's front door or the road. Rain drummed on the roof and blurred the windscreen.

'Wait here,' Danny said.

'I'll go,' she said. 'It'll worry them less if anyone's in.'

Danny doubted anyone would be. No lights on. No vehicles parked out front. Ruth was right, though. It was gone nine in the evening. If someone did answer the door, their hackles were less likely to rise if a woman, rather than a man, asked for directions.

'*Sprechen Sie Deutsch?*' he asked.

'Like a native,' she answered. 'It's not just the CIA who recruit kids from the top of the class.'

He smiled, the same smile he'd given during their journey here, first by car to Dover, where they'd put the British hire car on the Eurotunnel train, then by a different car they'd hired in Paris, and finally by this Merc which they'd collected in Berlin from a Mossad agent there. God only knew what story she'd told her fellow agent. Something about an assignment in Moscow, in Finland, she'd said. Danny had not been introduced.

Danny, of course, had stayed in the background throughout, still travelling under a false passport he considered safe. Ruth had switched IDs twice, but had been happy to deal with any officials. Their car had been waved through Passport Control at Dover and a cop had stopped and fined them for speeding east of Paris. Whatever nerves Danny had been feeling had been erased as he had sent them on their way after checking Ruth's licence, passport and the car's plates. Mossad fake IDs were as flawless as ever, it seemed.

Unbuckling her seat belt now, Ruth twisted round and half climbed into the back seat to retrieve her coat. She had great legs, Danny observed, not for the first time, and stopped himself staring. He'd been trying not to glance at her too often during the long drive in case she'd noticed. Hard not to stare, though, at someone as striking as her . . .

She was beautiful, but not in a conventional way. He reckoned other people might be more inclined to describe her as intimidating. Her physical condition was part of it, but not all. There was also the way she stood, the natural authority with which she occupied a room or even a car. If she had something of the athlete about her, then she had something of the actress too. Poise. Self-awareness. As if she knew people would stare. As if she were never quite fully relaxed.

Then there were the details. Her black hair, lush as cat's fur, asking to be stroked. And the light blue eyes that contrasted with her dark skin.

She twisted back into her seat and threaded herself into her coat, arching her back as she zipped it. Turning up its collar, she took her black peaked cap from the glove compartment and put it on, tucking her hair up under it to protect it from the rain.

'And I thought the weather in England was bad,' she said, in perfect German, with a slight Munich accent, Danny observed – clearly practising, occupying a role, knowing in a couple of minutes it might become real.

She chambered a round into her SIG Sauer P226 pistol and stuck it down inside her jeans – which every operative had been trained not to do but did all the same – then opened the door and stepped out into the rain.

Danny watched her go, keeping the engine running. She'd left the passenger door open, in case she had to rush back. Danny approved, just as he did of her going out armed, even though there was no reason to expect any danger out here in the middle of nowhere in the middle of a cold, freezing night.

She was trained, the same as him. This wasn't her day job. This was her life. She'd filled him in a little on her past during their drive. How her father had been American-born, but had moved to Israel as a child with his parents, who'd then been killed in a bombing.

Ruth's father, she'd explained, had met her mother at university there, where he'd been lecturing in history. She'd been younger than him. 'A good ten years. Probably around the same age difference as you and me,' she'd added, in a tone that had suggested how outlandish such a gap was, maybe for Danny's benefit, or maybe as a joke. He hadn't yet decided which. 'And for a while,' she'd continued, 'Dad used to joke that he was in charge, before realizing it was the other way round. He ended up respecting her more than anyone he'd met in his entire life.'

Had that been for Danny's benefit too? To remind him that they were equals in all this? Or to warn him that he'd damn well better respect her?

If so, she needn't have bothered. Because he did respect her. Enough to be wary of her. Enough to think of her as a wolf that would lie down with a hunter and remain perfectly safe as long as that hunter provided the meat.

In other words, Ruth needed him as long as it suited her. That was how Danny saw it. To help her get her revenge. Which made her no different from him, he supposed. He needed her comms skills, in case Glinka and the Kid's trail went cold again.

This was just business. No matter how attractive he found her, no matter how much he'd liked just *being* with her on the journey, he needed to remember that.

He flipped the wipers on to see her better. She'd given up on the farmhouse's front door and was now peering through a small gap in the ground-floor window to its right, her gloved hands cupped round her face.

She turned and waved, beckoning him forward. He leaned across and pulled her door shut, then drove through the open gates and up the short driveway, winding down the window as she hurried back to the car.

'It's deserted,' she said. 'Not much furniture. A letterbox full of junk mail. I'll meet you round back.'

Danny drove to the side of the house, out of sight of the road. He stepped out into the driving rain and retrieved his bag from the back. Ruth was already inside by the time he got to the front door. Elegantly done, too. The lock looked intact. He couldn't see how she'd managed it. Must have used some kind of electronic pick, he guessed. Something smaller than the lock-buster or he'd have noticed it on her when she'd left. Little point in asking her about it: Mossad agents guarded their secrets with their lives.

It was as cold inside as out, but at least it was dry. Ruth was nowhere to be seen, as he slipped silently into the kitchen. He heard a creak, then saw her ascending the stairs leading up from the hallway, ignoring his presence as she continued her sweep of the house.

He trailed a gloved finger through the dust on the kitchen surface by the stove. It didn't look like anyone had been in here for months.

'Clear,' Ruth said, returning to his side.

Danny tried the tap. It was rusted and it took a good hard twist just to make it budge. It shuddered and groaned. A trickle of stinking water spattered out into the aluminium sink, then nothing. The supply must have been cut off, he supposed.

He tried the gas stove next. Nothing. He checked in the cupboard beneath and found an orange metal gas canister.

Crouching, he lifted it: it felt about half full. Flipping the switch on its top, he stood and tried the stove again. This time he heard the hiss of gas. Ruth held her lighter to the stove's central ring and a trembling blue flame appeared.

'Quite the domestic couple, aren't we?' she said, snapping the lighter shut.

As Danny watched her drawing the curtains over the only two windows in the room, muffling the drumming of the rain, he left the stove burning, and looked at the paint peeling on the ceiling and the pale rectangles on the wall where pictures had once hung.

He shivered, wondering if they'd be better off sleeping in the car as they had done in shifts on the way there. But part of him craved a night lying flat on his back. As Ruth had recently reminded him, he wasn't getting any younger. His whole body, but most of all his spine, ached and he knew he needed rest before what he would – *hopefully* – face the next day.

'The only useable furniture is a sofa and armchair in the living room,' Ruth informed him, as if reading his mind. 'Everything upstairs is either infested with mice or damp.'

That settled it. Danny pictured himself snug in his new sleeping-bag – they'd stopped at a camping shop on the way – his head on a cushion on the floor, drifting off into a deep sleep.

'I'll fetch the rest of our gear,' he said.

He came back dripping from the rain to find the kitchen empty, but the gas stove still on. He was glad about that. It didn't make the place look homely, but it was better than coming back to find it dark.

He opened two tins of soup from the bag of food they'd picked up at the last town they'd passed through. Putting the two cans on the stove to heat, he rigged battery-powered electronic trip wires across the three ground-floor external doors. Another advantage of travelling with Ruth: she had plenty of kit.

Setting the last of the wires, he saw Ruth watching him from the living room doorway. As their eyes met, she turned and disappeared, as silent as a ghost.

CHAPTER 52

SCOTLAND

With dark clouds gathering in the sky and the rain still lashing down in rods, Ray Kincade stepped into the welcome fug of the pub.

He was cold, as well as disheartened. He'd walked the entire village, checking out the cars for rental stickers, and hadn't found a single one. He'd had no luck at the post office either. A couple of Americans had been in to send postcards home over the last few weeks, the grey-haired manager had recalled, but both had been women. There'd been no one else. And certainly no one, American or otherwise, who'd matched Ray's description of the missing friend he'd hoped to find staying nearby.

He had also drawn a blank in the local holiday lettings offices. The only places they'd currently rented were to Europeans.

It had occurred to Ray that the PSS Killer might be capable of passing himself off as European, might even be multilingual, if Ray and Danny's theory that he was ex-intelligence or military was correct.

He scanned the long, burnished wooden bar, reading the beer labels displayed on the pump handles, as he took off his raincoat and hung it on the antlered stand by the door. He'd drunk his first beer ever with his father on the day he'd enlisted. It had been Pabst, or Grain Belt, or some such insipid muck. His tastes had evolved since then: he'd developed quite a love for US craft beers and European imports.

'I'll have a pint of Bass, please,' he said, as he reached the bar.

Only a couple of other guys in there, he saw. Both were half his age, the same as the barmaid. She had a pretty face, but not nearly as pretty as Ray's wife's. He watched the beer being poured. Crystal clear and dark, it refracted the dim lights above the bar like jewels.

'Thank you.' He sighed as he took his first sip. 'A thing of beauty.'

'Visiting?' asked the barmaid.

'That's right. A bit of travelling and a bit of looking up old friends.'

'And which one brings you here?' The barmaid leaned forward, elbows on the bar, framing her face in her hands.

'Both, as it happens,' Ray said. 'I arranged to meet an old buddy of mine here. But I lost the address of where he's staying. His phone number too.'

'An American?' she asked.

'Yeah. Name of' – he spoke loudly enough for the men further along the bar to hear – 'Chuck Linska. Ten years younger than me, but bald, and built like a brick shithouse, as I believe you folks are fond of saying round here.'

This last comment earned him a laugh from one of the guys drinking at the other end of the bar. He noticed there were three glasses lined up. A door creaked and the owner of the third, a sandy-haired fellow who couldn't have been much more than eighteen, sauntered unsteadily back from the john to his seat.

'Good to see a Yank drinking something that's not lager,' said the oldest of the three men, red-faced but smiling.

Ray grinned. 'I gave up imbibing that kinda redneck goat piss around about the same time I learned to shave,' he said.

A laugh from all three this time.

'Well, at least you got a sense of humour,' said the Johnny-come-lately, with a bit of a slur in his voice. 'Not like one of your countrymen whose car I had to fix down at the garage the other day.'

Ray's glass stopped halfway to his mouth. 'An American?'

'That's right.' The younger man turned to his companions. 'The one I was telling you about, lads,' he told his friend. 'He's staying at the old lighthouse out at the point. No such thing as a please or thank-you with him. Doesn't even bother to answer when you say goodbye or hello.'

'Might be your friend,' said the barmaid.

'Could be,' said Ray. 'He can be a little brusque with

folks he don't know.' He shot the young guy a smile, just to let him know he'd taken no offence. Last thing he needed was him clamming up now. 'He a big fella?' he asked the young man.

'That's right.'

'Bald?' Ray asked.

'As a coot.'

He felt his stomach turn. He put his pint on the bar. He made an effort to keep the excitement from his voice. 'How far's the point?' he said.

'Two miles north,' said the oldest of the three men.

'And he's staying in a lighthouse there?' Ray checked.

'That's right,' said the young guy. 'It isn't in use any more. It's owned by some heritage group now that rents it out. The National Trust, I think.'

Ray began to fasten his jacket.

'I wouldn't go there this time of night,' the young guy warned. 'Half the track leading up there collapsed in the frost last winter. Still not been repaired. That man staying up there, that's why he came down to the garage. Nearly tipped his hire car right over. Needed me to drive up there with the tow truck to pull him out of a ditch.'

'We've got rooms here,' said the barmaid. 'You can go out and see your friend in the morning. I could even get you some supper, if you like.'

He turned his collar up. 'Thanks, but no thanks,' he said. 'This friend of mine, you've no idea how long I've been looking forward to seeing him again.'

CHAPTER 53

GERMANY

Danny joined Ruth in the living room, where he found her using her phone, her face illuminated by its ghoulish green glow. She'd laid her torch on the mantelpiece and its wide beam illuminated a good half of the room.

He noticed her glancing at the two missing fingertips on his left hand. Too long a story to go into now, he thought. He remembered how she'd nursed him in her hotel room following the explosion in the Kid's apartment. She'd have seen his other scars too.

She'd have read about his connection with the Paper, Stone, Scissors Killer as well, he supposed, just the same as everyone else in the world. And yet – in spite of all the other questions she'd asked about what had happened on the day of her mother's murder in London – she'd not asked him about it. She'd respected his past.

'Any luck?' he said. He knew she'd be checking to see that the Kid hadn't moved.

'Nothing. No reception. It must be the storm.'

She slipped her phone into the back pocket of her jeans

and nodded towards the fireplace, where plenty of wood and kindling had been stacked.

'You want to risk it?' she said.

'We probably shouldn't, but . . .'

She was right: it was a risk. A neighbour might drive by. Even the owners of the property might return. They might call the cops. And then there'd be another problem to deal with, another reason to move on.

'But why don't we do it anyway?' he said.

She didn't answer. The same as him, she was probably freezing her ass off and they'd both sleep much better if they were warm.

He set about laying the fire. She didn't object. He left her to light it and went to fetch the soup.

Bright flames were already licking away the darkness by the time he returned. She'd pulled the worn sofa and armchair to face the hearth and was perched on the sofa's arm, warming her hands.

He gave her one of the two soup cans, which he'd wrapped with a strip of tea-towel so it wouldn't burn her hands. He passed her some crackers he'd bought when they'd stopped for supplies.

'Thanks.' She took a sip from the can and sighed. 'God, who'd have thought canned tomato soup could taste so fucking good?'

He sat on the sofa, feeling the weight of the day fall from his shoulders. He took a swig of soup, scalding himself a little, but not caring, just glad for the luxury of heat, both inside and out.

He watched as Ruth peeled off her socks. As she stretched out her toes, he found himself smiling without knowing why, and hid it behind his can.

Dipping crackers into their soup, they ate without speaking, listening instead to the crackle of twigs and sap in the hearth. Finally Ruth stood, slipping off her jacket and placing her can on the mantelpiece, then switched off her flashlight, so that only the fire now lit the room, casting flickering shadows on the wall.

As she closed her eyes and slowly pirouetted, warming herself against the flames, he found himself gazing at her again, too dazed with comfort to resist, letting his eyes run over the slender curves of her neck and shoulders, down past her hips to her legs.

When he looked up, he saw she was staring at him too. But this time he didn't look away, not just because he'd been caught staring but because he didn't want to.

'I guess this is the part where if we're ever going to sleep together, then we do,' she said.

Danny couldn't help but blush, not because he was taken aback – a part of him had suspected, had certainly hoped, that this might happen here tonight – but because a voice inside him, which he'd been trying to drown with more professional thoughts, had been willing him to say exactly the same thing.

He thought about lying, about telling Ruth he wasn't interested, and acting like this wasn't something he'd considered since he'd swum back into consciousness in her hotel room as she'd walked towards him from the shower.

But he knew she'd see right through him. If she'd had the confidence to raise the matter, it meant she wanted it, and that she'd already worked out that he did too.

He thought about asking her why. But a Shakespearean quote rose inside his mind: 'There's beggary in the love that can be reckoned.' It came from *Antony and Cleopatra*, which he hadn't read since school. The line had been Antony's riposte to the wily Cleopatra when she'd asked him how much he loved her. It was the same line Danny's father had used whenever his mother had asked him to quantify his feelings.

He was under no illusions now. What Ruth was asking him had nothing to do with love. But at the same time, did he really want to know whatever pros and cons she'd weighed up? Did he really want to know if what she'd just said was down to what she was: an intelligence operative, who'd studied him, as she would any other mark, for weaknesses and tells, and had now decided to use her sexuality in an attempt to gain the upper hand?

Or did it matter if, instead, it was because of who she was: a woman who was drawn to him by liking or desire – just as any two normal people might experience when they met?

None of that mattered. In fact, the less he knew about her motives, and the less they discussed it, the easier it would be for them both. Why? Because that way, afterwards, they could focus on what they'd come here to do: capture the Kid and whoever he was with. They could reset their relationship to that of comrades, giving them both a greater chance of survival in what was to come.

That way they could avoid even thinking about becoming what they could never be: involved.

'Well?' she asked. Her blue eyes sparkled in the firelight, like shards of bright daylight as seen through the cracks of a dark room's door.

'Come here,' he said.

'Just like that?'

'Why not?'

'No preambles? No discussions? No flirtation?' she asked.

He caught something in her eyes then, behind the air of insouciance and mischief she was trying to project. Something darker. Disappointment?

Whatever it was, it threw him. Had he misjudged her? Was she looking for something more? He couldn't tell. He'd had so little proper experience with women since Sally and Jonathan had died.

He fleetingly thought of the series of girls he'd picked up in that lost year in California when his life had fallen apart, but he could recall neither their names nor anything they'd said. He remembered the women who'd come later, the ones he'd cared for, who'd made him remember himself.

He remembered Alice De Luca the first morning he'd woken up beside her when, rather than silently dressing and ducking out into the dawn, he'd stayed with her all day.

Only now poor Alice was dead, shot in the face by Glinka, as she'd opened her front door after Danny had left Lexie with her, wrongly believing that the two of them would be safe.

He remembered Anna-Maria, too, and how he'd entertained the idea of making some kind of real life with her. Of even asking her to get a divorce. Of the two of them and Lexie somehow learning to be a family.

But that chance had been snuffed out, like a candle flame in a gale. Even if Danny cleared his name with the authorities, he'd still be hounded by the press. He'd never get to lead a normal life. What right did he have to ruin hers too?

Ruth's face darkened with shadow as she stood and shuffled out of her jeans. She undid the buttons of her shirt, slipped it off, then her bra, and let them fall to the floor. She stood with her back to the fire, a silhouette as perfect as any artist's statue. She beckoned him towards her with outstretched arms.

But he hesitated. His feet wouldn't move. Where Ruth now stood, he imagined Alice falling after she'd been shot.

Ruth walked towards him. She unbuttoned his shirt, pushing it back over his shoulders and peeling its sleeves from his arms. She stepped into him then, pressing her naked skin against his. He felt her tongue parting his lips.

But he thought of Sally's sweet perfume, and remembered her instead, leaning out of the back of the taxi to give him her number, the first day he'd met her and had chased her down the street in the pouring rain.

Ruth was unbuckling his belt now, placing kisses on his neck, her breath warm against his skin. As she slid her hands between his legs, he felt himself harden.

But in his mind, he still saw Sally, as if the two of them were stepping towards one another to do this for the first time.

Sally.

Ruth's kisses were becoming rougher, hungrier. Her hands reached up behind his neck, twisting his head, pressing her lips against his. A soft moan escaped her as her hips began to grind.

But Danny's vision of Sally's face would not quit. Instead it grew more vivid and morphed jarringly, so that he saw it on the day the Paper, Stone, Scissors Killer had come for them. Her beautiful features stared back, warped by the duct tape stretched across them.

'Ker-murgh . . .'

Danny remembered screaming through the duct tape after the killer had finished with Sally and little Jonathan: '*KIIILL MEEEEE . . .*'

And now, as he opened his eyes and Ruth's face materialized out of the shadows, he gazed down at the bare skin of her shoulders cast golden by the glow of the fire, and hopelessness filled him, the longing of a child whose home had been burned to the ground, its ashes scattered to the winds, unable to return.

Everyone he came into contact with, he tainted or spoiled. All he brought people was misery.

He tried pushing the jumble of memories down inside him, into that locked, chained steel box in his mind, where time after time he had tried burying the sound of Jonathan's last torn breath, the look of terror in Sally's eyes and the burning hope, right up to the end, that had screamed her belief that he could still somehow save them – and her refusal to believe that he might fail.

Ruth was kissing him harder now and he tried to respond. As her hips continued to gyrate against his, he felt his teeth glance off hers and tasted blood. But again he saw Sally. He saw her dead face.

Ruth's eyes caught his. He pictured her not here but in the Kid's apartment: her knife flashing past him; his boot connecting hard with her stomach as he drove her desperately away; the feel of his pistol pressed to her face, as he'd attempted to force her to talk.

Just take her, Danny told himself. Give in to it. Give in to her.

But Ruth's hips were no longer moving and the passion, the hunger had gone from her eyes. Instead her brow was furrowing. With what? Incomprehension? Pity? Danny felt a twist of fear inside him . . . of shame . . .

As she pulled back, he waited for her to say something, to reject him, to speak of the coldness, the failure, she'd surely just sensed.

But she didn't. Instead she closed her eyes again. And this time, when her lips pressed against his, they did so softly, gently, as if whatever she'd seen, she was now trying to soothe it, defeat it, to exorcize it and absolve him of his pain.

CHAPTER 54

SCOTLAND

Doubt racked Ray as his eyes strained through the darkness.

Should he have called the police? Should he not have come here alone? An apprehensive voice inside his mind answered, *Yes*, to both questions. Because, out here on the point, staring up through the trees at the lighthouse, the wind blowing and the tang of salt in the air, he felt as alone as he'd ever felt in his life.

What did he really know? He had a parking ticket and the word of a drunk, none-too-bright car mechanic that a bald foreigner was staying here. That was about it. Hardly the kind of evidence he could present to the police. Not without revealing who he was.

What if the man staying here wasn't the man who'd tried to kill him at the farmhouse? What if he really was just some bald American on vacation? What Ray needed was final proof that the PSS Killer was here. And for that he had to see him with his own eyes.

He scanned the lighthouse again with his binoculars.

The building was L-shaped, with a stub of horizontal living quarters tacked on to the base of the tower. He'd already scouted right round it. The living-quarters windows were too small for an adult to fit through and there was only one door, which he was facing now.

The curtains were drawn, but light glowed through them, indicating that someone was in. A hire car was parked outside, but Ray couldn't be sure it was the one he'd seen speeding away from the farmhouse, and he'd glimpsed no signs of life since he'd arrived more than an hour ago.

It was tempting, all right, to sneak up to the door and listen, or get closer to the windows in case there was a gap between any of the curtains through which he might look, but Ray wasn't making the same mistake as last time. No way was he going inside that property, or even near it.

He'd been lucky to survive his encounter with the PSS Killer at the farmhouse. Be patient, he told himself. Whoever was in there would have to come out some time, either tonight or tomorrow. And that was all Ray needed. A glimpse to confirm what he already believed to be true.

An hour passed, long enough for the cold wind to cut right through his clothing and for him to wish he was back in the pub, shooting the breeze with the locals, and taking up the barmaid on her offer of a warm meal and a bed. His rib ached, too, where he'd bound his chest. He'd kill right now for a warm bath.

Then – bang.

He jolted. Had he been sleeping? He hadn't even seen

the lighthouse door opening, but now he saw the tall figure of a man walking from it, leaning into the wind, towards the car.

Is it him? *Is it?* Ray strained to see with his naked eyes, but it was no good. He slowly raised the binoculars as the man reached the vehicle, adjusting the focal dials, wishing to hell these were night-vision, dammit.

His heart lurched.

The man's back came into focus as he opened the door and the car's interior light switched on, bathing his entire silhouette in an ethereal glow. He looked so close that a surge of adrenalin raced through Ray, as he remembered how close he'd come to death in that farmhouse.

But *was* it him? Whoever it was, he was wearing a cap and had his collar turned up. Ray couldn't even tell if he was bald.

Turn, you motherfucker, let me see your goddamn face . . .

And then, for a tantalizing second, the man started to turn, bringing with him a bag he'd just taken from the passenger seat. He started to turn, only right there – at the exact point where he was about to reveal his profile to Ray – he hesitated.

Almost as if he'd heard something. Almost – impossibly, Ray told himself – as if he'd somehow *sensed* that Ray was there.

Every muscle in Ray's body tightened then. Every part of his being seemed to crane forward, desperate to see what he could not yet.

And then, just at the moment he thought his chance would vanish, just when the fear of failure inside him spiked up into a shrieking peak, the man did turn.

He turned slowly, so slowly that Ray now saw every detail of his features emerging through the binoculars' lenses, like the pieces of a fractured mosaic gathering into a whole. He turned slowly until he was in perfect profile, completely clear for Ray to see.

It's him . . .

It was.

Whatever microscopic spores of doubt had blown through the otherwise certain landscape of Ray's mind now vanished. This was the same man he'd fought and wounded in that farmhouse, the same man who'd tortured and murdered Danny Shanklin's son and wife . . .

He waited, his heart in his throat, unable to breathe.

Go back. Go back inside.

Because, after wanting nothing more than to see him, Ray now wanted nothing more than for the PSS Killer to vanish again. Because the second he did, the instant he disappeared inside that lighthouse, Ray would be getting the hell out of there, back to his car, from which he would be calling the FBI.

But the PSS Killer did not do what he expected. He did not shut the car door and carry his bag back to the front door of the lighthouse.

Instead he turned. He turned to face Ray Kincade. He turned to face him – and he smiles.

What?

A shuffling of leaves.

The cracking of a twig.

Both noises shrieked in Ray's mind louder than the wind.

He turned, too late. He glimpsed the figure standing there. White. Bald. Powerfully built. Over six feet tall.

CHAPTER 55

GERMANY

'And you're sure no one else can listen in on this?' Danny said.

'Certain.'

Ruth was sitting beside him on the passenger seat of the four-by-four. She had her laptop open in front of her, plugged into a power socket in the dashboard. A programme not dissimilar to Skype, but without branding, filled the screen.

'OK,' Danny said, into the phone clamped to his ear. 'Go ahead and dial in.'

A retro ringing sound, reminding him of the analogue phones of his childhood, trilled from the laptop's speakers. Ruth hit a couple of keys, passing the laptop across to him as she did, angling its screen away from her face so she couldn't be seen by whoever she was dialling.

That person was Spartak. His face filled the screen now. He looked oddly younger than Danny remembered. Or maybe he looked younger than Danny felt. Christ, he wondered, what kind of toll would these last weeks have taken on him? The last time he'd looked in a mirror, he'd winced at the crazy, tired eyes that had stared back at him. At least Spartak had got himself some rest. He'd need it too, because Danny needed him again.

He cut off the disposable phone from which he'd contacted Spartak minutes before to instruct him on how to dial.

'You look like shit,' Spartak said jovially. 'What the hell have you been doing since I last saw you?'

'Just trying to stay alive.'

'And who's been helping you do that?'

'What do you mean?'

'Oh, come on, Danny! The first thing you asked me just now was how quick I could make it to Germany and then you told me to download this shit-hot cloaked comms system that I've never even heard of before. Now, as much as I love you, my American friend, I'm thinking either you're shit-hot fucking lucky to have got out of England without my assistance, or someone is helping you . . . and I'm also thinking that, whoever that person is, they have some pretty high clearance access to get hold of a communications application like this. So, you going to tell me their name?'

Danny glanced across at Ruth, who shook her head.

'Just someone,' Danny told him. 'Someone competent. And someone who wants to find these scumbags and make them pay every bit as much as I do.'

Spartak slowly nodded, accepting that this was as much as he was likely to hear. 'Very well,' he said. 'Well, the good news is that we are at least one step closer to finding out exactly who the Kid is working for.'

'Go on,' Danny said.

'I got my hands on a list of the guards who were stationed at the Soviet Biopreparet in 1990 when it was raided and the smallpox was stolen. And, based on how old you say Glinka is now, I've narrowed the list down even further. Better still, I have photographic records for each of the shortlisted individuals.' Spartak's head dipped as he studied his keyboard. 'And they are coming to you now.'

Seconds later, a file appeared in the comms app's inbox on Danny's laptop. He glanced across at Ruth and raised his eyebrows expectantly. She nodded. He returned his attention to the screen, clicked the mail package icon and watched its contents balloon into a window alongside the one still showing Spartak's face.

Thirty thumbnail images, each of uniformed young men in the prime of their lives, came into view.

'Take your time,' Spartak said. 'The intervening years will have changed this man's appearance.'

But Danny didn't need to take his time.

Glinka.

He saw him right away, staring out at him from the screen. Yes, his hair was longer, a little darker and slightly less receding. And, yes, his neck and shoulders seemed broader, less powerful, less honed. But there, staring at Danny, were the same unmistakable features. The same intensity in the eyes.

This was the man who had destroyed his life. Of that there was no doubt.

'Kirill Sergeyevich Dementyev,' he said, reading out the name beneath the thumbnail image, at the same time clicking on it so that it filled the left half of the screen, as though the man and Spartak were now standing side by side.

'You're positive?'

'Yes.'

'Good. Now wait. I will look this piece of shit up and see what else we can find.'

Danny watched Spartak typing into his keyboard, but his eyes were soon dragged back to Glinka – Kirill Sergeyevich Dementyev. Now that they had a real name, he could begin to speculate. Who was he? What were his real motives in all this? Were there people who knew him as someone else entirely? Did he have family? A home?

Whatever he had – whatever he cared for most – Danny would take it, he vowed.

'Here we go,' said Spartak. 'Following a demotion due to insubordination and dereliction of duty, Dementyev deserted, only to surface again two years later, arrested for a bank robbery in Murmansk. Seems he got unlucky. An armed plain-clothes officer was in the bank at the time and got the drop on him. But then, before being handed over to the military by the police—'

'Wait,' Danny said. 'At the time of the robbery, was anyone else arrested?'

More typing at Spartak's end. He wondered what

Russian governmental database Spartak was currently – and, no doubt, illegally – accessing, and which of his contacts had got him in. He knew better than to ask.

'Just one,' Spartak said, a slow smile spreading across his face, 'and, from what you've told me about this particular elfin blonde *shlyukha* already, I'm guessing you might recognize her too.'

Another rattle of Spartak's keyboard. Another file reached Danny's screen. Another face that was impossible to mistake.

Glinka's woman.

The blonde.

'Yes,' Danny said. 'That's her.'

'Name of Vera Yaroslavovna Shepkin,' Spartak said. 'She was arrested alongside him in the bank. Seems like the weapons they took with them were replicas. A mistake they didn't make the next time.'

'What next time?' Danny's heart was racing now. Not one name, but two. The depressed part of him that had expected the Kid to have made as thorough a job of blitzing his associates' past as he had done of his own was exulting now. Because now they'd discovered their names, the trail might lead them to so much more.

'Two more robberies occurred in nearby cities in the next two months. Both were blamed on Dementyev on account of certain similarities as to how they accessed the building – ramming vehicles right through the front windows. No replica weapons this time. Six dead civilians and two dead armed guards were left behind.'

'But why was Dementyev out and able to do this? How come he never did time?'

'Because someone broke him out from the police station the same night he was arrested for the first robbery.'

'Who?'

'That I don't know. Just that it was someone incredibly violent and incredibly smart. Three police left dead. No one saw a thing. All the cameras had been disabled.'

Danny toggled the images on his screen, staring back into Dementyev's cold eyes. Murderous eyes. Intelligent eyes. A man with a plan for everything. Even for when plans went wrong. 'Forget what they did next,' he said. 'What about what they did before?'

'What do you mean?' said Spartak.

'Where did they come from? Who were they before they chose this life?'

'You mean family?' said Spartak.

'Someone must know who they are.'

As had happened with the Kid's sister, Danny knew that finding out who these two were still in contact with from their past might lead to finding out where they were now.

Spartak focused on his screen. The sound of typing took over for a minute.

'If we're planning to move in on the Kid,' Ruth said softly, so softly that Spartak didn't even look up from his work, 'we cannot do it alone. We need *him*.'

Glancing across at her, Danny saw she was staring at Spartak.

Her meaning was obvious. Two of them might be enough to track the Kid down. But to stand a chance of capturing him? They'd need the Russian too.

'I can find nothing,' Spartak said. 'At least, not on this police database. No mention of any relatives being sought in connection with these crimes. But that does not mean they don't exist. I know people, operatives, who can help. Only, Danny, you must realize this: it will take time, my friend.'

Danny thought of his daughter alone in the UK. He thought of those who had died because of Dementyev, Shepkin and the Kid. He already knew the last location the Kid had called from and how he might still be there.

'We're not waiting,' he said. 'We're doing this now.'

'But, Danny—'

'No,' Danny said. 'Ruth here is going to tell you the GPS coordinates of where the Kid last was.' It didn't matter that Spartak knew her name. He'd be meeting her soon enough. He stared hard into Spartak's alarmed eyes. 'And you're to meet us there this evening. Just you. But come armed and ready to finish this thing for good.'

CHAPTER 56

SCOTLAND

Opening his eyes – as he tried to shriek in pain, only to find that his mouth had been taped shut – the first thing Ray Kincade saw was his own reflection in the flickering candlelight. A full-length mirror had been positioned on the wall five feet in front of him. Horrified, he saw he'd been tied with black rope to a wooden chair and was naked and bleeding from his chest and thighs, where someone had slashed him repeatedly with a blade.

Someone . . .

He knew who . . . and strained now to turn his neck to look. But he felt his throat tighten and in the reflection saw a rope had been tightly tied round that too.

Was he here, the creature who'd done this to him? Was he watching him right now? *How the hell long have I been unconscious? Was I knocked out? Tasered? Drugged?*

All Ray knew with absolute certainty was that he was never leaving this place. This was where he would die.

'We don't yet know why you are here, but we will find

out,' a man's voice said, from deep in the shadows to Ray's right – calmly, almost in a whisper.

We? At first the word made no sense to Ray, but then he remembered being outside the lighthouse, spying on the PSS Killer, who'd looked up and had stared back at him from beside the car. Then he remembered the snapping of the twig behind him, and how he'd turned to see another person standing there – a second white, bald, powerfully built man, over six feet tall – who, impossibly, had looked exactly like the PSS Killer.

'You've clearly been paid to find us, Mr Kincade.' A second voice, sounding exactly like the first, this time coming from the depth of the dark shadows to Ray's left.

Mr Kincade. Oh, Christ. They must have taken his wallet from the glove compartment in the car. Along with his computer and phone. They'd probably moved the car by now to somewhere it couldn't be seen, so no one would ask questions about why it had been left there abandoned.

The voice on the right: 'We think we know who sent you.'

Movement: Ray detected it in his peripheral vision, both to his left and to his right.

The voice to Ray's left: 'You're going to help us find them.'

Help *us* . . .

Ray's mind raced. Could it be possible that there were two of them? He didn't want to look. He didn't want his

worst fears confirmed. He wished he was unconscious.
A part of him wished he was already dead.

Two men simultaneously stepped in towards him, one
from the left and one from the right. The candlelight
illuminated their pale skin, making them look like they
were made of wax.

They watched Ray as his eyes flickered disbelievingly
between them. They were identical in every way, right
down to their plastic disposable shoes and clothing. And
even though their faces were half concealed by surgical
masks, he could see enough to know that their faces were
identical too.

But if these men – these brothers, these twins, whatever
the hell they were – derived any modicum of pleasure from
revealing their existence to him, it did not show.

They did not even blink. Their eyes betrayed no glimmer
of amusement or triumph. All Ray registered in their flat,
merciless expressions was the cold fact of his capture. He
was theirs now. To do with as they wished.

'Danny,' the twin on the left said.

'Shanklin,' said the twin on the right.

Ray saw the blood-soaked surgical scissors then. They
were gripped in the fist of the twin on the right. Was that
the instrument that had been used to slash his chest and
thighs?

'You are going to tell us everything you know about
him,' said the twin on the left.

Ray's eyes flicked towards him. Gripped in his gloved
hands were a rolled-up magazine and a fist-sized rock.

The brother on the right told Ray, 'Where he is . . .'

Ray tried to shout. To swear to them that he didn't know. But all that came out was a muffled scream.

A sudden movement to his left. A fresh explosion of pain. Ray roared in agony. Something – the rock the twin on his left had been holding? – had hit him so hard in the side of the head that he could barely believe he was still conscious. He could feel blood running down the side of his scalp, trickling over his neck. In the mirror, through his blurred vision, he saw it dripping onto the floor. His hearing felt all wrong. His skull was on fire. Had this monster just fractured it?

Ray tried with all his might to stand, to tear himself free of the chair, to run. But he couldn't move an inch, the ropes had been tied so tightly. The chair didn't move either. It stayed exactly where it was. He remembered the little vampire tooth-marks in the floor of the dead family's farmhouse. This chair he was tied to now had been nail-gunned to the floor.

'In a moment, you're going to tell us whether you've already informed Shanklin that you've tracked us here,' said the twin on the left.

'Then,' said the twin on the right, 'you're going to tell us how to contact him.'

Ray saw that the twin on his right, as well as holding the scissors, had Ray's phone.

'And after that, you're going to tell us how we can find her . . .'

Her?

The way he said it . . . the way he looked . . . It was the first emotion either of the twins had shown.

'*Her*,' repeated the twin on the right.

'Lexie,' explained the twin on the left.

Oh, sweet Jesus, no, thought Ray. Not Lexie. Not Danny's little girl.

'You see, she's ours,' said the twin on the left, stepping in close to Ray now and gently stroking his fingers along the curve of Ray's ear.

'She needs to witness us,' said his brother. 'To understand. She must give us what is rightly ours.' He crouched beside Ray and looked steadily into his eyes, then rammed the scissor blades deep into the largest of the weeping gashes on Ray's thighs.

Tears ran down Ray's cheeks as, again, he tried to scream.

'Because, just like you,' hissed the twin on the left into Ray's ear, as his brother continued to twist the scissor blades, 'Lexie Shanklin needs to *see*.'

CHAPTER 57

GERMANY

Danny Shanklin, Spartak Sidarov and Ruth Silver walked in a straight line at twenty-yard intervals through the woods. Each was heavily armed and wearing camouflage fatigues.

'Smoke,' Spartak said, his voice crackling through Danny's earpiece. 'Approximately one kilometre ahead.'

Danny slowed his pace. Ahead the flat ground gave way to a gentle downhill slope. Through the trees in the distance, he now saw a thin column of grey smoke rising into the pale blue sky and, a few yards further on, the tops of the buildings down in the base of the valley. A farm, it looked like. Several barns and a main house made of stone.

'Watch out for trips,' Danny muttered into his mike.

His eyes were already aching, working overtime, searching for IEDs, as they had been since he and the others had left the vehicles a couple of kilometres back, in the patch of woodland where they'd rendezvoused.

The woods here, he saw, ran right the way down the slope of the valley to the farm. Meaning it might be

possible to get close without anyone noticing them. Still
no sign of any sentries. Which could be down to the fact
that it was only just gone dawn. Whoever was in that
building might still be asleep.

He flicked the safety off his AK-9, imagining both
Spartak and Ruth doing the same. Spartak had supplied
them with the weapons. Danny had smiled as his old
comrade and friend had watched Ruth check hers
thoroughly, before deeming it fit for purpose. Spartak
hadn't needed to say anything. The admiring look he'd
shot Danny had been enough: *one hell of a woman*, it had
said.

'All clear,' Ruth's voice murmured now.

'I see no one either,' Spartak agreed.

'Then let's close in,' Danny said, setting off down the
slope, faster now, his eyes still scouring the ground before
him, searching for traps.

They'd checked the GPS signal before they'd set off
from the cars. It was still strong. It still hadn't moved.
Even if the Kid and the others weren't there, the comms
equipment belonging to the Kid, which was sending out
the signal, still was.

Three hundred yards, two hundred . . .

'I still see no movement,' Spartak said.

'Nothing,' Danny agreed.

'Wait.'

Danny took one more pace, then froze. It was Ruth
who had spoken last.

'I see someone, more than one . . .' she said.

'Where?'

'Directly in front of my position . . .' She was on their right flank. 'To the right of the main farmhouse. I see three people. All are seated. None appears to be armed.'

'Spartak?' Danny said.

'I still see no one.'

'Hold your position, Ruth,' Danny ordered. 'Spartak: on me.'

Danny was in the centre of their line. He zigzagging swiftly through the trees, with Spartak in silent pursuit. They passed Ruth's position without speaking and continued another hundred yards. 'Cover us, Ruth,' Danny said. 'We're moving in.'

All three AK-9s were fitted with silencers. If these people were sentries or obvious combatants working for Dementyev, Shepkin and the Kid, then Danny and Spartak would be able to neutralize them fast, and would then be in a position to recce the main buildings up close.

But – and Danny's professionalism slipped, his breathing stuttered, his heart leaped to his throat – the three faces he saw as he moved in on the location pinpointed by Ruth did not belong to anyone working for either Dementyev, Shepkin or the Kid. Because the three people sitting at the rough wooden table in the small cobbled farmyard to the right of the farmhouse *were* Dementyev, Shepkin and the Kid.

Sitting ducks.

Inevitably, that was the phrase that rose in his mind

as he stared in disbelief at the scene unfolding in even greater clarity as he continued to close in.

His mind could hardly grasp the fact that they were finally there, quite literally in his sights. Any second now, with three squeezes of the AK-9's trigger, they'd be dead. He could feel his forefinger tightening, as if it had a will of its own, as if all the hatred he felt for these three people were coursing down his arm into his fingertip, desperate to be unleashed.

But no. He needed them alive. And something else . . . This felt wrong. Where were the sentries? Why wasn't any of the three armed? How, after all the planning they'd done and the precautions they'd taken until this point, could they have left themselves so exposed?

Twenty yards. Danny was still in the cover of the trees and the undergrowth. They hadn't yet seen him. They were deep in conversation. None of them had even looked up.

The farmyard was lower than the ground he was approaching from. It was walled and a short flight of stone steps led down into it. His eyes scanned the surrounding area and the overlooking windows. But there was nothing anywhere to indicate that he was walking into a trap.

'Let's do it,' he said into his mike.

He stepped out into the open, half expecting someone to open fire on him, unable to believe he really had got the drop on them like this.

A crackle of dirt beneath his feet. *Now* they looked up. All three. They each stared into his eyes.

But it was too late, Danny thought triumphantly. He

was too close. Even if they had handguns tucked into their belts, or heavier hardware hidden under that table, his AK-9 would rip them in half before they'd get a single shot off.

Looked like they knew it too. None of them moved. In his peripheral vision, he saw Spartak emerge into the open beside him and march towards the steps. Danny moved steadily forwards too, keeping his distance from his friend. He stopped at the edge of the high ground, so that he was staring down into the courtyard and right into the Kid's eyes.

'I bet you thought you'd never see me again,' Danny said. He was staring only at the Kid, but his words were meant for Dementyev and Shepkin too.

But the Kid's face showed neither fear nor surprise.

'Quite the opposite, actually, bruv,' he said. 'You see, you're late. We've been waiting for you here for over an hour.'

CHAPTER 58

Thud. Thud.

Danny turned in horror to watch Spartak, who was positioned at the top of a small flight of stone steps, lurch forward as if he'd been punched hard twice in the back. He swayed for a moment, teetering on the edge of the top step, as though he might fall. But instead he rocked back on his heels, and seemed to regain his balance.

Another thud. And this time Danny saw blood burst from the side of Spartak's neck. The big man slowly tipped then, like a forest tree being felled. He didn't reach out his hands to protect himself. Instead his face broke his fall with a sickening slap. His body slithered down the steps head first into a patch of overgrown weedy ground in the yard below. He didn't make a sound. He didn't move.

'Lower your weapon,' a voice Danny recognized only too well said behind him.

Ruth . . .

He felt a burning sensation in his gut. Something much worse than anger. It was the same thing he'd felt just a moment ago, when his eyes had locked on the Kid. He'd been betrayed again. This time by her.

'Do it now,' Ruth said, still behind him, 'or I'll execute you too.'

He could barely believe what had just happened. She'd just killed Spartak. She'd shot him from behind in cold blood.

His eyes fixed on the Kid. He wasn't smiling. Not yet. But he would, Danny knew, the second he lowered his AK-9. *Just kill him*, a voice in Danny's head said. *You're as good as dead anyway. Pull the fucking trigger. Let his death be the last thing you see.*

But a more powerful memory filled his mind. Of Lexie. If he killed the Kid now, Ruth would take him out. But if he didn't, there might still be . . . He might still find a way to do what he had always done: survive.

'OK.' His voice was trembling. From the adrenalin. From the rising fury inside him.

He slowly crouched and did as he was told. He put his weapon down.

The Kid's smile, the one he'd been expecting, was unleashed. A grin of amusement, of triumph, the expression of an expert player of games, who had planned everything perfectly and had now won.

He slowly ran his tongue across his lower lip, as though tasting the moment.

'You didn't really think I'd be dumb enough to let you track me across Europe using a GPS code, did you?' he asked.

Danny thought back to Ruth's hotel room . . . to how she'd nursed him back to health . . . to how she'd told him about stealing the Kid's router from his apartment before the explosion . . . to that program he'd seen running on her computer that she'd said had enabled her to track the Kid's location across the globe . . . All lies. She'd been working for the Kid the whole time.

'Or rather,' the Kid said, 'you must have believed it. Because why else would you be here?'

Danny said nothing. He glanced at Spartak, his corpse mostly hidden by the weeds. His friend. A man he had thought was practically invincible. He still couldn't believe he was gone.

'Kind of persuasive, isn't she?' said the Kid, a lascivious twinkle in his eyes.

Die, Danny thought. *I pray I get to watch you die.*

But even as he thought it, he could feel this hope fading.

'Bring him to the barn,' the Kid said, looking past Danny to where Ruth was standing behind him. 'And you two,' he added, looking down at Dementyev and Shepkin as he got up, 'hurry our friends inside along. I want everyone gone from here in the next half-hour.'

No, Danny thought. The Kid hadn't just *said* this to Dementyev and Shepkin, he'd *ordered* it. They worked for him, not the other way round. Another error Danny had made. The Kid wasn't just the brains, he was the boss.

He shot Danny another half-smile now, almost as if reading his thoughts, then turned his back on him. He walked across the courtyard and into the farmhouse, whistling as he did so. It was a tune Danny was meant to recognize and did – that old Burl Ives number, 'Ugly Bug Ball'. Another drop of poison. Another kick in the guts. Because that was the tune the Kid's niece, Beyoncé, had been singing when he had called at their house. The Kid hadn't been alienated from his sister at all, he now understood. She must have phoned him the second Danny had left and told him where he would be heading next.

Allowing Ruth to meet him at the Kid's apartment. And allowing her then to win his trust.

'You heard,' she said, behind Danny now. 'Move.'

He glanced over his shoulder at her. She didn't try to avoid his eyes. But something about her face was different. Any beauty he'd ever seen in her was now gone. She looked through him, like he wasn't even there.

'Do it now,' she said.

He thought back to the night they'd spent by the fire. He remembered holding her. He remembered their first kiss. But all of it had meant nothing.

'Down the steps,' she told him.

He forced himself to look away, to stop thinking about her. He had to see her as she saw him. She was nothing to him now, except an enemy.

He did as she'd commanded. He walked towards the steps, but stopped when he reached the top. Spartak's body still lay in a heap at the bottom.

'Down,' Ruth said.

His mind was racing. One on one, he knew he could take her. But Dementyev and Shepkin were still watching them. And both, Danny now saw, were armed. Dementyev was wearing a shoulder holster, which was visible beneath his open denim jacket, and the blonde, Shepkin, had a pistol butt protruding from the waist of her jeans.

Danny walked down the steps. He had to step over his old friend's body. He'd seen more bodies than he cared to remember, many of them people he'd been close to, over the years. But the sight of Spartak left a part of him feeling dead too. And he knew it already. They wouldn't even bury him. They'd just leave him there to rot.

Dementyev – the man he had known as Glinka, the man who'd shot so many of those civilians in London – smiled now as Danny walked towards him. He and the blonde gripped their pistols in their hands.

The blonde stepped in beside Danny and twisted him smartly round so that he was facing Ruth again. This time she did look at him, gazing into his eyes unashamedly, clearly trying to read him, an amused smile playing across her lips.

The blonde frisked him and stripped him of his handgun and ammo clips, then took his rucksack, along with his comms. She tossed the rucksack to Dementyev, who looked through it, before dropping it on the ground.

'I'm going to enjoy watching you learn how you will die,' he told Danny.

The blonde said nothing. She just spat hard into Danny's face. She looked like she wanted more than anything for him to react. So she can kill you, he thought. So she can take you down herself.

He felt her saliva trickling down his cheek.

'Into the barn,' Ruth said.

Up ahead a black-haired, powerfully built man opened the barn door and stepped outside, a submachine gun in his fists. No silencer. No need out here, Danny realized. If they were going to execute him by shooting him, no one would hear.

Watching you learn how you will die . . .

Dementyev's words echoed through Danny's mind. It was only then that he was struck by the strangeness of what he had said. He remembered when he'd first met Dementyev in the Ritz Hotel before the massacre: he had gone there thinking he was going to be offered a hostage retrieval job. Dementyev's English had been flawless.

It was a promise of something hideous to come. Danny would learn something terrible, and soon.

CHAPTER 59

They were injecting people. Civilians. As Ruth and the black-haired guard marched Danny across the cavernous interior of the barn towards a concrete bay set into its side, he saw that twenty or more men and women in civilian clothing were gathered there. Some were sitting on the floor, or packing bags. Others queued for their turn in a chair, where a woman was methodically loading syringes, then injecting their contents into these people.

'Into the pen,' Ruth said.

The concrete bay. It was a slaughter pen, Danny now saw, as he stepped through its waist-high metal gate. There were drainage holes in the floor and a tap with a hose fixed to the washable concrete wall. This was where whoever owned the farm would normally bring livestock for slaughter.

'Shackle him,' Ruth told the guard.

She covered Danny with her AK-9 while the guard did as instructed. He used metal handcuffs, looping their chain around one of the bars on the metal gate. Then he stepped back, leaned against the opposite wall of the pen and lit a cigarette,

'Why didn't you just kill me,' Danny said to Ruth, 'when you first had the chance?'

'You mean back in London?'

Her eyes twinkled. She might think nothing of him, he realized, but she still clearly thought enough of herself and how she'd tricked him to be happy to gloat.

'Yes,' he said, 'after the explosion in the flat. When I was unconscious. Why didn't you just finish me off then?'

'Because we needed to know what you knew,' she said. 'Because we realized when you broke into the testing facility at Pripyat and slaughtered the team there that you could not have been acting alone. And we couldn't afford to leave any loose ends or risk someone else coming after us. So we needed to find you. And that was when Adam's sister called.'

Adam . . . the Kid . . . Again Danny remembered the look in Beyoncé's mother's eyes as he'd handed her the envelope containing five thousand pounds. She must have known even then that she was going to phone the Kid the second Danny had left. He thought he'd been so clever. But, as with Ruth, he'd been a fool.

'And so you staked out the apartment in London,' he said.

'And when you showed, all I needed to do was to win your confidence.'

'But we both nearly died,' Danny said. 'He – Adam – the

Kid – your boss, he tried to blow us both up, remember?
We only just made it out of that apartment block alive.'

'Oh, Danny,' Ruth smiled, 'you still don't get it, do you?'

'Get *what*?'

'There was never any danger. The injury to your head?
That was me. I knocked you out.'

'But the explosion was in the papers . . .'

'Yes, because after I'd knocked you out, got you into my
car and sedated you, I went back and rigged the apartment
to blow. So that you wouldn't suspect . . .'

'And then?'

'I kept you drugged and interrogated you for two
days to find out everything you'd been up to. All about
Spartak Sidarov. That was when we decided we needed to
neutralize him too.'

Danny remembered the video conversation he'd had
with Spartak on the laptop when he'd identified Glinka
and the blonde as Dementyev and Shepkin. It was Ruth
who'd said they needed back-up. It was Ruth who'd
insisted he bring Spartak here today.

'So that's it?' he said, hating her afresh, remembering
how she'd killed his friend. 'Everything about you is a lie?'

'That's a melodramatic way of putting it, Danny, but,
yes, it's also probably true.'

'Even your name.'

Another half-smile. An apologetic shrug.

'And your mother wasn't Anya Silver, was she?' he
guessed. 'She wasn't one of the victims of the massacre
outside the Ritz.'

'I'm afraid not, Danny. Not even a distant relative. But enough of the small-talk, eh?' she said. 'It's high time we got this show on the road.'

CHAPTER 60

Ruth shouted a name Danny didn't recognize, and the woman injecting the civilians nodded and gathered up some equipment. She left the person she was with and walked over to the slaughter pen.

'What the hell's going on?' Danny said, as the woman – grey-haired and in her early sixties, with eyes that wouldn't meet his – loaded a fresh syringe.

But even as he asked, he saw Dementyev and the blonde walking towards him, quickly, as if they knew something wonderful was about to happen and wouldn't miss it for the world. And Dementyev's words came back to haunt Danny.

I'm going to enjoy watching you learn how you will die . . .

The smallpox.

Sweet Jesus, they were going to inject him with the hybrid smallpox.

'Hold him,' Ruth said.

The guard grabbed Danny. He pressed his whole weight down on him, pinning him against the concrete wall and the metal bars that fixed the gate to the wall. Danny bucked. He fought. But it was useless. He couldn't free his hands from where they'd been shackled.

The grey-haired woman came through the gate into the pen. Danny tried to twist out from under the heavy guard, but all he got for his efforts was a punch in the back of his head. He rammed his elbow back into the guard's gut. This time the man reared back before throwing his full weight up against him, slamming Danny's head against the gate bars and the concrete wall so hard that Danny heard something crack and thought he was about to lose consciousness.

He felt someone taking his jacket sleeve and rolling it up. With the last of his strength, he twisted his neck round – only to see the grey-haired woman gritting her teeth with determination.

He cried out, not from pain, but from the realization of what was happening, as she slid the needle into his arm. Dementyev and the blonde leaned over the gate, clearly enjoying the show.

'I can see from your eyes,' Dementyev said, 'you've already guessed what this is. And, of course, you had the privilege of seeing for yourself how effective it is when you visited our facility in Ukraine.'

'Go to hell,' Danny said.

But Dementyev just laughed. 'Oh, no, my friend, that is where you will be going. And very, very soon.'

The grey-haired woman stood up, her empty syringe's needle now dripping red with Danny's blood. The blonde blew Danny a kiss. Then she and Dementyev turned and walked away.

The guard let go of Danny and followed the grey-haired woman out of the pen.

Only Ruth remained. She gazed down at her prisoner with neither hatred nor pity. She stared at him with a mixture of boredom and cold resignation, as a farmer might who had brought an animal there to die.

'Those others . . .' Danny said. Through the bars of the slaughter-pen gate, he could see the grey-haired woman injecting another civilian, who just sat there unguarded, as if receiving nothing more than a flu jab.

It was the Kid's voice that answered: 'What about them?' He stepped in beside Ruth and slipped his arm around her waist, watching Danny carefully, again no doubt hoping for a reaction.

'Why are they letting you do this to them?' Danny said. *Why aren't they fighting?* The men and women, all young and of varying ethnicities, weren't resisting what was going on. *Why aren't they panicking or trying to escape?*

'Because they have paid for the privilege,' said the Kid.

'The *privilege?*' Danny thought he must have misheard.

'Of becoming weaponized.'

'Weaponized?'

'Yes,' the Kid said. 'What better way to serve their masters, their beliefs, and state their case to the West, than to become carriers . . . distributors?'

My God, Danny thought. These people were the clients. They were the terrorists who'd bought the hybrid smallpox. And this was how they were going to use it. They were going to spread the plague themselves.

'Once they leave here, they'll split up and travel to different countries,' explained the Kid. 'Doing everything in their power to share.'

'You're out of your mind,' said Danny.

'No, Danny. I'm just a businessman,' said the Kid. 'I'm just doing what I can to get by.'

'Do you have any idea how many people are going to die if you go through with this?'

'Every idea,' said the Kid. 'That's one of the reasons I was able to charge so much.'

'And what about you?' Danny said, turning on Ruth, still not quite able to accept that she was just as crazy and immoral as the Kid.

But all she did was slip her arm around the Kid's waist, to signal to Danny that they were one.

'You do know you could catch it too?' Danny said, desperate now to say something, anything, that might help to change their minds.

'Not if we've also made sure to have an antidote synthesized,' the Kid said. 'Which we have.'

Danny's blood ran cold. All the answers. Always. This was who the Kid had been, forever one step ahead of Danny, forever destroying other people's lives, at absolutely no expense to his own.

The grey-haired woman called out and waved across. She was already packing up her workstation, Danny saw. Ruth checked her watch.

'It's time we left,' she told the Kid. She turned to Danny. 'Have a nice life.' She grimaced. 'Or death. Whatever.'

She turned and walked away.

'I would shake your hand, bruv,' said the Kid, 'but . . . hygiene, you know? So instead I'll just say goodbye. And I really do mean it this time. We will never speak or see each other again.'

Danny didn't answer. The Kid gave a disappointed little shrug, then he smiled slowly, knowing it would be the last glimpse of his face Danny ever got. Then he turned and walked away with Ruth.

Danny watched them go. The black-haired guard followed. Then, one by one, the civilians left also, taking their bags with them. Until only Danny remained.

CHAPTER 61

Danny looked down at the cuffs. Stainless steel. Tight around his wrists. No way was he going to be able to slip or snap them. He looked desperately around for something to pick the lock. But the slaughter pen was spotless. His heart filled with despair.

He stared at the needle mark on his arm. The smallpox would already be working its way through his system. He was screwed. He would die. Even if by some miracle someone found and freed him, he would still die and their reward would be that they would end up infected too. He pictured Commandant Valentin Constanz Sabirzhan. He'd give anything not to go down like that, to go down fighting instead. But it was too late now. Way too late.

Hideously, he pictured Lexie, too. What if one of these people was booked onto a flight to the UK? What if Lexie got infected? It would be his fault. He'd been fooled by the Kid. He'd been fooled by Ruth. If something happened to Lexie, he'd have no one to blame but himself.

Danny slumped. He felt as if all the energy had been sucked from him. But he'd forgotten he'd been shackled to the gates, and as he slid to the floor now, he jarred his wrists painfully.

And that was when he heard it – a cracking sound, the *same* sound he'd heard when the black-haired guard had slammed his head against the bars and the wall. At the time, Danny had thought it had been his own bones making that noise, but he knew now that he had been wrong.

And his heart began to race. He sat bolt upright. He looked at the metal gate and saw where the noise had come from.

The gate's wall bar to which he'd been shackled had been fixed firmly to the concrete wall when it had been built. But Danny saw that it wasn't any more. In fact, it was loose, which it hadn't been when he'd first been shackled to it and had checked. It must have come loose when that psycho of a guard had decided to slam all his weight against Danny, damaging not just him but the gate.

Danny worked feverishly at it now, twisting the bar back and forth, first a millimetre, then two, then an inch, until – his heart leaped – it gave, twisting away from the wall. Only two inches, but enough, surely. Yes, he discovered. Enough for him to slip the chain of the cuffs through the gap.

Outside he heard a diesel engine roar into life.

He was already up and running straight across the barn to the door through which he'd come. He edged it open and looked outside, but could see no one. He opened it wider, but still the coast looked clear.

Hearing a vehicle drive away – a vehicle he was already too late to stop – Danny made a run for it. He'd seen that his rucksack was still where they'd stripped it from his back and dumped it by the table. He grabbed it and sprinted back into the relative safety of the deserted barn, where he hurriedly rifled through his belongings, cursing himself for not having a second handgun inside.

But at least he had a working mobile phone, he remembered. He had to contact Lexie. He had no way of knowing how many armed guards were still around this compound, or whether he had any chance of getting out alive. And even if he got away, where would he go? He was infected, as dangerous as the terrorists. He had no way of knowing how long the hybrid he'd been poisoned with would take to kick in.

He had to tell Lexie to find a way anonymously to warn the authorities. And to tell her to go somewhere even more remote than where she was now. He had to persuade her to stockpile food and water and get clear of the pandemic that was about to be unleashed.

He called the numbers for the disposable phones he'd left with her. He tried one, another, then the last. But she didn't answer any of them.

Think, he told himself, fear running through him, not for himself, but for her. If she wasn't answering, he needed to tell someone to find her, to protect her, to make certain that she came through alive.

He would have called Spartak. But Spartak was dead. So who else was there? Who else could he trust?

Ray Kincade. Yes. He was in the UK. He could reach Lexie within hours.

Danny rang his number. 'Pick up . . . Pick up!'

But the phone went through to voicemail.

'Ray,' he said. 'It's me, Danny Shanklin. There's something I need you to do. It's my daughter, Lexie. I need you to go to her now and get her somewhere safe. I'm going to give you the address and then I'm going to tell you why . . .'

Just as he hung up, he heard another engine starting outside around the back of the barn. He ducked out into the courtyard again. He didn't remember Ruth, Dementyev, Shepkin or the Kid searching Spartak's body for weapons. He might still have his AK-9 on him. With that, maybe Danny could stop these people leaving here. He had to try.

He made a break for the steps, but slowed as he approached the overgrown patch of weeds where Spartak had fallen. He stopped. Because Spartak's body was gone. And so were his weapons. They must have taken the weapons with them, Danny guessed. But could they really have taken the huge Ukrainian's body too?

A rattle of automatic gunfire. Then another. Two more short bursts. The noise was coming from the other side of the barn.

CHAPTER 62

Seconds later, Danny peered around the edge of the barn to witness something impossible. Spartak Sidarov was crouched behind a stack of firewood, his AK-9 up and firing.

Directly in front of him, a dirt track stretched into the distance. On the horizon, Danny could make out the shape of a white minibus, no doubt full of the terrorists who'd just allowed themselves to be infected with the hybrid disease.

Closer, a black Jeep had slewed to a halt at an angle with its back tyres shot out. Its passenger door was open and the unmistakable figure of the blonde was lying motionless on her back on the ground.

Someone – or possibly more than one person – was hidden from view on the other side of the Jeep and was returning fire at Spartak in short, sharp, controlled bursts. Danny remembered Dementyev on the balcony of the Ritz methodically mowing down civilians on the street below, using just such a style. Was it him? Or the Kid? Or even Ruth?

This last question was answered with a blur of movement barely yards away to Danny's left. Ruth. She was
darting between where she'd been hidden behind a small
outbuilding and a clump of bushes. He could see what she
was up to right away. She was trying to flank Spartak, to
get around behind him. Danny saw the glint of a pistol
in her right hand. Spartak was so focused on whoever
was shooting beside the Jeep that he wouldn't see her. He
wouldn't stand a chance.

And even though he was still cuffed and without a
weapon, there was no way in hell Danny Shanklin was
going to stand for that.

He waited until the very last moment. Ruth – or
whatever the hell her real name was – was making her
final run, this time from behind the clump of bushes to
the cover of a tree fifteen yards to Spartak's rear. Once
there she'd be able to close in on him and shoot him in
the back of the head.

Danny broke cover the second he thought he was out
of her peripheral vision, running as hard and as fast as he
could at her from just behind her and to her right.

The first she saw of him was when he was less than five
yards away. There was a lull in the gunfire and she must
have heard his footfall. The look of complete shock on
her face switched almost instantly to a blank expression
he'd seen in close combat so many times before. She was a
professional. He was now just a target, nothing more.

But as she brought her handgun round to fire, he
changed his angle of running. Just enough. Enough for

her to fire and to miss. Enough for him to hit her then with everything he'd got. To smash her backwards, so that the two of them ended up sprawling in a tangled heap on the ground.

Danny knew from fighting her in the Kid's apartment that she was good. Good enough, certainly, to best him with his hands cuffed as they were. Which meant he had to finish her now, before she got up.

She rammed her elbow hard into his face, and again. But he didn't try blocking it as instinct and training had taught him. Do that and she'd have the chance to break free. Instead he took the pain, then twisted underneath her, hooking the cuffs' chain over her head and jerking it hard back against her throat.

Her whole body flexed as he cut off her air supply. Again she tried slamming her elbow into him, but again he took it, hooking his legs around her now and using his full body strength to pull the chain tight.

She still didn't quit. She tried rolling left. And again. Her pistol – the SIG Sauer P226, he glimpsed it – just out of her reach.

She jerked her head forward, then brought it smashing back into his face. He felt his cheekbone crack, but when she tried the same move a second later, he knew her strength was leaving her. He had won.

Her last movement was to twist her head round as far as she could, blood flecking her lips, the last of the air hissing from her lungs, enough that, for just a second, her eyes met his. An instant of desperation, of begging, but then she was gone. He watched the light die in her eyes and did not let go until he was certain she was dead.

He pushed her off him. Breathless, he rolled to his left and picked up her handgun. He checked the magazine and saw it was half full. It was only then he realized that the firing had stopped.

'Stay the hell down, you fat fuck.'

The voice was Spartak's. Danny struggled to his feet and looked across to see that the position his friend had previously been occupying was now deserted. He edged forward, his arms up in a firing position, not knowing what the hell he might find next.

What he saw was Spartak, by the Jeep, his AK-9 trained on something on the ground before him.

That something, Danny saw, as he closed in, was Adam Gilloway, a.k.a. the Kid. To his right, out of reach, was a machine pistol. To his left, unmoving, with the middle of his face now nothing but a bloody hole, were the remains of Dementyev.

'It's me, Danny,' he called, in warning.

'I know.' Spartak glanced at him and flashed him a grin.

Danny drew level with Spartak. The Kid was semi-conscious. He was bleeding heavily from his chest. His eyes connected only briefly with Danny's, a look of total disbelief, before he rolled shuddering onto his side.

'Unfortunately it's not fatal,' Spartak said. 'And good work back there, taking that bitch down,' he added. 'I guess that's another life I owe you, eh, my friend?'

'Talking of which,' Danny said, 'the last I saw of you, you were actually dead.'

'No,' Spartak said, 'merely nearly dead.'

'Merely nearly?'

Keeping his AK aiming at the Kid, Spartak raised the side of his combat jacket to reveal the bulletproof vest he was wearing underneath. 'I never did fully trust that woman,' he said. 'She was way too good-looking for you, huh?'

Danny smiled. He couldn't help it. He couldn't believe his friend was alive.

'And your neck wound?' he asked.

'I have a thick neck, my American friend,' Spartak said. 'Or hadn't you noticed before? It will take more than one fucking bullet to cut through that.'

Danny looked up, hearing something.

'Oh, shit,' he said, 'is that choppers?'

'Yes, but do not worry,' Spartak reassured him. 'They're just some friends of mine.'

'Of yours?'

'Yes.'

But this time when Danny looked at him, he saw the grin had been wiped from his face. Any hint of humour had gone with it. Danny didn't like this. Not one little bit. 'What kind of friends?' he said.

'Friends who want back what was stolen from them. Friends who want to talk with this man, Mr Kid.'

Before Danny could say anything else, three helicopters appeared on the horizon. All had civilian markings on

them, but were clearly military in spec. Two peeled off
to the right, which was in the direction the dirt track
leading away from here went. It was the same direction
the minibus had gone. The bus's passengers wouldn't stand
a chance. Seconds later, the sound of heavy machine-gun
fire rattled across the valley, but was almost as quickly
drowned by the approach of the third chopper, which now
circled above Danny and Spartak, then wider again above
the farm and outbuildings. It set down in a paddock less
than fifty yards away.

Danny watched several heavily armed men climb out
and start running towards them, spreading out into an
attack formation as they came.

'Again, I say don't worry,' Spartak shouted, as the
chopper's rotor slowed and the noise diminished. 'These
people are not here to hurt you, but to help.'

CHAPTER 63

'Which of you is the medic?' Spartak demanded in Russian, as the first three men from the helicopter reached them.

A young blond man stepped forward and asked, also in Russian, 'Which is the one who needs the antidote?'

Spartak nodded towards Danny as four other men from the chopper knelt beside the Kid, frisking and binding him, then laying him out on a stretcher and starting to tend to his wounds.

The blond medic, meanwhile, took a loaded syringe from a pack in his jacket. Without ceremony, he rolled up Danny's sleeve and injected its contents into his arm.

'Who are these people?' Danny asked Spartak, when the two of them were left alone.

'My people.'

'*Your* people? You're telling me you're one of them? One of the hardliners? You're one of the people responsible for stealing this smallpox back in 1990 and keeping it hidden since?'

'We keep it for good,' Spartak said. 'Not evil. For our country. You understand?'

'No,' Danny said. 'All I understand is that this hybrid has been responsible for my whole life being trashed. And it nearly just got turned into a global pandemic.'

'And yet it hasn't. Everything instead has ended well.'

Danny looked around at the corpses of Dementyev, his woman and Ruth. He could hardly believe what he was hearing. Because if Spartak was part of this hardline Russian group, as he claimed, that meant he'd been part of them back when he, Danny and the twins had raided the facility in Pripyat. 'You've been using me right from the start,' he said.

Spartak wagged a finger at him. 'No, my friend. Not using, but helping. We have been helping one another.'

'No,' Danny said, 'you've used me to lead you to the Kid. To get your precious hybrids back.'

'Yes, but I have also helped you to capture him too. In this, we had a common goal.'

Danny was too tired for this bullshit, for this double-speak. He saw more men walking towards them slowly from the helicopter. One was being pushed in a wheelchair. He recognized the two men walking either side of him as the Ukrainian twins, Viktor and Vasyl. 'I thought we were friends,' he said.

Spartak looked genuinely hurt. 'But we *are* friends, Danny.'

'Friends don't fucking lie to each other.'

Spartak shrugged heavily. 'Sometimes even friends

have to,' he said. 'If they have a previous loyalty. Such as I do to my people. To my country.'

'So what now?' Danny said.

'Now,' Spartak said, 'we take Mr Kid over there . . .'

Danny looked across to see the Kid being carried on the stretcher to the chopper.

'. . . and we remove him to a special facility where we can talk to him at our leisure, after which we will, among other things, ensure that he confesses to the atrocities committed in London, thereby clearing your name . . .'

'And the smallpox?'

'What about it?'

'What's to stop him telling the press about it? Or MI5? Or the CIA? What's to stop him doing a deal?'

Spartak smiled. 'He will not be speaking to any of those people.'

'Why not?'

'You'll be able to read about it in the media in the next few days. The whole story about how he was arrested in Moscow, confessed to masterminding the London attack and provided compelling evidence to prove this, then unfortunately hanged himself in his cell before he could stand trial.'

'You're going to kill him.'

'No, Danny. Not me. What?' Spartak smiled. 'Do you think I look like a murderer?' His grin, which Danny knew so well, momentarily flickered back into life. 'No,' he said, 'there is someone else who will have the pleasure of doing that.'

Danny followed Spartak's gaze towards the stretcher with the Kid on it, which had now come to a halt beside the man in the wheelchair. Danny couldn't hear what he was saying to the Kid, but he recognized his profile and the chewed-off ear.

'Commandant Valentin Constanz Sabirzhan,' he said.

'Yes,' Spartak said. 'It seems a lot of people are coming back from the dead today.'

'But I thought you passed him the pistol.'

Spartak frowned apologetically. 'I gave him the antidote. I had to tell you he was dead or you would have called in the authorities to help him. And the existence of the hybrid would have become known.'

'More lies.'

'Necessary lies, my friend. Necessary secrets. Just like the hybrids themselves, which will vanish again and this time stay hidden for good.' He rested his arm heavily on Danny's shoulder. Danny did not push him away. 'And no one, not even you,' he said, 'will be able to prove they ever existed at all.'

Necessary lies . . . Danny watched the men carrying the Kid continue their walk towards the waiting helicopter. When the Kid had said goodbye to him in the barn, he'd been right. They would never speak to one another again.

CHAPTER 64

WALES

It was less than forty-eight hours since the shootout at the farm in Germany. And Danny – thanks to Spartak and his associates, who'd arranged diplomatic transportation – was now at the end of his journey, in the back of a taxi that had brought him from the private airfield, where he'd entered the UK, to the flat he'd left Lexie hidden in.

Danny paid the driver and got out. He looked up at the balcony of the apartment, but Lexie was not there, even though the sun was shining down from a blue, blue sky. He'd tried calling her countless times on the phones he'd left her with, but still hadn't had any luck. A part of him wondered if she wasn't answering on purpose, as some kind of punishment. Another part thought she might have seen the news that had been breaking and had simply hightailed it back to her former life and friends.

The thought of that worried him sick. His concern wasn't to do with MI5 or any other spook agency trying to get hold of her to use her against him. Far from it, events had come to pass exactly as Spartak had said.

The media had today begun reporting in a frenzy how Adam Gilloway, a.k.a. the Kid, had been arrested in Moscow and had confessed – with overwhelming accompanying proof – to being paid by the Georgian Secret Service to mastermind the London attack and the assassination of Georgia's own UN peace envoy.

He'd furthermore admitted that his aim had been for the attack to be blamed on the Russians, thereby polarizing international opinion in favour of Georgia's claims on the disputed border states of South Ossetia and Abkhazia. And he'd also provided incontrovertible proof of Danny Shanklin's innocence, before going on to hang himself in his cell to avoid standing trial.

All of which meant – also as Spartak had predicted – that Danny Shanklin's name had been cleared. Before leaving Germany, Danny had met with Crane/Melville, in InWorld™, who'd agreed to broker debriefs over the next few days with MI5 and the CIA to get them off his back.

Danny had already settled on his story. He'd say nothing about the smallpox. What would be the point when he had no proof? He'd tell them he'd escaped from London and had hidden with his daughter. He had been nowhere and had done nothing other than that.

No, what worried Danny, and the reason he'd hightailed it back to Wales just as fast as he could after the Russians had pronounced him free of the virus, was the PSS Killer. He was in the UK and, no matter how many times he had tried calling Ray Kincade, Ray still hadn't answered.

Maybe, Danny had reasoned, this was because Ray had

received Danny's first message. Maybe he'd come here to find Lexie, as instructed, and had taken her somewhere safe. Maybe there was a message waiting in the apartment for him, telling him how to get in touch.

He hurried up the stairs and unlocked the apartment's front door. He could see Lexie's boots on the rug in front of the TV, where she must have kicked them off. He walked through to her bedroom and then his, but she wasn't in either. He checked the bathroom, but it was empty too, although her toothbrush and washbag were still there.

It was only when he walked through into the kitchen that he saw it. A white envelope had been pinned with a magnet to the fridge.

That was when he felt the first dart of panic rising inside him. The handwriting on the envelope was both elegant and precise.

He stood in front of the fridge and just stared at the envelope for several seconds, before reaching out and opening it.

The note inside read:

SHE LOOKS SO MUCH LIKE HER MOTHER.
IT'S SO GOOD TO SEE HER AGAIN.
WE WANT TO SEE YOU TOO, DANNY.
NOW LOOK INSIDE THE FRIDGE.

Hunted

Emlyn Rees

ISBN: 978-1-84901-884-5
Price: £7.99

How far would you go to protect your family?
How fast would you run to save the people you love?

Danny Shanklin wakes up slumped across a table in a London hotel room he's never seen before. He's wearing a black balaclava, a red tracksuit and a brand new pair of Nikes. There's a faceless dead man on the floor and Danny's got a high-powered rifle strapped to his hands. He hears sirens and stumbles to the window to see a burning limousine and bodies all over the street. The police are closing in. He's been set up. They're coming for him...

Fast and furious from the very start, *Hunted* is a shot of pure adrenalin.

'A furiously fast-paced, brutally violent, action- and sex-packed international thriller.'
Daily Mirror

'Hunted gives new meaning to the phrase "fast-paced". Filled with clever twists, stylishly written and populated with characters who are as real as our friends and family (and enemies!), this thriller moves at breakneck pace from first page to last. Bravo!'
Jeffery Deaver